GW00569186

THE TIME WRITER
AND
THE MARCH
A HISTORICAL TIME TRAVEL ADVENTURE

THE TIME WRITER
BOOK TWO

ALEX R CRAWFORD

Spilled Red Ink
PO Box 731
Garrisonville, VA 22463-0731
spilledredink.com

Names: Crawford, Alex R. | The Time Writer and The March.
Title: The Time Writer and The March / Alex R Crawford.
Description: Spilled Red Ink trade paperback edition. | Virginia: Spilled Red Ink, 2022.
ISBN 9781953485045 (softcover)
Spilled Red Ink eBook edition. | Virginia: Spilled Red Ink, 2022.
ISBN 9781953485069 (eBook)

Subjects: BISAC: FICTION / Historical. | FICTION / Fantasy / Historical. | FICTION / Science Fiction / Time Travel.

Content Warnings: *mild language, violence, war, PTSD, mild discussion of nudity and sex*

READING ORDER

The Time Writer Series:
    Prequel: *The Time Writer and The Cloak*
ebook and audiobook available for FREE download to newsletter subscribers
    https://bit.ly/CloakB4

Season 1: 1750s Virginia - French & Indian War
    Book 1: *The Time Writer and The Notebook*
    Book 2: *The Time Writer and The March*
    Book 3: *The Time Writer and The Hunt*

Season 2: 1690s - The Golden Age of Piracy
    Book 4: *The Time Writer and The Escape*
    Book 5: *The Time Writer and The Chase*
    Book 6: *The Time Writer and The Surrender*

Visit my website for early releases, special offers, and to purchase ebooks, audiobooks, signed paperbacks, and exclusive merchandise.

alexrcrawford.com

INTRODUCTION

Beware of doorways through time... and not minding your business.

Author and unwitting time traveler, Amelia Murray, finds herself stumbling back in time to 1755 in Colonial Virginia. The colonies are on the cusp of the French and Indian War, and General Braddock and his troops are sent from England to defeat the French invaders.

Preventing the war, saving lives, and putting her nose into the middle of war plans is the least of her concerns. She needs to survive the streets of Alexandria with Bouchard, her former captor, on the loose, find her betrothed, Captain Spencer, and try not to get killed in battle.

How will she convince Benjamin Franklin to mind his business and help prevent the march by not providing equipment?

Can her relationship with Henry keep her in 1755 or will she find her way back to 2020?

The Time Writer and The March is a Historical Time Travel Adventure exploring 18th Century Colonial America and Braddock's March, through the wit and mindset of a 21st Century woman.

Dedication and Ramblings

For my ayesayers and naysayers:
I'm still making stuff up.

Content warnings *found on the Copyright page include,*
but aren't limited to: violence, war, PTSD, discussion of
nudity and sex, and a few more listed. I'm sure I missed
something that someone finds disturbing to their good senses.

Amelia is a brusque Gen Xer, full of fight and snark.
Neither she nor I am perfect. Life is a learning process, and
I'm continually learning. I never intend to offend anyone.

If I missed a warning that you find disruptive to your
reading enjoyment, I apologize in advance. I'm not blaming
it on the fact that my tarot cards are in the shop, but I'm
supposed to get them back next week.

Grab a drink, sit back, relax, and enjoy the
adventure.

Washington, and my time in the past, I could do my job and write about it.

"Are you ready for me to move out?" I screwed the lid back on the protein drink and sat it on the table. My fingernail found its way to the edge of the bottle. I picked at the label—it wouldn't budge. "I know I've been acting weird since I got back a couple of weeks ago, but I feel more lost now than I did when I was traipsing around battlefields with George Washington and Henry. Who knows why I was sent to that time? And now, all I want to do is go back. Does that sound stupid?"

"No. You really fell hard for him."

"The painting of me in the museum said that I was his wife. I know I didn't marry him before I left. Doesn't that mean that I need to get back? I just don't know how that is supposed to happen."

"Or," Beth said as she reached across the table and took the bottle away from me. The nervous picking, apparently, irritated her. "Maybe he marries someone that looks like you."

I choked down my oversized bite of banana. "With the same name?"

"You had said you saw a younger version of me and Hector—they even had our names. Perhaps, Lord Henry finds your ancestor, and that is who he marries."

"I... uh...." My hand ran across my forehead. "I hadn't thought of that possibility. Am I that naïve?" I shook my head. "Of course, he couldn't marry me. I'm stuck in the twenty-first century with no way to get back to seventeen-fifty-four." I stood up and tossed my banana peel into the trash. "I'm going to get dressed and start unpacking boxes."

Deflated, I went to my room and plopped face down on my bed. I wasn't special after all. The time I spent in 1754 would be a memory that I couldn't prove happened. I was just a normal person, set to do normal things for the rest of my life.

Four boxes of kitchen utensils, pots, pans, and dishes were emptied by noon. I gathered up the brown packing paper and crammed it into one of the empty boxes. Artemis nudged my hip as I leaned over the boxes, trying to get a few more wads of paper crammed into it. If she nudged any harder, I would have ended up face first in the box of paper. "Hey girl, is it time for a walk?" I scratched behind her ear.

It was Wednesday, and I had been here for two weeks. My SUV left at Fort Ashby, where I had visited and traveled back in time through the door of a cabin, was returned to me but was at my house in Fredericksburg. Hector had left for work before Apollo had awoken me. Beth left for the university after breakfast. She was teaching two classes on the *Effects of pre-War for Independence in Colonial America* in the morning and would come home after office hours this afternoon. The summer session was almost over, and she would get ready for the fall term. With her living in Williamsburg and me in Fredericksburg, I felt I would not see my friend as much.

My daughter, Hannah, picked up a waitstaff position at one of the many restaurants that dotted Colonial

Williamsburg when she was not in class. I spent the day with Apollo and Artemis, Beth and Hector's two very large Irish Wolfhounds. Our routine was simple: Apollo would nudge me awake, breakfast, unpacking, and a visit to the historic district—the dogs' large presence always attracted the attention of the tourists. How could they not? Apollo, the larger of the two, could rest his head on the kitchen counter. Oh, and he must have thought that it was funny when I sat half a smoked turkey and Swiss cheese sandwich on the counter and ran upstairs to grab my phone. Stupid human. Without effort or getting on the counter, he snatched it, and in one swallow, it was down his gullet before I could fuss at him. He just walked by and grabbed it. The nerve! Artemis, on the other hand, was taller than my 5-foot-1-inch when she stood on her hind legs. She would have to make a bit more effort to reach my sandwich by placing her front paws on the counter. Not only did I find paws on the counter or the possibility of dog slobber on my food disgusting, but I also really missed my food options for the four months I was stuck in 1754. I gained a new appreciation for smoked turkey sandwiches and sparkling beverages available with little effort, instead of the squirrel that I trapped when supplies didn't get to us in a timely manner while at Fort Necessity with Washington, and the boiled water to kill any bacteria that would cause us to get sick.

I would drag the dogs with me, mostly for the security I felt when they were around, but they also seemed to enjoy the activity and attention they would receive from the tourists. However, that meant I couldn't go into any of the museums. Leaving me to stroll by Henry's house and stare at it from the outside, like I was some sort of stalker. The thought of going back became an obsession. I would open doors, thinking that one would be the one to send me back to him. I would hold my breath, fling a door open, and found nothing spectacular on the other side. Just another room and occasionally a closet. It had been less than a month and I could remember the taste of his lips and the warmth of his breath as it tickled the little hairs on the back of my neck as we rode together on his horse, Louis.

I asked Henry his choice of horse names. Why not Lightning or Thunder or, even, Buttercup? I thought it odd that he would pick a French name, considering the constant conflict between England and France. Why did he give his horse a French name? "I will defeat the French on the back of King Louis." It was a way to jab a finger at the French. I don't think the French ever knew the name of Henry's horse. He was quite amused at his choice of horse names. I supposed I should be thankful he didn't name his horse Amelia. I'm not sure how I would feel about him riding around on my back. It was odd to me. He found it amusing. I suppose it was eighteenth century humor I would never understand.

Leashes on, and we were out the door. The historic district was a short distance from the house. We walked down the quaint street with historical two-storied, Colonial-styled houses built out of brick. The front door centered with symmetrical windows on each side. Some were more modern but kept the same feeling as the older ones. When I traveled through Williamsburg in 1754, most of the houses Apollo, Artemis, and I passed didn't exist. By now, the dogs knew the route, and what was once a slow and leisure stroll had turned into a sweaty adventure. It was the middle of August on the southern coast of Virginia, and the air was heavy with humidity and heat. We weaved our way through the streets and tourists to Hannah's restaurant, *The Salty Dog*, for lunch on the outdoor patio, and a big bowl of water for the pups. During the summer, the wait to get in would be two hours. It pays to be a regular, and the mother of one of the waitstaff. To be fair, I think it was all about the attention the Irish Wolfhounds brought to the restaurant. The dogs loved the attention, and the old tavern loved the attention the dogs would steal from the competitors. That day didn't differ from the rest. I sat there nibbling on my beer battered fish and potato wedges, while countless people came up to take pictures with the dogs. Apollo was thirty-four inches to the top of his shoulder. He could be an imposing beast if he wasn't such a big softy. Artemis was not as tall as Apollo, but she was just as gentle as Apollo. As gentle as they were, I knew if I ever was in danger, they would defend me.

Lunch and rest completed, we headed towards Henry's house. It had been a couple of weeks, but every time I walked the streets of Colonial Williamsburg, it felt like I was back there and any moment I would turn the corner to see Henry. The tourists that ran around snapping pictures, staring at their cell phones, and wearing tee shirts and shorts brought me abruptly back to reality. None of it was truly the same, not even Henry's garden was the same as I had remembered it.

We approached the front of the red bricked, two-story house, where I would often stand and stare, thinking I might catch a glimpse of Henry through the window. Or perhaps Millie, the young indentured servant that worked for Henry, would open the curtains and window to air out my room and let the sun warm the floor. *Ha! My room.* I hadn't stayed more than a couple of days, and to claim it as my room, I just shook my head. If I should claim anything as my room, it would be a tent in the middle of a field in the mountains of Pennsylvania. That is where I spent most of my time when I was pulled back to 1754. But the life with Henry in Williamsburg, that was the life I longed for in my dreams.

Apollo slowed down as we walked down the paved road that led to the Governor's palace at the end of the loop. Historic homes and buildings lined the outer part of the loop. Trees lined both sides of the narrow road. Twisted and contorted trunks, too wide for me to throw my arms around, led to green, leafy canopies. In the middle of the loop, sat a long and wide grassy area. Families sat in the middle or under the trees. Squirrels skittered across from one tree to another. People in historical costumes went about their day, walking up and down the streets and in and out of buildings. A woman in a blue striped petticoat, with matching coat, a white apron, and a bonnet and straw hat, to protect her from the sun, sat on a bench and embroidered a square of white cloth. An older, gray-haired man, in an indigo coat and breeches, tipped his cocked, or tricorn, hat as he walked past me. It almost felt as though I could see Henry leaving the Governor's palace and head towards me. The palace was a large, bricked building, flanked by outbuildings on either side. A white metal gate sat in the middle, closing off the front of the house and requiring visitors to enter through a controlled side. I was not looking to enter; only reminisce of my last night and the people I met in 1754. Artemis pulled me in the opposite direction, back towards Henry's house and the street that would lead us home. A yellow wagon, pulled by two horses, clomped past us. An older man and woman sat in the back and listened to the carriage driver tell them of the history of the buildings they passed. I must not have been paying attention to what was going on around me, as Artemis continued to pull me away from the palace. It was more than the wagon that set her nerves ablaze and raised the hair on her back.

"What's up guys?" I said to my furry guardians, as if they would return my question with an answer. I nearly crashed into the dogs when they did a full stop in front of me. Apollo haunched into a protective stance and a deep, guttural growl came thundering out of him. Something— or someone—was scaring the hell out of these two dogs. Whatever it was, if it scared them, then I wanted nothing to do with it. My stomach tightened as I looked around for the source of terror. My eyes locked on to what the dogs had sensed as dangerous. Out from behind one of the many trees which lined the street, a tall man with dark hair and eyes, dressed like any other tourist, emerged and stood about twenty feet in front of me. Without hesitation, I turned around and readied to run. Kyle, shifted his stare from Henry's house and back towards me. *What in the hell is he doing there?* They had banned him from the museum months earlier when he they arrested him for nearly destroying the portrait of the woman that hung in the library. The woman who looked just like me, if I had lived in the mid-seventeen hundreds, and had the same name. She was the wife of Henry. My Henry. But it couldn't have been me. We were to be married, but I was thrust back to the 21st century before that could happen.

That had to be some sort of odd coincidence. Right? There was something that drew me to Henry's house, but I had been there with him. It would have been my house as well, and I felt as though I had a duty to protect it, but there was nothing I could do about it now. Self-preservation was more important. I shook my head to shove the confusing thoughts away. What did Kyle have to do with any of this?

"Amelia!" Kyle yelled from behind me. "Stop. I need to talk to you."

I didn't turn around. There was nothing he could say to me that would make me stop. I didn't trust him, and I would not stick around for him to prove why I had that distrust. Artemis changed directions back towards Kyle. The leash yanked from my hand. I should have kept a better grip on it, but the force of a protective wolfhound proved to be stronger than me. The other leash cut into my hand as Apollo continued to pull me away from Kyle. I turned to look back towards Artemis, Apollo continued to pull me. As much as I wanted her to protect me, I didn't want someone to think she was a danger to anyone other than Kyle. I looked over my shoulder, "Artemis. Come." Heavy feet pounded away from me. The sound of paws hitting the pavement approached and slowed down next to Apollo. The dogs slowed down as we approached the walking district full of tourists. I picked up the leash that trailed behind Artemis. Out of breath from our trot and the adrenaline that coursed through my veins, we headed back to the house at a quicker pace than our leisure stroll that brought us to the historic district.

When we moved out of the district of shoulder-to-shoulder, sweaty tourists aiming for a photo in front of every building, I pulled out my phone to send a text to the group chat of Hannah, Beth, and Hector. If Kyle was in the area, he might know where I stayed, which could put everyone in danger. I needed to keep everyone safe, including myself.

ME

Kyle here dogs chased

HANNAH

Call cops

I stopped dead in my tracks. I couldn't text with both hands holding leashes. My hands trembled as I pushed and missed the letters I typed.

ME

No cops. I don't think. keep an eye out

BETH

No office hours. Heading home now

HECTOR

Agree w H Call cops

ME

omw house

I couldn't prove that Kyle was stalking me. I felt uncomfortable around him and couldn't explain why. He had the uncanny knack of showing up... well... everywhere. I didn't want to accuse him of anything that I couldn't prove. Innocent until proven guilty and all that. But this wasn't a court of law. This was the court of Amelia Murray, and Apollo and Artemis clearly agreed with me.

When we arrived at the house in record time, I checked the doors and windows to make sure they were locked. We went in through the back door, where I unclipped the leashes. Apollo and Artemis entered before me. I was hardheaded, but I was not that brave or stupid to go bounding inside without precautions. The possibility of Kyle or an accomplice's arrival before us lingered in my mind, and the dogs would surely find them. I stood at the backdoor, holding their leashes while they patrolled. No growling. No barking. They came back and looked at me like they couldn't understand why I was still standing outside. Of course! They wanted treats. "Thank you for protecting me today." I rubbed their big, furry heads. "Who are the good babies that get a treat?" The dogs danced around me and stared at the cabinet that housed their treats. "Well deserved today, you two."

I pulled a cold bottle of water out of the refrigerator and took a few sips. The water in the dogs' water bowl made a splash over the edge as I tossed a handful of ice cubes in the bowl. Overheated and adrenaline pumping through me, I needed to cool and calm down, and so did they. The sound of the mechanical garage door opening was followed by two Irish Wolfhounds prancing around the door that led to the garage, howling for the return of Beth.

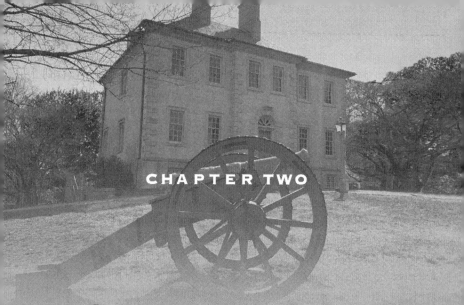

CHAPTER TWO

"*A*melia," Beth shouted as she made her way through 300 pounds of dog. "Are you okay? What happened? Are you safe?" I leaned with my back against the counter, sweat trickled down my spine. "Is he here? Why didn't you let me know you were here?"

In two steps, I was in front of Beth, hugging her. "I'm okay. We just got home. Apollo and Artemis checked out the house before I came in." Artemis wagged her tail and nudged my hand, asking for a rub behind her ear. "I just walked in and grabbed the water. I was about to send a text."

I grabbed my phone out of my back pocket. Some habits are hard to break—and a phone in my back pocket was one of them. I waved my new cell phone in my hand. I had lost my last one somewhere under a tree root in modern-day West Virginia, in 1754, when the French military unit, led by Ensign Jumonville, captured me. Considering the way modern women's clothes are made, I was lucky that I had pockets, and that the back pocket was big enough to hold my phone. I missed the giant pockets of the 18th century–large enough to fit a bottle of wine. "I need to text Hannah and Hector and let them know I am safe, and you're with me."

"You should have sent a text minutes ago. I damn near had a heart attack." Beth stepped out of the hug to grab treats for Apollo and Artemis. I had given them a treat only moments before she walked in, but those two deserved all the treats they could get. "Why is it, lately, that you are always in the middle of some sort of crisis? Which gods did you piss off?" Artemis caught the small dog biscuit Beth tossed in the air. Apollo stared at it as it flew next to his head and cracked into five pieces on the ground. No effort to catch, but he leaned his head down to pick up the pieces scattered around his front paws.

"Good question," I said as I put the phone away after sending the text. "I'm guessing I've irritated at least six different gods, and that was just in the last three minutes." My head shook at my unfortunate situations. "I don't know how I got wrapped up in this madness, but I think my quiet days at home are about to be on a hiatus."

Beth walked over to the cabinet next to the refrigerator and pulled out three wine glasses and placed them on the counter. She rummaged around in the drawer until she found the wine bottle opener. "I was serious about you getting back to work. It should help focus you. You should probably see a therapist while you're at it."

"I was thinking about that, actually." I sat down at the kitchen table and propped my feet up on the chair next to me. "Not the therapist part. What can I tell them? Oh, I'm jumpy and might have PTSD from being held captive by a French military unit, where I was regularly beaten until I escaped. Then I went to a battle, was almost assaulted, and then witnessed people dying. And, by the way, this all happened in 1754." I let out a small laugh. "No, I can't speak to anyone." I picked at an imaginary spot on the table. "What I was thinking about was the fact that I spend my days unpacking your boxes. Not that I mind, it's the least I can do for you and Hector. Then the dogs and I go for a walk. We have lunch. We come back. You come home. Then the day is done."

I moved from picking at the imaginary spot on the table to playing with the placemat. My wedding ring, that I would twist around my finger when my anxiety raised, was absent from my finger. I had lost 22 pounds by the time I got back to the 21st century. My ring was loose, and my clothes hung from my body. The constant traveling, hiking through the Allegheny Mountains, and the lack of a consistent meal, was the weight loss plan that I had no control over. I had to admit that I liked the overall results, but I was comfortable in my skin before the weight loss. I had to get comfortable with my new normal. Whatever that meant for me. "With everyone's schedule and my car being in Fredericksburg, I've only been around here." I waved my hand around and Beth placed a glass of wine in it. "I haven't finished the research for the book."

"Are you still going to write it? I wasn't sure if you were ever going to do it. You basically lived it. What more research do you need? Maybe you can work through some of your issues if you will not speak to a therapist."

"I prefer to pretend everything is fine and I'm coping. It's the world around me that isn't coping with the past." To avoid eye contact, I spun the placemat around in circles. I could feel the heavy, disappointed stare from Beth. "I don't know. Maybe I need to take a different direction. I'm thinking...."

Apollo's ears perked up. Artemis raised her head and tilted it to the side. Something—or someone—had sparked their attention. I sat straight in my chair and gulped down. Beth pulled out her phone and followed the dogs to the front door. Hector would have come in through the garage. I took a deep breath, grabbed my phone, slid over to the counter, and drew a knife from the block that sat on the kitchen counter. Kyle had found where I was staying. My heart was going to thump out of my chest. I followed Beth, ready to back her up, if it came to it.

"Hannah," Beth sighed with relief as she flung the door open. "You nearly gave us a heart attack."

"I nearly gave you one?" She gave Beth a quick hug, pushed her way past the overly excited dogs, rubbing their heads along the way, and threw her arms around me. "I was so worried about you."

"I can't breathe," I gasped out. I held the knife out of the way and held on to her with the other arm. "Really, I'm fine. Apollo and Artemis took good care of me until Beth showed up. Did you leave work early to be here?" I pulled out of her tight embrace before I passed out from lack of oxygen.

"No," Hannah said as she shook her head. We followed Beth into the kitchen. I shoved the knife back into the knife block and grabbed my glass of wine before sitting down at the table. Apollo and Artemis plopped in the middle of the kitchen floor. "My shift finished when you sent the last text. I wanted to see with my own eyes that you were okay."

"You sound like me, now." I snorted out the reply and took a sip of the white wine Beth had poured for me.

"I thought I had lost you forever." She took my glass out of my hand, took a sip, and slid into a chair at the round kitchen table. I scrunched my nose and took it back. I might not drink it all, but she was eighteen, and I refused to let her down my glass of wine. "You were gone for months and didn't let me know you were safe." Hannah played with the placemat. We hadn't only our looks, but the same nervous habits in common. "I just needed to know that you didn't disappear again."

"You know, I didn't disappear on purpose." I reached over and grabbed her hand. "I wouldn't do that to you."

"I still have doubts about the whole time travel thing." She said, flailing her arms about in a grand gesture. "And you're trying to get back to Henry?"

"Sweetie, I..." My mouth hung open, unable to form any more words. She was correct. I was trying to find my way back to Henry. It was a hopeless pursuit, since I was not sure how time travel worked.

"You've made it very clear that he is more important to you than I am."

"I never said that." The world of emotions came

crashing down on my chest. I couldn't breathe. "I didn't choose to end up in 1754. But when I did, I was terrified, and all I wanted to do was to get back home to you. Then, I met someone that was a friend, a protector, and then became so much more to me."

Hannah's eyes watered. The tears were ready to burst out of me. I gripped her hand tighter and sucked in a quivered breath. I needed her to know that I was here for her. "Then I was thrust back to this time. My feelings for him, for you, for my life here, and my life there, are all over the place. I was happy to be home but..." my voice cracked, and I gulped down a breath to regain my composure, "I feel lost without him and without you."

Hannah looked at me. Her mouth opened, but no words came out. Her lips opened, closed, and made shapes to form words. Tears slowly trickled down her cheeks and edged off her chin.

"You are always my first love. You know that." I let out a deep breath.

I looked over at Beth. I hoped she would say something. Anything. I wanted her to save me. This was my mess, and I needed to figure out how to not alienate my daughter, but I searched for help. "Hannah," I began. I drew in another deep breath to give myself a moment to think. She sat there, sobbing. She was going to explode at me. I knew it. I didn't want her to leave. "Sweetie, I won't leave you again. Well, not on purpose. I will stop looking for a way to return. You are the most important person to me." I gulped down the entire glass of wine. "Please, I don't want you to hate me over this... over him.

I can't stay here forever. I'll pack up, go home to Fredericksburg, and everyone and everything can get back to normal."

"It's not that," she said. Beth handed her a box of tissues. "I was so worried about you when you disappeared. It was me who harassed the police. I tried getting the FBI involved and spent months not knowing if you were dead and now... now you're ready to throw what I went through to the side like I am fine with you leaving again. And you are ready to jump into some other guy's bed. I still have a dad. Well, had a dad."

"So, what do you want from me?" My voice went up a few octaves and my temper flared. "I don't know what to do, or say, to make it up to you." It was useless to hold back the tears. I grabbed a handful of tissues and blew my nose. "We're never getting your dad back. He's dead and there's nothing that either of us can do about it. Someone was determined to take him away from us. I loved him— still do. And I know you love him, we always will."

"Yeah, well... I don't want to be an orphan. Couldn't you go back and warn him? You're a time traveler now."

"I'm not sure how it works, but I don't think I can."

"Can't you find a guy in this time? I mean, there must be a million of single men out there." She flailed her animated arms around again. Her emotions were on full display, full on drama queen like her mother. "Get on a dating app or something. A two hundred fifty-year-old guy isn't your only option."

"You're right," I said. What was I thinking, trying to find my way back to Henry? He moved on–to one of my ancestors that had the same name and looked like me–but he moved on without me. I needed to do the same.

"If you have nothing planned for tonight, maybe you can give me a ride home? It will give us some time to talk." I looked for a smile from her. A faint one slid across her lips. "Maybe we can pick up dinner from *Betsy's Biscuits*? You can stay the night in your old room. We can watch movies and eat junk food until the wee hours. What do you say?"

I could see the rise and fall of her chest as she inhaled deep into her lungs. "Let me run back to my apartment and grab my stuff. I'll be back to pick you up." Keys jangled in Hannah's hand, and she was out the front door in two seconds flat.

"Well, now that we've got that settled," Beth said as she smacked the table as if her hand were a gavel and she was the presiding judge. "I'll grab a box from the garage, and you can throw your new wardrobe in there."

"Wow," I shot her a look. "You are quick to kick me out."

"I'm quick for all of us to get back to normal. Don't get me wrong, I'm going to miss you unpacking these boxes. I'm sure Apollo and Artemis are going to miss your walks and lunches in the district."

"Won't you miss me?" I raised an eyebrow at her.

"Really? I just want you to be okay and not worry about you."

"I just want everyone to be careful." I held up my hand to stop the conversation. "Kyle is still out there being super creepy. I'll be fine." I pulled my phone out and opened a shopping app. "Look, I'm going to order cameras for around the house and will give all of you permission to view the live feed. You know... just in case." A few clicks later and the cameras would be at the house in two days.

"Good idea, Amelia," Beth picked up her phone and read the text message that came in. "Hector will be home in a couple of minutes. We'll come by this weekend, and he will install the cameras while we head over to the bookshop to visit Maggie." Beth placed the phone face down on the wooden table. "She mentioned something about being on another case."

Our friend Maggie owned *By the River Bookshop* in downtown Fredericksburg. Somehow, she was always getting involved in the Burg's drama and solving the odd crime here and there. Being in the middle of the town, she was amid the action and thrived on it. The only mystery she couldn't solve was the murder of my husband Todd and my disappearance. I think she missed her calling as a private investigator or an FBI agent. She claimed she liked the quiet, slow life of owning a bookshop, but she couldn't help but get involved. I think that is one of many reasons I love her. She always seemed so daring and ready to jump in to help others. Sometimes, without regard to her own safety. Occasionally, Beth and I would get dragged into her adventures when we were around. She kept our sleepy little town exciting.

"Sounds like nothing has changed," I said with a snorted laugh. Of course, everyone else's lives were the same. I was the only one who had their life thrust into the past. For me, it was exciting, an adventure of a lifetime.

Now, my adventure was over, and I had to return to my old life. "Other than your move from the Burg to here, not much has changed for you either."

"What were you expecting when you came back? That the world would be different?" I followed Beth to the garage to get an empty box. "Life continued when you were gone, but it didn't change for everyone, just you." Her pointed finger looked as though it would stab me. "You should think about it being like a vacation."

"That was not the vacation I would have planned." I grabbed a roll of packing tape from the junk drawer in the kitchen as we headed up to my room.

"Ah, but it was a vacation where you had an adventure and found a hot guy. You just couldn't—you know—continue the relationship afterwards. Kind of like a summer fling."

"You make it sound so... I took a summer break from college and hooked up with a hot guy and we will never see each other again," I mocked. "This is not like the movie *Grease*. I'm not Sandy and he's not Danny. We will not run into each other at the pep rally."

"No. I make it sound like a forty-year-old woman went on an adventurous vacation a met a hot guy to fool around with."

"There wasn't much fooling around. The time gods saw to that when they decided it was time for me to come home before the two of us... well... you know." We trudged up the stairs, down the hall, and into my room. Apollo was close to my heels. "And he ends up marrying someone that is my doppelgänger." I pulled out of the drawer the few new clothes I had purchased and haphazardly threw them into the box. "Because it sure in the hell isn't me. I'm here with no way back. It's weird."

Beth plopped down in the floral accent chair in the corner near the window that looked out to the backyard. She moved the curtain to the side and peered out back. "Did you ever find out what happened with Henry or your evil twin?" she asked, letting the curtain drop back into place.

"Nope. The museum had little info." The small box stuffed full and taped shut. With a small wardrobe, I could have thrown everything in a few grocery bags. "I tried searching for him on the internet but couldn't find anything. It's like at some point, he just disappeared. Or they didn't record what happened. I don't know. I wish I could find out more about what happened to him. Even the wiki pages have absolutely nothing on him. It's like he disappeared into thin air."

"Kind of like you did to us and him." Beth sat down next to me on the bed and wrapped her arm around me.

"Yeah," I said as my shoulders dropped. I rubbed my face to chase off the tears. "I'll be fine. Really, I'm fine. Yeah, I'm good."

"Who are you trying to convince? Me or you?"

"I love you." I wrapped my arm around her and gave a squeeze.

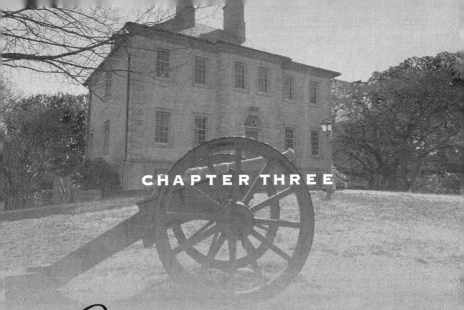

CHAPTER THREE

"*M*om, I swear if you cry one more time, I'm turning this off."

I sniffed up my tears as a pillow flung from the other side of the sofa smacked me on my left shoulder. The motion caused the wine to wave back-and-forth in daring waves in the wineglass's bell.

"Aw, come on. It's so sweet. He loves her so much. And she loves him." I motioned towards the television screen. "I mean, look at that. How can you not?"

"You're a sap."

"I'm okay with that." I took a sip of the sweet and fruity pink wine. "It's why I enjoy watching this movie. Guaranteed to make me cry."

"Mom," she said groggily. "If you go back, I will try to understand. Just know I will miss you."

I looked over at Hannah, leaned on the arm and curled up on the other side of the sofa, her head supported by her left arm, her heavy eyes squeezed tight and opened in a sudden jerk. It was late. "Hey, why don't you head to bed? We can finish watching this later."

"Mmm... yeah...." Hannah mumbled her response and padded up the stairs. I clicked off the television, and left our glasses and the remnants of our dinner from *Betsy's Biscuits* on the table, and followed her up.

The next morning, after breakfast at *Betsy's*, Hannah dropped me off at the house and headed back to Williamsburg for her lunch shift at *The Salty Dog*. I needed to clean up from the night before and to get my life back on track. Cleaning, groceries, and security cameras were all on my to-do list.

I stood in the garage, looking at my SUV, returned from police evidence and not driven in nearly five months. This was the first time since I had been back that I was alone. Not just people out for the day, but by myself. No dogs to walk. No one around. Alone. Maybe I should get a cat.

I wanted to jump in the car and drive to Fort Ashby. Who was at the house to stop me? No one. I opened what seemed to be a hundred or more doors, with coins in my hand. I threw coins on the ground. Nothing recreated the time slip. An itch in the back of my mind told me it might be Fort Ashby that was my portal there and Henry's house my portal back. I promised Hannah that I would stop looking for a way back, but my curiosity picked at me. I was like an addict looking for my next time slip fix. Or was Henry my addiction?

"Get in the car and go buy groceries." I had to

convince myself to stay put and avoid heading to West Virginia. "Groceries and a couple of extra security cameras, just in case." Security cameras were to arrive the next day, but I questioned if I had bought enough. I wanted every inch of the perimeter covered so Kyle couldn't slip in undetected.

I sent Hannah a text to thank her for visiting and to tell her I loved her. I had to keep myself grounded to the present and remember who was most important to me. Hannah and my friends.

I passed the freeway on my way to the grocery store. It took all my willpower not to jump on it. Groceries—check. Security cameras—check. "See, Amelia, that wasn't so hard. Now, was it?" It was. It really was. I knew it would eventually get easier, but until then, the itch lingered.

I opened the blinds to fill the house with the late August sun. I had to admit, while in 1754, I missed the modern conveniences, such as flushing toilets, hot showers, travel that took only hours instead of weeks, and central air conditioning. Good. Think of the positive things: you like modern appliances, grocery stores, the internet, and food delivery.

The buzz of my cell phone pulled me out of my mental list of things I appreciate. I answered, not knowing who was on the other line. New phone with Hannah, Beth, and Hector as the only contacts listed. "Hey, Amelia," Cora's voice flitted through the phone. I knew the sing-song voice was going to turn into a lecture from my editor. "Got your email. Glad your back. Listen, I hope you had time to write while you were on your little vacation. I need your draft in 5 weeks."

"Right. I'm getting on that." I lied through my teeth as I opened the door to my office and looked at the mess. Someone had gone through my things looking for clues as to where I could have gone. Drawers half-opened. They piled notebooks eyeballs high on the desk. My notebook I took with me to 1754 was not among the stack of filled, empty, and half-filled notebooks piled haphazardly on top of my desk. My small, brown leather notebook with the dates of George Washington's battles, sat covered with mud and Jumonville's blood, in a glass case in the *Henry Spencer House and Museum* in Colonial Williamsburg. It was going to take a good part of the week to get my house back together.

"What about your outline? We were supposed to meet weeks ago to discuss it." The sound of her fingers feverishly typing on the keyboard clicked-and-clacked through the phone. "I haven't seen it."

"Right. I'll get that for you by next week. I lost my notebook and need to recreate it, so... yeah... I'll get that to you. Next week. End of week. No later." I felt like a child disappointing her favorite teacher. She had to know that I made all that up. At that moment, I had no notebook, no notes, and nothing on my laptop. The police had my laptop in their custody since it was in my SUV when I left it at Fort Ashby, in West Virginia. I hated disappointing my brilliant editor. She was busy, and I wasted her time with losing my work when I spent four months in 1754. Time for me to step up and earn my living as an author, and I needed her to make that happen. I couldn't screw this up. Slipping through time couldn't delay the launch of my next book. *Get her off the phone and get to work, Amelia.*

"Did you finish your research?" I knew the expression that she made without even the need to see it. It was the one she had given me before. Raised eyebrow, pursed lips, and the feeling that I was about to say something that wouldn't make her angry, just disappointed in me.

"Actually," I began. The truth couldn't be told outside my small circle of people that already knew what had happened to me. "That is exactly what I was doing while I was out of the loop. I was doing a deep immersion in Colonial America, specifically seventeen fifty-four. There was much to learn about what happened at Jumonville Glen and the defeat at Fort Necessity." I had to hide so much from everyone about my travel through time that it felt odd to speak with conviction. Of course, there was no way I was going to tell her about the time travel. However, I would not lie.

"Good. Good." The keyboard continued to click. "I'll look for your outline next week." She paused for half a second. "Next week outline," she was firm. "First draft in five. Don't disappoint me, Amelia."

"Okay, well, I better get right on that..." I needed to get her off the phone so I could start my outline. I had only made a couple of plot points, places of interest, and notes on some characters.

"It's good to have you back. We'll set up a video call in a couple of weeks."

We said our goodbyes, and I collapsed at my desk. I could feel my blood pressure rise, causing a sharp pain in my shoulder. Heart attack or stress? Neither one fit into my plans. A bottle of wine later, I finished cleaning my office, organized my supplies, and set up my modified work schedule to accommodate the tight deadline. If I locked myself in the house only to leave to go to the grocery store for quick and easy meals, then I might squeak by. Fortunately, living through the events of 1754 and having them so vivid in my mind would allow me to finish my outline in record time. The words flowed through my fingers when it came to writing my story. I told the story to Beth and Hannah, replayed it through my mind over-and-over. It was all I could think about for the past month.

The tight deadline delayed my visit back to Fort Ashby for another couple of months. I couldn't afford to take the time out of my writing schedule to visit. It would still be there when I sent the manuscript to Cora. I would visit and see if my theory of in one door, out the other held true. If it did, at least I knew which door I had to go through to get back home. This time, however, I would let Beth and Hannah know I was going to test the theory. Maybe I would bring one of them along with me—just in case.

Saturday brought Beth, Hector, and Hannah to the house for a visit. Add that to the list of delays to finish the manuscript. Getting back to normal brought comfort to my chaotic life.

Hector mounted and connected security cameras around the outside of the house, down the driveway, front doorbell, backyard, and the sides of the house, and a few hidden cameras angled down the sidewalk. No one could get inside without my knowledge, unless a helicopter dropped them on the roof. I chuckled at the thought. I've entered buildings through time portals. Why would I think that the roof or chimney was the only way to enter my house undetected? My primary concern was creepy Kyle. I wanted to make damn sure he would not drop through the roof or emerge through time portals. At least, I hoped he wouldn't.

"Do you think I need to add a camera inside?" I asked the group as Beth, Hannah, and I stood around watching Hector connect the last camera.

"Mom, how is anyone going to get in here? This place is guarded like Fort Knox."

"Whoa, I don't want to see you naked by accident," Hector said and caught himself before he slipped from the top of the ladder.

"Are you saying you want to see me naked on purpose? Besides," I began, with my hands placed firmly on my hips, "I don't wander around the house naked."

"Oh, goodness. Hector is in for it now," Hannah said in a whisper to Beth, who already shook from hiding her laughter.

"What's wrong with me being naked?" I continued, with a smirk cut towards Beth and Hannah.

"It's not... I wouldn't... you're... I love my wife." Hector quickly finished the connection and descended the ladder. I snorted out a laugh. Beth tried not to laugh at him. That failed miserably. I thought she would fall over from laughter. She grabbed her side and leaned over, gasping for breath.

"Of course you do, lover." Beth said and smiled towards her lobster-colored husband. "We are destined to be together forever. And we have the fully clothed Amelia to thank for that." She nodded her head in my direction. I smiled at the memory of the double date where Todd and I introduced them to one another. We had moved to Fredericksburg from Poland, when Todd was reassigned to Washington, DC, because of his job with the State Department. I had met Beth when I interviewed her for information on a book I was writing. Todd knew Hector from work. Together, we knew they would be perfect for each other. It was as though they were meant to be together. We just needed to help them find each other. A whirlwind romance later, and the next year the married couple helped me cope with the sudden death of my husband six years ago.

"You two are adorable." I smiled at them and wrapped my arm around Hannah's waist. "Okay, team. Let's check out the app and camera angles before Hector puts the ladder away."

I set everyone up with a login, gave each permission to monitor the cameras' live feed, and view past events. If something happened to me in the house, at least they would have the video evidence of whomever was responsible—namely, Stalker-Kyle.

The old restaurant in the historic district of Fredericksburg, *Betsy's Biscuits*, was close to the house and filled to the brim with diners. The tourists wrapped up their day and filled every available restaurant before leaving or heading back to their hotels, homes, or continued their journey up and down I-95. Businesses found along Caroline Street were once row homes or businesses erected over the past 250 years. Above the shops, restaurants, salons, and bars, you could still find apartments. Fredericksburg had been a busy port town during colonial times, and George Washington's childhood home, now known as Ferry Farm, ferried people across the Rappahannock River.

Maggie, owner of *By the River Bookshop*, amateur sleuth, and owner of Pom the orange tabby cat and Fritz, an over-stuffed, red, short-haired Dachshund, lived above and the shop. She promised to stop by after work and have dinner with us, as Betsy's was a short five-minute walk from the bookshop.

Breakfast and lunch were *Betsy's* busy time, especially on the weekends. Saturdays were the toughest days to get a table—morning or night. Maggie ran down the street from B*y the River Bookshop* and put us on the waitlist. She could have called over to Betsy to make the reservation, but I'm sure she wanted to pick up a cinnamon roll biscuit topped with strudel for the morning. It was one of the more popular deserts in Fredericksburg and guaranteed to sell out before the Saturday nighttime crowd made their way through.

Betsy's offered seating indoors in the building's front, small tables with long benches stretched out along the walls. The tables could fit two comfortably. We would pull two tables together to fit our larger group. Two and four-people tables filled the center of the room. The kitchen was to the left, and down the righthand side of the room was a hallway that led to a bar area, with a few more tables, and the door to the back deck which offered outdoor dining.

The outdoor dining area in the back side of the building was inviting, but we decided against it. We worked our way through the front dining area, down the right side of the seating in the back. The roar of conversation filled the room. Plates and silverware clanked together. A boisterous group, seated in the corner, enjoyed loud conversation and laughter. Two tables over, a toddler proved the day had been too long and loudly protested every bite his mother offered him. His infant sibling wailed in a carrier on the bench next to the mother.

"You never told me where you disappeared." Maggie's voice flittered over the wail of overheated and exhausted children. I glared at the father who sat there, ignoring the commotion, and continued to eat his biscuits smothered with gravy and chunks of sausage. When Henry and I found the orphaned Tamhas in the woods after we had buried his murdered parents, we had to care for him until we met up with Tanaghrisson and his people adopted the infant into their tribe. Henry helped every step of the way. He had no reason to help, but he did. The father next to us could take a hint on what it means to be a true father.

"Oh. I... uh... I was doing research and lost my phone." I hesitated to tell Maggie the truth. She was quirky and seemed to know everything about everyone, but she didn't need to know that about me. I didn't want the entire town to think I was an eccentric author that was counting the days to be committed to a psychiatric ward. I knew she was curious and wanted to know where her friend had been, but this was one of those times that I knew to keep my mouth shut. "It was a strange situation–really. But I'm back now and I'm ready to get back to work. Speaking of work, I heard you were on a fresh case." A change in topic was in order.

"Come by next week. I have a new batch of orders that require your John Hancock on them." Readers that wanted my signed books ordered them through Maggie's bookshop, which required me to make frequent trips to sign batches of books. Some wanted personalized notes, which I loved to do, but I fell behind when I wasn't around for a few months. It would take me days to catch up, days I didn't have to spare with my deadline quickly approaching and Cora down my throat.

"Will do." I made a quick mental note. "New case?" Time to refocus her away from my disappearance.

"Oh, so you know the old Woods' house on Caroline Street?"

"Which one is that?" Hannah interjected.

"It's the big white one on the corner of Caroline and Wolfe," I answered. I swallowed hard. The house she mentioned was familiar to me. I had stayed with Elizabeth Woods, a friend of George Washington, when I was in 1754. She was a younger version of Beth, and I was certain she must have been her ancestor.

"Well, there have been several break-ins. They wanted to add security cameras, but it is one of those old historical houses," Maggie said and shoved a chunk of fried potato into her mouth. She paused a moment to chew. I think she used it for dramatic effect. "Well," she said as she swallowed hard. "There have been break-ins, but nothing stolen. They don't know who is doing it. It's all really scandalous."

"Why don't they put up security cameras?" I questioned. "Hector finished installing mine this afternoon."

"You should get a restraining order while you're at it." Hannah gave me a disapproving look with her piercing blue eyes.

"I'll work on that," I said, looking back towards Maggie and taking a bite of my biscuit. "Cameras?"

"Oh! They can't." Maggie picked up another chunk of her O'Brien potatoes. Besides the french toast, the O'Brien potatoes with chunks of bell pepper and onions, were my favorite. We would have to watch her eat the entire pile before she would tell us the entire story. And I thought I was the only one that used twenty words when it only required five. "They put in a request to the council, but it's one of the protected buildings. Being one of the original ones and all that..." She flittered her hands about. "Every little change needs to get approval."

"Why don't the police set up extra patrols or something?" Beth chimed in.

"Well, you know how they are during tourist season. Unless it is something that would stop people from coming—which it won't—they're not getting involved." Maggie had a love-hate relationship with the local police chief. "So, the family asked me to help them solve the case."

I wondered if this had anything to do with my visit there in 1754 and my return. Not likely, but it felt as though everything was tied to me. "What ya got?"

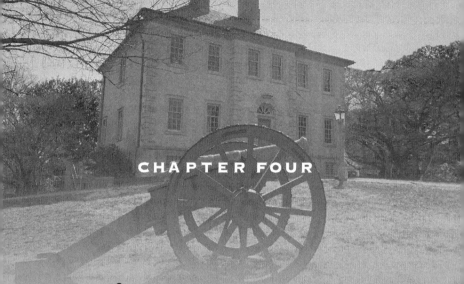

CHAPTER FOUR

*I*f you would have told me six months ago that I would go from time traveler to a private investigator on a stakeout, I would have called you crazy. Yet, there I was, on a stakeout with Maggie and Beth. The buzz of Caroline Street had disappeared along with the tourists. The call of frogs and the bugs swarming to lights was the only big thing to happen to downtown this late at night. Sure, there were the college students cruising home–rambunctious and half-stumbling–after drinks in one of the local bars. Other than that, it was quiet... and boring.

"Looks like it's a bust tonight," Beth tried to stifle her escaped yawn.

"I'm ready to crawl into bed and get a few hours' sleep." My heavy eyes burned from trying to stay open.

"It's only three. What if they come later?" Maggie questioned our dedication to her mystery. I don't think she ever slept.

"Mags, come on," I pleaded. "We need to head back to my house. We'll meet up at Betsy's at nine for brunch."

"Fine. Fine. Don't say I've never showed you a good time." She made a joke, but I knew I disappointed her we were bailing on her.

"Nine. Be there," I said. Beth and I crawled out of Maggie's little red sedan. For someone that went on stakeouts, her choice of car colors was not stealthy. I would have thought a red car would stick out like a sore thumb. But what did I know? I drove a black SUV. I could lose my car in an empty fast-food parking lot.

We headed back to my car, parked on Princess Anne Street in front of Maggie's bookshop. The historic district of Fredericksburg was comprised of one-way streets. We had to drive down two streets, turn left, turn left again on Caroline Street—where we would pass Maggie and her stakeout—go down further, turn right on Lafayette Street, and to my house. It might have been faster to walk.

"Do you think that car is following us?" I kept looking in my rearview mirror at the set of headlights that stayed a short distance behind us, but made every turn we did.

"Maybe?" Beth repeatedly switched from looking in the side mirror to the rearview, then over her shoulder. "It's not like there are that many ways to get through here." She sucked the air out of the car in a panic. "Maggie might be in danger."

"Do you think Kyle is the one breaking into the Woods' house?"

"You know, I was wondering if he was. You told me

that my ancestor lived there, but what do you think Kyle has to do with the break-ins?"

The light turned green, and I turned left to head back through downtown instead of continuing my path home. "Send her a text. I don't think she should stay out there alone. The headlights might be—I don't know—nothing? I'm paranoid, is all."

We pulled up next to Maggie's car and stopped, headlights closed in. "Hey, we've got some stranger-danger stuff going on. Let's save this for another night." She nodded and waved as she drove off. Thank goodness she didn't argue with me. Maggie headed to her house, and Beth and I headed to mine. Hector and Hannah waited for us outside. I looked in my rearview mirror again. The car had turned left down the street behind us. I needed to get my paranoia under control.

"I think I should get a dog instead of a cat."

"Or a gun," chimed in Beth.

"I don't want a gun. I've seen what they can do." Pulling into the garage, I turned off the car. We took a moment before heading inside. "I bandaged up and watched men die from gunshots. It is not pretty."

"You were in a war. Of course, they shot men." She stepped out of the car. "And that is exactly why you should get a gun—to make sure you are safe."

Hector and Hannah stood outside our doors. "I'm thinking about getting a dog," I announced to the group as I got out of the SUV.

"What?" Hannah scrunched her nose at me.

"Like one of those purse dogs?" Hector held his hands up to show a dog smaller than a loaf of bread.

"She wants one for protection." Beth shook her head in disapproval. "I told her to get a gun."

Hector and Hannah simultaneously said a long and dramatic "oh" in response.

"I don't want a gun. Besides, a dog would keep me company while I'm home alone."

"You could move to Williamsburg and live near us."

"I don't want a dog or a gun." Near the door, I kicked off my shoes. "I like this old house. It's quaint. I'll think about moving." Hannah squeezed me in a tight hug of excitement. "I said think."

The following week, I stayed busy at my desk, recalling the events of 1754 and Washington's actions and how they helped fueled the rising tensions between the French and English during the start of the French and Indian War. I, conveniently, left out my involvement in the death of Jumonville. History books—or the men that wrote them—felt the need to keep my name out of it, and I went along with that. How could I possibly explain to Cora that I went into the past and it was because of me they killed Jumonville? It helped writing the events and the emotions that went along with them. It was not a great alternative for a therapist, but it helped.

I remembered those events like they were yesterday. My fingers tapped at my keyboard faster than I could ever imagine. Outline finally finished and sent to Cora. Manuscript was well on its way with four weeks left to finish. I was determined to finish on time so I could take a

visit to Fort Ashby in October. I would take Hannah or
Beth with me, just in case I slipped through time. They
needn't worry about me again. Also, I had no intention of
slipping during the cold and snowy winter in the
mountains, so I slip in October or, maybe, never again.

When I was not pounding furiously on my keyboard, I
spent the rest of my time scrolling through hours upon
hours of security footage. Every shadow, bird swooping by,
early morning bunny hopping through the backyard, and
spider crawling across the lens was caught on camera. Kyle
was nowhere to be seen. He hadn't visited the house or try
to call me. I could finally breathe again. Until one
morning, while I was quickly scrolling through footage,
while I sipped on my pumpkin spiced coffee with a sweet
pumpkin spiced foam, I thought I caught a glimpse of a
figure. Kyle or a ghost? *It had to be Kyle!* I sent a copy of
the footage to Hannah, Beth, and Hector, looking for
unanimous affirmation from the group. First thing after
coffee would be a visit to the local police department and
file a request for a restraining order.

At the beginning of October, I sent my manuscript to
my editor, and I was ready to get back to Henry in 1754.

ME

I want to go to Fort Ashby

BETH

... ...

ME

I know what you're going to say

BETH

… … …

ME

Don't say it. Just come with me.

BETH

Hannah?

ME

No

BETH

??

ME

you know ((skull and crossbones emoji))

Next weekend? It's a long one. Winchester?

BETH

Hector?

ME

I guess. What's with the one-word replies?

BETH

Class

ME

((poop emoji)) sorry. Later.

My weekend clothes sorted and packed. I folded the

dress I wore when I came back from 1754 into my bag. My satchel was lost or stolen during the battle at Fort Necessity and the new one I had ordered arrived the previous week. Traveling through time spends an inordinate amount of energy. Using the word hungry does not seem like I could do the trip any justice. Famished and exhausted. Knowing that time travel required a lot of energy, and I wanted to be prepared. I loaded up with energy bars, jerky, a canteen for water, matches, a utility knife, soap, toothbrush and paste, and a coin.

Hector drove the three of us to Winchester on Friday night. We checked into *The Winchester Inn. The Inn*, in the historic district, dated back to the 1800s. I was supposed to stay there while do my research last April. Time travel changed those plans for me.

Our rooms were next to each other on the second floor. In my room, a large queen-sized bed with a thick white comforter sat center stage. It reminded me of a fluffy cloud. I knew where I was headed. I would not have the luxury of a comfortable bed or a hot shower. Which made me appreciate my long shower and good night's sleep even more than I normally would. Henry was worth the discomfort. Resolved to find my way back to him, I knew deep down, Hannah would be okay.

After breakfast, I changed into my light blue dress that Miss Elizabeth Woods had given me in 1754. I stayed with Elizabeth during George Washington, Henry, and my stop in Fredericksburg on our way to Williamsburg. I had showed up at her house wearing the dirty uniform from soldiers that were killed during the battle at Fort Necessity. The dress I had been wearing during the battle was filthy, head-to-toe from mud and blood. Heavy rains turned the battlefield into a mud pit, and it looked as though it soaked the entire muddy field into the dress. Sergeant Lovett found my clothes, which I am sure came from our dead compatriots. The thought sent a shiver shooting down my spine.

The young woman took sympathy on me and provided me with two dresses. I had a dark green dress for everyday-wear and travel, and the silk light blue dress for dinners and events. I traveled from 1754 in the blue silk dress, so that it was what I was going to wear on my way back. The dress would be inappropriate for me to travel in, but it is better than the skinny jeans and boots I was wearing the first time I traveled to 1754. It would have to do.

We loaded up in Hector's car and took the fifty-mile drive from Winchester to Fort Ashby in West Virginia. My stomach twisted into knots–I was going to be sick. Did I have everything I needed? I knew I wasn't nearly as prepared as I could have been. Money, gold, jewels—I didn't think of that until we approached the fort. I would have to figure out that part when I got to the other side of the time portal.

Hector pulled into the small parking lot. There was a car parked in one of the spots. "This is it?" He asked. "Who did you say lived here? The pirate woman?"

Beth laughed. Her story of Mrs. Ashby's family possibly being pirates led me there during my first research trip. "I didn't say she was a pirate, but her family might have been."

I gave a wink to Hector as he looked back at me through the rearview mirror. Pirates. "This is it. Fort Ashby." My heart raced a million miles an hour. I thought it might jump out of my chest. I took a deep breath. "Let's do it." I left my cell phone in the car. It wouldn't do me any good two hundred sixty-five years in the past.

"I'll walk you to the door, but I'm not going in," Beth said. "I have my love here and I'm not going to seventeen-fifty-four to look for another one." She rubbed Hector's arm as a reassurance. He took his hand in hers, brought it to his lips, and kissed it.

We got out of the car and looked around the fort's footprint. The fort that was built in 1755 by Captain John Ashby no longer stood. A concrete outline of where it once stood was out in the field. The museum was on the righthand side of the parking lot. There was a log cabin built around the time of the building of the fort–although it was not there in April 1754–that stood to the left. It was that log cabin I had entered and transported back in time. I hoped to repeat that process now.

I approached the cabin, took a deep breath, patted my new satchel, and grabbed the door handle. I looked back at my friends. They gave me support throughout this adventure and I wanted to remember them. "Please, tell Hannah what happened. I'll try to figure out to send you a message and let you know I'm safe. Not sure how. But I will." I smiled at them. "Here goes nothing!"

The metal door handle was cold from the chilly early

morning of October. I hadn't thought to bring a cloak or extra layers of clothing, but I made sure I had food–I've my priorities in order. I twisted the door handle. Locked. Hector and Beth were standing behind me, waiting for me to slip through the time.

Beth had a look of concern on her face and gave a half-smile. She asked, "Did you need a coin? You mentioned you found one each time you slipped through time."

"Is that like a payment to the time gods?" Hector questioned. He reached into his pocket, pulled out a quarter, and tossed it to me.

"Let's try this again," I said. I kissed the coin for good luck and held it in my fist. I grabbed the door handle, filled my lungs with the air of the 21st century, and gave it a firm twist. Locked. Over and over, I tried opening the door. It didn't budge. I pulled an old coin out of my bag and tried again. Nothing. The prick of tears teased at the corner of my eyes. "Maybe the museum?"

"Maybe," Beth began. "What if it doesn't happen?"

I hadn't thought of it not happening. My entire plans for the rest of my life depended on me turning that door handle and slipping through time. "Let me try the museum first." I choked out the words. "Then we can go."

Despondent, the sidewalk to the museum felt like a million miles long. I held up the coin, grabbed the door handle, and it opened. Success! There was no swirl of wind, smell of cherry wood, bright light, or the pull of the time slip. What I found was a friendly museum employee sitting behind the counter. Failure. "Welcome to the Fort Ashby Museum." Her voice was delightful and probably surprised that someone was here to learn about the old fort. She looked me up and down. "Wow, you must be a dedicated re-enactor."

"What?" I sputtered out.

"Your dress." She pointed to me. I had forgotten that I was wearing a colonial era dress.

"I... uh... right." I felt a tear roll down my cheek. She was not what I had expected to see when I opened the door. "Do you know when the cabin will open? I was... um... hoping to see inside."

"I can take you on a tour, if you'd like, but you can look around here." She waved around the room. "Do you have questions about the Ashby's or the fort or the war or colonial America? By the looks of it, you could probably answer my questions."

She smiled at me. My lip quivered as I struggled to smile back. Beth placed her hand on my back and gave it a rub. A reassuring squeeze of Hector's hand on my shoulder was the final straw to the tears. I couldn't stay in there any longer. My heart broke into a million pieces. That was the only way I knew to get back to Henry, and my hopes were crushed.

"Thank you for your time." Beth called out to the woman. "Let's go, Amelia."

"Are you Amelia Murray? The author that went missing here?" The woman asked as we were leaving. "I knew I recognized you." She pointed her finger at me. "The police were out here looking for you. We should call them."

I turned around to leave. "Different Amelia."

CHAPTER FIVE

In the dark recesses of my closet, hides a colonial era dress, along with the dress, you will find the memories of the life I once lived in 1754. I couldn't fit in it the way I did when I traveled back to the 21st century. I had comfortably filled into my size ten clothes. That was a distant memory as well. *Betsy's Biscuits* kept me fueled. Although I couldn't let go of it or donate it to a museum, it remained hidden from sight. Every time I looked at it, my heart ached at the memory of what could have been. I gained a new outlook: no time to live in the past, look towards the future.

To push the memory of my time with Captain Lord Henry Spencer out of my memory, I stopped writing historical fiction. The chance of running across the history of his demise seeded a great sense of fear and regret in the pit of my stomach. It's possible I could have found out about my ancestor he ended up marrying. I didn't want to know about the children they could have produced, or if I resulted from that union. *Because... ew.* That would mean that I almost slept with my—how many greats?—great grandfather. No. I found it best to move on.

Six months had passed and with a restraining order firmly in place, there had been no sign of my stalker, Kyle. Cozy mysteries were my new literary focus. Small town murder solved by a local based on Maggie and her adventures. I thought writing about mysteries Maggie solved would be a wonderful distraction. In the middle of March, my editor, Cora, would be in town and wanted to meet to discuss the next book series. She was in Washington, DC, for a conference and wanted to meet in Old Town Alexandria.

"You know, I can see through your tricky ways." I gave Cora a hug before I sat across from her at the table in *Gadsby's Tavern.* The tavern, built in the late 18th century, sat on a corner and was connected to a hotel. We worked our way through the bar area and back towards one of the dining rooms. Dark wood covered the lower half of the walls and framed the doorways and windows. A few diners sat at tables dispersed about the two dining rooms. It would get busy later, but during that time, I would enjoy the quiet lunch with my friend and a wicked cider with rum.

Cora loved her job, which she often told me, but I was afraid she would soon retire. She was in her early sixties, and I probably added to her head full of gray hair. She stood a few inches taller than me, and gave the best hugs. Her arms wrapped around me like a comforting blanket.

"I don't know what you're talking about. You always

loved to have lunch at a historic tavern." Cora's southern drawl and charm made it difficult to be upset with her. Her dark brown eyes sparkled with mischief. "However, if it inspires you to write historical fiction again... you'd make mama happy."

A quick smiled shot across my face. "Your mom will love my new series. You can't tell me she wouldn't love to sit down with a fun, cozy mystery."

"I just don't get it. You have such great reviews from the historic series. War, George Washington, love... you had them hooked."

I couldn't tell her the reason I couldn't write historical fiction set during the French and Indian War was because I was there and my heartbreak of leaving Henry was too fresh and painful. Thinking about what I lost and what he meant to me, it crushed me to know I would never have that again. I knew two hundred sixty years later he was long gone, but his memory was still fresh in my mind. Once, I had promised myself that I would learn the proper protocol of women in the mid-1700s. When do I curtsy? Lord? Lady? Mistress? Your Excellence? How do I lace up my own stays? When will indoor plumbing become a thing? It was all a foreign language to me. Henry had tried to provide a book on etiquette, but it was more about how to be a good wife of the 18th century, not what I really wanted to learn. I left it behind when I could no longer bear the thought of never being with Henry again.

The waitress set our plates down. I got the fish, delicately battered and fried, and thick chips, with a side of tangy coleslaw. They styled the plates after the old tavern pewter-styled plates. They really went for historical immersion. I had to stop for a moment to regain my composure. Memories of my tavern meals with Henry flooded my thoughts. A young barmaid, Eloise, called me old, and I blew up at her, causing the crowded tavern to stare in my direction. I made quite the bold scene. Looking back, it embarrassed me at my reaction to her comments. A snorted laugh escaped at the memory. Grabbing a few fries in my hand, I laughed and turned my head away from Cora.

"I might revisit the series later. Right now, though, I want to talk about solving crimes." I shifted in my wooden chair. "My cozy mystery series would be based on Maggie. Do you remember my friend that owns *By the River Bookshop*, in Fredericksburg? When she isn't in the shop, she is inserting herself into Fredericksburg police cases. With her loud and friendly personality, she knows everyone. My books will be based on her store and could bring more business to her little shop, offering her the opportunity to hire more help. Mayhap, she could solve more crimes. It was a win-win for both of us." *Mayhap?* What was I doing? Channeling Henry and his overuse of the word "mayhap?"

"Mayhap? You have a chip on your shoulder." She looked over the brim of her pewter mug of warm cider, giving me the look of 'I know you're hiding something from me.' "What do you have against history?"

"I'm not angry or have anything against history," I said through an overly stuffed mouth full of fried potatoes.

"And I don't have a chip on my shoulder. I just need a break."

"No, really." She pointed to my left shoulder. "You have a chip on your shoulder."

Looking down to my left, an inch-long chunk of potato laid precariously on my shoulder. I picked it up and shoved it into my mouth with the rest of the crispy logs of perfection. No sense in wasting a perfect fried potato.

Cora agreed to give the new series consideration, and I agreed to plot when I got home. We thought I could have the first outline completed by the end of May and the first draft completed by the end of September. Plenty of time to make the change.

The tavern had plenty of empty tables during lunch. We stayed and chatted while enjoying our meal, without the rush of clearing the table for the next guests. I had another spiced cider with rum, which required me to walk off the booze before driving home. I could be such a lightweight.

"You should go visit the Carlyle House a couple of blocks over," Cora said as we were leaving the tavern, giving a flick of her head in the house's direction. "Built around the same time as your last book."

"First of all, why would you know that? It sounds like a set-up." I eyed her suspiciously. "Are you hoping that it will inspire me to continue the series?"

"I'm just hoping that you will enjoy yourself. Go on tour. Explore the grounds." She wrapped her arm around my waist as we went down the steps and headed towards the parking garage. "You might find what you're missing there."

"Inspiration?"

"Your love for history. Now, shoo." She flittered her hand at me. "And I expect to hear from you soon. I'm serious, Amelia. You need to churn out the words."

Waving her off, I continued towards the parking garage on South Union Street, the street which ran along the Potomac River. The Carlyle house stood to the right of me on Cameron Street, and on my way back to my SUV in the garage. Somehow, I missed the old house on my way to *Gadsby's Tavern*, but there it stood in its 18th century glory. Standing in the courtyard, I looked up at the large windows adorning the front of the house and hoped the ghosts of the original owners remained hidden in the halls and basement. There was no reason for me to go in there, I told myself. I turned to walk away, refusing to take the chance of running into a ghost of someone that I knew lurked about the old mansion. A cannon stood in the courtyard's corner, a reminder of our defeat at Fort Necessity. We left our artillery, weapons, supplies, and our wounded with the French. I swallowed down those memories, desperate to leave behind those past months.

As I turned to leave the courtyard, a ghost of a different kind caught my eye. To call Kyle a ghost was a bit of an exaggeration. He was not dead, as much as I thought his death would make my life safer. Nevertheless, he still haunted me. I thought he had given up on stalking me months ago. He watched me from across the street. He hadn't given up, he just got better staying hidden in the shadows. I would know him anywhere. The overcast day dulled his dark brown hair and darkened his brown eyes. He wore a long black trench coat over his lanky body. I wondered what he was trying to hide under it. It seemed bizarre and out-of-place to anyone that wore long trench coats anymore. It was mid-March, temperatures in the fifties, hardly stalker trench coat weather. He started towards me with a sinister glare in his eyes. No. That couldn't be happening. I sprinted across the courtyard towards the French Blue front door and up the five concrete steps. Footsteps pounded on the pavement behind me. He closed in behind me. I reached out toward the door handle, grabbed it firmly, and gave the knob a turn. It was locked! My fist pounded on the door. "Please, someone. Let me in." No answer. Kyle's footsteps slowed down behind me. There was no time to run around the side.

Kyle panted at the bottom of the steps. I continued to smack my hand on the door. I tried the handle again. Locked. He put his hand in his jacket pocket. Was going to pull out a gun and shoot me? I would become another ghost of the Carlyle House. He pulled out his hand and yelled, "Amelia, catch!"

Instinctively, I caught whatever he threw towards me. I looked down at the object in my hand. Thankfully, it was not a grenade. A coin? *He stalked me that entire time to give me a coin?* I didn't want to take the chance that he could have a gun in the other pocket. I knocked again on the door. No answer. I tried the handle again. It turned, and the door opened. *Oh, thank goodness someone unlocked the door for me.* I threw the door open, quickly entered the house, and slammed the wooden door behind me, plowing my back into the door to hold it closed and prevent Kyle from following me inside.

A blinding light pierced through the room. The smell of cherry wood burning in a fireplace permeated the air. The wind blew around me. I knew what was happening. This happened to me before. Once at Fort Ashby, when I was sent back to 1754. The other time was at Henry Spencer's house in Williamsburg, when I returned to the 21st century. The urge to enter the light overcame me. I could hear aggressive pounding from the other side of the door. Kyle struggled to get in. The handle clicked in desperation. I didn't lock the door behind me. Why couldn't he get in? Thankful that he remained outside, I turned back towards the room and let the thoughts of Kyle and the trouble he brought with him left my mind. The light enticed me towards it. Inviting, like a warm brownie, begging for me to take a bite. Henry filled my thoughts. As it happened before, it happened again. Everything went black.

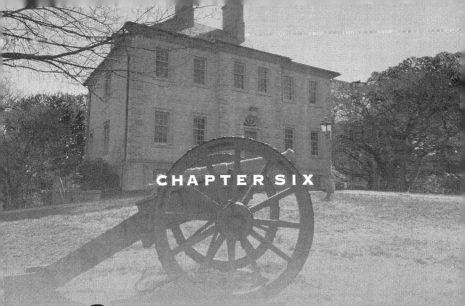

CHAPTER SIX

"*M*istress, are you well?" A woman's voice woke me from my slumber. Dragging my hand across my forehead, I struggled to gain my composure.

I opened my eyes to see a concerned, young, black woman, dressed in a colonial-style brown cotton dress, kneeled next to me. Was I seeing what I thought I was seeing?

"Hm?" I closed my eyes tight. Confusion swirled. Hundreds of thoughts and memories crashed through my head. They rolled and bumped into each other, like a child spilling their entire bag of marbles. I slowly opened my eyes again to find the view hadn't changed. The specter of time brought be back to Colonial America—back to Henry. At least, I hope it did and that this woman was not an employee of the Carlyle House in full costume.

So much could have happened to Henry in the seven months that I had been away. My head spun in a million different directions as I continued to lie on the floor. Traveling through time drained my energy. Even though I just had lunch, I was famished. I tried to regain my thoughts and closed my eyes. I could hear footsteps across the wood floors running away from me. Excited women's voices permeated through the wall from a nearby room.

I thought about the last time I had traveled through time. I wore a pair of skinny jeans, a white pullover shirt, knee-high boots, and a blue corduroy blazer. It was scandalous for Ensign Joseph Coulon de Jumonville and his second in command, Bouchard—that abusive bastard—to see me in such a state. They looked down at me and considered me a spy for the British. I had been on a fact-finding expedition for the last book I wrote, when Jumonville had found my notebook containing the dates and locations of Washington's battles. I became a punching bag as they tried to pull information on the upcoming maneuvers from me. Excuses for the way I dressed formed in my head.

When I got dressed that morning, I had slipped on a pair of straight-leg jeans and brown loafers, pulled on a green V-neck sweater, wrapped a lightweight, black knitted scarf around my neck, and a threw on a lightweight brown tweed blazer. Appropriate attire for a woman in the 21st century. It was not appropriate for a lady of the mid-18th century to wear. How was I going to explain my clothes this time around? In my pocket, I had my debit card, cell phone, and key fob for my SUV that was parked in the parking garage. It was doomed to be towed—again. No notes to brand me a spy. No money to buy clothes. I would be reliant on the generosity of my hosts. I hoped they would not throw me out of the house, thinking that I was a men's-clothing-wearing vagrant.

Multiple sets of feet clomped across the wood floors and got louder as they closed in on me. I had to think of a story of how I got there, but my thoughts were still in a fog. *Think, Amelia, think.* I played the invalid card, hoping to garner sympathy for my situation. I remained on the floor with my eyes closed.

"Penny, call for Cate." A woman's voice called from above me. "Mistress?"

I fluttered my eyes open. Exhausted from time travel, feigning weakness was not a struggle. "Where am I? Who are you?" I said in a weakened voice. Confusion was not a struggle either. My head continued to spin like a cyclone. Parched, my throat and tongue felt as though I had swallowed a gallon of sand and asked for the Sahara Desert for seconds. "Water?" *Keep it simple, Amelia.*

I looked at the young woman leaned over me. She appeared to be in her mid-twenties, with fair skin. Her brown hair, worn down and pulled over her shoulder, was tied with a green ribbon. Soft brown eyes looked at me with concern. I looked over her dress, trying to get a sense of when I had slipped through time. She wore a light green petticoat and matching bodice. More than one woman dressed in mid-18th century clothing confirmed to me I had traveled back in time. Again. I needed to figure out to when. Calculations of the time it would take for me to walk to Elizabeth Woods' house in Fredericksburg started squeaking through my head like rusty cogs. Two or three

ALEX R CRAWFORD

days to walk. No food. No shelter. No way to make a fire.
No problem. The woman called out over her shoulder,
"Penny. Cate. Bring water." She looked down at me. "Are
you able to move, Mistress? I cannot have you laying in the
middle of my entry." A quick, concerned smile spread
across her lips.

"Who are you?" I struggled out as I ran my hand across
my forehead. Words and thoughts escaped me.

She looked at me; her face spoke volumes. I must have
appeared to be a madwoman to her. "Mistress Sarah
Fairfax Carlyle, wife to Major John Carlyle, master of this
house."

"Major?" I struggled to put two thoughts together.
"Major John Carlyle?"

"Yes, Major John Carlyle of the Virginia Forces."

"Where is Washington?" I should have asked about the
date. But I didn't want to seem too deranged and thought
to ask where George Washington was in order to piece
together the year.

"Washington?" Her voice and eyes dripped in
confusion.

"Yes, George Washington." I snapped back. Deep
breath. "I beg your pardon, Mistress Carlyle." Hunger
took over my temper. I took another deep breath to regain
control of myself. Fortunately, I could pull a tidbit of
information from the deep recesses of my memory. I had
to remind myself that George Washington had two older
half-brothers, Lawrence and Gus. Sarah Fairfax Carlyle
was a sister to Ann Fairfax Washington, Lawrence's widow.
"I am acquainted with George Washington." My hand

rubbed over my exhausted face. "I hoped to locate his whereabouts."

She grabbed my hand and helped me sit up. "I suspect he is currently at his home." She looked me over, probably wondering why I was wearing odd clothes. Well, odd for the 18th century. "Why would you come to Alexandria to find him?"

Penny and another woman, who I assumed was Cate, another enslaved woman, rushed into the entry. Cate lifted a glass of water to my lips. It felt like a monsoon season had arrived in the desert in my mouth. The water sloshed around my empty stomach, reminding me I needed to find food before I turned into a *hangry* grump.

Too late.

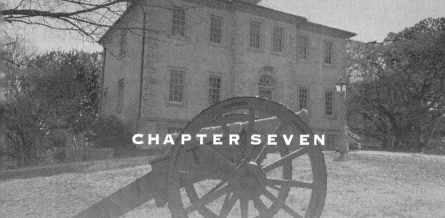

CHAPTER SEVEN

"*I* am not entirely sure how I arrived here. Perhaps I was taken hostage?" I shook my head in disbelief at my situation. I went into the past prior to that day, but didn't think it could happen again. Being taken hostage by the French when I arrived in 1754, I knew that would help explain my strange attire and how I could have arrived. I hoped this would work again. "That is why I'm dressed like this." I motioned to my clothes. "I would like to inquire about the date, as well."

"Today is the eighteenth day of March in the year of our lord seventeen fifty-five." The women helped me up to my feet. "They held you hostage? That sounds dreadful. Who would do such a thing?"

"The French. That's who." I was short with her, and it was not a lie. They had taken me hostage for over a week in April 1754. A year had almost gone by, and there I was back during the beginnings of a war. I had to find my way to George Washington. He would know where I could find Henry. Maybe I head south to Williamsburg. It would be unrespectable and dangerous for me to head there on foot, by myself, alone on the road. Nope. A shiver ran down my spine. I would have to make different plans to find my way to Williamsburg. When I last spoke with Colonel Washington, it was at the celebration at the Governor's palace in Williamsburg. He swirled and danced around with as many young ladies as he could snag that night. He loved to dance, and as I recall, he was quite the dancer. I snuck out the back door with Henry before the expectation of my dancing skills—or the lack of them, I should say—were to be put to the test.

"I pray it is not the French that are imprisoned here in Alexandria. That Drullion does nothing but complain. I dare say, cannot envision him taking you hostage."

Drullion's name didn't ring a bell. Why did they have the French imprisoned here? I had to find out more. "The French that are imprisoned here... I mean... how did the French become imprisoned here, in Alexandria? I didn't think they got close to here. We had French hostages from the skirmish at the glen when they... we... killed Jumonville, but I thought they moved them to Winchester."

With Penny on one side and Cate on the other, the women gently helped me through the foyer, up the stairs, down the hall to the right, and into the first room on the right. It was a well put together bedroom. A tall chest of drawers in one corner, two upholstered chairs, and a four-poster bed. I could only guess this was Mistress Carlyle's bedroom.

"I only know what my husband had mentioned to me." She motioned for Cate and Penny to assist me into one of the floral chairs. The floral fabric matched the drapes on the windows and the bed. Mistress Carlyle sat down in the chair across from me. "Cate, will you bring Mistress... I apologize. I don't believe you gave me your name."

"Oh, yes. That was so rude of me. Mistress Amelia Murray." With my hand placed on my chest, I gave a tilt to my head in a half-assed bow. "I... um... am... was... I don't know. I was betrothed to Captain Henry Spencer. At least, I was supposed to be... I believe." My thoughts stuttered in my head. "But they took me hostage, and now I'm here."

"Mistress?" Cate interrupted.

"Yes, please prepare tea," Sarah said to Cate, without looking towards her. Her eyes scanned my face, and no doubt, my odd attire. Cate curtsied and left the room, leaving me alone with Mistress Carlyle.

"You are Mistress Murray?" Sarah's eyes widen to the size of saucers. "It was the French who captured you and were with Colonel Washington."

"You heard about me?" I thought I was a forgotten memory. Quick to show up. Quicker to leave. The heat of my embarrassment flushed up my neck and made its proud display through my fair skin. The freckles couldn't hide the pink hue. "But how?"

"Colonel Washington is a relation of mine." She next to me and ran a hand over my head, looking for any bumps or cuts. It was understandable. They had found me sprawled out on the floor of the foyer. "My sister, Anne, was wife to Lord Lawrence Washington—God be with his soul—Colonel Washington's older brother." The look of excitement crossed Sarah's face when she spoke. Finally, we were getting somewhere in this conversation.

"Colonel Washington spoke of me?" The last I recalled, he thought of me with indifference. With my quick opinion on his lack of battle skills, he was quick to dismiss me. He didn't appreciate my tactics... even though I was correct.

"He told the story of the ball in Williamsburg and how you disappeared that night. It was all quite the scandal with Captain Spencer. Everyone thought you ran away from the captain. I was to attend with my husband, but we couldn't make the trip, you see." She stared off into the abyss of the sunny window. Something had troubled her about the trip, but she was not ready to share that with me.

My legs wobbled under me as I tried to stand up. "I didn't want to leave that night." My voice cracked, overwhelmed with emotion. I collapsed back into the chair. "I need to let Henry know I'm here and safe."

"Please, Mistress, you are in no condition to walk. You need your rest." She ran her hand across her midriff, which allowed me to notice her round, pregnant belly. Her dress was a lovely light blue silk embroidered with red and blue birds. Yellow and red flowers danced and twirled their way around her body and hid her stomach when she stood. When she sat, her round belly snuck out from under her loosened stomacher, there was no denying she was with child. "I will send word to Colonel Washington regarding your safe return. He will know where to find Captain Spencer."

Tears pricked at my eyes. I had given up hope of ever seeing Henry again. I wanted to run out of the room and race around Virginia looking for him. That was a silly idea. I could barely stand up, let alone run around the entire state of Virginia. And then, there is the whole business of running–my least favorite activity. "Of course. I hate to impose on you, but until I can find Henry, I need a place to stay. I don't have a place to stay, or clothes, or any money." The feeling of being lost and alone overwhelmed me. Alexandria was in friendly territory and the Carlyle's home would allow me to be safe until I could figure out where I needed to go next.

"Of course, Mistress Murray. I am certain Captain Spencer will be pleased to hear of your safe return and that we took great care of you until he can retrieve you." She reached across, grabbed my hand, and gave it a reassuring squeeze. When she grabbed my hand, a rush of comfort ran through me. "Now, let's see what we can do to get you out of these indecent clothes and into a proper dress befitting a lady. I will have Penny send for the tailor."

I presented her with my open and empty hands. "I don't have money to pay for clothes or anything else, for that matter."

"Of course, you don't." She let out a heavy sigh, leaving me to feel as though I was an inconvenience and intrusion to their otherwise quiet household. "The major will negotiate with Captain Spencer when he arrives."

Cate arrived with tea, biscuits, and cold meat and

cheese. Still famished from the unexpected time slip, I wanted to devour the entire tray of food. It was difficult to refrain from taking it off the table and dragging it to bed with me. Sarah sent her to find the tailor.

"Do you have a spare room for me? I..." Exhausted, I wanted to sleep for a week. I didn't want to deal with the tailor. Food and sleep—and finding Henry—was my only concern. "I mean, I have nowhere to go." The tea was too hot to take more than a sip. Instead, I took the opportunity to refill my empty stomach with a slice of ham and a chunk of the white cheese.

"We received notice that General Braddock and Governor Dinwiddie will arrive next week. We can spare a room until then. I'm sure we will get you on your way before they arrive."

"What's going on? Why are they coming here?" With a surge of energy, I bolted upright in my chair and rattled out my questions. In the future, there will be a road called Braddock's Road. I remember seeing the name while driving in the Washington, DC, area. It must be the same Braddock, although I wasn't too familiar with why he would have a road named after him. Instant regret rushed into me. I researched more about what happened after I left, but I ignored it and resolved to not traveling back in time.

Sarah sat back in her chair after taking a plate with a biscuit and cheese from the nearby tray. "Soldiers started arriving a few days ago. They traveled from England." By the look on her face, I wasn't sure if she was annoyed or excited about the activity that would bring. Their arrival would fill the small port town of Alexandria. "Major Carlyle received notice they were to make plans to engage with the French. The Major handles the commissary and has been busy ensuring there are enough supplies for the journey."

"Oh, of course. You had mentioned some French soldiers being here... in Alexandria," I said, wanting to find out more about them. My stomach clenched, thinking about the possibility that Bouchard could be among them. During my time with Jumonville and Bouchard, I hadn't heard the name Drullion. It couldn't possibly be the same defeated group from the glen. Or was it? The group at the glen was not the same group that held me captive. Some were the same, of course. Jumonville, Bouchard, and a handful of familiar defeated faces looked at me that morning. I assumed they had picked up a new group after they had taken the fort—on the fork of the Ohio River— from the colonials. I took a sip of the cooled down tea. A yawn escaped. Rest. I needed sleep.

"You must need rest after your ordeal." She must have read my mind. "Penny is getting your room ready. We will wake you when the tailor arrives. Cate will find you something to wear until then." Sarah stood up, showing it was time for me to leave her room. "Major Carlyle will want to speak to you when he returns from his appointment."

Penny waited for me at the door. "Thank you, Mistress Carlyle. Your generosity is greatly appreciated."

I gave a small curtsey. It was not elegant, but it was an improvement from my earlier attempts at 18th century customs and courtesies. Meeting in the principal's office later sat rough on my mind, but expected.

Penny led the way down the hall to the other side of the landing. On the right, we entered the bedchamber. Late afternoon light seeped through the window on the other side of the bed. On the small stand next to the bed, Penny left a pitcher of water and a glass. All these fluids meant I would eventually have to find a chamber pot. One of the minor inconveniences I would have to deal with in order to be with Henry. I dreaded the thought of using one, but I would have to put aside my desire for modern conveniences to be with him. A chair across the room had a chamber pot mounted to the bottom of it and a lid to cover it. It was almost like using a toilet without the flush. This was a step up from my previous experience at the Lovetts' home. When I fell into a fevered sleep for a few days after I had escaped the French, Henry took me to the home of Sergeant and Mistress Lovett. That time was such a blur. I had spent many days being abused and tortured by Bouchard, that I fell ill. My body was exhausted from the daily beatings and long trek from Fort Ashby, in West Virginia, to Fort Duquesne, in Pittsburgh. It shut down. With the help of Mistress Lovett, Henry, and Ruth, her enslaved servant, I could recover.

I stripped down to my sweater and underwear, unlatched my bra and pulled it out through an arm on the sweater, and crawled in bed. The fatigue was overwhelming, but my brain ran laps around the room. I continued to think about Henry. When was I going to see him? How would he find me? I traveled through 260 years, for him. I tried to convince myself that I could wait another week. Finally, I dozed off for a few minutes, utterly exhausted.

In a daze, I remember the tailor came to the house and took measurements. I would need jackets and petticoats to travel in, clothes for dining, formal wear, and another set for regular day wear. Then there was the need for bed gowns, shifts, stays, stockings and underpinnings. My loafers would work for now, but I would need to find a cobbler and have shoes made. I had no desire to wear my hair in a cap, even if that behavior was viewed as disrespectful for a married woman of my age. However, I was yet to be married. If Henry still wanted to marry me was up for debate. I worried he had forgotten about me. Or, perhaps, he was upset that I had left him alone in his room on the night we were going to make love. Maybe he had moved on to find another woman. No. I had to take that thought out of my mind.

When I visited the *Lord Henry Spencer House and Museum* in Williamsburg, in the 21st century, I remembered the portrait of a woman that looked like me and named Amelia. I had previously thought that it was someone other than me, since I couldn't figure out how to travel back through time. But there I was, back in 1755, so he must still want me. I would find him. The excitement kept me tossing and turning throughout the night. They say patience is a virtue. I never claimed to be patient or virtuous.

CHAPTER EIGHT

"*M*istress Murray, my wife tells me you are to be married to Lord Henry Spencer." Major Carlyle bowed as I entered the room. In his mid-thirties, he was of average height, a little round in the middle, but not exceedingly so. He wore a red uniform jacket with silver buttons going down the front, a red waistcoat, red knee-length breeches, white stockings, and black shoes. He topped his head off with a brown wig.

I gave a low and respectable curtsy to Major and Mistress Carlyle when I entered the parlor. While we waited for my clothing to be made, I wore one of Sarah's dresses. It was a green linen petticoat and jacket. They embroidered the bodice with silk red and blue flowers. Out of respect for the master of the house, I wore a dreadful cap. Although she was my height, she was slimmer than I was. I had lost twenty-two pounds when I was in 1754, and now weighed a comfortable 142 pounds, give or take ten or fifteen pounds. However, Mistress Carlyle was a size or two smaller than me. Fortunately, clothing could be more flexible around the middle. It was the arms that were a bit too tight for me.

"Lord?" Mistress Carlyle looked at me with confusion. "I thought he was just one of Colonel Washington's captains."

"Oh, yeah," I said nonchalantly. "He's a lord son of a duke of something-or-other. I don't recall." I flittered my hand around the air to shoo off the conversation. Henry felt uncomfortable with the discussion of his title and family, and I sure would not speak out of turn about it, considering I knew little about it myself. "Governor Dinwiddie had asked him to join the Virginia Regiment. He wanted people he could trust." I looked over at Major Carlyle. "You know how persistent Governor Dinwiddie can be, I'm sure." Henry and I hadn't discussed his peerage enough for me to remember of which seat or how or what. His older brother held the title of Duke and adopted Henry's son to pass the title down to him. Henry left England when his wife Caroline died in childbirth. He didn't discuss the details of his circumstances. Her death must have been devastating to him. I didn't understand how he could have given up his young son so easily and leave, he wasn't willing to tell me the entire story. I made a mental note to ask him about it when we finally get the chance to talk. It was different leaving Hannah. As an adult, she required less from me than a young boy.

Major Carlyle pondered what I had said about Dinwiddie. "Yes, yes." He said with a gruff. He cleared his throat. "I will inquire the whereabouts of Lord Spencer.

You are welcome as our guest until you can make further arrangements."

With a curtsy, I said, "Thank you, Major Carlyle. Your generosity and kindness are greatly appreciated. Truly, I am honored to be your guest." I laid it on thick. I needed his respect in order to not be thrown out on the street, and I was sure he understood I was grateful to him. It was thoughtful and kind of him. However, I knew he would expect financial compensation from Henry. All in due course.

Later that morning, I itched to get out of the house. The last time the sun shined on my head was the day before when I had left Cora in front of *Gadsby's Tavern* and made my way to the *Carlyle House*. With enough sleep and food to make me content, I needed to be refreshed with the crisp springtime outdoors.

The Carlyles lined the garden behind the house with trees, and plants ready to flower. Off to the side, laid another garden, trellised and prepared for fruits and vegetables. To the right were three small buildings. They were simple. I assumed they were indentured servant and enslaved people's quarters. I didn't see an outside kitchen, which I thought was common. Henry's home in Williamsburg had a kitchen in a separate building, to the side of the dining room. There was no such building at the Carlyle House. When Henry's staff served breakfast, we sat in the dining room, and they brought the food to us from the kitchen next door. Although improper for me to sneak into the kitchen in the basement, I wanted to get a feel for where things were located.

Beyond the gardens, I could see the masts of the ships docked on the Potomac River. Seagulls cawed and yelled overhead, as they signaled their claim on a meal. Men carried crates up and down the dirt road that ran along the side of the property. Crackle of wagon wheels over the dirt path and the roar of conversation and laughter brought the port alive. It was a busier port than I had expected. In the 21st century, there was a wharf with shops, slips for small personal boats, and people. Lots and lots of people.

"More soldiers are due to arrive today," Mistress Carlyle said as she approached me from behind. I stared out towards the river. "Mayhap your captain will be among them."

"Do you know when they are supposed to leave to engage the French?" I asked, hoping she would know if her husband was to join the group or not. I couldn't rely on the thought of Henry's arrival with the rest of the soldiers.

"No, Mistress Murray. I would not have been told." She said with a slight laugh. She must have thought I was a fool to think she would be privy to the details of military movement. Henry had shared that information with me, but our circumstances were a bit different from the Carlyles' conversation. "They will travel to Annapolis by the beginning of April. General Braddock has sent notification to the Governors, Colonel Washington, and the Major. We will know soon enough."

I turned towards Sarah and asked, "Mistress Carlyle, do you not desire to scream at the lack of knowledge of the goings on?"

"You have too much free time to think about these

things, Mistress Murray. Would you like to come inside and embroider with me?" She turned towards the large, tan-colored bricked home. Open curtains to my room on the left swayed with the light breeze that carried the smell of the port and swirled its way through the open windows.

"Not yet," I said, knowing full well that my embroidery skills were terrible and an embarrassment to all of womankind. "I would like to walk to the market."

An exasperated exhale escaped from her petite frame. "Of course you will need an escort." She seemed appalled at the thought that I would wander off to the market on my own.

"And money. You know... just in case. I am certain Lord Henry will be more than happy to pay you back when he gets here," I said matter-of-factly. It was a matter of fact that I had no clue if he would pay my debts and I despised to beholden to anyone else for my well-being.

"I will have to request it from the Major. And let's hope your captain can pay your debts."

I suppose she had a point. We were going on hopes and assumptions I would have my debts paid for by Henry. We didn't know where he was or if he would show up with the rest of the soldiers.

Cate escorted me to the quick jaunt to the market. I wasn't sure what I had hoped to find, maybe a notebook, ink and quill, and any other little trinket that caught my eye. Hannah needed to know that I was alive and well, but I had to figure out how to get her the message. Retail therapy and incorporating myself into the area hung at the top of my list. The market square was a couple hundred yards away from the Carlyles' grand house. Major Carlyle could monitor the activity from his bedroom window if he so chose.

Shops, inns, and tenements surrounded the large square on three sides. We wandered past merchant carts, stalls, and storefronts. Merchants called out to shoppers as they wandered past. As we approached, the roar of conversation and the call of fish, tobacco, and produce for sale rang through the crisp morning air. The crowd of people stifled my breath. I was certain the entire populace of Alexandria emerged into the market that morning. A woman walked by selling a meaty hand pie. She wore a dark brown skirt and jacket, with an off-white bonnet on her head and a worn apron down her front. She carried a woven tray with a length of rope tied to the handles on each side, placed around her neck for support. From the aroma of bacon that wafted past me, I would guess it was pork. It reminded me of the time that I had stumbled upon a renaissance fair when I traveled to Edinburgh, Scotland with my daughter, Hannah, and my late husband, Todd. A woman on the streets of Edinburgh sold hand pies, and my stomach ached to try one.

Chickens clucked and pigeons cooed from nearby fowl baskets. The large woven reed baskets were about eighteen inches wide and two feet tall, with a woven lid on top, and little reed bars which allowed passersby to gawk at the creatures in their little prison. They crammed four or five birds into the small container. I would squawk too, if I had to stay in such close quarters until they hauled me off to die. No. I wanted to imagine they were hanging out with their friends until they found a spacious home to lay eggs and eat bugs until they were old and cranky. Happier thoughts would prevail.

Two stalls down from the chicken-man was the basket-man. The short, squat man with a ruddy face called out to shoppers while he wove a basket. I slowed in front of hanging baskets of various sizes. The one near the back of the stall with a long leather strap caught my eye. Gathering baskets with large, looped handles sat on a table. Fowl baskets, like the ones the chicken-man contained his chickens and pigeons in, lined the front of a table. A market basket with a woven handle would loop perfectly on my forearm and would collect my shopping. I turned and smiled at Cate, looking for her approval of my choice in the basketry.

Out of the corner of my eye, I thought I saw a familiar face. I did a double take. It couldn't be. My stomach dropped to my toes and my mouth dried into a desert. Bouchard stood across the market, staring at me with death deep in his eyes. I froze. Panic set in. The blood coursed like fire through my veins. I frantically searched for a quick way out of there. Maybe he didn't see me? I was going to be sick.

"Cate, we need to leave now." I snatched her arm with urgency. We didn't have time to mess about the market. People crowded around the stalls, making it difficult to make a quick escape. I could hear his shouts from behind. He wanted me dead. He always wanted me dead. I was going to be killed in the middle of a crowded market and no one could stop him.

We pushed our way through the crowd. An old man bumped into me with a firmly placed elbow to my side and nearly knocked me down to the ground. Cate caught me by my elbow. We neared the edge of the crowd. I held onto Cate's hand, not wanting either of us to get lost in the crowd. We needed to get back to the house. Back to safety. Another man knocked into me. I kept my head down, but could see his white linen breeches and socks, with black buckled leather shoes. I had to escape. Bouchard was closed in on me. My chest weighed heavily on me, suffocating me. The entire world imploded.

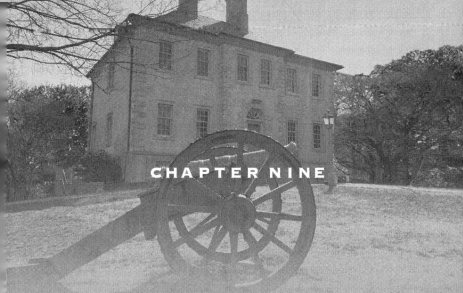

CHAPTER NINE

A firm hand grabbed tight on my upper arm. I was not fast enough. *Was he going to shoot me? Stab me? Snap my neck?* The blood pulsed through my veins. It throbbed in my ears to the point I couldn't hear the surrounding crowd. I yanked my arm, desperate to get away. He would not let go. I yanked again. His fingers dug into my biceps. Cate pulled away from my grip. Tears threatened to burst out of my eyes. I squeezed them shut. "No," I yelled with an ear-piercing scream. If he was going to kill me, then I wanted everyone to witness it. He would hang for it.

His grip tightened around my arm. "Amelia, please. Stop." His voice was deep, strong, and with a hint of desperation. I stopped in my tracks. I would recognize that voice anywhere and through all of time itself. My feet refused to move. I opened my eyes and looked towards my captor. White trousers. *What was Bouchard wearing?* Not a Virginia Regimental uniform. I followed up the red waistcoat and blue coat with red lapels. A brass gorget hung around his neck. My knees buckled as my eyes met Henry's blue eyes staring with fire back at me. He reached around my waist to prevent my collapse to my knees. I knocked on the hilt of his sword as I threw my arm around his waist to hold on for dear life. The chaotic world no longer existed. The sounds and movements of the people, animals, and even the breeze that flowed from the nearby Potomac River became a blur.

Speechless, I stood there, mouth agape. Henry found his voice. Thankfully, one of us did. "How are... where did... my love? I thought I had lost you."

"I... I... I was lost. I'm here. You found me." I grabbed the lapels of his uniform jacket. I had to hold on to him, in fear that this was a dream. Adrenaline coursed through my body. I struggled with my breaths and gasped for air. "Bouchard. Over there. Chasing us." Behind me was a horde of people that hid my assassin.

"Come. Grab ahold of your maid." He pulled me by the hand through the crowd. I clamped down on Cate's hand. Protection from the front and back. Would it be enough? I was afraid he could still harm me. I held my breath until I knew we were out of sight of Bouchard.

We rounded the corner away from the market. There were fewer people on the side street. My ears and lungs burned from the chaos. "Where are we going?" I gasped out a shout as I ran behind Henry. At six feet tall, his legs and strides were much longer than mine. My short legs struggled to keep up with him. Cate, light on her feet, trailed behind us.

"I need to get you to safety. Then, I'll find Bouchard and..." I stopped dead in my tracks. Cate crashed into me. Henry skidded to a stop and turned to face me, not letting go of my hand. "My love, we need to keep moving."

"Henry, please. Just... just... stop for a moment." I refused to budge. "Bouchard will not chase after you. He knows you will kill him. He will wait until he finds me alone." I sucked in air. "Besides all that, why is he allowed to slither around the streets of Alexandria? Shouldn't he be in jail or hanging from the end of a rope?"

Henry pulled my hand to his mouth and kissed my knuckles. I missed those lips upon my hand. "Then we need to make sure you are never alone. I will not let you leave my side ever again. I cannot..." He took a hard gulp to swallow back the tears. He cleared his throat and his voice lowered. "I cannot lose you again. When you left, my world become nothing. I dared not eat or sleep. You invaded my every thought. I searched for you everywhere I went. I..."

I squeezed his hand. "Let's get Cate back to Carlyle's. That's where I'm staying." The three of us gasped for breath, both from adrenaline and exertion. I released my death grip from Cate's hand. I felt bad for the woman. My grip will have cut off the blood supply to her fingers. Henry offered me his arm and Cate followed behind us back to the house. I squeezed his forearm. I wanted to feel him in my hands, never to let him go.

The walk back to the house was quick. My short legs went a hundred miles an hour, trailing after Henry's long stride. I wanted the walk back to the house to last the rest of the day. Just the two of us together. We needed to get to know each other again. Seven months passed since we last spoke. I wondered if he had changed. I know not only did I gain my back with my pre-kidnapped weight, but I had been moody without him. My friends and Hannah called me—oh, what was the word?—insufferable grump.

This version of Alexandria differed greatly from the thriving city of 21st century. It was a new town in the beginning stages of becoming a thriving community. The dirt streets, lined with small wooden and brick buildings, pulsed with merchants shuttling goods to and from the docks. Major Carlyle's home was the most impressive building in the area. It was built out of sandstone, transported from Aquia, thirty-five miles away. I was familiar with the quarry. It was nearby my home in Fredericksburg. It would be the same quarry they would get the stone for steps and walkways throughout Mount Vernon. George Washington selected the stone for the building material of many of Washington, DC's government buildings. The quarry sat along Aquia Creek, and boats and ships transported the stone up the Potomac River to Alexandria and the future Washington, DC.

"Major Carlyle was to send a note to Dinwiddie and Washington on my behalf." I finally spoke up, when my breathing and pulsed had slowed from the chase. I felt as though I needed to make an excuse for my lack of letting Henry know I was in 1755.

Henry slowed his pace. "I hadn't heard from any of them. When did you arrive?" The snap in his voice screamed of anger. Or was it irritation? Either way, his tone showed that he was not happy with me.

"Yesterday. In the afternoon. I'm not sure." My head shook. "I showed up at their house." I turned to look back at Cate. She was nearby, which kept me from saying much more. "We can discuss my arrival later."

"We have much to discuss later." Henry said and squeezed my hand that was firmly placed in the crook of his arm. My heart wanted to thump out of my chest. He either was no longer upset with me, or he would blow his top at me later. I voted for no longer upset with me.

Cate left us at the front of the courtyard and entered through the side door—the servant's door. We crossed the front, went up the steps, and entered through the front door of the house. I wanted to take him upstairs to my room, discuss what we have missed from each other's lives, and finish where we had left off those seven months ago in Williamsburg. That would have to wait until later, much later.

A white male servant dressed in dark blue livery trimmed in white approached and led us to the parlor on the left to wait for Major and Mistress Carlyle. We sat on the sofa. I could hear the Carlyle's young son, William, crying upstairs. They had moved the toddler into his parents' room, instead of his own room with his caregiver, to prepare for the arrival of the soldiers. It had thrown off his routine, and he didn't seem pleased. The stress of the change in the household already wore on the Carlyles. I was a nervous, excited little ball of fire. "I meant to ask you earlier," I began. We had a moment to ourselves, and I was ready to inject myself back into his life. "Where are you staying?"

"I arrived..." he was interrupted by the arrival of the Carlyles. We stood up to greet our hosts.

"Captain Spencer, grand of you to join us." Major Carlyle entered the room, more animated and robust than I had seen him since my arrival. "I had just sent the dispatch for your whereabouts only hours ago. How you fair with such haste?"

"I arrived this morning to join Braddock's troops and ensure all was well for Governor Dinwiddie's arrival next week." Henry said, as they invited us to sit back down. "We should receive around two thousand soldiers and will require provisions during the stay and our onward mission."

"Two thousand soldiers will descend upon Alexandria?" Sarah gulped out her questions. "How long will they stay?"

"Mistress Carlyle, the entirety will not arrive until our departure. A small contingent will use Alexandria as headquarters. Others will remain in Fredericksburg, Winchester, and additional locations. As for the length of the stay, that is yet to be determined. General Braddock requested a meeting with the Governors to discuss our strategy. The General and his staff will continue to Annapolis after their arrival." Henry turned to look at Major Carlyle. "Have you heard from Colonel Washington? After Williamsburg and the reduction of the Virginia Regiment, I heard he had resigned his commission. I had hoped he would join us."

Two thousand soldiers? That's more soldiers than I expected, enough to start a war. *No. It is too soon to go to war.* However, the taste of war lingered in the crisp March air. It would be here soon enough.

"Today is the day the heavens smiled upon you. The Colonel wrote me last week to tell me he will join General Braddock here in Alexandria."

"Brilliant," Henry exclaimed and smacked his hand upon his knee. My body jumped from the sudden outburst. He seemed genuinely happy to hear that he will meet back with Washington. His smiled left his face as quickly as it had appeared. "I must digress from the jubilation and discuss a manner of great solemnity. I am concerned with a distressing situation that involves my betrothed in the marketplace." *Betrothed? Did the handsome young captain still wanted to marry me? A forty-one-year-old woman?* A smile crept across my face.

"I assure you, we sent her with an escort." Major Carlyle's face reddened. "I will see to that slave's lashings myself."

Henry raised his hand in protest. "I assure you, Major Carlyle, Mistress Murray was in the presence of her escort." He lowered his hand and stood up. I could see the look of distress race across Henry's face. "It would not have mattered if she was there or nay, for Mistress Murray was certain to be murdered by a man that should be imprisoned."

"Captain, who is this man?" Carlyle huffed out and jolted out of his chair, meeting Henry's stance.

I pulled Henry's hand and invited him to sit back

down. If he didn't stop pacing like a caged tiger, I would jump out of my skin. "He is one of the French we took as prisoners in the glen." Henry looked over at me and held my hand. "Bouchard is roaming the streets of your town. That is the man that..." He stopped. I didn't want to hear him discuss my distress over Bouchard. He knew it would embarrass me.

"Ah, yes. Bouchard. He is one of the French soldiers on parole." Major Carlyle sat back in his chair. "Ensign Drullion has been quite... quite... difficult. Do you see? He constantly insults our sensibilities. We offered him, Bouchard, and a couple of the cadets their parole. We secured the rest of the privates in the gaol."

"Major Carlyle," I interrupted. "While it is true that I was at the glen on that fateful morning and would like no other than to see the men imprisoned, my concern is strictly of Bouchard. He was the man that caused me great physical distress prior to the incident at the glen. When I was held captive, you understand?" I tried to swallow down the lump in my throat that was choking the life out of me. The memory of my captivity made my head spin. Bouchard took great pleasure in the daily beatings.

"Mistress Murray, I have heard of your involvement in this matter. General Braddock and Governor Dinwiddie have sent notification to have the French transported to England. The officers, to include Bouchard, are to be sent to Hampton and then on to England. The rest of the men are awaiting transport as the merchant ships allow." Major Carlyle tried to ease my worries. Nothing would ease them until I knew Bouchard was out of the country or dead. I didn't care either way, but I preferred him to have a painful death at the end of a hangman's noose. "Please, I behoove you to understand the situation. I am a gentleman. Those French officers are gentlemen, and it is required that they be treated as such. I am sure Captain Spencer can explain the finer details in a way that you may understand."

I could feel my blood boil. My ears burned with rage. Henry grabbed my hand to hold me back from stomping across the room and telling Carlyle exactly what I thought about the situation, and my understanding of it. Before I could go full-on crazy-person rage at Carlyle, Henry interrupted me. "Thank you for your consideration, Major Carlyle. I believe Mistress Murray will require a walk in the garden to temper her understanding of the situation."

"Of course, please dine with us this evening and we can discuss settling Mistress Murray's expenses."

"Cheap bastard." I said under my breath. I turned and smiled at the major, hoping that he didn't hear my indiscretion. My teeth gritted incredibly hard, preventing me from speaking ill of my host, I thought I had cracked a tooth.

"We would be honored," Henry said as he stood up and reached his hand out for me to take. I had a terrible feeling that I had embarrassed him.

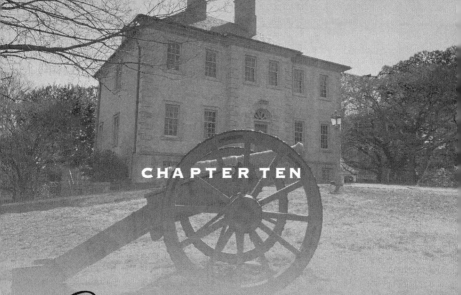

CHAPTER TEN

"*Y*ou don't expect me to run around here naked, do you?" I thought I would start the conversation before Henry could. The evening had turned cool, as it often does near the water in mid-March Virginia. "I didn't think he would ask you to pay him back. He's a rich merchant and has his hands in all kinds of trade. Including human trafficking." I refused to lower my voice, despite the look Henry gave me. "I won't feel guilty for taking money from his slavery business. Just look at this place." I waved my hand back towards the Carlyles' large home.

"I'm not concerned with the costs." Henry looked towards the Potomac. We stood at the edge of the terrace overlooking the garden. "I'm concerned about your safety."

"Well... I," I interrupted.

"Will you let me finish my thought?" He snapped back. His terse response took me aback. "We discussed this situation months ago in my library. It was the one agreement you made for our marriage. You need to learn to control your temper when in the company of men like Carlyle." He looked back towards the house, in search of our host or his ears.

Fire emanated from my nostrils like a dragon ready to barbecue and devour her prey. I had placed my hands on the balustrade, ignoring the coldness of the white stone, and refused to look at him as I fumed. I refused to break down in tears. As he placed his hand on top of mine, I could feel the heat turn my skin on fire. Piercing it like a hot poker. I wanted to pull back, but he took it and raised it to his lips, planting a soft kiss on my knuckles. He turned my hand over and kissed the inside of my wrist. It calmed my temper but heated my soul. He played me like a piano, and he was a master composer. His gentle touch of my skin made my heart sing the love song of the ages. "Walk with me." It wasn't a request. It was a statement to which I couldn't refuse. I would walk with him to the end of the earth if he asked.

We took the wide stone stairs to the left of the terrace and strolled into the garden. The evening air off the Potomac River brought a wet chill that settled deep into my bones. Throughout the garden, trees showed small buds on their branches. It was too early in the season for flowers to emerge, but they gave warning of the impending warmth of the summer. In a month's time, we would see the blooms of spring. Unlit cressets hung from poles and lined the path through the garden. Smoke bellowed out of chimneys, filling the air with the sweet smoky scent. It reminded me of the smell of cherry wood smoke when I slipped through time. I couldn't figure out the significance of why that scent. Would I ever know the reason for how or why I slipped through time? The rambunctious sound of the wharf dulled. Gulls no longer squawked overhead, having returned to their nests—or wherever they went—for the night. The sailors and merchants stopped their work for the evening and would start up again early the next morning.

"You know it is killing me to say this, because I think he was completely out of line, but I'm sorry I lost my temper in there." I interrupted the silence. I didn't want him to be upset with me, but there was something about being in his presence that empowered me and allowed me to be bold. We snaked our way through the garden as the evening sun dipped behind us. The amber light warned us of the impending darkness. "I'm only upset that I made you angry with me."

"Amelia, my love, it matters not if he was out of line. You need to control your tongue for propriety's sake."

"Did I really agree with that? I thought it was more like a curtsy here-and-there. Use this fork. Teatime is at four. That kind of thing." We stopped near one of the trees that lined the path. By that time, it was dark and the cressets that lined the path were still unlit. Two men moved from cresset to cresset, lighting the wood in the metal baskets that hung from metal poles with torches they carried. "This was not what I wanted. I couldn't keep my mouth closed."

"For the love of... why must your refuse to

compromise?" Flames from the cressets reflected in Henry's eyes, which made them appear to burn with anger.

I wrapped my arms around myself. "Is that what you want? A subservient woman to keep her mouth closed?" I turned my head away from Henry. I didn't want to see the answer to my question on his face. It was 1755. I thought I understood the relationships between men and women of the 18th century.

"Do you believe Sarah is subservient? She may not always agree with her husband, but she will not allow herself to say it in front of guests. They discuss it and John carries the burden of their decision." Henry grabbed me by my shoulders to force me to look at him. "The decision that they made together. Let me be that for you. Allow me to carry our burdens."

A flash of light from the other side of the servant quarters caught my eye. "Bouchard." I called out and ducked in fear that a bullet was headed in my direction. "He's trying to shoot me."

Henry formed a cocoon around me with his body. "Get inside," he growled.

I lifted my skirts and ran towards the house, up the stairs, and through the back door. The door slammed shut behind me, alerting the occupants of my distress.

"Mistress Murray," Major Carlyle rushed out of his office. "Why are you making such an uproar?"

"Bouchard," I panted out. "Henry. Gun."

"Good heavens," Carlyle rushed back to his office and barreled out with a pistol in hand.

There was a push on the door behind me. Someone tried to get in. Bouchard must have shot Henry and was determined to kill me next. Carlyle motioned for me to move out of the way, his pistol in hand. The door burst open. Henry ran in, chest heaved as he searched for breath. He found me standing against the wall in the foyer. He drew me into his body and wrapped his arms around me.

"Are you certain you saw Bouchard?" He panted, out of breath. "You heard the shot?"

"Uh... no... I don't remember. There was a flash. I thought..." I looked up at him.

"Did you see a pistol?" Henry's blue eyes bore straight through me. He questioned me and my intentions. *Did he think I said that to garner attention and sympathy?*

"I... it was dark. There was a flash," I said as I looked down towards the floor, ashamed of the spectacle I caused. "I'm not sure what I saw. It's scared me he would find me ever since I saw him this afternoon."

"Mistress Murray," Carlyle interrupted. "You certainly know how to cause a rumpus."

Henry cut a look at Carlyle. He drew me in closer to his body and planted a kiss on top of my head. A deep sigh escaped my lips. I wrapped my arms around his waist, rested my cheek on his chest, and closed my eyes. The thud of his heartbeat slowed. It was at that moment that I knew all would be well between us.

Without letting me go or looking over at Carlyle, Henry asked, "When will we dine? Mistress Murray will want to freshen up. She had quite an excitable day." Relief spread throughout my body as Henry took control of the situation.

Excitable? Ha! That day had been almost too much for me to handle. I would have to contend with a dinner and hear about how expensive my stay has been—and I had only been there since the prior afternoon!

They would serve dinner in a little over an hour. That would give me time to change into one of Sarah's spare dinner dresses. Henry would run back to where the few soldiers that had arrived that afternoon were camped to make sure things were in order and return prior to the evening meal. It was the longest hour of my life.

Another tight-fitting jacket. My arms felt like stuffed sausages in the sleeves. I wondered how long it would take for the tailor to finish my wardrobe. Shoemaker would be next on my list. My loafers were suitable, especially since my feet were hidden under the skirts. I had hoped to find a shop while at the market, but Bouchard's arrival changed those plans. Later that evening, I hoped to discuss our future, but Carlyle dominated Henry's time.

They served dinner in courses. The cook prepared an onion soup, lamb, rice, boiled cabbage, and fried potatoes with bits of crisped ham. The wine flowed as quickly as the conversation. I was thankful that Carlyle held off business discussions with Henry until after dinner. Henry had been in Williamsburg with Governor Dinwiddie when General Braddock had arrived with his soldiers from England. Not one to be in the middle of politicking, Henry left a week ago from Williamsburg to Alexandria, and arrived only that morning.

"At the camp with the soldiers," Henry answered Carlyle's question regarding Henry's lodging arrangements.

"We cannot have a Lord staying in a cold tent when he can stay here." It was common, even expected, for dignitaries to stay at manor homes while traveling. He would compensate Carlyle, of course. I sat up straighter in my chair. Henry? Staying here? With me?

"Oh?" I gulped out my response.

Carlyle shot me a look. Apparently, he had forgotten that I existed. "That is to say... he can stay in one of our spare rooms. We can discuss the arrangements and business after dessert."

"Mistress Murray." Sarah took a sip of her wine. "The tailor sent a note this afternoon stating he will be ready for a fitting of one of your frocks in the afternoon after next."

I was not sure when that was supposed to be. My guess was in two days. "Will he be coming here for the fitting, or am I expected to go to his shop?"

Sarah laughed. "He will come here, of course. We cannot have you vexed by running into the French devil while out to have a fitting."

A dessert of sweet meat and brandy had me ready to loosen my stays. I had dropped twenty-two pounds from the constant traveling, walking, and lack of regular meals. I happily didn't keep it off and could return to my old wardrobe. If they continued to feed me like this, I was sure to purchase a larger wardrobe upon my return to the 21st century—*if* I found my way back to my time.

After we dined, the men moved into the study, while

Sarah and I moved to the music room. We might have stayed together, since it was the four of us, but the men had to discuss my expensive little habit of wanting to be clothed, fed, and Henry's accommodations.

"I would like to thank you and the major for your warm welcome." Cate brought in glasses of wine for us. We sat at the card table but had no interest in playing cards. "You have a lovely home. How long have you lived here?"

"Just on two years now." She didn't seem too interested in striking up a conversation. She stroked her growing belly. We had a few too many glasses of wine and a long day behind us. Sarah looked as though she could fall asleep standing up.

The deep laugh of men congratulating each other on their negotiation skills rang through the foyer and seeped into the music room. I looked up from my nursed glass of wine when the door opened. The soft glow of the candles danced across Henry's face. I stood up, and he met me within three strides. The biggest, stupidest looking grin crossed my face. It was like I was in a dream. He took my hand and brushed a soft kiss across my knuckles. I gave a quick curtsy. "All is well, my lord?" He cut me a look and smiled. I was dying to know where he was staying the night. By the look on his face, it would not be at his tent in the encampment.

"I will stay here this night," he said with a smirk.

I held my breath and squeaked out, "Oh?"

"Of course, since the two of you are unmarried, there will be separate rooms. We will not have debauchery under my roof." John bellowed out authoritatively from across the room. It was his house, his rules, but he was roughly the same age as Henry, which made him younger than me. I wanted to snort out a laugh. It wasn't like I was a maiden, never experiencing the private touch of a lover or a husband.

"Of course, Major," I said as I gave a nod of my head to him. "I would expect nothing less from you."

I wondered if he knew of half of the rumors that ran about Fredericksburg and Williamsburg about his beloved Colonel George Washington. When we were in Williamsburg, the women I had met talked about George's desire to marry. I'm not sure how much was gossip and what was the truth, but they had told me he had asked at least one of the eligible women for her hand in marriage before the ball. He was young, he in need of the money of a well-off woman of the gentry. I knew he would eventually meet and marry Martha Custis. He would not let marriage keep him chaste, but he was not here under Carlyle's roof. Apparently, my honor would be in question if they left us alone in a room together before marriage. *Cheese and rice!* 18th century decorum strikes again.

"I will be down the hall," Henry whispered close to my ear. I could feel his warm breath tickle the hairs on my neck. "Meet me down here after all is dark and silent."

The blood rushed to my cheeks. The candlelight couldn't hide the surprised look on my face.

"Yes, of course," my voice echoed in the room. I wanted to ensure everyone knew my innocent intentions. "It has been quite a long day. If it pleases you," I stood back and looked around the room to our hosts, "I think I will go to my room. We can discuss any further arrangements in the morn." I gave a deep curtsy. I embraced the dramatic flair and skittered up to my room.

I figured the sooner I could get everyone to their rooms, the sooner I could sneak out and meet with Henry. We had only a few moments alone since I was back, and we spent half of that arguing over my temper. We needed to time to reconnect. To fall in love again.

CHAPTER ELEVEN

"I'm a grown-ass woman." I said out loud to myself. No one was in the room with me to hear my declaration of age or independence. Penny had already turned down my bed and the fire in the fireplace across the room had taken the chill out of the air. The house was quiet. I laid in my bed in my shift and waited for John's snore to signal that everyone was asleep. My heart raced. My fingers thrummed across my stomach. Nervous energy took over. I couldn't just lay there in wait. I jumped out of bed and paced the room. The moon glowed behind a few stray clouds as I pulled the curtain back. Padding barefoot across the room, I opened the door to listen for anyone one stirring about the house. I was being ridiculous. What would happen if they caught alone us? Would they force us to marry? Big whoop-di-do!

The chilled night air lingered throughout the house, so I pulled a blanket off the bed, wrapped myself in it, and with tender steps, as to not squeak the floorboards and alert the sleeping occupants, I slithered down the stairs to the music room. The moonlight peered through the window, casting a soft blue glow across the floor. I sat there in the darkened room, waiting for Henry. Why didn't I go to his bedroom instead of the music room? I changed course and head to his room. His room sat across the upstairs, landing on the other side of the house from our hosts' bedroom. The Carlyles would be none-the-wiser of our liaison. When I crossed the room to leave, the door suddenly opened. I jumped and squeaked out a startled scream when a hand clasped over my mouth and an arm grasped firmly around my waist. I wanted to scream and fight, as my nerves stood on high alert until I recognized those powerful hands. They belonged to Henry.

Henry removed his hand from my covered mouth to caress my face. His thumb ran across my cheek and his fingers through my loose, wavy auburn hair. His hand slipped beneath the blanket and pulled me closer to his body. He wore only his shirt and breeches. There was not much material between the two of us. The cotton blanket dropped to the floor as I ran my hand up his chest. I could feel the muscles under the thin linen tighten under my fingertips. His heart pounded in his chest. It pounded for me. Our lips met and were very messy and absolutely passionate. I wanted to devour him. I could taste the sweet brandy that lingered on his warm tongue. He was delicious. My head spun and knees weakened. I released the breath I held. He pulled me tighter and closer. He was intoxicating, and I was addicted to him. To his touch. To his mouth. *To his... oh, my*! I could tell he wanted me as much as I wanted him. It had been far too long to think about our last night together and what almost happened between the two of us. If only I hadn't slipped back to my time before we could go further.

He closed the door with the flick of his foot, and we moved deeper into the room. Hands explored each other's wanton body. The blood coursed through my veins like a wildfire. I ached for his touch. He pressed me against the card table. His lips found their way to my neck. His warm breath heated my soul. He stopped and pulled away. "I shouldn't have done that."

"What was it you shouldn't have done? Stop?" I panted out like a depraved teenager. "You're right, you shouldn't have done that."

He caressed my face. His hand was warm and inviting. "I shouldn't have taken my liberty with you." Make up your mind! Either stop or don't, but the back-and-forth sent my hormones into a tailspin.

"I'm pretty sure I was a willing participant." It disappointed me in the change in direction of the interlude. I searched for the discarded blanket in the moonlit room, finding it near the door, and wrapped it around me. "How many times are we going to get close and one thing or another keeps it from happening?"

"Amelia, please." Henry reached out for me as I tried to leave. My body was on fire, and I needed to cool it and my emotions.

I took a deep breath and sighed. "It's okay, love. It really is. I had assumed that we would spend the night together. And... well... we should've talked about it. I guess?" I shrugged my shoulders and headed over to the window, unwilling to let my emotions get the best of me and flee, and looked out over the garden. What I didn't understand was his hold up. When we were in Williamsburg, we were about to spend the night together. When I had gone to my room to use my chamber pot and freshen up from our evening at the Governor's Ball, I had slipped back through time to the 21st century, and this time, the god of time stayed silent. "The thing is," I turned to face him. His face glowed in the moonlight. "I had spent months obsessing over you. You haunted my every waking thought." I choked down my emotions lingering in my throat. "I wondered what would have happened that night I left. Now, when we have the opportunity, you stopped mid-kiss and I must respect your decision, as I would expect you to respect mine. But that doesn't mean I'm not disappointed."

Henry stood there without saying a word. I searched his face, hidden by shadows and the only light coming from the moon that played hide and seek with the clouds, to understand what he was going through. It made little sense to me. He had been married. His son lived in England with his brother. I wondered if he was concerned that I may get pregnant and die in childbirth, how his wife, Caroline, had seven years ago.

"Amelia," Henry whispered out my name. "I love you. You must know that."

"Honestly, I wasn't questioning your love for me. You have done more for me—and treated me—better than anyone else. I've told you some crazy shit and you keep coming back for more. So, yeah... I'm pretty sure you love me." I shifted over to the nearby chair and pulled the blanket tighter around me to shield myself from the cold and the tension in the room. A cloud of hesitation hung heavy between us. I could sense there was more to his story than he was telling me. "So, if it's not the lack of love, what is it? Don't I turn you on?"

I was no longer a young twenty-year-old woman. My body showed the signs of being forty-one. I had given birth. Over the years, I gained and lost weight. I had stretch marks and saggy skin. He was five years my junior and in peak physical shape. He worked his body and looked great in a pair of tight breeches of his uniform.

"Am I too old? Too saggy? Not what you're looking for?" I had to face the possibility head on. "I thought I felt your passion." He looked away from me. "I'm sorry if I'm embarrassing you. That is not my intention. I don't want to pressure you into anything you are not ready for... that isn't fair to either of us. But something is amiss."

Henry walked over and sat in the blue floral occasional chair across from me. He leaned over with his elbows on his knees and wrung his hands. The clouds had moved on and the moon was high and bright in the night sky. "Allow me to ask you about..." he trailed off. He ran a hand through his hair. I had seen him with his hair down and not pulled back with a leather thong, once, maybe twice. And that was when we were at Fort Necessity, preparing for the fort's defenses. The other time was when we had stumbled upon the cabin in the woods, where we found

Janet and her husband's mutilated bodies. Strands of hair fell out of his queue while he dug the couple's grave. So many men during this time wore powdered wigs—it was the sign of being a gentleman. I don't know how they could stand the heat of them. Henry chose to not wear a wig and would powder his natural hair during formal events. I remember seeing him with his hair powdered at the Governor's Ball. To me, it seemed an odd style—the whole wig wearing bit—but who was I to talk? I showed up in the 18th century wearing jeans. I wore my hair uncovered like a wanton harlot—slight exaggeration—it was unbecoming for a woman my age to expose her hair, as I often did.

"I need a drink. Brandy?" He asked, walking to the decanter left on the table earlier that evening. One glass downed in one gulp, and another poured. He handed me a glass and sat down across from me, spinning it around in his hands, looking for what he wanted to say to me.

"I was married," he began.

I interrupted him. "Right. And married people have sex. Your wife was pregnant twice. So, I know you know what..." He held his hand up to stop me.

"Please, this is difficult enough without you interjecting."

I feigned zipping up my lips, locking them, and throwing the key away. He looked at me like I had lost my mind.

"Yes, as I was saying. I was married," he continued, and took another sip of his brandy. "Caroline was pregnant twice. Neither were my child."

I sat closer to the edge of the chair.

"My brother, Charles, implored me to marry Caroline and raise the child as mine. You see... my brother is married to Margaret. Caroline was Charles's mistress and daughter of Lord and Lady Percy. It would have been a scandal for Caroline to have a child without a husband and known as the mistress to Charles." Henry paused and took a stuttered breath.

I didn't want to interrupt. I wanted—no, *needed*—to know more. He needed my support. I reached for his hand. He trembled under my touch.

"Charles insisted we live in the home with him and Margaret. He said it would be best to keep us as family." Henry sniffed and gulped down the tears and took another drink. "It had nothing to do with being a large, loving family and all to do with bedding my wife. I laid with her once—our wedding night—as it is required to consummate a marriage." He sounded matter of fact in the telling of his story.

His voice lowered to a near whisper. "At first, she laughed. Then she cried. Then she screamed at me and told me never to touch her again. And I never did. I haven't touched another woman since... since... well, you."

"Oh." I took a deep breath and sat deep in my chair. The brandy was warm as it trickled across my tongue. I needed liquid courage. "What about prior to Caroline? Were there... I mean... did you have any experiences before her? Any women?"

"Have I bedded any others? No."

Cheese and rice, this was heavy. I closed my eyes. I

THE TIME WRITER AND THE MARCH

fought back the tears. His brother was a class one asshole. Charles nor Caroline deserved him. Hell, I wasn't sure I did either. I raised my glass and took another gulp of the liquid fire.

"What about Margaret? Did she know about any of this? I mean, it was happening in her home."

Henry hesitated before answering. "She turned a blind eye to his indiscretions. She couldn't carry a child to term and now... she may never be with child. You had asked before how I could leave my son with my brother, that is why. Though I may love him, he is not truly my son."

"I'm trying to wrap my head around all of this," I said as I rubbed my forehead. Thoughts circled through my head like a million shooting stars. "You have only bedded one woman—once—on your wedding night nine years ago. None before. None since."

Henry sighed heavily and sat back in his chair. Tears on his face glistened in the moonlight. His white shirt drowned in the blue light. He was a vulnerable vision to behold.

"The one time you were with a woman, she was an absolute she-devil." If Caroline wasn't already dead, I would have travelled to England just to knock the shit out of her and kill her myself. "I am so sorry, Henry."

"Why are you sorry?" He finished his glass and went to pour another. "You had nothing to do with Charles or Caroline."

"When you finally let down your guard, I disappeared on you. It wasn't by my choice, mind you. But that was another rejection you didn't deserve." I shook my glass around, judging how much of the amber courage that remained. The rest of the bottle was where I wanted to drown my tears. "I come back here and... well... I shouldn't have expected you to want to jump into my bed." I finished the glass in a last gulp. The pain in my chest felt like my heart imploded.

"My heart ached when you left me. I was not sober for months." He sat his empty glass on the card table to his right. "Dinwiddie disbanded the regiment. They sent those that stayed on to the frontier to build forts. Washington resigned instead of accepting the position as captain."

"What about you? Did he send you to the frontier?"

"Ha! I hoped he would have asked. I looked for a fight." He rubbed his hands against his breeches. "No. He thought I would drink away all the rations." He stood up, walked over to me, and took my empty glass out of my hand and placed it on the table next to his. My eyes followed him through the room as he walked over to the window overlooking the terrace. "No. It was a dark time for me. He thought it best that I stay in Williamsburg and suggested I find another woman."

"I'm happy you didn't." I walked over to him and wrapped my arms around him from behind and rested my cheek on his back. He had an intoxicating, sweet, earthy scent. He grabbed hold of my hands to prevent me from letting go of him. It made no matter; I didn't want to let him go. I would have held on to him forever, if I could. "You know, the night of the ball, the women wondered how I could snag the most eligible bachelor in Virginia." A smile spread across my face. "Maybe that's why Washington was rejected so many times. They were holding out for you." I kissed him on his back.

"There was no other but you." He raised my hand to his lips. "If I couldn't have you, I would have been willing to die a thousand deaths."

He turned around to face me and drew me into his arms. I hoped he had finally found his soul's peace with me.

CHAPTER TWELVE

"*T*omorrow, Amelia. They will fit tomorrow you with a jacket that doesn't squeeze your arms like sausages." I looked at myself in the small dressing-table mirror in my room. I wore a simple brown jacket and matching petticoat, kerchief, stays, stomacher, and shift borrowed from Sarah Carlyle. At least my shoes fit. Soon I would find something practical, made of black leather, a buckle or ribbon, and a low heel. I couldn't see to spending more than needed on my wardrobe, since my length of stay was always uncertain.

The three hours of sleep from the previous night showed across my sullen face. Henry and I ended the night not as either of us planned, but with a better understanding of where we stood. We decided it would be best to wait until a better time to further our physical relationship. Marriage might be in our future, when—no, *if*—we could find the time. I knew what I wanted and would wait for him.

I headed downstairs to take breakfast and a very large, very caffeinated pot of coffee. Then set out to find a shoemaker. With Bouchard still wandering the streets of Alexandria, Henry insisted on escorting me to the market. I reminded him he would be not only responsible for my safety, but to fork over the cash for my little shopping spree.

"As much of an asshole as your brother is, at least he made sure you weren't destitute. Trust me. It totally sucks not having any money and completely depending on the kindness of strangers." I gave Henry a nudge with my hip as we walked to the market. He didn't flinch at my comment or the nudge. "Are you paying any attention to me? You seem a million miles away."

"Hm?" His response proved that he was, in fact, a million miles away.

"I said, at least your brother sent you here with money. I don't know how you would have been able to afford me without it."

He looked at me and scrunched his eyebrows together, a look of confusion crossed on his face. "You give him far too much credit. He sent me with nothing. I left with the clothes on my back, my title—if you can call it that—and what little coin I had in my purse." He paused for a moment, and a smirk crossed his face. "And took the one thing I knew would infuriate Charles."

He piqued my interest. "What was that?" Oh? That naughty devil. That was not a side of him I had expected.

"The portrait of Caroline that hangs in the parlor."

I snorted out a laugh at his answer and covered my

mouth with my hand as to not draw too much attention to us as we continued to walk through the crowds of people and sellers in the market to find the shoemaker.

"And here I thought you hung her portrait out of the loss." Now, it was my turn to look at him in a state of confusion. "I don't understand. You're obviously rich. You have land, a house, and you have not questioned spending money on me. How?"

"A brilliant mind for business." He stood straight and seemed to grow a few inches with that answer.

"But you didn't start off here, in the colonies, with the money. You cannot make something from nothing." My pace slowed as I made calculations in my head to figure out how he had done so well for himself. Audible squeaks of the rusty wheels of my brain screeched through my ears. "Did you rob a bank? Hijack a plane? Break into Fort Knox?"

"That's an adventure for another day." He chuckled and gave my hand that rested in the crook of his elbow a reassuring squeeze. "Let's find you a shoemaker."

We found the shoemaker at the end of the busy marketplace. He lined his small shop wall from floor to ceiling with wooden shoe forms and a few samples of what he could produce. There were slippers, bespoke shoes with heels for all occasions decorated with embroidery, lace, ribbon, and bobbles. A pair of tall-shafted riding boots and simple daily wear shoes with buckles and ribbons caught my attention. That morning, a shipment of leather from England arrived, along with bolts of silk in pink, a light blue with a floral print, and a rust-colored brown.

Against my protests, Henry had him fit my feet for four styles scheduled for picking up the following week. We ordered a pair of plain black with a half-inch heel and a simple metal buckle for my everyday wear. I demanded a pair of men's riding boots, like the ones Henry wore. He insisted I would not need them, but I knew better than to believe him. The two men outvoted me and left me a bit grumpy about my lack of riding boots. Henry ordered a pair of pink silk slippers with a soft leather bottom, so I would not sneak around the house barefoot. Ha! He knew me well enough to add those to the list. Henry insisted I have a pair made for formal events, which were bound to happen in the next couple of months with the group of men scheduled to arrive within the next week. I picked out a dark blue silk with tiny red roses embroidered, and the tongue trimmed in white lace. The last pair was an evening shoe for dressing up for non-formal events and dinner when the expectation was to dress for the occasion. That pair was a black leather one-inch heel with a black ribbon. They needed to be versatile in looks and function. My loafers would have to last me longer. If I wanted any other types of fabrics or leather, there was the requirement to wait until the next shipment came in from England. I found it ridiculous that the crown required the colonies to buy supplies and goods from them instead of allowing the trades to flourish. Soon, higher taxes would be demanded and sow the seeds of revolution. That would wait on the horizon for another twenty years. As we walked back to Carlyle's house, I wondered where Henry and I would live during the revolution. Would he fight alongside

Washington? I needed to get that thought out of my head. We were about to embark on the current war. I needed to make sure we survived the next few years. I could worry about the Revolutionary War afterwards.

Henry stayed on high alert throughout our trip to the market. His eyes shifted and head moved from left-to-right, looks over his shoulders, in a constant lookout for Bouchard. That snake slithered about the town, waiting in a bush or under a rock to lash out and attack me. The fear of his vicious strike kept me indoors, hidden, and miserable.

That afternoon, Henry left with John Carlyle for the day to order supplies for the inbound troops. Sarah reminded me that Governor Dinwiddie, General Braddock, and his entourage would arrive the following week. We would plan a dinner and figure out sleeping arrangements for everyone. "I would like to mention, we would need one less bed in the house if that man of yours would marry you before the crowd arrives." She rubbed her pregnant belly. She was five months along, and no one would notice that she was pregnant, with all the layers of cloth worn, but now and then, I would catch her caressing her unborn child. Her little boy of eighteen months, William, played in the corner with his nursemaid.

"Ha!" I blurted out. I couldn't contain the snorted laugh. "You are preaching to the choir."

Sarah planted a side-eyed look of confusion in my direction. "Mistress Murray, you say the most peculiar things."

We had made a floor plan of the house and cut out

pieces of paper to show pallets and beds. It was like playing a game of Tetris. Fit all the pieces in halls, bedrooms, even the music room would end up with pallets. The men would stay a few nights before heading to Annapolis for the meeting with the Governors. Henry would join Braddock and Dinwiddie, leaving me alone while Bouchard skulked about the town. My stomach twisted in knots at the thought of him leaving me for even the day.

"Bingo! We got it!" I shouted out as I placed a cut out pallet in the hall. "It will be tight, but for only a couple of days."

"Brilliant." Sarah smiled at me. "Bingo?"

"Oh, just a silly word of excitement." She considered what I had said with amusement. We sat in the study writing our lists and making the plans. The front door slammed, causing us to nearly jump out of our skin.

"That will not be enough," stormed Henry, as the men stomped through the front door. "Where else can you order supplies?"

"There are others I can call upon." John's voice was even toned. "This whole affair may end a week after next, and we can get the regulars back on their ships to England."

"Ah, there they are." Henry took off his cocked hat and gave a bow to us as he walked into the room.

"We were working on the sleeping arrangements for next week," I said, and shot a smile to Sarah. "Since I'm your betrothed, Mistress Carlyle suggests we—you and I, that is—get married as soon as we can arrange it. Sleeping quarters will be overfilled and we need extra space."

Henry laughed and brought my hand to his lips and placed a tender kiss. "Very well. If Mistress Carlyle says it must be so, then it must."

The sound of the slap John gave to Henry's back caused me to jump. It reminded me of the sound of Bouchard and the smacks he gave me when I was held hostage, firm, loud, and uncalled for. I gritted my teeth and closed my eyes tight to push out the memory. "Let's leave the ladies to their work." Carlyle looked over his shoulder to Sarah as he left the room. "Have tea sent to in." Henry gave me a sympathetic look over his shoulder as they left the room. I gave the request to Cate and helped Sarah upstairs to her room. She would steal away moments of rest, as the pregnancy tired her.

After tea, Henry invited me for a walk in the garden. "Are you happy?" Henry asked as we walked down the steps from the terrace into the garden.

I squeezed his arm. "Very." A stupid grin spread across my face.

"When you thought about coming back... here... to this time, why did you pick here and now?"

"I didn't. I tried going back to your house, but walking through doors never worked to bring me back. It's a museum now. Well, in the future. I knew... well, I thought... I was supposed to come back, but I didn't know how."

A squirrel ran across our path and skirted up an apple tree. "How did you know?"

"Our portraits are in the library. I went on a tour of your house in Williamsburg and the first time I was there, when I went back, there was only Caroline's portrait and a portrait of you in the library."

"What portrait? I have not sat for one."

"And neither have I," my voice rang with excitement. "So, here's the thing. There was this guy, I told you about him, Kyle... total tool. Anyway, the portrait of me was getting restored because he took a knife to it."

We had walked along the path through the small garden and stopped next to a tree at the end, close to the wharf. Henry looked down towards me. "Why would he destroy your portrait?"

"Good question. Never got the answer. But I'm guessing he must have been pretty upset with me, wanted me dead, or something. I don't know. Not sure what I could have done besides not want to go out with him." An icy chill ran down my back and I shivered from my toes to the top of my head. "But then, I couldn't figure out how to get back and the tour guide said she was named Amelia, and she was your wife. So, I thought you might have married one of my ancestors or something like that."

"It appears as though the good lady leaves a trail of men in wants of her death." He tried to hide the laugh that lingered beneath the surface of that comment. Kyle, Bouchard, and I'm sure there were more. And I thought I was likable. "Do you have an ancestor named Amelia in Williamsburg?"

"No. Not that I know of. Were you looking for a replacement?" A small laugh came out of me. I took a moment to race through my memories. I had known little about my ancestors; it could have been possible. "Well, I couldn't figure out how to get back. I even put on my dress that Miss Elizabeth Woods gave me in Fredericksburg and headed back to Fort Ashby. I thought maybe Ashby was the way here and your house was the way back. You know, one-way in, one-way out sort of thing."

"Is that how..."

"Stop interrupting." I held my hand up in protest. I knew it was a long story, but my mouth yammered a million miles an hour, and I still had much to tell him. "There is so much more. So, get this... Fort Ashby's door didn't work. Frustrated, I decided it couldn't have been me in the portrait, blah, blah, blah. I stopped doing research and had no clue what happened to you or me or whoever the woman was in the portrait. I was devastated and lost without you, and promised my daughter, Hannah, that I would stop trying to get back." The snap of my fingers was sharp. "Remind me later. I need to find a way to get her a note."

"How do you plan on doing that?" he asked. "Or am I not permitted to interrupt?"

I stuck my tongue out. "I'll figure that out later. Tomorrow... I don't know. We'll figure something out." I tossed my hands about. With the craziness of my story, it took me aback that was the seemingly improbable part of it. "Okay, so, a few days ago, I met my editor—don't worry about that part—and we had lunch at *Gadsby's Tavern* which will be by the marketplace, and she was trying to convince me to write historical novels again. She suggested I visit the Carlyle House—which becomes a museum— and that's when shit hit the fan. I was looking at the front door, walking up, going to take a tour, and guess who I saw?" I didn't give him the chance to answer. "Kyle! I ran from him. I didn't know what he wanted other than to kill me. Why do people keep wanting to off me?" *Am I the problem?* "He chased after me, threw a coin at me, and I ran in the door. And presto-change-o here I am."

Henry stood there and stared at me. He did that thing that he does... contemplating what he was going to say and drive me crazy with lack of quick reaction. I would just burst something out, without a care how it came across. "How did he know about the coin?"

I shrugged my shoulders. "Don't know. I tried going through doors holding coins, but that didn't work."

"Do you still have the coin?"

"No. That's the weird thing about it. Every time I've slipped through time, I had a coin. Then, when I wake up... no coin! Also, no energy. Famished. Confused. I swear, I'm not crazy."

Henry looked out towards the wharf, back at the house, then down at me. Was he searching for the truth? Or was he just trying to take in my story?

"Are you looking for something?"

"I already found what I was looking for, my love." He stopped, took a deep breath, and smiled. I recognized that smile. It was the one he gave when he thinks he produces a brilliant idea. A self-congratulatory smile. I looked up into his deep blue eyes. He offered me his arm, and we started walking through the garden towards the house. "Would you like to know what John and I were doing today?"

It was my turn to be confused. "I thought you were

securing supplies for Braddock's soldiers."

"Aye, that was part of it. The other was a stop to the tailor. He will be here this evening, soon, in fact, to fit you in your wardrobe. I requested he hire additional help to complete them by this Friday."

"Um, today is Wednesday. That doesn't give much time for Friday. Besides, other than the fact that I'm stuffed into this dress, why the rush?"

"Do you have plans for Saturday?"

"Find Bouchard and slit his throat?" I snorted out. "Is that a good plan?"

Henry laughed. "I have a less bloody idea for Saturday."

I raised an eyebrow at him. "Now, you have me intrigued. Did you already off him for me? Are we going shopping? A picnic in the park? Hot date under the stars? What?"

"Do you ever slow down?"

I stopped mid-step and looked up at him. "Nope! You should know that by now." He gave a slight tug, and we continued our walk towards the house.

"Mayhap, you can squeeze in a wedding somewhere in between assassination and a picnic in the park."

Dead stop. My feet wouldn't move. My stomach dropped to the non-movable feet. "Wedding? Like... our wedding? Or someone else's wedding?"

Henry turned towards me and gathered my hands in his. "Our wedding." He let out a small laugh. "I spoke to the minister, and with some financial convincing, he will come here to marry us. I already spoke to John about it.

Unless, of course, you want to get married in the church. The rendezvous will be more of a public display. There are complications in the legality of our marriage."

"Not a chance."

"You don't want to marry me?" Henry's shoulders dropped.

"Of course I want to marry you. I meant about the whole church thing. When have you ever seen me step inside a church?" I shook my head. "Don't need a church wedding." I brought his hands to my lips and kissed them. "I just need you. Let's do it. Saturday. Here. What about in the garden or on the terrace? Weather permitting. Do we have a reception after? I don't know anyone here. I only know Elizabeth, Mistress Lovett, although that would be improper to invite her, and, of course, Lieutenant Hector Bennet. Will Colonel Washington be here?"

"Did you want to delay it in order for you to decide how we are to be married and invite your additional guests?"

"Nope. I was trying to figure out how much I could squeeze in between now and then... you know... to drive everyone crazy as a bridezilla."

"A bridezilla?" His voice was low and gruff. He pulled me close with one arm and caressed my face with his right hand. "Whatever will I do with you?"

"I can think of a million different things that you could do *to* me," I said with a flirtatious smirk. "However, that will have to wait until our wedding night."

He leaned down and kissed me gently on the lips. I could swear that every bone in my body left me.

CHAPTER THIRTEEN

arch 22, 1755

There is only one word to describe that morning: *chaos*. I was stuck upstairs in my room with last-minute alterations being made to my dress. The tailor didn't deliver my new wardrobe until early morning, but a few of the seams had to be taken out. How could I resist the best bread and freshly churned butter made by the Carlyles' cook? Two seamstresses accompanied him to the Carlyle house. They sewed and altered while I bathed. I received my every day, black, plain shoes from the shoemaker; the rest were in process of being sewed, stitched, and cobbled. The plain ones would have to do.

The fabric I picked out was a plain, light green silk, the color of a new leaf. Cream-colored lace trimmed the sleeves and around the neckline. I planned to learn how to embroider and would tackle the cream bodice later. I don't know why I thought that would be a good idea for me to take a needle and my clumsy hands to a cream silk. The thought of me sitting still long enough to learn how to embroider was beyond my imagination.

Sarah planned a party for that night with a few of the local families. She had put more effort into the event than she needed to, considering she should have been laid up in bed with her pregnancy issues. Instead, she pulled herself up and got to work with wedding plans. Henry introduced me to society in Williamsburg at the Governor's celebration of our battle at Fort Necessity, but this was a different group of people. Her people. I inquired if someone sent word to Washington, only to find out that he had gone down to Williamsburg and would return to Alexandria next week with Braddock and Dinwiddie. I sent a note to Elizabeth in Fredericksburg, but it wouldn't get there in time for her to attend. Thoughts of an intimate wedding with the people I considered friends danced around my head. Besides, I would have loved to brag about George Washington's attendance at my wedding.

Bathed and dressed, I sat while Penny styled my hair with her uncanny ability to tame my natural wild curls. The top portion of my hair, pulled back out of my face. We left the rest down to fall into ringlets. Sarah insisted I wear a wig, but victory was mine and I avoided the overheating wig. Overwhelmed and in a panic, I didn't need or want too much fuss made over me. That day should have been spent with Hannah, Beth, and Maggie by my side. A simple wedding with close friends and family.

A knock at the door pulled me out of my daydream. I

looked away from the mirror that caught my distracted stare. Sarah walked across the room, dressed in a lovely floral print on a dark blue silk ensemble. Her eyes raked over me, sizing me up. No comment. I supposed that meant I was passable. "We should get started before the weather comes in." She looked out the window that faced the backyard garden and the docks. Rain clouds threatened my hopes for a ceremony in the garden. If we didn't start soon, it would relegate us to somewhere indoors. They had set the house up for the after party, which was scheduled to be a house full of people, food, and dance. Musicians would set up on the stairs landing to ensure music filled the house. One of my greatest sources of anxiety in all the eighteenth century was dancing. I might throw in some barely moving slow dance as a middle school dance, but my minuet skills were a dumpster fire. I could fake my way through the multitude of utensils in a formal dinner, but the coordinated dance was out of my league. *Just get through the wedding, Amelia.*

Sounds of laughter and jovial conversation leaked their way through the house and up the stairs. No one else seemed to be nervous. Why was I? Light from the late afternoon sun fought with the gloomy rain clouds. They filled the terrace with a few familiar faces and the crowd of the others that stood around were unfamiliar to me. My stomach clenched. I felt the blood surge and pulse through my body. Every vein was ready to explode out of my body. Hyperventilation wasn't an option. I looked around to see if Bouchard's familiar face was anywhere around the perimeter of the property. Rain ruining my wedding would be preferable to seeing him. No sign of Bouchard. A deep breath and I was ready.

Guests filled the terrace, becoming a backdrop to the space around me as it all became a blur. Henry was the only person I could focus on. He was dashing in his full military uniform as he stood in the garden next to the minister. A break in the clouds let the light shine through the trees like a spotlight on us. Our eyes locked as I walked towards him. I wanted to drown in his deep blue eyes. My breath escaped me the length of the walkway down the stairs and to the center of the garden. Our onlookers gathered at the balustrade at the edge of the terrace and looked down into the garden where the three of us stood.

The minister, dressed in black breeches, coat and frock, wore a white, frilly cravat that peeked out around his neck. He began in a deep baritone voice. It didn't suit his small stature of a few inches taller than me. I had to do a double take to make sure it was truly him that spoke. "Dearly Beloved, we have gathered here today in the sight of God, family, and friends, to witness the joining of this man and woman in holy matrimony..." The rest of what he said didn't matter, I could focus only on Henry.

He continued with a short sermon about being faithful to each other. My pulse surged through my ears, making most of what he said sound like the teacher from the *Peanuts* cartoons—a blur of indistinguishable words. There was something about being obedient to this man, and that is when the giggles brewed inside of me. Clearly, the minister knew nothing about me. Honor, love, be faithful? No problem. *Don't laugh. Don't laugh. Don't laugh*. My lips pressed together firm, to suppress a laugh. It ended up being a snort. A loud, obnoxious, very un-lady-like snort. Henry shot a slightly annoyed look, while the attempt to contain his laughter didn't go unnoticed by me.

"If you can continue," said the minister, unamused at my antics.

Henry leaned over and whispered, "He awaits your answer to say I will."

"Oh! Sh... sorry." I caught myself from making the situation worse in the minister's eyes. "Yes, of course I will take him as my husband." Take that, eligible women of Williamsburg! The most eligible man in Williamsburg is off the market.

The minister handed Henry the ring. It was a simple band, much like the one I had received from Todd on our wedding day. I had stopped wearing that ring months ago. When I had lost weight, it slid easily off my finger, with the high probability I would lose it. Although I would always have a special place in my heart for Todd, he was killed, and I finally allowed myself to move on. The ring sat lonely in the jewelry box at my house in Fredericksburg, two hundred sixty years in the future.

The spotlight from the heavens shone on the ring, casting a brilliant light from it. Delicate. He slid it easily on my finger. A perfect fit—like the two of us. He held my hands in his and brought them to his lips. Henry leaned towards me. "I inscribed the word timeless inside the band." My grin split my face in two, to the point my cheeks hurt. One simple, perfect word.

The minister interrupted our moment, "I present to the congregation, Lord and Lady Henry Spencer."

Jubilation rang across the terrace and through my body. It was like I was lost in a dream. I waited for my alarm to go off right when I got to the good part. Too good to be true.

As a married couple, we joined the additional guests that arrived and gathered in throughout the house and spilled onto the terrace. He had kissed my hand a dozen times during the walk from the garden, up the stairs, across the terrace, and inside the foyer. The moment we walked inside, the clouds burst open, and everyone pushed their way inside. Rain poured down in buckets. Unpredictable springtime in Virginia strikes again. Any thoughts of escape to the garden for a private moment disappeared. They would force us to be social and not smuggle to a dark corner away from our responsibilities.

Although I'm sure Henry compensated him, John opened his cellar and let the wine and spirits flow. As I feared, as the guests of honor, they expected us to lead a dance. I suppose the crowd would not be ready for my rendition of the Roger Rabbit or the Cabbage Patch. No popping and locking? No one would be ready for that, not in a million years, well, maybe 230 years. "Can't we just do some sort of slow dance where we stand indecently close to each other and barely move?" I begged of Henry. "Just a little foot shuffle? I'm not sure your toes can handle my graceful moves."

Henry stood in front of the gathering crowd and cleared his throat. "I must apologize to all of you. I am a

ALEX R CRAWFORD

terribly uncoordinated and would prefer that I maintain my dignity—and the toes of my bride—and decline to partake in the dance." He turned to me and took my hand. "However, it would bring us great pleasure to watch you enjoy the festivities. Eat. Drink. Dance. Make merry." He placed my hand in the crook of his arm and led me out of the room.

"I swear, if I didn't already marry you, I would have married you for that alone." I pulled him close to my side.

"You're easy to please."

I let out a small laugh. "My love, you do not know how easily I can be pleased."

That stopped him in his tracks. I was not sure if I had said the wrong thing or not. The last time he was intimate with a woman was on his wedding night with Caroline. It had become a humiliating and scarring experience. Even though I knew he wanted to be with me, concern loomed that he would avoid our first night together as a married couple.

He grabbed a bottle of apple brandy and two glasses from the table in the foyer. "I'm paying good coin for this party; we should enjoy every drop."

"I agree," I said as I stood in front of the green bottles displayed on the table. I decided on another bottle of the apple brandy. "We don't need the glasses. Let's get stupid drunk and do stupid shit." I raised the bottle to my lips and took a swig. "Streak in the park? Toilet paper the neighbor's house?" Another hearty swig. "Dance on tables? Fornicate on the front lawn?"

He let out a chortle. "You are going to be the death of me, Lady Amelia."

"Lord Henry," I gave an exaggerated curtsy, ignoring men and women shuffling about the foyer and picking trays of cheese, meat, and fruits. "You may have mentioned that before, and I haven't killed you yet." I smirked and raised the bottle to Henry in a toast. We clanked the bottle necks together and took another swig of the brandy. "Let's go raise some hell."

"The rain continues," said Henry as he looked towards the back door that led to the terrace.

A raised eyebrow and another swig of brandy. "I just got this dress and I refuse to get it wet. We could strip naked and run outside in nothing but our birthday suits."

"Or," he began. He grabbed me around my waist and pulled me close. I could feel the heat of his body burn through the layers of my clothes. "We can disappear upstairs."

"We can..." I looked over my shoulder at the stairs. People moved in and out of the foyer to various rooms. Some looking for food. Some looking for more drink. Others for entertainment on the dance floor or to play cards. A roar of laughter came from the music room, which contained four tables for playing cards. None paid attention to us, they wanted the entertainment. "I'm pretty sure no one would even notice us missing. I mean... you might notice if I was missing, but..." His lips hit mine before I could squeak out another ridiculous, nervous comment.

Bottle in one hand and the other holding each other's

hand, we snuck upstairs to our room. Truth be told, it was almost a sprint up the stairs. During the wedding, they brought Henry's belongings into my room. There was no assumption that we would spend a night apart, and they would give his room to General Braddock upon his arrival. I looked forward to this night for—what seemed like—forever. I reminded myself to slow down and go at Henry's pace. His inexperience and emotional trauma in the bedroom would be something we both had to overcome together.

Stopping in the doorway, a glance around the room showed someone had expected our arrival. Of course they had. Candlelight from a million candles—only a slight exaggeration—radiated throughout the room. The light from the fireplace danced across the floor, the flames crackled, and the radiating heat took the chill out of the room. Henry closed the door behind us with a flick of his foot.

CHAPTER FOURTEEN

"Okay, so here's the thing." I turned to Henry. "I've had a lot to drink... I mean... I plan on drinking more... but I digress. At some point, I'm going to have to pee." I looked over to the chamber pot chair in the room's corner. "The last time I left the room to do that... before we had... well, you know. It threw me back to the 21st century. I'm not ready to leave you. But... oh, gods of time..." I broke out in a cold sweat. "I'm not sure I can pee in front of you, either." I put my hand to my forehead and rubbed it. "This is so stupid. I know I'm being stupid. I'm not sure if I'm able to use the chamber pot in front of you."

Henry looked at me like I sprouted another head. "What do you do in your time? Do you not use a chamber pot? Or do you always use an outdoor privy?"

"Oh, heavens no. We have bathrooms and toilets and indoor plumbing." As soon as the words left my mouth, I realized how much of an ass I sounded like. "That is to say... we have private rooms inside the house to perform those functions. Usually without an audience, unless you have children or pets. They never can seem to leave you alone long enough to use the toilet in private."

He took a deep breath, ran his hand across his cheek, and took a swig of brandy. "You realize people use chamber pots every day." He glanced at me and then over to the chamber pot chair that taunted me in the corner.

"But I haven't had to use one in front of you." I took a swig of the brandy. Liquid courage to use a chamber pot in front of my new husband.

"You fell hard on the floor using one at Mistress Lovett's house." He snickered. "I thought I had to rescue you from it."

"That was the first time I used one. I hoped you hadn't noticed it, or me, splayed across the floor. It mortified me." I took another swig of brandy. The rain continued to tap like an intruder at the window. "The rest of the time I squatted behind a bush... in the woods... and used leaves when I needed to wipe." After that declaration, I needed another swig or two of the brandy. If this conversation lasted much longer, I would be completely drunk off my feet and not care where I used a chamber pot. "It was embarrassing for me, but it was at least private."

"I see." Henry stared at the chamber pot chair in the corner, scraping his hand across his chin. It was his turn to take a couple of swigs of the apple brandy.

"I would rather you didn't, actually." My face scrunched in embarrassment.

He laughed. A loud, body shaking laugh. My lips

pursed and face contorted into a small, pinched scrunch. The blood rushed to the surface of my skin, causing me to blush a vibrant shade of lobster. "Wife, we will find a dressing screen and place the chair behind it. It would distress me to no end to know that you were uncomfortable around me. And I will be damned if I will allow you to escape to the future to use a private chamber pot or privy."

"Husband, if it were that easy, I would drag you with me to enjoy the solitude and enjoyment of a flushing toilet and running hot water. You would question why I would want to come back here." I lifted my green onion-shaped bottle of brandy to my lips to hide my incoming laugh, and almost shot the brandy out of my nose—there was a slight burn in my nostrils from the brandy's attempt at escape.

We tap danced around the real reason we came upstairs. It was not to discuss chamber pots, my embarrassment of its use, nor the flushing toilets of the future. Conversation bounced around as we sat in front of the fireplace, about everything but the elephant in the room. The elephant being the bed behind us. He was difficult to read. Do I make the first move? Would that be too bold for him? *Ah, what the hell.* Someone had to do it. I gulped down more liquid courage than I should have and almost choked on it.

I stood up and walked over to his chair. "Do you mind?" I asked as I approached and motioned to his lap. He took my hand, kissed it, and pulled me down to sit on his lap. His soft lips were warm, and his tongue tasted like the apple brandy we overindulged in. I couldn't tell where his mouth ended and mine began. He was gentle, passionate, and delectable. My body ached to be with him. I ran my hands across his chest and tugged at his jacket.

"It will be easier if I stood." He said as he pulled his lips away from mine and slid me off his lap.

"Will I get a striptease?" He raised an eyebrow at my question. "You know... do I get a show? Throw money at you? Tuck it in your thong?"

"Christ, woman! What in the devil's name are you talking about?" His cheeks flushed crimson.

And there we have it, folks. Amelia does it again. Open mouth, insert foot. If I could keep my snarky comments to myself, I might have already been in bed with that gorgeous man. Instead, I turn the mood from passion to confusion in zero point two seconds.

"I was hoping I would get a sexy little show from you while you undressed, is all." I unpinned my jacket from the stomacher. "A little something like this..."

I used the music that stirred up the stairs and throughout the house as my muse to undress. I cannot say the removal of pins and layers down to my stays and shift was sexy. It was work. A stupid smile spread across Henry's face, amused by my shoulder rolls and booty shaking, non-sexy movements. I lifted the front of my shift to gain access to the ribbon that tied my stocking in place. Henry's hand stopped me. He kneeled on the floor in front of me, picked up my foot, slid my shoe off my right foot, and placed my foot on his chest. He slowly slid his hand up my leg, pushing my shift to my knee. Too many sips of apple brandy made it difficult to steady myself. His free hand slid up my calf and untied the pale green ribbon. He rolled my white clocked, silk stocking down, removed it from my foot, and placed a kiss on the top of my foot and then my knee. He repeated the process with the other leg. A gasp escaped my lips. Standing up, he brought me closer to him, reached around and planted a hand firmly on my bottom. He moved his hands up and unlaced my stays, while he placed delicious kisses on my lips and neck, until I slinked out of it. He tugged at the billowing fabric of my shift, gathered it up in his hands, and pulled it over my head.

My hands quickly found their way in front of my forty-one-year-old and very exposed body. I suddenly became extremely aware of every sag, stretch mark, and late-night trip to the kitchen for an extra scoop of ice cream. It is all fun and games when you're covered from top to bottom under three hundred layers of clothes. It is quite another when you are standing naked for the first time in front of the man you love.

He took me by both wrists and held my arms out to the side of me, drinking in my body. I closed my eyes, embarrassed. I didn't want to see if he would look at me in disappointment. His warm hand caressed my face. "You are beautiful." A pause hung on each word.

I opened one eye, then the other. I was not sure if he was talking to me or someone else. "Your turn." I flicked a hand at him. "And I expect some ass shaking."

He handed me my bottle of brandy, took a swig from his, and commenced to remove his clothes in the same swagger I had provided, down to his shirt. "Take it off slowly," I demanded. And he did.

He stood there, naked and exposed to me. I took another drink of the brandy and moved over to him. My hands wanted to touch every inch of his body. His thick body didn't hide the muscle tone that proved that he was not afraid to work hard. He was strong and defined. He had a few light strands of hair that dotted across his chest and a happy trail that led further down his body. I walked around him to inspect his backside. It didn't disappoint. "You, my love, are spectacular," I said as I slid my hands down his back and gave a small smack on his rear end.

He looked over his shoulder at me. "You look at me as though you are judging a horse you intend to purchase."

"Oh, you misread my intentions. I'm not looking to purchase you." As I circled to the front, I kissed him on his back and continued to run my hands over him. "I already own you. You are mine forever until the end of time itself."

He swooped me into his arms and carried me to the bed, where we spent the rest of the night ignoring our party guests, learning more about each other, and listened to the rain.

CHAPTER FIFTEEN

*O*ver the next couple of days, there was much to plan. Sarah kept to her room most days, exhausted and ill from her growing pregnancy. General Braddock, Governor Dinwiddie, and their entourage were due to arrive in three days, on Tuesday, March 25th. Neglectful in sufficient research for the time after Braddock's arrival, I offered next to no information to Henry about the upcoming movements. I remember hearing about Braddock's March, so I knew they would not tidy things up with the next few weeks and have him and his troops on their way back to England, like Major Carlyle had hoped. No. we were in for a battle with the French. Without knowing how or why, we would end up there—wherever "there" proved—left many questions, but it would leave an impact on our future interactions and battles with the French.

When we were not preparing for the arrival of Braddock, or visiting the small band of troops encamped nearby, Henry and I spent our time cavorting in the bedroom. "You know," I interrupted the silence and snuggled up next to him in the bed and tickled my hand across the hairs along his stomach. The mid-afternoon sun filled the room and cast a light across his face, as if the heavens shone down on us. "You're pretty good at this. I thought you said you didn't have experience."

"I said I had bedded one woman, one time." He rubbed my arm. "I had done... that is to say... I was not inexperienced in other ways."

"You tease." I poked at his side to make him squirm. "Do we ever have to get out of bed? Can't we just live here?"

"They arrive tomorrow, my love," he said as he tamed my wild curls, which fell like a waterfall around my face, "and you know how Dinwiddie can be when he blusters about."

"I think I can handle Dinwiddie. He seemed easy enough to conquer with my charming personality and ravishing good looks." A smirk crossed my face as I snuggled in closer. "What do you know about Braddock?"

Henry took a deep sigh and thought about how he wanted to answer. When he did that, I knew it was more complicated than he was going to let on. "When I was in Williamsburg with them, he took command and was determined to make sure things went the way he had planned. He does not want to be here any longer than required."

Fair enough.

"Why do you think they sent them here? Weren't you

guys, the colonial soldiers and whoever, taking care of things? As you like to remind me, it's not like we're technically at war with the French."

"After losing the fort that the French have named Duquesne, and Necessity, there is concern about the maintenance of our trade routes and our ability to manage."

I raised my head to look at Henry's face. "No. That can't be it." I shook my head in disbelief. "We can't go to war over something as simple as trade routes."

"What did your study of history tell you about the war?"

"Not much that I had found. I only scratched the surface. I remember a little from school, that was forever ago. Besides, that would require me to study the time more instead of moping about the town until I focused on the future instead of the past." My fingertips mapped his chest. His body reacted to my tease of the small tufts of brown hair that speckled across it. "And to be quite honest, the focus for this time period is more on the Revolution which will happen in twenty years, or the Civil War in a hundred years. It was a bigger deal... gaining our independence, cousins' war, and all that. This all doesn't feel right."

"Does it not happen? Has history changed for you?" The cadence in his voice quickened.

I shook my head. "No. Nothing like that. It's," it was my turn to stop and think how I should answer. "I thought if we were to go to war, it should be for something other than money that lines the pockets of the investors in the trade company."

"We've gone to war in the name of religion." He sat up in the bed. I rolled onto my back and pulled the white linen sheet over my nude body. "They have fought wars over simple misunderstandings. We will go to war over financial gain. We are foolish men, on the path to idiocy."

"If you go to war, then I'm going with you." I sat up to look into his eyes and pointed a finger into the middle of his chest. "So, you better decide if dragging your beloved into a pit of stupidity is worth it." I laid back down with my head across his lap.

Henry laughed. "It is not my decision if we go to war or not. Lest you forgot, you have told me it will happen." He played with a stray tendril of my hair. His voice was calm and collected. "You will not enter battle again. You can stay here with Sarah, or I can send you to our home in Williamsburg, but I will not allow you to go into danger again."

"You don't get to make that decision for me." My voice squeaked and ears seared. "If you go, I go. Plain and simple. I don't know how you can make it happen, but you will." I shot up to sit and yanked the sheet up with me. "Besides that, you better get me a wagon and a horse. You just bought me a pile of clothes that I will need to bring with me. And blankets. A tent. Oh! Maybe a tent thingy that I can put over the wagon, so I don't have to sleep on the wet ground." The bed shook as I plopped down into the firm mattress made of straw and topped with a feather pillow top.

"Enough." Henry snapped. I nearly hit the ceiling. "You are not going. And certainly, will not bring the entire contents of a house. No. No. I will not allow the mother of my future child to go into war."

I stopped and stared at him. "I never said I was pregnant." Confused at his statement, I bolted up and left the sheet behind. "I can't get pregnant."

"You have a daughter." His eyes glared at me. "I bedded you more times than I can count in the past three days. How can you know that you're not with child?"

I took a deep, slow breath. "Maybe this is something we should have discussed before we got married, but I had told you when we found Tamhas, and I gave him to Tanaghrisson's people, that I'm told old and cranky to be a mother." I massaged my temples to stave off a headache that lurked in the background. "I hope you didn't think I would magically change my mind because you are good in bed." My jaw clenched at the audacity. "Not only that, but it is also physically impossible for me to be with child."

His brow furrowed. "I do not understand. You have proved to not be barren."

"Well, I can explain that, but it involves medicine and surgical procedures from my time." It took more explanation than I fully understood to tell him about anesthesia, surgery, and hysterectomies. He either understood what I told him, or he didn't. I could never tell. Terminology and my odd phrases from the future were sometimes met with questions and explanations. Other times, I think he thought it was another odd thing I would say, and it would be more trouble than it was worth to find out what I had meant.

"It matters not." Henry's voice was gruff and determined. "You are not to go." He got out of bed, slipped his breeches on, and searched for his shirt that had been haphazardly discarded earlier that afternoon.

"Captain Lord Henry William James Spencer, would you stop and listen to me?" I scurried out of bed and grabbed my shift, puddled halfway under the bed. His full name and title pierced off my tongue like poison. Henry's nostrils flared and shot out fire in response. "I did not travel two hundred and sixty years through time and space for you to abandon me. I don't care if you must make a deal with the devil himself. You are to make it happen. I'm going with you. Like it or not." I punched a pointed finger in his direction.

Boots and stockings, waistcoat, jacket, and hat in hand, and he was out the door. I stood in the middle of the room with nothing but my shift in my hand and a crushed heart.

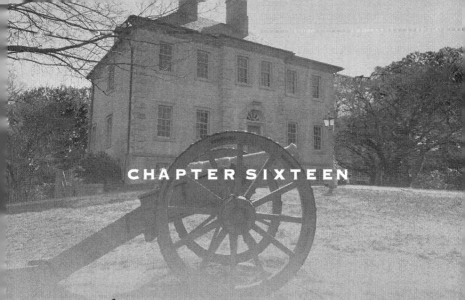

CHAPTER SIXTEEN

*D*inner was a quiet affair. We prepared for the impending deluge of guests. John and Henry had spent the rest of the afternoon visiting troops and at the warehouses. They didn't return until sometime late that night. I had gone to bed alone and experienced a fitful sleep. Blankets twisted and wrapped around me. I would wake up, straighten the blankets up, attempt to sleep, only to repeat the process less than an hour later.

The early morning sun crept over the Potomac River, slipped through the bedroom curtains, and pried my eyes open. I wasn't sure how long I had slept without my cell phone to check the time a hundred times throughout the night. I turned over and looked at Henry's empty, unslept in, side of the bed. My hand wiped away the tears from my wet cheeks. How would I fix the mess I had made between us? I couldn't back down and stay in Alexandria or Williamsburg when I needed to go with him on the march.

Getting dressed to receive the guests was first on my

list. Well, I supposed it was second or third. A cry over how I can royally screw things up was first. I laced up the front of my sage silk jacket with rose color lacings over my rose-colored stomacher with a floral print and headed down the stairs. The activity and voices coming from downstairs drowned the gentle rustle of the matching silk skirt out. My new pair of black leather shoes, with a short heel, arrived the day before—tight. They would require some breaking in. I was half-tempted to put my loafers back on. The half sleeves on the jacket would allow me to help around the house, without damaging the end with food, tea, or dust. I debated on wearing my white kerchief and opted to leave it in the room, along with the ridiculous cap Sarah insisted I purchase. Married or not, I didn't want to cover my rambunctious auburn hair. If exposed hair was a sign of wanton and immoral behavior, then my husband—wherever he hid from me—could deal with the comments from the men.

As I reached the bottom of the stairs, I patted the bun at the nape of my neck. Without the cap, I could have worn it down and in fixed curls, but I lacked the skill and the enthusiasm to pull myself that much together. Everything in place. With my head held high, I would not allow my anger from Henry's night out show. Wafting through the house, the savory smells of breakfast tickled my nose and caused my stomach to protest its emptiness. The kitchen, below the dining room, allowed the delicious aroma of the kitchen to inhabit the house. I entered the dining room and expected to be alone to grab a few pieces of meat, freshly baked bread, and whatever fruit or vegetable I could find. The typical breakfast in the Carlyle house. Instead, I found Henry in the room, sopping up bits of yolk on his plate with a chunk of bread. The blood drained from my face and churned the pit of my stomach. His absence impacted me more than I had expected and the sight of him acting as though he wasn't distressed by our tiff made my blood boil.

Convincing myself that I was a level-headed adult and not an emotional toddler was difficult. "Morning," I said flatly, refusing to look at him. *Great job not acting like an emotional toddler, Amelia.* I walked to the buffet table and plated a fried egg, slab of ham, chunk of bread, and cooked medallion carrots. All were leftovers from the dinner the night prior, except for the egg and bread. Sitting across the table from Henry would give me the best angle to show that his absence couldn't get under my skin. I could be as stubborn as he was.

Henry finished his tea, stood up to leave, and said, "A messenger arrived a few moments ago. Dinwiddie and Braddock will be here this morning. I shall attend to Carlyle." And he walked out the door. What the actual hell was going on with that man? I shook my head in disbelief and finished what little food I could stomach.

Commotion from outdoors took over the sounds of clanking plates being carried down to the kitchen for cleaning. The last time I had seen Dinwiddie was the night of his ball in Williamsburg, and I had disappeared after our introduction. Would he remember me? There was no time to wonder and speculate. I would find out soon enough. I joined the rest of the household outside to welcome our guests. The servants

scurried to line up on either side of the entry path. John and
Sarah stood at the head of the group. Sarah's paled skin looked
sallow in her dark blue dress. Henry and I took our place next
to each other and stood behind them. It reminded me of one
of the receiving lines I had to go through when Todd and I
attended events at the embassy. Pomp and circumstances were
not my forte, but I took part in what was required of me with a
smile and an attempt to be a supportive and dutiful wife.

We received an entourage of military powerhouses. As
the men approached on foot and carriages from the port
within a short walk from the Carlyle house, Henry leaned
towards me and briefed me on their names and titles.
General Edward Braddock, Commander-in-Chief of His
Majesty's forces in North America, led the group of
uniformed men. The sixty-year-old leader of the
expedition wore his red jacket and waistcoat over his white
britches and tall boots. My expectation of him to be tall
and commanding proved to be false. I found him to be of
average height and a bit thick around the middle. His face
bore a long, pointed, straight nose, which gave him an air
of arrogance. We would not get along—I could feel it deep
in my gritted teeth.

Commodore Augustus Keppel, Commander-in-Chief
of His Majesty's Ships and Vessels in North America,
dismounted next. Henry stated he had briefly served with
the Second Viscount. "Married?" I asked, raising my
eyebrows.

"No. However, you are." Henry's reply was quick. My
mouth dropped wide open in the most detestable manner.

He gave me the look of "now is not the time for conversation." I wondered if he was jealous of the young Viscount's good looks. He was young, around thirty years-old, he wore a brown wig, and was handsome in his blue naval uniform. Henry saw me raise an eyebrow at the Commodore. I did it to annoy Henry more than my interest in the man. Henry leaned over to me again. "We shall see if he is wearing his teeth today." *Oh, I see.* We didn't have time for my conversation, only time for the conversation he wanted.

I shot a look of confusion. Was he saying that to poke fun at him or me? I know George Washington started losing his teeth at a young age. Maybe it was more common in the 18th century than I had realized. "What? No teeth? Toothless?" I whispered out, leaning in towards my husband. Henry nodded in response to my questions. A gasp escaped me. "But, how?"

"Scurvy." His eyes flicked back towards the incoming group.

He didn't need to point out Lieutenant Governor Robert Dinwiddie, acting governor of Virginia. I had met him in Williamsburg the previous summer. The man looked the same to me. He was around sixty years old, round about the middle, and it looked as though he received a bit too much sun on the ship. He tenderly wiped the sweat that ran down his beet-red face with a linen cloth. The suit he wore was light brown and had matching breeches, waistcoat, and coat. His gray wig plopped on his head didn't help his innate ability to overheat with the exertion of the quick jaunt from the docks.

Captain Robert Orme, the thirty-year-old Aide-de-camp for Braddock, followed behind the rest. He was tall, gangly, with brown hair and eyes. He wore his hair pulled back and no wig. I couldn't decide if the wild locks were due from their recent travels or if he didn't care enough about the formalities, as if he didn't have—or want—much to prove. I suspected he had better things to do than to follow Braddock around and joined the group out of obligation and duty.

"Ah, Captain Spencer, good to see you arrived," Dinwiddie said to Henry as he approached us. Henry gave a tilt of his head in a quick bow. Henry would have stayed out of the impending war if it was not for Dinwiddie's influence. I couldn't understand why Henry was always ready to do as Dinwiddie asked. Henry's father had died in a riding accident when he was young. His brother became head of the household at the young age of fifteen. Charles was too young and arrogant to be a proper mentor to Henry. Henry looked towards Dinwiddie as a fatherly figure, although I'm not sure he would admit to those feelings. "Mistress Murray, pleasure to see you again. You gave us all a worry when you vanished like the wind."

I curtsied deep to Dinwiddie upon his approach. "Governor Dinwiddie," Henry interrupted Dinwiddie's criticism of my disappearance. "Might I introduce you to Lady Amelia Spencer, my wife?"

My cheeks flushed. In one flail swoop, Henry not only defended my honor against the governor, but he used his title in that defense. He preferred not to use his title. As second son and brother to the biggest asshole known to mankind, he tried to keep his distance from the aristocracy. A deep grin crossed Dinwiddie's face. It was the look of pride, not mockery. "Congratulations on the nuptials," Dinwiddie said with a deep bow.

Carlyle approached and interrupted the welcomes and accolades. "Let us get inside before the rain comes in." He ushered everyone towards the door. Deep black clouds rolled in from the horizon into the dark gray sky above. Weather during the spring into the early summer in Virginia was unpredictable, at best. Soldiers and sailors carrying trunks and bags followed our group into the house. The Carlyles barked out orders, and the men disbursed throughout the house to the respective rooms. The addition of the people and their belongings made the house seem quite small and quite loud. I panted for breath as I felt claustrophobic. However, the tapping of the rain outside told me I was too late to escape to the garden. The garden was a place of quiet refuge for me, and now I was stuck inside with the heat and excitement from the hoard of locusts that descended upon Alexandria.

Earlier in the day, Cate and Penny had moved Henry and my belongings—including my screen to keep the chamber pot private—to the bedroom across from the Carlyles' room. Braddock was to take our room, Dinwiddie across the hall, Orme had a pallet on the landing—which, was the size of a small room—at the top of the stairs, and Keppel would return to his ship at the end of the day. Sarah and I managed the household tasks while the men planned for their trip to Annapolis. They were to leave in a week to meet with the rest of the governors, which would allow me the opportunity to breathe. I was not used to that amount of activity in the house. Other than my wedding day, it was an unruffled household.

"Are we going to have enough wine to get through the week?" I asked Henry during our midday meal. Three bottles of wine went down like water and Braddock requested more. Carlyle's nostrils flared while he requested Cate bring more wine from the cellar.

"Perhaps an ale should be served tomorrow?" I later said to Sarah. "Something less likely to get them intoxicated so early in the day. Maybe just tea?"

"Mayhap, it will calm down tomorrow. After all, they have been traveling and require laxation." She let out an exasperated breath. Her stays and the baby pushed on her lungs. "Surely, they cannot drink all our wine in a week." The look on her face didn't convince me she believed what she had said.

"I believe you give them not enough credit for the ability to throw back bottles of wine as if Jesus Himself was turning water into wine in front of them." I looked over at my friend as she counted the number of bottles that remained. "Sarah, they went through five bottles this afternoon. They will go through twice that tonight. Maybe tomorrow we should try to stick to tea as much as possible."

"I'll have John put in an order for more wine. He will charge it the commissary account."

"Don't count on being repaid for it. The English aren't known to repay debts to fund military campaigns."

She looked disappointed at hearing me say that. Her household budget dissipated before her eyes, and she could do nothing to stop it.

"They won't be here for much longer. A week... tops... then they're off to Annapolis." I didn't know how long they would be in Annapolis before they started the march towards Fort Duquesne, but whatever the time, it would not be long enough. The Carlyles couldn't keep up with the drinking and carousing of their guests.

A night filled with drinking and eating ended with Henry and me in our room, alone for the first time since breakfast—when the tension was thicker than the gravy on that night's roast. I finished brushing my teeth at the washstand, washed my face, and sat down on the dressing table chair to take my hair out of the bun. Henry put a hairpin on the table after I removed the ribbon. I sat there and allowed him to finish. A rush of emotion overtook me. I watched him in the mirror as he ran his fingers through my hair and pulled out the tangles. The tension was heavy. Neither one of us knew what to say to the other. Apologies? I was not about to apologize for telling him I would go with them to battle. What would I have to apologize for? He is the one that didn't come to bed last night. Thoughts of him visiting a gentleman's club or brothel stung through my heart. Perhaps he stayed at the camp with the soldiers. It didn't matter. He ran away instead of staying at the house with me. He was the one that should apologize. The thoughts ripped at my insides. I had to know why he stayed out all night.

I gulped down the anger that festered in response to my racing imagination of his whereabouts. "We should talk," I blurted out. I never said I was subtle. "You can be pissed off with me all you want, but you ran off yesterday and I woke up alone. I need... you need... I... where were you?" My chest heaved as I seethed with anger.

Henry walked over to the chair in front of the dark fireplace. Candlelight dotted throughout the room, casting shadows across his face. The rain had brought in cooler temperatures, but we knew it would not last. We refrained from lighting a fire, which left the cold air—or the uneasiness—to bite at my skin.

"I was occupied," Henry huffed out. My stomach clenched and my jaw tightened.

"With whom?" Jealousy surged through my veins. I feared his answer would be one I would not want to hear, but I had to know.

"I wanted to wait until it was confirmed, but I see that your anger will not allow for that." He pulled off his ribbon and untied the leather thong that kept his hair in a braid, and let it fall to his shoulders. It should have been me running my fingers through his hair instead of him. "I was planning for a servant to accompany Bouchard, Drullion, Boucharville, and Sable on their voyage to Hampton for transport to England. You need him as far from here as possible."

The blood drained from my face, unnerved by the sound of Bouchard's name. I pushed the thought of him out of my mind. I stayed indoors or would venture through the garden and stayed away from the marketplace. All to avoid him and his name. "You would do that for me?"

A sympathetic laugh crossed out of Henry. "Wife, you look over your shoulder and jump at every loud sound. You refuse to breach these walls. I cannot allow you to be a prisoner when it is he that shouldn't be allowed to terrorize you." He came over and pulled me into his arms. "Besides, Drullion has been causing quite the perturbation among the townspeople. He stands and shouts rhetoric in the marketplace day in and day out."

"Oh, I see." I didn't know how else to respond. "When will they leave?"

"We have been sending the French prisoners on merchant ships, as space allows. The plan was to send the officers after, but Braddock was unsure about allowing them to be on parole, and their behavior and your wellbeing hastened the need for their departure." He continued to hold me in his arms. He stroked my hair while I pressed my cheek against his chest. It brought a sense of comfort and the care from him eased my soul. "Bouchard and the others will depart in the next couple of days. The rest will continue their transportation on the merchant ships. Rest assured; you will be safe."

I knew I would be safe; he would ensure that. "Thank you," I said as I looked up at his face. I was an ass in thinking he was off at a brothel. He had never given a reason for me to think such disturbing thoughts. I knew being intimate with a woman brought him distress. How could I think a brothel would ever be an option for comfort for him? Now I needed to convince him I would not let him spend another night out of my bed. Even if that meant I would ride into battle with him and the rest of the troops.

The sex that night was gentle. The pain we experienced over the past couple of days needed careful mending. As I laid there afterwards, feeling his chest rise and fall with every sleep-induced inhale and exhale, I knew we were back where we needed to be—together as a resolute partnership.

CHAPTER SEVENTEEN

*H*enry spent most of his next couple of days with the troops. They prepared for a military review for the upcoming Monday. Braddock wanted to see what he was working with—troops, equipment, and an excuse to have a celebration and more booze. The troops housed in the other locations would not join us until it was time to depart on the march.

After the review, the local gentry would get together for a celebration. Cakes, pies, roasts, and more wine were on the menu. Other households were bringing dishes, which helped ease some of Sarah's and my tension. John Carlyle was counting the money that left his coffers and mumbled something about recompense and an early grave.

The sun shone down on the sea of red uniforms that filled the parade field. Henry was not officially assigned with the English soldiers, but was brought on as a Virginia Regiment leader by Governor Dinwiddie. Henry sent a message to his troops the previous month, when

Dinwiddie insisted he join the fight in order to monitor Braddock. Washington, stubborn from the request to take on the rank of captain, resigned his commission and would need more convincing to join the entourage. Most of Henry's company were eager to join the march against the French. They had already met the French on the battlefield during the battle at Fort Necessity and wanted payback for our lamentable defeat, and an opportunity to make a bit more coin for the pockets.

I joined the women and the gentry on the sidelines, decked out in my light green silk dress—the dress and the humidity stifled me—in order to watch the pomp and circumstances of the inspection and reception of the troops. I wore a large, brimmed milk maid hat to keep the blazing sun off my face. The unpredictable spring weather brought a clear and sunny day on the 31st of March. It would make for a lovely reception afterwards. Rain the previous week threatened the reception to take place in the Carlyles' house. Sunny weather would allow us to enjoy the open-air celebration.

Braddock, flanked by his Aide-de-camp, Captain Orme, watched the soldiers march around the field and line-up in formation. Cannons, horses, rifles, and soldiers were on full display. Squinting to focus on the faces across the field, I searched for Henry and his company. I found the ragtag group at the end of the block of other soldiers. English Regulars were in company formations, and they kept the Virginia soldiers separated from them, but still on the field, showing their support and presence. Henry stood in front of his company, looking strong and proud. He was one of the taller commanders. His unit looked a bit worn, but they stood there proud and sure. If I strained my eyes hard enough, I could make out Sergeant Lovett, Private MacDonald, and Private Johnson.

Lieutenant Hector Bennet stood next to Henry. He looked like a clone of my friend Hector Bennedet, Beth's husband, from my time. In fact, I had met Elizabeth Woods in Fredericksburg, who looked identical to a young Beth. Would these two younger versions of my friends would meet? I thought about hosting a party at our home in Williamsburg after the upcoming battle and would invite the young lieutenant and Elizabeth to attend. I hoped I could play matchmaker for the two of them, like I had in my time.

Before plans of parties and matchmaking, Braddock and his troops would set sail for England, and we could get back to normal. Well, until the next conflict. Surely, Henry and I couldn't afford the wine requirement to keep Braddock and his men fueled. Concern about John and Sarah financing this affair lingered in my mind. They were supposed to get reimbursed for the commissary, which included getting supplies and food for the troops, but reimbursement from the crown was slow, if it even existed. Sarah complained once or twice to me about it. I offered to ask Henry to speak to Dinwiddie, but she shook it off and said John would take care of it. It continued to trouble her, and the stress it caused her pregnant body concerned me.

We gathered near the parade field for a celebration. They made speeches. Back-slapping congratulations on the troops were handed out left and right. White open tents dotted the area for respite from the blazing sun. Food and drink lined tables and trays carried by enslaved men. A band of musicians kept the entertainment going. To make the day better, I was no longer concerned about Bouchard ruining my life. They put him and the rest of the French officers on a ship headed down to Hampton, near Williamsburg. From there, they found their way on another transport ship—one with better accommodations than the merchant ships they put the other soldiers on— and sent to England.

For the first time since I arrived in 1755 Alexandria, I felt as though I could leave the confines of the Carlyles' house without the threat of being killed by Bouchard. I walked down the street without being on the constant lookout for him to attack me. It was a tremendous weight off my shoulders. I could relax and enjoy myself and took in a deep and wondrous breath.

Henry released his troops and found his way over to me. I chatted with Sarah and other women of the local gentry. A roar of laughter and conversation spilled through the crowd. Henry practically pulled me around the party, introducing me to everyone, like I was his prized cow. I would have preferred to stay with the small group of women. Instead, I felt as though he was parading me around the field for inspection—showing me off like the soldiers were showed off to Braddock. There were too many people to remember their names. I recognized a few from our wedding reception. I tried to commit their names and faces to memory. No sooner as I thought I had it down, we moved on to someone else. As much of a disdain as I felt for being in the social setting and on display, I enjoyed being outdoors and around people without looking over my shoulder.

Braddock and a few of the other soldiers appeared overly friendly with a few of the women. The heat of the day and the wine lowered their inhibitions. "Can we get out of here before Braddock dances on tables with a wine bottle in one hand, and Miss Langley in the other?" I pleaded to Henry. He raised an eyebrow at me, glanced over towards Braddock, and nudged his head in a "let's go" movement. Private MacDonald had taken Louis, Henry's horse, named after King Louis of France, back to the stables. So, we walked back to the house.

Henry thought he was amusing riding his French named horse, Louis, after the king, into battle against the French and told everyone who would listen of his jest. If only we could win a battle, that would make it more amusing to me. We had spent weeks on the back of the chestnut-colored Narragansett Pacer, traveling from one end of Virginia to the other. I refused to ride side-saddle, as was customary for women during the 18th century, and would walk funny by the time I dismounted. As much as I enjoyed riding close to Henry, I had mentioned to him I would like a horse for myself and, possibly, a wagon. I thought it made sense. And I'm sure Louis would appreciate having one less person on his back. A few extra pounds on me didn't need to find their way to the back of Louis. A push and a nudge on that request was in order. I wasn't sure when the troops would move towards Fort

Duquesne, but I wanted the opportunity to get to know the horse before we left.

Henry and I avoided the "I'm going with you into battle" conversation, both of us stubborn to the gills. Eventually, the conversation needed to rear its ugly head. Apparently, I thought there was no better way to spoil a good time as we walked around the field than to bring up our source of contention.

"So, I was thinking," I began. Deep, long, cleansing breath.

Henry looked down at me. "Why do I have a feeling you are going to raise a conflict?"

"Lord Henry William James Spencer," I spit out like a mother about to discipline her child. "As I was saying... I thought I will not stay here... in Alexandria, that is... when you leave." I wasn't about to add to the fact that I was planning on leaving with him. "With that being the case, I'm going to need a horse and possibly a wagon so I can get back to Williamsburg or wherever I decide to go."

"When I leave, and you head to Williamsburg," his voice resolute, "we will find transport for you on a ship to take you to Hampton. Then we can find transportation for you to Williamsburg." I could tell I might have met my match. He was seeing through my devious plan.

"I would like to stop in Fredericksburg along the way and visit with Elizabeth." Think fast, Amelia. He's going to see right through this. "I would think the best way would be for me to have a horse and wagon or carriage or something."

"Amelia, my dearest," Henry pleaded over the music,

bellowing in our direction. I knew I was going to get an earful with that introduction. "You realize it will be dangerous for you to go with us." As I predicted, he saw through my devious plan. "You have met General Braddock. It has been only a few days since his arrival. You observed how he is in manner and decorum. Why would you want to spend more time with him than necessary?"

"Why are you going?" I countered. "You couldn't possibly find him more interesting than me."

"I gave my word to Dinwiddie when I was in Williamsburg." His voice dripped in defeat. In that moment, I realized he didn't want to go on this fool-hearted campaign but felt obliged to because he had given his word to Dinwiddie. "I cannot betray my word to him. And I don't want this to come between us."

My mind raced around at possibilities. *What if I could stop this war?* Could we find another way to maintain the borders without the fight? "I'll make you a deal."

The late afternoon sun still offered warmth as we walked to the left of the field and headed towards the house. We had taken our time during the walk, as it offered us one of the few opportunities to be alone outside of our bedroom.

Intrigued, Henry raised an eyebrow. "Unless you're offering to stay here..."

"Help me try to stop this march. If we stop it... well... then... maybe... just maybe, we can stop the war."

"What about the borders? The French will continue to push the boundaries. We will lose more of the Ohio and then they will push for more. The proprietors of the Ohio

Trade Company will insist we maintain the boundaries and trade routes."

"We'll figure something out. First, we stop the march." I had no clue how we were going to make that happen. I didn't know if changing the course of history was possible. Once, I had told Henry that we needed to make sure things happened the way they were supposed to happen. I explained the idea of the butterfly effect. One little change in the past could impact the entire future. Was that a risk I was willing to take?

"And if we don't?" he said with a heavy sigh. We turned the corner, gaping at the Carlyle house, standing like a mountain on the horizon.

"If we cannot change the plans and the course of the future, then you tell Dinwiddie you resign and allow him to be upset with you. Or you take me with you." I refused to make it easy for him. "Either way, they will not separate us."

"What happens if you go and you see me die?" His voice was solemn. "Or if something happens to you and you die. Then what?"

"All I know is if you go, then I go. You stay, then I stay." I squeezed his arm as we approached the front of the house. "We are a team. We're in it together. Team Spencer."

He brought my hand to his lips and gave it a kiss. "I hope this works and I can keep you out of harm's way."

"I'm not sure if you've noticed this or not, but I'm always in harm's way." I said with a snort. "Team Spencer. Should we get matching tee shirts?"

"Do you mean a team of horses for a wagon?"

"No." I scrunched my nose in confusion. "I mean, like a sports team." Then it hit me. "Wait. I guess you don't use it in that context yet. Forget about it and the matching tee shirts."

Cate met us at the door. She was a wonderful help to me during my stay at the Carlyles' house. After my debacle at the Lovetts' home, when I told the Lovetts' enslaved woman, Ruth, that eventually there would be no more enslaved people in the United States, I had learned to keep my mouth shut. All I knew to do for Penny, Cate, and the other enslaved people was to treat them with respect and appreciation.

"Good afternoon, Cate. Has it been quiet with all of us out?" I knew it had been quiet, but I also knew as soon as the crew came back, it would be loud, chaotic, and stressful.

"Yes, Mistress Spencer," she answered with a curtsy. "Would you like me to have cook prepare you afternoon tea?"

"Do we have any food leftover from this morning?"

"No, mistress," Cate said, her voice seeped with disappointment. She didn't like to let me down, and I didn't like her disappointed.

I wanted to offer to go to the kitchen and scrounge around for a snack. "Maybe we can go to the tavern?" I turned to Henry. "There really is no reason for them to start anything for us. They'll be busy tonight when the group returns."

He knew I didn't like to put anyone out unnecessarily,

expect for maybe him. I may have found a bit of pleasure in pushing his buttons. *Push. Poke.*

After changing into our everyday clothes, which consisted of my dark blue cotton petticoat and jacket and Henry in black britches and a plain blue coat and waistcoat, we headed to the tavern at the docks, which was a short walk from the house. *Horst's Tavern* always had a lively bunch. With the soldiers and the gentry at the parade field, everyone else must've called it an early day and headed to the tavern. The ruckus snaked down the street. Someone sang loud and off key as we turned the corner. "We can go back to the house, if you would prefer a quiet evening," Henry said with a look of apprehension twisting across his face.

"You'll be with me. We'll be fine," my voice cracked, and I took a tighter grip on his arm. I wasn't sure if I was trying to convince him or me. Definitely me. "I'll let you know if it gets too crazy for me." The drunken debauchery reminded me of the time I went to Edinburgh, Scotland, with Todd and Hannah. I ended up in the middle of a renaissance fair and down to a tavern by the docks. I met a group of men that I swore were pirates. We drank and laughed. I thought nothing more about it and had believed that I had traveled back in time during that trip. I was gone for a few hours and Todd convinced me I was confused and lost. Doubt filled my thoughts.

A man faced towards the wall, propped up with one uneasy hand on the wall and the other held his prick as he pissed away four gallons of beer. His shoulder length hair fell about his face. Henry gave me the look of encouragement to leave. I shrugged. "I've seen worse at frat parties when I was at college. Just you wait until I tell you the story of New Orleans and Mardi Gras. It will make you blush."

"You have seen worse than this? A lady shouldn't be around this," he said, flailing his hand about, like he was trying to show me the world of drunken revelry for the first time.

"I'm not having them cook anything, and this is what we have around. Everywhere else is closed because of the review of the troops and the party. So, we eat here, or we don't eat at all, and I'm famished."

"Christ, woman." He said, opening the door. "Don't start any fights."

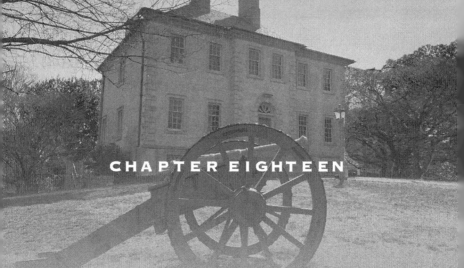

CHAPTER EIGHTEEN

"See ya later, alligators." I threw up my hand, gave a peace sign, and snorted out a laugh as we left *Horst's Tavern*. "Aren't you proud of me? I made friends and didn't start any fights."

Henry held me by my waist as my legs felt like gelatin. "I believe you had a bit too much to drink."

"What I believe, my good Lord Husband, is that I require a piggyback ride back to the house." I stumbled over my foot and caught myself before I face planted into the street.

Henry looked down at me. The moon behind him caused his face to have an ominous darkness over it. "You want a pickaback? To the house?"

"A what?" I tried to focus on what he said, confusion and the inability to see his facial expressions overpowered my drunken thoughts.

"Pickaback?" He slowly questioned me.

I stopped and swayed. "I said piggyback, not

pickaback. What the hell is a pickaback, anyway?" I snorted another laugh. Pickaback. This place had strange words.

"What is a piggyback?" Henry countered. "You asked for whatever that is."

"You know, a piggyback ride? I climb on your back," I said as I motioned towards his back. "And you give me a ride home. Piggyback!" I was proud of myself for getting through that explanation of a piggyback in my slightly intoxicated state.

"That is a pickaback, not a piggyback." He laughed at my foolishness.

"No." I stumbled over my other foot this time. "That's a piggyback, not pickaback." I poked my finger into his chest.

He took my hand in his. "It is unbecoming for a lady to have taken too much drink in public. I need to get you home now." He swooped me into his arms. "I do not understand. You had the one jug of ale."

"I think Charlie swapped my drink out for more. Every time I turned around, it was magically full again." I snapped my finger. There was not enough flick of my finger to cause an audible snap. Just a pathetic, muted thud. "Just like that." Another pathetic attempt at a snap. "Magic."

By the time he carried me, we were less than a mile to the house. "If anyone approaches us, you will feign a foot injury. They cannot know that you have no control over the drink. I should have stopped you."

"I'm fine. Really. I can walk." I struggled to extricate

from his grasp. That made him firm his hold on me. I gave up in defeat. "Listen, I didn't realize I had too much until it was too late. It was fun..." I threw my hand out like I was on a carnival ride. I had been pent up and stressed about Bouchard and the upcoming march to the French that I let myself go. It was easy to let my hair down in the tavern. The other patrons were drinking, singing, eating, and having a grand time. They expected nothing from me, just to join in on the fun. In my time, it would not have been a big deal. Go to a bar, have one too many, call a cab, fumble too long trying to get the key in the front door, stumble into the house, and wake up the next morning with a killer hangover while lying on the bathroom floor. By the look on Henry's face, I can see that is more than frowned upon, especially with someone of his standing in the community. We went in through the garden, through the back door, and he helped me stumble upstairs to our room, where he unceremoniously deposited me on the bed.

It didn't help that I got the giggles. "Are you going to take advantage of me in my... my... my drunken state?" I snorted with laughter.

He put his hands on his hips and stared at me. "I most certainly am not. In fact, you need to stay in here for the rest of the night. I cannot have you like this," he said as he wagged his finger at me. "I cannot have you embarrass me anymore and not in front of Braddock. How could you possibly become more inebriated from the walk from the tavern to here?"

"Henry... I..." I knew I had acted like a fool. When we had discussed getting married in Williamsburg, I had agreed to represent him in public. That I needed to remember that I would hold the title of Lady Amelia Spencer, wife of Captain Lord Henry William James Spencer. I was acting like a stupid college girl, released out into the wild for the first time. How did I let myself get so drunk in public? "I'm sorry." I said soberly. "Will you help undress and light some candles? It's getting dark in here and I don't want to be alone in the dark."

He helped me undress down to my shift, brought me a jug of water, and promised he would return later with food. I laid back, closed my eyes, and could feel the world spin a hundred bazillion miles an hour. Thumps of heeled shoes across the wood floor. The rumble of laughter and conversation wafted through the house. My head spun. I closed my eyes and crashed.

I woke up later with my bladder ready to pop. Sitting up, I swayed and realized I was still drunk. I stumbled behind the screen in the corner, which hid my chamber pot chair. At least I didn't have to squat over the pot like I did when I was at the Lovetts' house. I fell ill and remained in a fevered daze for three days. When I finally had the wherewithal to use a chamber pot on my own, I stumbled and crashed onto the floor. Henry rushed in and found me sprawled on the floor and a lovely shade of crimson from the embarrassment. I didn't need him to rush in that evening, so I minded my uneasy feet, used the chamber pot, wiped my hands clean, and headed back to bed. A steaming mug of willow bark tea in the morning would be on the menu.

"Stop banging on the damned door," I shouted, and covered my head with a pillow.

Henry rubbed my hip and said, "Go back to sleep, my love. I'll take care of this."

I grumbled a curse or two, rolled over with my back facing the door, and crushed my eyes closed. The morning sun found its way through an offset curtain and tortured me with its cheery mood. I drew the blanket over my head in protest. The sound of the linen of Henry's breeches rubbing against his skin and his feet padding over to the door rang like the morning church bells. Sleep would elude me. There was no sense in fighting it.

"Tell him I'll be down." Henry shut the door and went behind the screen.

"Who was it?" I grumbled out.

"Orme. Braddock wants to meet," he called out from behind the screen.

I reluctantly edged myself up on my elbows. My head throbbed. "You don't think he wants to yell at you because I... um... I was a bit drunk last night?" I ran my hand across my brow, attempting to wish away the pain.

"He hardly took notice of your absence. They had much to drink and then came back and finished a couple more bottles of John's stock. He mentioned the review went well and took another bottle to celebrate."

"Did you tell them why I wasn't down there?" I sat up in the bed—sluggish and clumsy—propping the pillow behind my back. There was no use hiding my hungover shame under the blankets.

Henry pulled on his shirt and tucked it in. He moved

THE TIME WRITER AND THE MARCH

over to the chair, sat down, and pulled on his stockings and boots. Within 4 quick and long strides, he walked over to me, ran his fingers through his hair a few times, handed me his leather thong and ribbon, and sat on the edge of the bed. I pulled my fingers through his hair again, made sure he was tangle free, grasped his hair and braided into a queue and wrapped the strip of leather around and tucked in on itself. A half-assed bow was all I could manage. He leaned over planted a kiss on my lips. "You taste like the tavern."

"That's a nice compliment. Thanks so much." I twisted a smirk in his direction. "I feel like the tavern made me its bitch last night." Running my tongue across my teeth, I rubbed my hand across my brow again. "Will you have Cate bring me some willow bark tea and something light to eat? I don't think I'm heading down soon."

"Would you like hot water to bathe?" He lifted an eyebrow in my direction. He tugged on his light blue linen waistcoat and coat and leaned over the mirror to tie his white linen neck stock.

I lifted my arm up and smelled my pit. That was godawful. I regretted it the moment the sharp tang hit my nostrils.

"I will take that as an affirmation." He spurted out a hearty belly laugh out as he reached the door. As the pillow I flung sailed haphazardly in his direction, he slid out the door and shut it before he fell victim to my onslaught. I threw myself backwards on the bed, yanked the blanket over my head, and growled.

By late morning, I was finally ready to join the world

of the living. It would be a quiet day, with the slight stir of my hungover compatriots. Perhaps the men would head over to the encampment and check things out. Sarah may need my help to prepare menus, lists, or some other household chore.

The house was quiet. No rumbling of the men. No business of Sarah running to-and-fro barking orders and stressing over her guests. I was half-tempted to sneak back upstairs and crawl back into bed. Out the back door, I found Sarah seated at a small table engaged in conversation with Mistress Dalton, as they both sipped on tea. I didn't want to interrupt or try to explain my absence from the night prior. It would not have been without scandal—something that none of us wanted to endure. I headed back upstairs, undressed, and crawled back into bed.

Later that afternoon, Henry came in to check on my wellbeing. Understandably, he was concerned when he didn't find me sputtering about with Sarah. It was unlike me to hide away in bed all day. I wanted to be busy, just not that day. "Braddock, Dinwiddie, and Orme head to Annapolis in two days." He said as he crossed the room and plopped on the side of the bed next to me.

"Get your dirty boots off the bed," I grumbled, and rolled over to face him.

"I can see the rest has not improved your mood."

I shot a glare at him. He moved his feet off the side of the bed, laid across it with his head on my lap. I ran my fingers over his brown hair, straightening the flyaway strands. "Sorry, I'm not grumpy. Just bored. I should have grabbed a book or something. I've been up here brooding all day."

He reached over and rubbed my blanket covered leg. "Are you feeling ill, my love?"

"No. Not really. Just a bit hungover and blah. Sarah and Mistress Dalton were on the terrace." I flicked my head towards the window that overlook the terrace.

He continued to run his fingers up and down my leg, sending shockwaves up and down my spine. "Did they not invite you to join them for tea?"

"I avoided them like the plague." I twisted a lock of his hair around my finger and made little ringlets. "It was probably best for everyone."

"Mayhap, you would drink less the next time we go to the tavern and not require lying in bed the entire next day."

"Oh, I'm fine. Just a bit bored. Besides, you can't tell me you weren't having a good time with them. You had joined in the sailors singing of the sea shanty. Yo ho-ing with your bottle of rum and a lovely lass. Where did you learn that?"

Henry tucked his arms behind his head as he stared at the ceiling. "I picked things up here and there."

"That's vague. Do I need to call Scooby and the Gang to solve this mystery, or are you going to tell me?"

He seemed a bit unsettled at my inquiry. Taking a deep sigh, he answered, "I sailed around before settling in Williamsburg. I might have been on a merchant ship or two, sailed with some... interesting?... types. That is all."

"That doesn't seem like the complete story." I

humphed. "What secrets does my husband hide from his dutiful, innocent, and highly respectable wife?" Sarcasm dripped from my tongue.

Henry was in another world. A past life that haunted or drew him back. I couldn't tell.

Commotion erupted downstairs. He popped out of bed. "Saved by the bell," I called after him as he ran out the door. "I might as well see what is going on in the land of the living."

By the time I finished dressing and made my way downstairs, the commotion dissipated. "What's going on?" I found Henry in the parlor with Dinwiddie, Braddock, Orme, Keppel, and Carlyle. Braddock shot me an unwelcoming look. He obviously didn't approve of my intrusion. I straightened my skirt and checked my hair.

"Mistress Spencer," Dinwiddie stood and gave a quick bow. "You were missed last night and this morning."

"Thank you, my friend." I said, as I gave a curtsy to the room. "I felt a bit under the weather, but all is now well."

"The French kidnapped Mistress Spencer... what was his name?" Dinwiddie asked. He was trying to sing my accolades to Braddock, but remained a matter of fact about it.

"Sieur Jumonville, Bouchard, and their gang of not so merry men."

"Yes, Jumonville." Dinwiddie escorted me over to a chair at a table in the parlor. "Didn't you have that Half-King scalp him?"

"The French pay for the scalps of the English. The

honorable Tanaghrisson was just returning the favor." I quipped.

Braddock sat there and didn't interrupt mine and Dinwiddie's conversation. For the first time since I had met him, he was quiet and not blustering. I knew that would not last long. Dinwiddie turned to Braddock and said, "Mistress Spencer was at Fort Necessity with Washington. She helped Doctor Craik with the injured."

Braddock sat back in his chair. "Did she?" His voice was flat and unimpressed.

Was this a trial? Was I being judged? Rolling back my shoulders, I answered, "I did. I also escaped from the French and told the soldiers at the fort on the forks of the rivers... the French are calling it Duquesne..." I flittered my hand about matter-of-factly, "about the impending attack. Lives would have been lost, not just the fort, if it were not for my intervention."

"They should have defended the fort," Braddock spit out.

"They would have been annihilated." I sat ramrod straight in my seat, at the ready to pounce. "If those few men would have tried to fight the thousand French soldiers, you would have still lost the fort and unnecessarily lost those men." I could see Braddock was getting irritated with me. As a woman, he didn't see my place anywhere near a battlefield or involved in the logistics, regardless of my knowledge. I glanced over at Henry, surprised he hadn't stopped me by then. He cracked a smile in my direction. I was not the only one that was tired of the bluster, and he knew I could handle my own. "It was best to hand it over and live to fight another day. I must commend the decision of the soldiers that day. For it was not cowardice, but courage to know when to fold their hand and accept defeat."

"That defeat is why they implored me to come here. To take back that fort and show the French that we will not cower to them."

"With all due respect, your Excellency," I began, knowing full well it would be difficult for me to give him respect. "It is a shame that you had to travel here to assist in the fort's recovery and boundary lines. I am quite certain, a man as noble as you, has much more important things to do back in England. However, if it was not for that defeat, then we would not be aware of the powerful presence of the French in the Ohio. We would have thought that they were minding their business away from us. They showed their hand. They sent you here to help show them ours. I hope you are ready for their fighting style. At Fort Necessity, again, another defeat, terrible." I shook my head. "Besides the terrible loss, we learned their fighting style and gained an insider to their operations, in their political prisoner, our very own Captain Stobo, who remains with the French at Fort Duquesne. You would take great heed to listen to your counselors on the subject."

His reaction could have gone one of two ways. He could have listened to me and my informed opinion. Or he would fly off the handle. I braced myself in my chair for the backlash I saw bubbling under his skin.

Braddock's face reddened. "Captain Spencer," he

huffed out. "Your wife should learn to control her tongue."

"Your Excellency," Henry stepped forward from the sidelines where he had stood and bowed to Braddock. "Her tongue is one of the many reasons I had to make her my wife. She saved the lives of countless men. She is loyal and as intelligent as any man, myself included."

I wasn't sure how to take that last bit. I shot a look at over to Henry.

Dinwiddie's shoulders shook in his struggle to contain his laughter. "Let's drink a toast to sharp minds," he lifted his glass to me. "And sharp tongues."

CHAPTER NINETEEN

"*I* guess they're off to see the wizard." I leaned over the balustrade on the terrace and watched the men leave on ships towards Annapolis. The white sails disappeared down the Potomac, then up the bay. It might have been faster if they left on horses, but as I discovered, they refused to listen to me.

Henry looked at me, raised an eyebrow, and shook his head. He gave up long ago on trying to figure me out. We strolled down through the garden—my hand firmly placed in the crook of his elbow—and down towards the docks.

On the third of April 1755, Dinwiddie, Braddock, Orme, and Keppel left for Annapolis to meet with Governor Sharp, the governor of Maryland, and the other governors of the colonies. Quiet and calm fell upon the Carlyles' house. "Since they are gone for a few weeks—at a minimum—what should we do?" I poked at Henry, hoping to get out of the Carlyles' space for a little while.

"We set sail for Williamsburg and settle you into our

176

house." Back to the old discussion of sending me away while he battled the French. "I will return before Braddock and Dinwiddie's arrival."

"Or..." I drew out a long "or." "We could buy me a horse, maybe some armor, chain mail, sword, AK-47, tank, and I stay with you."

He glowered in my direction, absent of comment. We strolled towards the house from the docks.

"Henry, there are several concerns that I have about leaving you." I looked over at him, wanting to see if he paid me any attention. He was. "The first one is I'm sure I'm supposed to be here with you. You must be the reason I keep popping back to this time. The first time, I had assumed it was because I was researching Washington's movements. I had been thinking about him, what he was doing, and next thing you know... I'm in 1754."

"Washington has remained secluded." He pulled me to the side to avoid a very large deposit from an enormous horse. "He has business to attend at Mount Vernon before joining us."

"Exactly! That's why it can't be about him. It must be about you. What if I'm here to protect you?" I hadn't thought of Henry as the reason for my time travel. At first, I assumed it was to observe Washington, make sure history happened the way it was supposed to happen. Then I met Henry and fell in... Infatuation? Amusement? Love seemed too serious of a word to attach to my feelings before I slipped back to 1755. However, that changed my thinking of why I was sent through time to 1754. But that didn't explain why I was sent back to the future. "If I hadn't stopped you on the road to the fort, you would have arrived with the French taking it and they could have taken you prisoner or killed you."

"Then why did you leave me?" He sounded dejected. Time travel and how, when, or why it worked eluded me.

"Until recently, you didn't need me. You were safe. Depressed. Sad. Angry. But safe." It was making sense to me. We walked across the garden to the terrace. "I arrived in 1755 before you were to run off to join the fight against the French. That can't be a coincidence. Can it?"

Henry took it all in. Listen. Contemplate. React. "What if you are correct?"

He looked over the garden towards the docks. Tall sails raised over the buildings like white-capped mountains as they approached the docks. Gray rain clouds billowed in the distance as they continued out to sea. The cherry tree at the back of the garden flowered. Spring was in full force. My mind chased the reason for my time travel.

"Why would you question your brilliant wife?" As I grabbed him around his waist, I let out a small laugh. I felt the deep breath escaped him. I brought down my excitement level to match his. No sense in working him up more than he already was. "I've been right about a lot of things," I began as I tried to work it out. My thoughts jumped back-and-forth around my head. "I know something is supposed to happen with Braddock. He has a damn road named after him... or he will. I can't control... or at least I don't know how to control... slipping through time. What happens if you leave me in Williamsburg or here and I slip? You wouldn't know what happened to me.

No. No. I need to be here, there—or wherever—with you."

He turned to look at me. As he stared deep into my eyes, he searched for the truth in what I told him. He couldn't deny that it made sense. They have sent me to protect him. I just didn't know how I was going to do it. With a determined look, he said, "You will need a horse."

"And a wagon. I have lots of clothes." I shrugged my shoulders. "Apparently, I don't know how to pack light. What else can I say?"

"Why do you need to bring that light green silk dress into battle? Are you going to defeat the French with a minuet? Or have you forgotten our wedding?" He shook his head. "No. We can send your clothes and the items you brought with you from your time to our house in Williamsburg. I have enough coin to get you a horse, a small wagon, and any other small supplies we may need over the next few months. If they can decide on the funding, I will receive my captain's pay, and that will be enough to get us home." He pulled me into his arms and planted a kiss on my forehead. We stared into the horizon, worried about what was to come next.

A week later, we received notice of the meeting's postponement, and everyone headed to Carlyle's house. A few of the governors couldn't—or wouldn't—show up in a timely manner and Braddock grew impatient and disappointed in what he learned about the Maryland route towards Wills Creek. Prior to leaving Williamsburg, Captain Orme sent a message to George Washington at Mount Vernon. They invited Washington to join the entourage. After some negotiations, he agreed to join the growing crowd in Alexandria. Washington was hesitant to join Braddock, since he had resigned his commission the previous year and didn't want to take a demotion. I can't say that I blame him. He focused on family at that point and the need to find a wife to run his household and estate.

During one of his visits to Williamsburg, Henry told me that George had asked no less than three eligible ladies for their hand. All refused. I laughed when he told me about George's disappointment. He had complained to Henry that he wasn't sure if any woman would ever marry him. He needed someone to help elevate his standing with the gentry, and with his resignation with the regiment and his minimal land holdings, he was not the prize those ladies were looking for in a husband. I am sure in thirty-four years, when he is the first president, regret may cross their minds. Henry considered introducing him to some women in Alexandria when they got back from Fort Duquesne.

"Don't worry about that. He will do just fine in a couple of years. He will marry a very wealthy widow," I said to Henry as we laid in bed one night, my head on his chest, moved up and down with the rise of his breaths. With the activities throughout the day to get ready for the arrival of the governors, it was one of the few times we could spend together.

"Please, tell me her name is not Amelia," Henry said as he tucked a lock of hair behind my ear. "It would distress me to learn of my demise and you marrying that young buck."

I laughed. "Cheese and rice. Not a chance." I planted a kiss on his chest. "Her name is Martha Custis. I believe that is her name. She has... or will have... a couple of children with her husband before he dies."

I could feel the tension radiate across Henry's chest. "Martha Dandridge Custis? Daniel Parke Custis's wife?"

"Suppose so," I said with a shrug. "Hadn't really thought about it. I always thought of her as just Martha Washington." I knew the brief history of Martha Washington, prior to her marriage to George. "If he is rich, then it might be. Supposedly," I said as if I was a teenager gossiping with one of my girlfriends. "He was one of the most eligible bachelors in Virginia. They marry. He dies. She's wealthy. George needs the society standing, and she needs a new husband. Botta boom. They get married."

"That is not what I expected." He laid further back into the bed. I wasn't sure if he was talking about Washington getting married or Custis's demise. "Yes, Custis is wealthy, much more than I. Met him twice in Williamsburg."

"I know! It's totally crazy. I mean, good ol' George is good looking. Has some wealth. Loves to dance. Women just don't seem to want to marry him."

"I would have thought his lady friend, Miss Woods, in Fredericksburg would have married him."

"I think fate has other plans for her." A jaw-cracking yawn escaped from me.

When I mentioned the word fate, Henry's ears perked up. "What do you mean?"

I explained to him about my friends from the future,

Beth and Hector, and how they looked identical to Elizabeth Woods and Lieutenant Hector Bennet. Lieutenant Bennet had served in the Virginia Regiment with Henry. Prior to the recent parade, the last time I had seen him was after our defeat at Fort Necessity. Henry and I had traveled to Williamsburg and Bennet had stayed with the men that went to Alexandria before they were all sent back to their homes. I hadn't thought about asking Henry about him and his current martial endeavors. It was not like they sent me to play matchmaker with him and Elizabeth, but I had a feeling they would hit it off if they met.

When I had told Beth and Hector about their 1754 versions, they didn't mention they had traveled through time. So, we had to assume it was their ancestors. We wondered if there was more to this time travel business than we had originally thought. I would have expected Beth and Hector to have said something if they had traveled through time.

The next morning, we continued the preparations for the assembly. Major Carlyle stayed in bed for the day. He felt ill again. I think the stress of the commissary was taking its toll on him. The pregnancy hung heavy on Sarah, and with little Willie toddling around the house, she took respite when the opportunity allowed. Henry took on some of Carlyle's appointments, while Sarah and I prepared the house.

"We will need to stack the guests up." I said as I stared at the layout of the house. Sarah and I were playing musical beds again. Concern grew with five governors–

whomever they were bringing–Braddock, Orme, Washington, Henry, and myself. "Keppel will stay on his ship again. Maybe he can fit others if needed." I moved a pallet cutout on the map of the house. "We can use the music room."

"Whoever the governor brings with him will have to stay in the same room." Sarah shook her head and shifted a few pallets around the map. We would pack the house to the brim with guests. I was reluctant to give up my room and move into an inn, but it was looking as though that would be the case. "Servants can stay in the servant quarters or in the hall."

"Cate has slept on a pallet outside our door before they headed to Annapolis. We can bring her into our room." I pointed to a section on the map. "We can fit at least four men in this section at the top of the stairs. Orme slept there last time." I moved another cutout pallet into that section. "If we extend the privacy panel out a little, we can fit one more pallet and still give them some privacy."

We planned on receiving ten men and a few servants. Henry and I could keep our room and I wouldn't have to rough it in a tent with the troops nor head to the inn over *Horst's Tavern*. After my overindulged merriment, I wasn't sure if I was ready to show my face there for at least another month or two. Which was a shame, because they had a delicious fish chowder.

CHAPTER TWENTY

By mid-April, everyone settled in, and the meeting of the masterminds was to begin in Carlyle's parlor. I was not sure how many people they packed in the rooms and who slept in which room. Sarah and I had devised a grand sleeping plan, but that seemed to fly out the window as soon as everyone started showing up. Bodies piled throughout the house in a drunken slumber. We moved the chairs from the dining room, music room, foyer, and any other spare chair we could find into the parlor for the assembly. They didn't invite me. Bastards. They didn't believe a woman's place was at the table. I had to remind myself this was 1755 and it would take another 250 years before I would be accepted into their ranks.

Where there is a will to be involved, there is a way to make it happen. And I had every intention of getting my freckled little button nose in the middle of their discussion. Fortunately for me, every door and window were opened to allow air and people circulation.

Nonchalantly, I brought drinks, food, remove a plate, or find some other way to saunter through the room in order to listen and eye Henry as he sat against a wall away from the chaotic planning.

"Wagons! We need wagons and horses!" Braddock's thunderous demands reverberated throughout the room. The tray of tea I carried shook as I nearly dropped it at the outburst. "How are we supposed to take back the fort without equipment?"

I slinked my way through the room and stood next to a man seated off to the side. The occupant of the chair next to him left to find the privy. I plopped next to him and balanced the tray on my lap, hoping I would remain unnoticed. Looking over towards the man, he glanced at me. We each gave a quick smile, and he added a nod. I couldn't place the face, but he seemed familiar to me. He appeared to be in older than me, in his mid-fifties, perhaps. He leaned towards me and whispered, "Does any of this pomposity interest you?"

"I like to know what's going on," I whispered. I looked over at the man, dressed in brown from head to toe. Well, his shoes were black leather, with an intricate buckle. "Why are you here?"

"They desired the Postmaster General to attend, to confirm the passage of their correspondence as they go about this escapade." The man sat back in his chair and stretched out his legs.

I cocked my head to the side and looked over at Braddock's face as it turned fifty shades of red. Leaning in close to the postmaster, I whispered, "I suppose for logistical reasons, that makes sense." I leaned in closer. "However, if you ask me, and I know you didn't, but they are completely unprepared and don't know what they're getting themselves into. Braddock's blustering is going to send John, Major Carlyle, into a twisted ball of stress and make Sarah a widow." We both looked over towards John as he wiped the sweat from his brow. It was warm in the room, but not that warm to cause the profuse sweat.

Carlyle stood up to address Braddock, the governors, officers, and other civilian men. I could see his stomach clench. He had to drag himself out of bed to attend the meeting. The activity took a toll on his health. "We cannot get the required supplies of wagons, horses, and the men to drive them." He held out his empty hands. "We lack the resources."

My seat mate leaned over towards me, "I shall rescue our host from the humiliation that Braddock seems to enjoy giving upon him."

"Have you heard of the phrase 'mind your business'?" I cocked an eyebrow. Well, I attempted to cock an eyebrow. It turned into two eyebrows being raised. As much as I practiced, I still couldn't do the one eyebrow cock to respond to a ridiculous statement, even if it was my own. "As much as I adore John, you might make things worse. Unless you want to feel the wrath of Braddock..."

The man patted my shoulder as he stood up. "If I may," he began, grabbing the attention of the room. "General Braddock, gentlemen, I may have a solution."

Braddock shot an annoyed look over to the man. "What is it Mister Franklin?"

"It would seem that you decided to have this assembly in the wrong location," said Mister Franklin. Braddock shifted in his seat. Touché, Mister Franklin. "You assembled in Virginia, which, with all due respect to Governor Dinwiddie and Major Carlyle, is not the best place to find your supplies. Yes, Virginia is a merchant's dream. Trade moves through here with great ease. Major Carlyle has done quite well for himself as a merchant."

Mister Franklin looked about the room to ensure he had everyone's attention. All eyes focused on the man that stood next to me. I looked around to see if anyone had noticed me sitting there. Of course, Henry would notice that I had made myself a fly on the wall. I am sure he would think that I was somehow involved in Mister Franklin's oration. "However, you need not of a merchant to get your wagons. Mayhap, what you need are farmers. If you had your assembly in Pennsylvania, it would have brought me great pleasure to welcome you and buy your wagons, horses, and drivers." John Carlyle looked a bit relieved that someone had removed the attention from him, and he plopped down in his chair in a slump. I was not sure how much longer the man could handle running the commissary, nor Braddock, for that matter.

Braddock spoke up, "You could get the one hundred fifty wagons, four draft horses each, and drivers?"

"Of course, it comes with a price." Mister Franklin tipped his head toward the stirred assembly. "Farmers are reluctant to dispose of their means of work and income without recompense."

Braddock let out a huffed breath. "We have ten thousand sterling for it."

"Ten thousand may get you thirty." Franklin shook his head. "Fifty thousand fund your requirements."

Braddock laughed. He was used to the English way of getting men and equipment. The lords would provide the men and equipment, they would pay for it, and seek reimbursement later from Parliament. Taxes left the colonies and made their way to England, so there was no one to demand conscript, unless they were using enslaved people—and they were not willing to give them up and take them out of the fields. Any required supplies came at a cost.

"Thirty thousand." Braddock rebuffed. "Eight hundred on the outset. Send a warrant for payment for the remainder."

"How will we pay the thirty thousand?" Someone on the other side of the room asked.

Another man stood up. "I'm not paying for this." I shot my head around in an attempt to see who made the statement. My short stature kept me from peering over the men's heads.

"Nor I," shouted another. The discourse volleyed about the room.

Mister Franklin sat back down as the men argued about funding the battles.

"Well, Mister Franklin, it looks as though you didn't mind your business and now have to get wagons and men without all the funding you will need." I no longer needed to whisper, as the ruckus of funding drowned out any other noise.

He laughed. "Mayhap, your assessment is well founded, Mistress. I may have my ways to get the wagons with that amount." He flicked a look towards Carlyle, who twisted less in his seat, but continued to wipe sweat from his brow. "And look at Major Carlyle." He gave a nod. "He looks less distressed. Speaking of minding one's business, what business do you have in here... Mistress..."

"Lady Amelia Spencer, wife of Captain Lord Henry Spencer," I said, holding out my hand to shake his. He took it and raised it to his lips. Being wrapped up in the debate, proper protocol flew out one of the open windows. "Please call me Amelia. And as far as my business here..."

"Oh, I have heard about your spirit. It is a great pleasure to make your acquaintance." He chuckled as he sat back in his in chair. "You can call me Ben."

"I knew I recognized you!" I practically jumped out of my chair. He was a younger version of the paintings I had seen of Ben Franklin, but as soon as he said the name, it hit me like a bolt of lightning. "You're Ben Franklin." It was not a question. It was a statement. A loud and excited statement. He twisted an amused look towards me. "No wonder you didn't mind your business. I'm not sure you would know how to live without being involved in one thing or another. Printing press, science, postmaster, founding fa..." I had to stop myself. He was not a founding father or an ambassador yet. They were not even on his radar at this point. We would have to wait for over twenty years before that happened.

"I see my reputation proceeds, the both of us." He chortled.

"I'm totally fangirling over your brilliant mind." I looked up and saw Henry headed my direction. The determined look on his face told me I was about to get an earful. Ben shot a curious look in my direction, then followed my eyes towards Henry. "Oh, it looks as though the tea is cold. I need to get a fresh pot. Please, excuse me, Ben."

As I slipped and twisted through the crowds of chairs and loud men, in the opposite direction of Henry, I slid out the door towards the back of the house. There were three doors to enter the room. One through the sitting room, where we welcomed guests. Two that entered from the foyer, one towards the front and one towards the back of the house. I thought I could try to sneak out to the back and avoid Henry. I was wrong.

"Amelia," Henry said through gritted teeth as he grabbed my arm. I had to hold the tray tight to keep from dropping it as I was pulled backwards. "What did you say to Mister Franklin? You were told to stay out of this."

"I was staying out of it. I just told him to mind his business," I said with a smug look on my face. After finding out who I was dealing with, I knew there was no way Ben Franklin could mind his business. His business was the business of being involved, whether or not he wanted to admit to it. It was impossible for him to retire and live the quiet life of a gentleman. He became a postmaster so he could send his printed materials without paying the fee. He couldn't keep out of this if he tried. "Besides, if he took care of the wagons, then that means that is one less thing John needs to worry about. And, if you hadn't noticed, your friend, John, is going to have an ulcer or stroke or die of a heart attack if he must deal with Braddock and this whole commissary thing much longer."

Henry's hands and arms flailed about. "You were supposed to stay out of the room." He pointed towards the parlor's open door. The loud conversation happening in the parlor kept anyone from noticing us or his loud, angry voice. "Braddock will ensure you stay with the Carlyles if he suspects you will contradict his every command."

"Eh, I'm sure you'll convince him." I shifted the tray in my hand to rest on my hip. It was getting heavy from the cups and tea. "Besides, I'm not causing problems. That was entirely up to Ben. I think he knew he could take care of the situation and help John."

Henry took the tray out of my hands and carried it as we walked towards the table in the foyer. "He's a postmaster, not a commissary officer, nor should you be familiar with him."

"No, my love, it is Ben Franklin. The man is a flippin' legend."

The foyer had a long table sitting in the middle. With the number of guests we had, we couldn't sit everyone down for a meal. We thought it would be best to set a table up buffet style, and people could grab food and find a place to sit. We converted the dining room to another sleeping location. Cate had placed a tray of sliced meat on the table as we walked up. I grabbed a roll and pried it open with my fingers. A piece of sliced beef caught my attention, and I slid it between the pieces of bread, making a sandwich. "Is he going to be another president? Lead men into battle? He will be too old for that in twenty years."

"Franklin? No. He doesn't fight. He is a character, though." I said through a mouth full of another piece of the sliced beef I pulled off the tray. Henry handed the tea tray to Cate. I handed him the sandwich and made another for myself. We headed towards the garden to get some fresh air and enjoy the meal. I ripped into the sandwich. It was mid-afternoon, and I had been going since early morning. With a full mouth, I garbled out, "He will be one of our founding fathers. He is, quite arguably," I swallowed down my bite and wished I had grabbed a cup of tea, "One of the most brilliant minds of this time."

"Will he get us the wagons?" Henry eyed me over his sandwich.

I shrugged my shoulders. "Suppose so." I turned to look towards the docks. Seagulls cawed as they flew in circles overhead. "I mean, Braddock will lead the men towards Pittsburgh." I looked towards Henry as he raised an eyebrow at me, questioning my statement. "Not Pittsburgh, well, not yet... Fort Duquesne. We know he will. I remember the name Braddock's March." I turned and looked towards the Potomac River and the gathering of ships at the docks. "If Franklin says he can do it, then he'll do it. I'm just wondering how he'll be paid back for it."

"I heard them mention they will send a request to Parliament to tax the colonies."

"They should tax the Ohio Trading Company. It's their trade route they're trying to protect." My ears burned and nostrils flared. I shoved the last bite of sandwich in my mouth. "Half those men in there are involved with the trading company." I said with a mouthful of food and a vigorous chew, stabbing a pointed finger in the house's direction. "They will benefit from this battle financially and have the colonists pay for it. This is going to cause problems further down the road. It's so wrong. How can we let this happen?"

"We cannot stop it." Henry laughed and took another bite of his sandwich. He seemed less insistent with scarfing down his sandwich than I was. "It is grander than us and that group of men in there will ensure it happens. I promised Dinwiddie that I would go, but you can stay behind. You have the option of traveling to Williamsburg and await my return."

"You know I can't do that," I said as I wrapped my arm around Henry's waist and rested my head on his chest. "I can't protect you from there."

"Braddock is not the only one troubled with the procurement of a wagon." He took another bite and swallowed before continuing. "I might have found a horse, but a wagon and a team of horses proved difficult to procure around here. Would you still go if I can only provide a horse for you?"

"As I see it, if I had my own horse, at least Louis wouldn't have to carry the both of us everywhere. I can go without a wagon. Hell, I would walk the entire way, if I had to, but I will settle with a horse of my own. I hope I don't need to remind you I will not be riding sidesaddle."

Henry wrapped his arm around my shoulders and kissed the top of my head. "I need to get back to the meeting. Washington arrived before I chased you out of the room."

"I need to check on Sarah." Exhausted from the day's events, my bed called me, but I knew Sarah needed me more than I needed a nap. At forty-one years old, I felt like I had lived two lifetimes. How did people survive the 18th century? There was always so much work to be done. I started to long for the automation and progress of the twenty-first century. But, thinking about the history I witnessed, the people I met, and Henry, kept me from searching for a door to slip back to my time.

CHAPTER TWENTY-ONE

I stretched out like a starfish in bed and searched for Henry. He slipped out before I woke up. The early morning light crept through the slit in the curtains and begged me to join the land of the living. I padded across the room, slipped behind the screen, and used the chamber pot. A light knock at the door startled me from my dazed morning ritual.

I popped my head around the screen to find Penny had entered the room. "Thank you. You know, I could have brought up my water," I said to Penny as she placed the pitcher of hot water on the washstand.

"I dinna mind, Mistress Spencer," Penny said, stealing a glance out the window as she opened the curtains. "It's quiet in your room."

I stifled the laugh that begged to burst out. It was only quiet during the day when Henry was working, and I had a lazy morning. We filled our nights with quiet conversation and making love.

Conversation and love making were in stark contrast to Henry's hateful first wife. The cruel heifer laughed at his inexperience the one time she allowed him in her bed. She was already pregnant by his brother and forced to marry Henry. They were cruel to him, and I could only hope that my love for him healed his troubled past.

"It's been chaotic around here lately." I walked over to the window and stood next to her. "They won't be here forever. I miss the quiet days around here, too." The view of the Potomac was always the same. Ships coming in and out of the port. Seagulls flying about the docks, looking for a meal to swipe out of someone's hand or off the ground. Carts of goods moved to the market on the road next to Carlyle's home. It was always a bustle of activity outside, but in my room, it was a quiet escape.

"Would you like me to help you get dressed, Mistress?"

"Penny, I think you are looking for reasons to avoid the madness downstairs." I smiled and thought about doing the same. "A penny for your thoughts." Ugh! Did you really say that to Penny? "That is, you can tell me what troubles you. I can sense your distress."

"With the drinking," she hesitated, unsure if she could speak freely to me, "the visitors are cruel."

"I believe most of them are cruel without the drinking." I patted her on the shoulder and turned away from the window. "Stay up here as long as you can before Mistress Carlyle requires your help. You can tell her you were helping me." I walked over to the trunk and pulled out my indigo cotton jacket and petticoat. My apron was white, with blue and red flowers printed on it. I pinned the top of it to the dress and had apron strings to wrap around my waist. I pulled the matching cuffs out from the bottom of the sleeves. The thought of covering my head with a cap caused me to cringe. It was bad enough that I couldn't throw on a pair of jeans and a tee shirt, but had to wear layers of dress. For some reason, a cap to cover my hair seemed to be my breaking point, my rebellion against the misogyny.

I peeked into the small dressing mirror and recoiled at my wild auburn locks. Exhausted from tending to the guests, I fell asleep without braiding my hair. I pulled a comb through the nest, which only intensified the chaos. The curls eventually smoothed out. I pulled my hair back in a chignon, pinned into place. I was ready to face the morning. "Was anyone stirring about before you came up?"

"Yes, Mistress," Penny finished making the bed. "Food is on the table. I will fetch you a plate."

"You know, the second you leave this room, someone will be ready for you to be put to work. No, I can make myself something. I can give you a few more minutes in here, but they will come looking for you soon." As much as I wanted to hide upstairs with Penny, I could no longer avoid management of the downstairs chaos.

Sarah's pregnancy left her sick and exhausted that morning, and I couldn't leave her to do the hard work. When we prepared for the men, we didn't expect the amount of people that had arrived. It overwhelmed the entire house. I couldn't imagine managing the chaos, a husband that looked as though he was about to have a heart attack from stress, and the addition of being pregnant. No. I could handle being overworked if it gave her a moment of respite. As I started down the stairs, the corner of my eye glimpsed George Washington without his boots. In his stocking feet, he stood as tall as Henry. Well, that sneaky devil. I hadn't noticed the height of his heel before, but they had to be a good two inches. I smirked at his tall tale and traipsed down the stairs.

More houseguests stirred, bringing the house to life. The empty wine bottles that were strewn across the house the night before were removed and replaced with teapots. Fresh bread, hard-boiled eggs, blocks of cheese, pickled radishes, and berry preserves were spread in bowls and trays throughout the table. I grabbed a slice of bread, slathered some butter and preserves on it, popped a pickled radish in my mouth, and plucked a hard-boiled egg to round out my meal. I took a cup of tea out to the terrace to enjoy the cool and quiet morning in the garden.

Elbows on the balustrade, plate resting next to me, and a teacup firmly in my hand, keeping me warm, I looked over the garden. Bees buzzed around the flowers. The Potomac blazed like fire from the morning sun creeping over it. A light breeze flapped the flags atop a ship's mast. The kitchen garden came to life. Flowers opened, begging the bees to taste their sweet nectar. Leaves spread, looking for the sun to warm them. The early morning dew sparkled on plants like glitter. I took a deep, cleansing breath and filled my lungs with the crisp morning air. The cucumbers were transplanted, and the vines climbed over the trellis. June would bring the fruits ready to harvest.

What they didn't eat fresh throughout the summer would get pickled or canned for meals throughout the colder months. One-inch onion tops peeked out from the ground. They would harvest and store them to get through the winter. Melons, squash, strawberries, spinach, lettuce, green beans, carrots, and cherries would grace the table in the coming months. Apples, more leafy greens, and pumpkin in the autumn. I smiled, thinking about the sweet and tender bounty. I had to stop my daydream and remind myself that we would be on our way to Fort Duquesne before long.

I gulped down the rest of the bitter tea—they had steeped it for too long and became cold—and strolled back inside to get the house ready for the continuation of the assembly.

"Do you have to go with him?" I asked Henry as he plated his food. "Couldn't you stay here? With me?" My inner child wanted to throw a tantrum and have him stay. After breakfast, he packed his bags with food, a change of clothes, and a few supplies. They had tasked George Washington to ride the route to Fort Duquesne to ensure Braddock a smooth trail. I remembered part of the trail the men had carved when I traveled with them the previous summer. It was rough, narrow, and taken over by nature over the past year if someone hadn't maintained it. It was certainly neglected. Washington and Henry both knew the area, and with the two of them and one of Braddock's men, they could travel there and back within the next week or so. I knew I couldn't leave Sarah behind to deal with Braddock and the rest of the guests by herself. I rubbed

Louis' neck as he brought his nose down to my shoulder and nudged me. "Bring him back alive and well, my friend." I whispered into his ear. He flicked his ear, snorted hot air through flared nostrils, and gave a stomp in response.

I stood on the front porch and watched the men ride west. I wrapped my arms around my waist, trying to protect my emotions. Deep breath and gulp down your tears. "Back to work," I said out loud, flattening down my apron, without a care if anyone heard me talk to myself.

I wandered down to the darkened cellar with a candle lit lantern in my hand to check the supplies. We were quickly running out of wine and brandy. There were a few bottles of gin and whiskey left. Another shipment would arrive in a couple of days, and with the rate these men drank, I was not sure we would make it until the delivery without a mutiny on our hands. Food stores looked just as bleak. Money to help fund the commissary was non-existent, and Major Carlyle would have to submit an invoice. The thought of him not being reimbursed niggled at the back of my brain. The request to Parliament to raise taxes to fund the campaign was to be sent at the end of the week. We would not receive a response before Braddock left for Duquesne, but according to him, he would already be on his way to New York to take care of the minor issue with the border and would have the funding approved.

Ben Franklin sent a note to his son to reach out to the local farmers. "Amelia." Ben took my hand and gave a bow over it before placing a kiss on my knuckles.

"Ben," I responded with a small dip of a curtsy. "It

appears as though you are leaving me here to brood over your absence. Are you off to mind your business? Or to poke your nose around a bit and give yourself more things to do?"

"Mayhap, upon your return, you and the captain will come visit my printing shop." He knew what sang to my heart. The printed word. Over breakfast, we had discussed my love for reading and writing. I played off the writing as a pastime and that I hadn't published. Well, in the 18th century I hadn't published a book. That said nothing for the thirty-two novels I published in the future. I was more than happy to accept his invitation and hoped that Henry and I lived through the next few months in order to take Ben up on it. My crazy imagination took flight and a wide grin spread across my face. I would get to see Benjamin Franklin's printing press and not the reproductions in the modern time Franklin Court Printing Office. To see the actual man—who I found to be quite charming and intelligent—at his press. I wished for a working cell phone or camera to take through time with me. If all electronics didn't have their energy drained when I crossed through time, then I could have visual proof of the fascinating moments that helped carve our history. Alas, the gods of time travel had a different plan for me.

When Washington and Henry returned a week later, the news was as unfavorable as expected. The path would not sustain the troop and equipment movement. Braddock, the orders follower that he was, stood his ground. We were to travel through the Virginia path to Fort Cumberland, then up to take Fort Duquesne from the French. There would be a group of men to widen and clear the path ahead of us. I remembered what it was like the previous year, when I was with Washington's group at Fort Necessity. The mission of our group was to expand the trail from Wills Creek to Captain Gist's trading post. The expansion would help move products and give the British a more established stronghold from the French. Unscrupulous negotiations with the tribal leaders led to the tribes losing more of their lands. There was a new half-king, Scarouady, the Oneida that had succeeded Tanaghrisson as the half-king. If Tanaghrisson thought Washington had difficulty listening to his wisdom and experience on the frontier, Scarouady would be in for a hard mountain to cross with Braddock.

Washington's unwillingness to listen to Tanaghrisson led to the half-king to take his warriors and left us to defend Fort Necessity alone. The French had their indigenous allies with them. It was nearly a slaughter of our fort. The stockade was too small to fit all the troops, which led most of them in the trenches for defense of the fort. Rain fell hard that day. Flints were difficult, if not impossible, to light. The already waterlogged trenches filled with more water and bogged down the men.

The French and their allies stayed in the tree line. Trees provided a canopy to offer them refuge from the rain, which allowed them to shoot at us when we couldn't shoot back. We were in the middle of the field, exposed.

They brought wounded soldiers to the surgeon, Doctor Craik, who I helped with my mediocre first aid skills. The volleys eventually stopped, and negotiations began. The French, led by Captain Louis Coulon de Villiers, Ensign Jumonville's half-brother, was upset that we killed his brother. Washington signed the surrender of the fort, with the admission that he assassinated Jumonville at the glen. I wouldn't say that it was an assassination, but Tanaghrisson struck an axe into Jumonville's skull after we captured him. Jumonville suffered with a bullet wound and held my notebook in his hand. Ready to accuse me of spying or witchcraft, I wasn't sure which, and Tanaghrisson refused to allow that to happen. It was a debacle, and I was in the middle of it. Tanaghrisson and I had an understanding from when I had met with him after my escape from the French. I am still not sure if I started this war or if it would have started no matter what I did. Regardless of what happened at Fort Necessity, the men didn't learn, and we would confront them on the battlefield once again.

Parliament in London decided how this was going to play out, and really had no clue what we were up against. I wanted Henry to pull out of this and send his troops home. There was a feeling deep in my gut that twisted and churned, telling me this was a bad idea. No matter what anyone had told Braddock, he was about to stick to the plan that was laid out to him before he had even left for the colonies. Things were different in America than in Europe, and not giving Braddock the ability to decide on the ground was going to lead to a tough mission, not that Braddock could think for himself. Honestly, I didn't know how bad it would be. None of us did.

roops descended upon Alexandria and formed columns, followed by wagons to pull artillery. A few supply wagons followed the artillery. At the end of the over a mile long train of soldiers, horses, wagons, and artillery, I walked with the other camp followers. Henry couldn't find a spare horse for me. However, he felt it necessary to remind me I could go to Williamsburg or walk with the other camp followers. He wanted me to go to Williamsburg, but the stubborn mule that I am, refused to leave his side.

Additional wagons from Pennsylvania would meet up with us further down the road at Fort Cumberland. Camps couldn't support too many men at once, so we moved in waves towards our destination. Colonel Dunbar moved his regiment through the rough Maryland route and would rally with us at Fort Cumberland. We were short on horses and wagons, which meant everyone had to carry more supplies and equipment than expected. In total, I counted around fifty of us women trailing behind our soldiers. Throughout the journey, we would help mend clothes, set up camps, prepare food, clean what we could, and were used as pack mules. These determined women would be ready to pick up a musket if necessary. They allotted us half-rations and we would not be at a camp for a long time. Which meant I would not have time to trap small game to help supplement our meals, nor would we be able to bake bread. Hard *biskits*, salted meat, and dried vegetables, made for a boring, but sustainable diet.

"You wanna pull yer skirts through like this." The woman next to me tugged at the end of her skirts tucked into the waistband, which formed a style of trousers. "Keeps it out of the mud."

Looking over at the woman and then to others around me, I realized my hanging dark blue petticoat collected more mud than their skirts. It reminded me of an old *I Love Lucy* episode. The one where she was in Italy and at the vineyard to squash grapes with her feet. In order to keep her skirt out of the grape juice, the Italian woman showed Lucy how to pull the back of her skirt between her legs to create–essentially–a pair of short pants. Sometimes, I could be a complete knucklehead. I had forgotten that I used that tactic when Henry and I found the cabin after my escape from the French. We had found a young couple murdered in their home. While Henry dug a grave for Tamhas's parents, I cleaned up the unfortunate and bloody mess. I stripped down to my shift to create the same function. Their assassins remained undiscovered, and that continued to haunt me.

"And yer shoes," she said, pointing to my feet with the pipe she pulled out from between her teeth.

I fought through the mud with every clomping step I took. The mud swallowed my feet and shoes. I tugged and pulled, hoping I didn't have to go elbow deep into the sticky, thick mud to fish out a lost shoe. The women had experience with the terrible roads and functioning in an environment that I had no business being in. I pulled off my shoes and kept ahold of them until I could wash and store them in the pouch I had slung across my chest.

"Thank you." I gave her a smile. "I'm Amelia."

"Brigid." She bit down on her clay pipe. The sweet scent of tobacco smoke escaped from her lips and caught the breeze to swirl around her face.

We set towards Fort Cumberland, leaving Braddock to head off to another meeting, intending to catch up to us down the road. Travel with the troops would take much longer for us to reach our destination. Moving the massive amount of people and equipment was no simple task. Henry would ride alongside his troops atop of Louis, and I would continue to wade in the mud with the other women and children. His company was too far ahead of us for me to see him on the march. Either I made friends with the women, or it would be a long and lonely road ahead.

June in Virginia continued to bring the rains. Days of early morning drizzle, followed by a blazing hot and humid afternoon. Hot and humid mornings would turn into a deluge of rain in the afternoon. Some days, there would not be a cloud in the sky, then the thunderstorms would roll in, bringing a downpour. It was difficult to stay dry. Clothes would soak through, leaving them heavy with water and sweat. The roads kept the moisture and never seemed to fully dry, which caused the trampled path to be nothing but mud by the time the women traipsed through it.

My feet were heavy with every step I pulled through the mud. The weight of the cannons bogged down the heavy carts. We pushed and pulled. Horses struggled to pull their legs out of the mud to move the wagons. I lost count on the number of horses that fell from being overworked or injured beyond repair. I feared Louis would suffer the same fate as the other beasts of burden. Hell, I felt like a beast of burden and wondered when it was my turn to fall from being overworked. Every muscle in my body ached. When we would stop for the day, as a woman, my day was not complete. They considered it a privilege to serve the needs of the men. Ha! I could barely lift my arms to move the pot filled with water to make a stew. It amazed me that a few of these women traveled with children, who we expected to work alongside their mother.

Day-after-day, we trudged along as we made our way west. Some days, we could make a respectful distance, maybe fifteen miles. There were too many days when the bogged down carts hampered our progress. A day of hard work pushing carts, carrying supplies, and standing over another dead horse, only to make it two or three miles down the path, was pure torture for the entire group.

I swore the gods tried to keep us from making it to

Fort Cumberland and then on to Fort Duquesne. However, the lords in London and their orders made us continue to push.

"You could have told Dinwiddie 'no' to this," I said to Henry one evening as we settled in for a well-earned dinner.

He looked down at the salted pork and the bits of carrots that were splayed across his plate. "If I stayed in Williamsburg, I would not have found you." He tore off a piece of the meat. "If I was not there to rescue you, who knows what Bouchard would have done if he caught you?"

I let out a snort. "He wouldn't have caught me." The pork was too salty. I hadn't rinsed it off well enough before cooking it. It would have to do. "I get it, you know." Henry raised an eyebrow in my direction at my statement. "Why was Bouchard so angry? I know why. He was loyal to Jumonville and to see him killed in the glen... he blamed me for it. I guess," I paused for a moment. "It was my fault."

Henry swallowed a large gulp of ale, trying to wash down the salt. He didn't complain. Good man. "It was Tanaghrisson that killed him, not you."

"For me. He killed him to get my notebook back." I shook my head. The sight of the axe splitting Jumonville's head, and the wet, slurping sound of his scalp being separated from his head, was too much for me to think about as I poked around my chunk of meat. What made it worse was how I learned that English and French paid for the scalps. Before then they only took hair. I didn't want to admit to Henry, but sometimes the memory triggered, and the moment haunted me at night. I knew that night would be one of those nights and fitful sleep was in my future. "Let's talk about something else." I shook off the thought.

"Right, then." He fished out a piece of hard biscuit from his broth. "What would my lovely wife like to discuss? The recent book you have read?"

I shot a death glare over to him. "Of course, I have all the time in the world while I'm pushing the back end of a cart, axle deep in mud and horse shit, while carrying this basket that is larger than I am on my back." I slowly gnawed on a chunk of pork. Barely able to find the energy to chew. "You sit atop of Louis all day barking orders. Perhaps, you should rest your precious voice." He let out a laugh. Truth be told, I would not know what Henry was doing most of the days. He was too far ahead of the cannons and the rest of us camp followers for me to see. I was bitter from the travel, cold, and constantly being dirty. Maybe I had become a bit too soft to handle the 18th century trials and tribulations of the march to war. "Do you know what I want?" I closed my eyes and took a deep breath.

"What would please my wife?" We sat on the ground outside our tent, next to the fire. I had prepared food for other men in Henry's company. They had taken their food and found a quiet place to rest their weary bodies. Henry slid down onto his elbows and plopped his feet out in front of him.

"A shower." The sly smile crept across my face. "A shower, massage, washing machine, and a nice soft bed." I sank further into the ground. "Oh! And room service, delivery, something I don't have to cook."

"I am thinking you prefer your time in the future than here with me."

"Oh, please." A snort escaped. "I prefer the conveniences of my time. I enjoy being with you. When we... if we... get out of here, I'm going to let you ravage me. I'm tired of the constant flow of people around us. We haven't had a proper time alone in forever." I cocked an eye open. His face split from one side to the other in a huge grin. "If you could only see it. Sure, there is crime on every corner. Violence. People shooting school children." An exasperated sigh escaped. "Car accidents. Drunk Driving. The list goes on. It sounds terrible, and it is. But there is air conditioning. Cars to travel from one location to another in a fraction of the time. Airplanes. Easy access to food and clean water. Flushing toilets, showers, and proper oral care. Then there is medicine to help with nearly anything. None of that stupid bleeding that surgeons around here think is going to help."

"Is that all?"

"Well, if you were there with me, it would be perfect. However," I pulled the end of my skirts out from the waistband and flattened the front of it down. "Now I get to stay in clothes that are constantly dirty and wet. I'm going to catch a disease out here." I shifted to my elbows and looked around the camp. Men and women migrated between tents and campfires. Exhausted laughter rolled through the rows. A man's raised voice—frustrated, angry, tired of the travel and mud—argued with another soldier.

"How are the men doing?" I sat up to look at Henry and took another swig of ale. "I don't get to see too much of what's going on in the caboose."

Henry cocked an ear toward the riled voices. "The... what?"

"Hm? Oh, the caboose. In the rear."

"A couple of men had to stop their march. Feet looked like they were about to rot off." Henry scrunched his nose at the memory. "Washington left us for a bit. He said he would try to catch back up with us at Cumberland."

"Is he okay? What's wrong with him?" I wasn't sure if my being here would change history. Washington heard my warning about the trip, but he was coming along as a volunteer, regardless of my opinion. I wondered if he had changed his mind. "Did he say screw it all and head back home? You know we could do that as well."

"No. Nothing like that. At the very least, I do not believe he has turned coat. He confided to me he has dysentery and requires to be treated by his surgeon." Metal clanked as he tossed his plate to the side.

"People die of dysentery. He needs to drink plenty of clean fluids, so he doesn't dehydrate to death. Can you send him a message? The surgeon will not bleed it out of him. He could probably use a dose of antibiotics, but they haven't discovered penicillin yet." I rubbed my forehead. Pain crept behind my left eye. "He isn't supposed to die now."

"For someone that was too exhausted to open her eyes not a moment ago, your worry about Washington has got you worked up. Should I be concerned? You're not looking for a younger man, are you?"

"Ha! You *are* the younger man. I've got six years on you." I shot a glance in his direction. "No. He is supposed to do great things," I said as I laid down on the ground. I didn't care anymore about the dirt. It was unlikely a few more layers of filth would make a tremendous difference. "I'm concerned that I've messed up the timeline somehow."

"You have barely said two words to him since your return. I am certain you have done nothing of the sort."

We cleaned up from our meals. The both of us dragging our feet to our pallets. Each day, the exhaustion piled on to the exhaustion from the previous day. That day was no different.

CHAPTER TWENTY-THREE

*O*ur small tent made for close sleeping conditions for the two of us. It was about seven feet long and about the same for width. With the top supporting pole standing at about six feet tall, Henry had to duck while inside. I still cannot figure out how the rest of the men fit six men into a tent. Head to toe? Nuts to butts? Dogpile? Dependent on the other women's situation, they either slept one woman in the tent with five men and cared for their household needs. Or, if she had children, they would sleep with multiple women and their children piled into one tent. Married to a captain occasionally had its privileges.

When Henry stirred early, he unintentionally nudged me awake. He might have been able to sneak out on any other morning, but the thought of somehow screwing with the timeline kept tossing around my head throughout the night.

"Where are you going?" I pried an eye open and

quickly shut it again. The sun hadn't made its grand appearance for the day, but a soft blue glow radiated through the canvas of the tent, and I had no intentions on beating the sun to morning salutations. "It's too early to get up." I blindly reached out to grab him back to bed.

He placed a kiss on my forehead. "Braddock called for me." And with that, he was gone and left the swish of the canvas flap in his wake. No kiss on the lips. I held up my hand in front of my mouth, blew out, and smelled my breath. I wouldn't kiss my mouth either. A visit to Annette, my dental hygienist, will be on the top of my list if I ever traveled back to my time. I pulled the gray wool blanket over my shoulders and closed my eyes.

I dozed off for what seemed like seconds before Henry came back and gathered the rest of his uniform and bag. "Come on, it's too early. It's not even light out," I said, feeling as though it was a school day and I had stayed up all night reading a book instead of sleeping. The air was cool, and I wanted to snuggle back into our make-shift bed for an hour or two longer.

"I have to leave immediately, but will return." His answer was quick.

"When will that be?" I seethed—ready to bite his head off.

"I will tell you when I return." He snapped in response.

I bolted up to sit and watch him prepare the rest of his small pack. "What if you don't return and then I'm stuck out here in this godforsaken mud pit alone?"

"You are resilient." Henry tossed left over hard biscuit,

salted pork, and cheese into his satchel. "We will catch up with you tomorrow."

Fire shot out of my flared nostrils. "Henry William James Spencer, stop being so damn cryptic and tell me what's going on." My voice was louder than necessary, but so was my temper.

"The walls have ears and there cannot be any word of what is happening." He said in a quiet, low tone, as he stood outside of the tent and looked around. "I cannot tell you who is going with me or what we are doing, but we will talk on my return. Do you trust me?"

"Of course, I trust you with my heart and soul." I placed my hand over my heart and took a deep breath. "What, or rather, who, I don't trust is Braddock. He doesn't listen to anyone but the yahoos over in London. I don't think he has our best interest at heart."

"He is a general and is following orders." He rolled up his blanket and tucked it under his arm.

"Is that what you're doing? Following orders?"

"Please, do not be angered." He crawled back into our little tent and kneeled beside me. His gentle fingers caressed my face. A sweet smile graced his beautiful face. Goosebumps sprung out of every follicle on my body. Even being angry with him for not telling me what was going on couldn't stop my heart from melting into a big, stupid, squishy puddle. His grin told me he knew what he was doing. "I will see you in a day or two." That time, he kissed my stinky morning mouth. If I would have known he was leaving when he went to meet with Braddock, I would have brushed my teeth instead of falling back to sleep and given him a proper sendoff. He left me alone in the tent to face the unknown without him. Eyes closed, knees pulled up to my chest, I sent a request to the universe to keep him safe.

Sleep would never happen for me, so I packed up the tent and prepared a morning meal for Henry's soldiers— well, not the entire company. Most cooked for themselves. Water boiled in my cooking pot for the stick-to-your-bones oatmeal. I debated on the amount to cook. Cooking for two made it easy to add a bit more to the others. Cooking for one, I didn't know how much to make, so I threw in more than I thought I would eat and let it simmer to a thick, sticky paste. Raisins and dried chunks of apricots added sweetness to the concoction. After a couple of minutes to cook in the pot, and the raisins plumped up to a juicy tidbit that bursts between my teeth. Lovett, Johnson, Thomas, and Hector Bennet would wander over, half-dressed for the day, to help us eat whatever I cooked. Except that morning. That morning, none of the usual suspects showed up for breakfast. *Curious.*

I ate my fill and pawned the rest on other hungered soldiers. That was an easy chore, considering that meant that they got a cooked breakfast. I packed up the rest of our camp. Washed up by the stream—this time, I was certain to brush my teeth and joined the other women.

While we walked, I mostly listened to their conversations, injected a comment here and there, absorbed what it was like to be a regular woman, instead of the gentry, during this irregular time. I suppose, to them, it wasn't irregular. Other than being a time traveler, I considered myself a regular woman and, for me, this was irregular. I wanted to know what it was like for them when they were not following their husbands into battle.

Mary-with-the-blue-dress-and-brown-hair—there were so many of them named Mary—was from somewhere around Richmond. She tried to tell me, but her description of the area meant nothing to me. Richmond, Virginia, was a place I had visited in the future, and I had no reference to the Richmond of 1755. I just smiled and nodded as if I understood her. Her husband was a day laborer turned soldier. Apparently, the pay was better, and it guaranteed them a meal. Her permanently red hands showed signs of the chemicals used to wash dishes day-after-day in the kitchens. The couple shared a room with another couple in a boarding house. Without his pay, she couldn't afford to stay at the house, leaving her no choice but to follow her husband to battle.

Mary-Millie's-mom towed behind her a four-year-old daughter, Millie, with flaxen hair and freckles sprinkled across her cheeks and nose—a spitting image of her mom —both wore brown dresses that matched their brown eyes. For the life of me, I couldn't imagine bringing a child along. She said, though it was tough work and keeping up with the caravan was difficult, they knew there would be food in their bellies and some coin at the end of the march. She relied only on her husband and had no other choice but to follow. It was a common theme among the women.

Others added that if something was to happen to their husband, they wanted to be there to take care of him. The way older-Mary-with-the-graying-hair spoke about her husband, I would have thought she wanted to make sure he was dead and received a widow's payment. She was a short, stout woman, with a clay tobacco pipe always between her deep yellow stained teeth that matched the yellow flowers printed on her apron. I ran my tongue over the front of my teeth and wondered what it would take to get more tooth powder.

Brigid, the woman I had met on the first day of our march, joined our little group. Brigid and older-Mary-with-the-graying-hair lifted their pipes to each other as a welcome. The same as a man might tip a hat or raise a glass. I stifled a snort at how appropriate the gesture was. It was kinda cute and fit their no-nonsense personalities.

Older-Mary-with-the-graying-hair pointed her clay pipe at me and said, "You say little, Amelia." I looked over my shoulders and wondered how many other Amelia's there were in our group. Did they have a nickname for me, like I had for them? *Was I Amelia-with-the-mud-up-to her-boobs?* I tried washing my clothes, but the mud stained them, and they never got fully dried before I was out marching in the muck again.

"How can I learn about all of you if I talk too much?" Truth be told, I was afraid to slip my story up. I wondered what they thought or knew of me. No respectable captain's wife would have agreed to being a camp follower. Turns out, I must not be too respectable, because there I was, a captain's wife, boobs deep in mud again. "A wise woman listens before speaking." And a wise woman should have stayed safe at home. I never said I was wise.

"We see you talkin' to that fancy captain," said Brigid. "You his wife?" She flicked her head at me.

"She's not his wife," interrupted the willowy Mary-with-the-blue-dress-and-brown-hair. "A captain's wife would be at their big house takin' care of the children and slaves." A dreamy look came over her face. There is nothing grand about thinking you own people, young Mary-with-the-blue-dress-and-brown-hair.

"Mistress then?" asked Brigid.

I shook my head and smirked at Brigid's question. "I'm not his mistress. If you can believe it, I'm his ridiculous wife, who insisted on tagging along on this ridiculous march." Looking around at my captive audience, who stared back at me like I was ridiculous. "Like many of you, I didn't want to be left behind by my husband." A few of the women nodded.

"You could be sittin' in your fancy house, sippin' your fancy tea, with your fancy servants, and you came out here?" Asked older-Mary-with-the-graying-hair with a snort of disapproval. "You must be soft in the head, or he must be sumpin' in bed."

The woman roared in laughter at the vulgarity, and at the expense of my dignity. The tingle and burn of my face turning twenty shades of lobster red made my eyes water. My mouth moved as it tried to form words. Only a mouse squeak came out. That caused them to laugh louder and me to shrink into myself. I thought older-Mary-with-the-graying-hair might have a heart attack as she choked on the pipe smoke and laughter. It would serve her right for laughing at my expense. Okay. I didn't want her to have a heart attack. I just didn't want to be the butt of her jokes. It was tough being in a strange time, doing something I never thought I would do, and at that moment, I felt alone.

"Ah, we're just having a bit of fun," said Brigid. She walked over to me, grabbed my hand, and patted it. "Just trying to lighten the mood. Take no offense. Why are you walking with us instead of riding in a wagon or on your own horse?"

That was a brilliant question, without a brilliant answer. "If I rode up there with the men, then how would I know what you ladies really thought of me?" I squeezed my eyes tight to fight back the tears. A nod and a squeeze of my hand were all Brigid could get from me. The embarrassment would leave, but the question of 'what the hell was I thinking when I followed Henry off to a battle' would continue to linger. After their light ribbing, the women engaged with me more during our trip. I suppose I had just been jumped into their gang of merry maids. I felt more at home with them than I did sitting in the large house with the Carlyles, but I still wondered what the hell we were doing on that march.

CHAPTER TWENTY-FOUR

*T*wo days after Henry left, he returned with the rest of the missing men. I started a full sprint towards him; he waved me off and hot stepped to Braddock's tent. With my grand gesture of excitement at his return rejected, I walked with my head down and finished setting up our tent. The cooking pot heated, while I wiped off the salt from the slab of salted pork. A little salt was fine for flavor, but it usually ended up being too much, and the meal became overly salted. Adding the hard biscuit helped absorb some of the salt from the broth and thicken up the brothy stew. After the meat received a proper sear, I would add water to the pot and make a stew. I missed having the fresh meat of the occasional deer we hunted while we were based out of Fort Necessity. Heck, even the squirrel was not too bad, nutty and lean. This constant movement prevented us from doing much more than eating hard biskit, a disc of bread, baked until all moisture is removed. It is more like a large, thick cracker.

In order to eat it, we soaked it in broth, wine, or lard. Dried and salt preserved foods, the occasional cheese if we could get our hands on it, and oats rounded out our cuisine. Not my favorite, but better than eating grass and bark.

I jumped at a loud thump of something hitting the ground behind me. I nearly dropped the long fork I used to flip the meat over in the pot. Familiar hands wrapped around my hips and slid across my midriff. Soft lips kissed my neck below my right ear. Sweat poured down my back, tickling its way over my buttocks and down my legs. The heat from the fire and the heat and humidity of the June day in Virginia were unforgiving. But with Henry now back from his secret mission, all was well in my world.

"Mmmm...," I groaned. "Mister Franklin, you must be discreet. My husband will be here soon."

"Could Mister Franklin cause you to make that squeaky little noise when I kiss you here?" Henry moved down my neck, oblivious to any onlookers.

"Perhaps, he could. He is quite handsy with the ladies, and I hear they like it." My eyes closed to take in the bliss. Henry nipped at my shoulder. "More of that, and I may forgive you for leaving me to sleep alone."

"I'll give you more if you have something in the pot for me." He sniffed the air and peered over my shoulder.

I reluctantly pulled away from him and peaked inside. The pork had a nice crust to it and the salt brine kept the inside moist and full of flavor. Rations of potatoes, which I fried alongside the pork, and half-wilted cabbage, thrown in pot in the final few minutes, rounded out the meal. A bit of water and hard biskit and we would have a thick stew.

I grabbed our bowls and piled food in them. Henry stripped down to his breeches and shirt. The temporary camp buzzed with conversation and movement. "So, when do I get to hear about your secret squirrel mission?"

Hector Bennet popped around the corner with Thomas, Johnson, and Lovett not far behind. They had stripped down to their breeches, shirtsleeves, and bare feet. It was too hot and humid for much more. Their noses lead the way over to us. "I suppose you four are hungry." I lifted an eyebrow at the hungry crew. "Grab your bowls and we'll see what I can scrounge up for ya." I looked over to Henry and said, "I expect to hear about the clandestine mission. Don't you dare think your hungry comrades are going to keep you safe from me or my inquiring mind." I shook the fork at him.

Before he could answer, the hungry crew joined us for an evening meal. Some nights they stole away to their own bed rolls or makeshift tents, tonight they plopped down with us. Whatever had occurred over the past couple of days lingered in their minds and kept them together as a gang. I served up what was left in the pot and pulled out some hard biskit I had planned on using in the morning to extend the food in the pot.

"Now that you have food in front of you and have settled in, who will tell me where you ran off to?" I smacked my thighs and looked around at the exhausted faces. A few startled at the smack. They looked back-and-forth to each other in silent communication. "And your answer may not be if you tell me, then you have to kill me. The lot of you will starve if it wasn't for me."

Johnson shifted around. *Ah, I found the weak link.* I mentally rubbed my hands together as if I was a villain hatching my evil plan. A piece of my leftover pork and a reminder of how much I've been in the trenches with them would be all that I need to convince him to spill the beans. Henry looked as though he was about to stop him from telling me, but he knew I would eventually find out. He nodded to Johnson in an approval to start.

Johnson took a bite of the pork I offered, ran his fingers through his dark brown hair, looked over his shoulder, and leaned in towards the center of our little circle. "General had us bury the pay." My eyes shifted to every man sitting around the circle. Each looked around to see if anyone could hear the conversation. That's not suspicious.

With a scrunched face in utter confusion, I asked, "What the actual fffff... why?"

The men looked at Henry for further explanation. "Coin is weighing down wagons, which he wants used for supplies and equipment and not to haul around the money. The men's needs are being met by the commissary and do not need to have pay until after the battle." Again, the men looked over the shoulders for prying ears. Henry continued, "We are losing support from the tribes. He ignores their wisdom."

"Yeah, we saw what happened the last time at Necessity." I shook my head. "Will they ever learn?"

Henry gave me a look as though I should have the

answer to that, being that I was from the future. He might have a point. Being that I am a woman, and I dealt with stubborn men, I knew they would not learn. I need not to be from the future to figure that out.

"He thinks we will lose a lot of men and sees no need to pay them if they die." Henry looked around again and brought his voice to a lower whisper. "We will have to go back and retrieve it after we take New York."

"If we even make it to New York." I blurted out and immediately threw my hand over my mouth.

Henry huffed a laugh. "Now, the good lady understands the situation. That is his point. More coin for the survivors."

"That's a stupid plan." Already annoyed with Braddock's inability to bend to a different fighting strategy, now, he was expecting to profit off the deaths of the soldiers. I couldn't imagine what would come next from him. "When everyone finds out they aren't getting paid, there will be a mutiny."

Henry grabbed my hand. "That is why no one is to discover the plan. They entrusted us to secrecy, and now you are as well."

"Oh, you know I won't say anything to anyone. I can keep a secret." I pulled my hand away from him and looked at the men. With a pointed finger, I began my lecture. "At least one of you better live to tell the tale, or else everyone's pay will be lost to time."

THERE WAS no such thing as being clean—the thick Virginia mud made sure of that—but we tried. We had left the edge along the Potomac River on our way to Fort Cumberland, which I had previously known as Wills Creek before they had built the fort, and crossed into Winchester.

Winchester brought back the memories of not only our previous brief stay when we had left Necessity, but during my time, when I was going to use it as home base to explore the various locations of Washington's battles. It was supposed to be a quick research trip that turned into the biggest research trip of them all. Thrown smack dab in to his first and second battles. The brief stay allowed us to restock supplies and have injured and sick men cared for and sent home if required. Most of them direly needed the pay and stuck out the pain.

Westward travel took us past the location that would eventually find Fort Ashby. No, Fort Ashby meant that one door that I knew was a portal between the two times didn't exist yet. It wasn't like I knew how it all worked, anyway. When I had returned to my own time, I had tried to open the door at the fort. It did me no good. A confused, yet incredibly thoughtful, museum's historic interpreter, Barbra, stared at the crazy woman as she burst through the door in 18th century dress. Disappointed that I was still in the 21st century, I stared at her. It was me. I was the crazy woman. If it hadn't been for Beth and Hector with me, I might have fallen onto the floor in complete defeat.

I looked over towards the vacant field where the fort

would eventually stand. No swirling lights beckoning me to slip through time. Instead of pining for a way home, I continued to follow the group step-after-step towards Cumberland. Remembering the trip when I was taken hostage by Jumonville and his group of men, I knew the walk to Cumberland should only take a couple more days.

"Are you lookin' for sumpin?" asked older-Mary-with-the-graying-hair. She nearly ran me over from my sudden stop in the middle of the trail to look at the empty field where I had woken up confused and at a different time. That was over a year ago, but it felt like yesterday.

I broke out of my trance. "No? Yes? Maybe?"

"Which is it?" We continued with the group.

"Maybe?" I kept in step with her as we crossed through the stream. The cool water rushed over my hot, tired, and dirty feet. I remembered a deeper pool of water not too far from where we crossed. I could have stripped down and washed the filth away. Bathing was a secondary or tertiary concern for us on the road. Walk. Eat. Sleep. Maybe bathe. I came back to our conversation. "They kidnapped me, the French did, last year. It was around here, and it brings up terrible memories."

The other women around us heard our conversation. "Did they ransom you?" asked older-Mary-with-the-graying-hair. Of course, she would be concerned about money. The chance for a widow's pay kept her tagging along with us.

"No." I looked around at my gathering audience. "I escaped."

Brigid piped in. "Did they beat you?"

"Yes. Not too severely, though." I grabbed my ribs when I remembered the few well-placed kicks from Bouchard. "Just enough to hurt me, but I needed to keep up with the group so they couldn't do too much damage to me."

Mary-Millie's-mom seemed to be invested in the conversation and nearly left Millie behind. "How did you escape?" The little blond girl carried a rock she pulled out of the stream. She tugged on her mother's brown skirt to gain her attention to show her mother her new toy.

"One night, I slipped away and ran to the fort under the cover of darkness. We had met up with other French forces and they were to take the fort at the fork in the river. It's now called Fort Duquesne."

"That's where we headed," said Brigid. "I heard the men talk about it."

"She knows that," said Mary-with-the-blue-dress-and-brown-eyes. She adjusted the basket she carried on her back.

Older-Mary-with-the-graying-hair asked, "Is that why you are following your captain? To get back at the French? I would do the same. You're a stronger woman than I am." She popped her pipe into her mouth and took a puff.

"Ha! Not even close." I looked around at the women who had become my friends after the endless days of walking and talking. "You ladies are absolutely remarkably strong women. You came from harder living than I have experienced and are so brave to follow these men into the unknown. I knew what I was getting myself into, so I'm at an advantage. You haven't had to deal with the French and their indigenous allies, but you followed. I could leave knowing I would be fine and taken care of. You don't have that option. No, my dear friends, it is you that are strong. Not I."

We made it to Fort Cumberland and memories of the previous time we were here came flooding back. When we left Fort Necessity after our defeat from the French, we trekked to Cumberland and then on to Winchester. As many times as I had gone through here, it felt familiar. An unwanted familiarity that told me we were closing in on our target.

A few days there to regroup, resupply, eat a decent meal, and get some rest was appreciated. We had finished setting up our tent and unpacked when there was a call for the officers to meet. Their meetings always seemed to last forever and a day. I think Braddock liked to hear himself talk. There was not much for me to do until we could get our food rations. I went looking for the other women so we could head down to the river to find a spot to clean up.

The weather had been dryer over the past few days. It replaced our muddy feet with hot, dust covered feet. A layer of dust an inch thick covered me head-to-toe, and I was ready to wash it off.

We gathered scraps of linens and clothes to change into, if we had any spare pieces. I had an extra shift that I could clean on the occasion. It would be nice to wash the layer of stink off and put on the clean shift. As we trekked down to the river, we heard the bugle sound again. I looked towards the noise—which, at that point, that's all it was... noise—and saw Henry headed my way.

"I'll catch up to you ladies in a minute." I waved them off. My bath would have to wait. Henry approached in a near sprint. I met him halfway. "I was headed to the river to wash up. Is there a problem?"

"Braddock has ordered that the surgeon will inspect all women."

"Why?" I gasped out.

"He wants to make sure they are healthy."

"What exactly does that mean?" I scowled.

"He doesn't want the soldiers to get the pox from the women."

"Syphilis? He is worried that the women are going to give the men syphilis?" I bowed my head and pinched the bridge of my nose. "These women are their wives, mothers, sisters. If the men don't already have it, they will not get it from them."

He grabbed me by the shoulders to force me to look at him. "You don't know if they have it or not."

I stepped back and pulled out of his grasp. "You're right. I don't. But I know I don't have it." My animated arms flailed about. I pointed towards the women. Towards me. Towards Henry. Towards Braddock. I was pointing at everyone. My neck grew hot as my face flushed. "What happens if they have it? It's not like they have penicillin to treat it. All the treatments are going to be painful for nothing. Let's not forget that the doctor is going to be touching one woman's nether regions after another, and not washing his hands in between his violating exam. No. Not going to happen. I refuse."

"This is not a request, Amelia. Braddock could send

them away. He won't have his army killed off by women." I shot him a look. "As the wife of a captain, you have the full right to refuse. Your propriety as a lady will keep you from the exam. The same cannot be said for the other women." Henry reached out to me. The heat of my fury burned into his hand, and he yanked it away from me. I am sure I shot lasers out of my eyes. "They must be examined. There is no choice for them, my love."

"Are the men going to be examined? Or is it just the dirty women?" My nostrils flared as I ground down on my teeth. Henry shook his head. "If the women are to be examined, I will be there with them to make sure they are taken care of properly." I wiped away the tear that escaped and turned my head away to look toward the defenseless women. It burned hot down my cheek. "It's the least I can do for them. I'm heading down to wash up. I'll warn..." deep breath, "inform the women of tomorrow's violation."

"Go gentle on them, if you please." Henry rubbed my shoulder. He thought it would bring comfort. It just irritated me to no end at that point. I didn't want to be comforted. He was supposed to be angry. I wanted to be angry, but that would do no one any good. I would gather my good graces before I made it to the river. That was a miracle all in itself.

*a*pparently, 18th century surgeons—if one could really call them surgeons—don't like to be told to wash their hands between exams. Doctor James Craik threatened me to be kicked out of the exam area more than once. He would not listen to me when I told him if one woman had a venereal disease, then It would get passed on to the next, with the unwashed hands-on exam.

"Please, if you don't wash your hands, could you not touch the women?" I begged the young surgeon, and by young, I meant he was in his mid-twenties. George Washington was a Lieutenant Colonel at twenty-two, and Craik was a seasoned doctor at twenty-five. They made me feel about a hundred-years-old. "All I'm asking is that you consider how the disease spreads from one person to another, and that cleanliness can help eliminate the spread of illnesses."

"Mistress Spencer," Craik said, nearly throwing his equipment to the floor. "You were efficient at tending to soldiers during the battle at Fort Necessity. For that, I am grateful." He sucked in a deep breath. "However, I find it of great concern you insist you know more about the medical treatment for the women."

"Lady Spencer, if it pleases you, Doctor Craik." My jaw ached from my clenched teeth. "Together, we saved lives that tragic day. Thank you for the care you provided to the wounded and dying." I had to massage his ego a bit. It was painful, but a necessary task. "I would like you to consider the possibility that, although I am but a woman, I may have some understanding about the care of women's health. I only ask that we maintain a clean environment for the women. Which, I might add, includes your tools and hands."

"I shall take your advisement into consideration." My gut told me he was just telling me that to appease me. "Will you escort the first woman?"

My shoulders slumped, and I let out an exasperated sigh. It figured. My words fell on deaf ears again.

"And Lady Spencer," Doctor Craik called after me. I looked over my shoulder as I pulled the flap back to the tent entrance. "Would you be so kind as to bring me water and soap?"

My face split with a huge shit-eating grin. It would not be enough to ward off all the infections, but it may help some. "Yes, doctor."

We set up the exam room in the church to keep away from the prying eyes of the soldiers. The church was small, barely large enough to accommodate the garrisoned men and their spouses, if they had any. It was a wooden structure with glass windows, instead of the cheaper stretched animal hide. We moved chairs over to the side and set up a table for women to lie down on for their intrusive exam. How this was authorized was beyond me.

After our tomcat display of hissing, baring teeth, and arching our backs, we got down to work. There was the occasional hiss, perhaps a scratch here-and-there, but we could comprise enough to get through the fifty-or-so women.

The strain of every step ached as I limped back to my tent. I spent the day gathering clean, hot water, being an advocate for the women, and holding a frightened hand when needed. It took its toll on my out-of-shape body. I thought I was prepared with the constant walking, hauling, pushing, cleaning, and cooking over the past month. Nope. My stupid, aging body refused to relent to my pleas of solidarity.

Midday meals had come and gone, and my stomach screamed as loud as my heavy eyelids. Dinner would have to wait, if we were to eat at all. I couldn't lift the heavy logs —that I once called my arms—enough to rub my eyes, let alone stir a pot. Where was the pizza delivery when I needed them? Pizza delivery would have to wait for another 250 years for me. Tonight, I would have to find the mental and physical strength to prepare a meal.

As I walked up to our little encampment, the fragrant scent of meat and smoke wafted through the air. Henry, Johnson, Lovett, Bennet, and Thomas lounged around the fire in breeches and shirts, laughed and took bites of stew. They were off in their own little chatty world, completely ignoring me as I hobbled towards them. My weakened knees couldn't hold me up any longer, and I collapsed on a log that Henry was leaning against, legs outstretched in front of him. He sopped up the last bit of his stew with a chunk of bread, leaned back, and jumped when he noticed a zombie sitting next to him. It was me. I was the zombie. Dead woman walking.

With my chin in my hands, elbows on my knees, and eyelids that hung heavy, I didn't have the energy to fuss about dinner. Or realize that they somehow made an entire meal without my help. My entire body and soul ached for a hot bath, room service, and a comfy bed. I was too tired to argue about prepping food.

A nudge on my leg, pulled me out of my catnap. With all the energy I could muster, which was not much, my eyes crept open with irritated slowness. What did they want? Couldn't they see I was exhausted and didn't want to do anything but sleep? Lovett held out a bowl of stew and a chunk of bread—that made me less irritated. My stomach grumbled loudly at my slow response to not shoveling the food down my throat as quick as possible. My body dared me to move faster. Henry raised a mug of what appeared to be ale and sat it next to me—crankiness dissipated. I mumbled something that I intended to sound like a thank you, but it came out more like a nasal grunt.

The spoon held heavy in my hand. I slowly chewed a chunk of the ham with my eyes closed. "Mistress Hockneck and a few of the other women wanted to show their gratitude." Henry placed a square of linen on my lap, so I could wipe the stew that dribbled down my chin.

Not sure if it was my brain exhausted from the day, but I had no clue who was Mistress Hockneck. "Who?" *Maybe she was one of the Marys?*

The quiet Hector Bennet spoke up. "Why would we know anything other than what the woman had told us? You are a woman. Would you not know their names?"

Hector's voice went through me like a lightning bolt. That insolent young pup. Had he not experienced the wrath of Lady Amelia Louise Lindsay Spencer to know not to talk down to me?

"How nice of you to notice that I'm a woman." I sneered. "And besides, you're lucky I know who you are. You hardly say but two words to me, and you sure are quick with your bowl to eat the food I cook." My level of patience with his misogynist attitude hit rock bottom. "I might know her by her appearance and her given name. However, contrary to your belief, women do not stand around gossiping about who is married to who. There is more to us than our husbands and what we can do for you men." Henry sat quietly. I didn't need him to defend me from the twenty-year-old Bennet. "When it comes time for you to find a wife, make sure she is your partner. Someone that has more to converse about other than you." I pointed my spoon at him as though I would dig his heart out with it. "Because if her only topic of conversation is Hector Bennet, the conversation will be utterly boring." I downed my ale in three gulps. I tried to make it more dramatic with one gulp, but I almost choked on it. Turning to Henry, "I'm done with him. You can school the young pup on how to pull his head out of his ass."

I turned and stumbled to my tent to peel off the day. As I laid down, stewing over what young Hector had said, I suddenly remembered that I couldn't figure out a way to send a message to anyone in my time. They would be worried after the past few months. I was safe for now, but I headed to a battle, and they may never know what happened to me.

The mannerisms of the young Hector Bennet pulled me back to my time with my friends, sitting around Hector and Beth's kitchen table in Williamsburg. For some odd reason, the 18th century Hector hardly ever spoke in my presence. I wasn't sure if it was because I was old enough to be this version's mother, or if I intimidated him. If he thought I was intimidating, just wait until Elizabeth Woods got hold of him. She had a way about her that makes it difficult to tell her no.

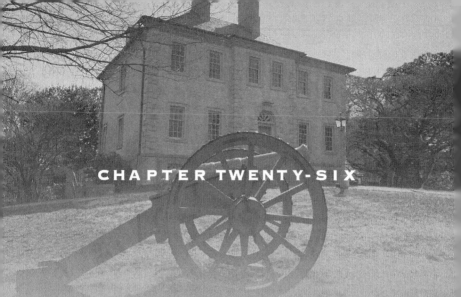

CHAPTER TWENTY-SIX

"*O*h, so you are Mistress Hockneck," I said to Mary-with-the-blue-dress. "Thank you for the food last night."

"Ye dinna look like ye could walk back to yer tent. We knew ye wasna gonna fetch a meal for those men." She dunked the shirt she was scrubbing back in the river. "Least we could do for ye."

"I wish I could have done more for you." I took a deep breath. Cold water swirled the suds around my hands. My eyes followed a few bubbles as they dissipated into the current. I twisted the shirt and watched the water pour back into the river. "You know, with the surgeon." It vexed me to make eye contact with the women, knowing I didn't have to go through the same indignities at the hands of Doctor Craik.

Even knowing her last name, I couldn't think of her as anyone other than Mary-with-the-blue-dress. I tried to use her given name, but it was easier to think of her as what she wore. Good thing there was not much of a chance for her to change her clothing. She threw a pair of stockings over the edge of her basket. "Ye did what ye could."

A roar of cheers poured over the embankment from the camp. Mary-with-the-blue-dress Hockneck and I stared at each other, gathered up the clothes, and threw them in the baskets we used to haul everything around. The wet and damp clothes weighed heavily on our backs. We worked our way up the embankment as quick as our legs would carry us. Curiosity of the celebration moved us forward. As we approached, the deafening cheers swept us up into the excitement. Neither one of us was tall enough to see what was happening, so we pushed our way to the front of the crowd of men. Four wagons piled with supplies, led by teams of horses, clanked and clomped their way into camp. Benjamin Franklin came through for our mission. Well, at least four of the one hundred fifty wagons we expected arrived. Over the next month, we would receive the promised wagons, additional horses, and extra supplies for the officers. I dreaded the day we would move on towards Fort Duquesne.

Another day of commotion helped break up the monotony of camp life. Usually, it was another wagon arriving with supplies. Really, there was not much for us women to do but worry about food and laundry most of the day. Oh, and sewing and cleaning and—at least in my case—trying to not think about air conditioning, showers, and flushing toilets.

Our allies, a group of the Haudenosaunee, arrived one day as I mended the bottom of my shift. It caught on a bramble while foraging in the nearby woods, tearing a hole in it. I had a spare shift, one of the few items of clothing I could bring with me, but needed to ensure I had one to change into so I would not wander around the camp naked. That would have certainly caused a stir among the men. When I had suggested to Henry that I wanted to bring my entire wardrobe, he scoffed and suggested we send the rest to his house in Williamsburg. Since I had to carry my necessities and other supplies, I would not admit it to him, but am glad I took his suggestion.

As the Haudenosaunee made their way towards Braddock's tent, I looked for my friend, Tanaghrisson. He was not with the group of men and women. I had hoped history had recorded it wrong, but it was true. He died a few months after saving me, my secret, and ultimately Washington, by killing Ensign Jumonville at the glen during our early morning attack on the thirty-four French soldiers near Fort Necessity. I scanned the crowd, looking for another familiar face. One woman I had met the previous year stood out from the crowd and talked with a young man while they walked towards the tent. She had spoken to me when I visited their village with Henry. She helped me find the woman that nursed Tamhas, the infant I had found in the woods near the cabin where the young couple was murdered, when all I could offer him was a cloth soaked in goat's milk. Her English was limited and broken, but I hoped she would speak with me. The opportunity to approach her would not come, as the women and the young men left. Followed by the rest of the warriors. Where were they going? We couldn't defeat the French if they left. I ran after them. Perhaps they were going to gather more warriors to join our cause. They continued to leave as they ignored more pleas for them to stay.

Henry stood with a group of officers outside of Braddock's tent. I was winded by the time I made my way across the encampment. The air was heavy with humidity, heat, and the disappointment that oozed from the men. "Where are they going?" I stopped a few feet away from the group. My hands rested on my knees as I bent over to catch my breath.

"Not now, Amelia," Henry said as he waved me off.

My jaw dropped, and my eyes narrowed from the sun and my anger. I was not sure which one burned hotter. That is not true. I knew my anger burned hotter than the sun. *Deep breath, Amelia.* I stormed off to catch up with the group of Haudenosaunee. This couldn't be it. Why would they abandon us? Didn't they know we needed them? I was too slow to find out.

We needed them. But the Haudenosaunee didn't need us. Nor did they deserve the disrespect they received from Braddock. He dismissed them as unneeded—especially the women. I knew there was a lack of respect for me and the women that trailed behind our soldiers. Braddock saw us as a nuisance, discounted as the weaker sex, an inferior species that was there to distract the men. What he failed to realize was the camp would not run smooth without us. We cleaned, cooked, mended, and nursed the soldiers, allowing them to focus on their mission. If needed, we would pick up a sword, pistol, or musket to fight to the death.

Their people respected the Haudenosaunee women as equals. They were warriors. When the women were dismissed by the idiot Braddock, the rest followed. I couldn't blame them for leaving us behind. How did this guy ever get a road named after him?

I would like to say I would have done the same if given the chance. However, I couldn't have left the camp with the knowledge of Henry staying behind. I was dedicated to him. His protector. I convinced myself that he was the reason the god of time sent me back in time, and I would not let my mission be a failure. Besides all that, I loved him, and I knew he loved me. Even if neither one of us said it to the other. All the love in the world and throughout history would not do either of us any good if we didn't get out of this alive.

We would have to fight without our allies. We were in this alone.

A heavy cloud of despair hung over my head; it seeped deep into my bones. As we headed to battle, and the women just took care of their daily business. No one mentioned to me any concern they had about what would happen to them if, or when, we encountered the French, but I felt it necessary to give instruction to the women. "Remember, ladies, stay near the back of the convoy." I looked around at the women and children that continued to gather around me. "Let the soldiers do the fighting."

"The French will not shoot us. We are women." A young woman's voice sounded from the back.

Standing on my toes, I looked for the source of the statement. "Ha! Don't rely on that theory."

"The godless savages will. They are taking our land and killing our families." Brave statements flew from the rear of the group.

"You are invaders to their land. The French and their indigenous allies—they are not savages—will see you as a threat." My nostrils flared and voice went up an octave. "And if they do not kill you, they will take you as slaves. If you are lucky, they will sell you back to the English." A faint reminder of a story history book lingered in the deep recesses of my brain. I knew what would happen. They would take women and children as slaves. Some sold to other tribes. They would keep others with their captor. And a few others would be ransomed. Who knew what would become of the women? Myself included. They could be set free or integrated into their society. If they tried to escape, it meant beatings, if not death. My shoulders sank. There was no suitable answer other than, "Don't get caught."

Militia from North Carolina joined our group. I pressed Henry about the group, not wanting to have any part of McKay's group woven in with the men. A group of his men tried to assault me on the night of our loss of the fort. Henry reminded me that Captain McKay was from South Carolina, and these men were from North Carolina. As we walked past a group of wagons, one man shouted to another, "Daniel Boone, it is about time you arrived."

I shot a quick look at Henry as we continued to walk past the group of five wagons, and in a low whisper, "He is a famous pioneer." I glanced at the young, twenty-year-old. "Well, he will be one day." As luck would have it, the handle on my pot needed a repair, and Boone made quick work of the repair with his blacksmith tools.

They split us up into two groups. Five hundred soldiers started their march a day before the additional thousand that included us women and other camp followers. They included general Braddock and Colonel Washington with the first wave of soldiers to leave Fort Cumberland. Every movement Washington made came with a wince. He piled pillows atop of his saddle to help pad his ride. I suggested to Henry a wagon would be more comfortable for him, but he quickly shut me down. Washington required to appear as a powerful leader from the seat of a horse, not the seat of a wagon. He needed to be on a horse. I thought he looked miserable and would fall off the horse and would look like an idiot sprawled out on the ground, writhing in pain.

Prior to our departure, wagoners mended wheels. Bakers baked biscuits. Cannoneers cleaned cannons. Riflemen reamed rifles. And women, well, we womened— basically; we did everything else the men couldn't or wouldn't do.

We readied our provisions to set out early in the morning. I put my spare shift in the basket, along with our kitchenware. Could I call my pot, ladle, bowls, and cups, kitchenware? I didn't have a kitchen, but an open fire. Eh, kitchenware sounded good enough. It was the simple things to focus on that kept my mind off our departure for Fort Duquesne in the morning.

The tent was too hot. Then it was too cold. Again, too hot. A rock jammed into my back—it hid from me. My mat was lumpy. I straightened it out—it lumped up again. My shift twisted around me. How could I expect to sleep if I my clothes twisted around me as though I were a mummy?

Henry snored.

CHAPTER TWENTY-SEVEN

July 9, 1755

My eyes squinted from the blazing sun. My well-worn hat provided little protection. Not a cloud in the sky lingered to save me from the heat. The pack on my back hung heavy with the replenished supplies. We slogged along in another day's march, knowing we would soon encamp prior to an actual battle. We crossed over the Monongahela and continued towards Fort Duquesne. I was prepared, or so I thought, to support Henry and his men on the field. I imagined it would be much like the movies where they line up and take turns killing each other until someone gives up. Out of nowhere, there were several volleys of fire at our front. I later learned that the advance guard lead by Colonel Gage had met a defensive line of French regulars. During Gage's rapid withdrawal to report his engagement, he met with Braddock, and his column rushed into combat.

"Why, after near three weeks of pushing and pulling

the big cannons, did that general leave them behind?" Brigid asked. She bit down on her pipe and fiddled with one of her faded blond braids that threatened to come undone.

I had asked Henry the same question at one of our daily stops. If luck was on our side, our sections would catch up to the other, we would camp together. Other nights, I squeezed in with older-Mary-with-the-graying-hair and Brigid. "Too heavy and wide to get through the steep and narrow pass. You saw the difficulty they had with the wagons." General Braddock abandoned the cannons somewhere near Fort Necessity in the Allegheny Mountains.

"Hmph," interjected older-Mary-with-the-graying-hair. "Seems odd to go to war without your cannons."

"We are not at war." I didn't add the 'yet' to that statement. "The general didn't want to waste our precious time with the cannons. Easy in, easy out. Or so he believes."

"Men." Snorted out older-Mary-with-the-graying-hair. "They take the easy way. 'Tis why I followed my husband. He either dies or he goes home. He will not be running away from me and leaving me poor." She chomped down on her clay pipe with determination.

With the sound of the not-too-distant flintlocks and muskets, all I could think of was where was Henry. How do I get to him? How can I protect him? Who did I think I was? Wonder Woman?

General Braddock raced up on his horse from the rear. He would lead his men into battle. Smoke from the gunfire filled the air. Lines of men fell as blood poured out of chests, wounded and dead. The Indians moved through the trees with skill and used the coverage to their advantage. We saw this happen at Fort Necessity. We knew this would happen again. Braddock focused on fighting like he would in Europe, "like gentlemen." These were different opponents, and he used the same strategy. My gut was heavy with disappointment and fear.

The English soldiers filed in their formal lines with the guns pointed into the heavy woods. They would be no match for the experience and fierce tactics of the Indians and the French. Shots rang out from behind trees. Soldiers dropped. Officers seemed to be the primary targets. Remove the head of the dragon, the rest will tumble with it. Confusion and terror filled the air and seeped into my thoughts. The women and I were behind the chaos, with the baggage wagons under Colonel Dunbar's command. Musket blasts and yells ensued nearly a mile in front of us, but wouldn't stay there for long. The whoops, yells, and battle cries pierced through the air and landed straight in my gut, like the bullets that flew past my head. Perhaps not all the bullets flew past my head, but you couldn't convince me otherwise. I hollered at them to run, but so many thought there was something they could do to help the men.

With the help of Brigid, the Marys, and a few others, we started tossing supplies off the wagons. We might get women and children away from the battle on the wagons faster than they could run. That was my hope, at least. "Stop," I shouted to the wagoners brought in from

Pennsylvania. They continued to remove the horses from the wagon shafts. "Stop," I called out again. "We need to get the women and children to safety. Please," I pleaded. As I ran up to another group of wagons, I recognized Daniel Boone. I called out to him by name. "Daniel, please help"

I turned and received an abrupt push of another man's forearm across my chest that knocked the air out of me and sent me lurching backwards as I gasped for air. I struggled to gain my footing as my arms flailed, looking for anything to grab hold. The ground came quick and hard, knocking any remaining air in my lungs out of me. Wagons, loaded with supplies, stood still in front of me. The horses threw up dust as the men rode them away from the battlefield.

The indigenous people that fought with French continued to move with precision through the trees. Few French soldiers following behind. They would soon work their way to where the women were still trying to figure out how they were going to escape.

Shots continued to ring out. If I looked hard enough —and I did—with Henry close to the melee, I searched for him. Along with my search for Henry, I could see Braddock in the distance. He went down with his horse. I was too far back in the line to see what happened. Next thing I knew, he was back up on a different horse, barking orders to the troops. Again, it happened. I'm not sure how many more times it happened before I didn't see him again. I was more concerned about getting the women to safety and keeping myself alive.

A wagoner waved his hand towards a group of women and they piled into the back of the wagon. They pushed, shoved, and piled in on top of one another. The two horses struggled with each step. Their legs lifted, necks strained out in front, and snorted in labored disapproval. A crack of the whip snapped through the air. I pushed behind the wagon. If we could get it going, I was sure it would fly away and take them to safety. It would not budge. Another crack in the air. No movement. They weighed the wagon down with no hope of escape. Sounds of musket fire edged closer to our location. The two men jumped out of the wagon and removed the tether from the horses. Surely, they would not leave these women stranded. I stood with my mouth wide open as they rode away. The sounds of screams and gunfire drowned out the sound of the hooves pounding the ground. Hot tears streamed down my face.

"Boone!" Where was Boone? Surely, he wouldn't have left us like the rest of the wagoners. He would become famous as a frontiersman. He wants to be a hero. Where was our glorious hero when we needed him?

Running away with the rest of the men. Some hero he turned out to be. "Boone, you coward," I called out to somewhere in the dust cloud of men on horses as they raced away from the fight. A musket round pierced through a wagon, sending a shard of wood flying past my face.

I grabbed the hand of a woman, and she yanked her hand back. Another hand gripped tight to the side of the wagon. My palms, slick with sweat, pulled her out of the wagon. A child behind her cried out for her mother. I waved my hand to coax her near the edge. She bent down, and I grabbed her under her shoulders. The young chestnut headed girl, only four years old, cried and fought against my pull as she tried to get back in the wagon. Blood poured from a woman in the wagon. She reached towards the child, her head lolled, and her face paled. "You need to run. Now," I yelled as I handed the child to another woman as she climbed out of the wagon. The woman grabbed the young girl by the hand and ran towards Fort Cumberland. It would be a long run if they could make it back safely.

CHAPTER TWENTY-EIGHT

R un!

CHAPTER TWENTY-NINE

*L*ike the damned fool that I am, instead of running away from the fight with the other women, I was on a mission. "Go!" I shouted at the women and children to run to safety, and I ran towards the gunfire.

A shot cracked into the wagon, splintered the wood. Shards cut through the air. Another shot rang out. I ducked and covered my face. More shards. Ear-piercing screams filled the air. Another crack of gunfire. Children cried. More shards. "Stop shooting at me!" Another shot. More splintered wood soared like high velocity confetti. I reached for my left biceps. It felt on fire. Blood covered my hand.

With a grunt and a scream, I peeled the basket straps off my shoulders. Pain surged in my left arm as the strap snagged on the gouge through my biceps. My knees hit the ground as my fist clinched, trying to squeeze away the pain. On all fours, I panted and groaned as I stood up. The blood was fresh and hot as it seeped down my sleeve. The sound of blood pounding through my ears left me deaf. Muffled sounds of gunshots and yelling seemed distant, even though I was in the middle of the chaos. There were bodies lying everywhere. Some men still fought, but many were dead or teetering on the thin line of life and death. Mary-Millie's-mom laid dead, half hanging out of an abandoned wagon. This was not the battle that I signed up for.

Indigenous warriors moved through the chaos, pillaging supplies and scalping the dead and some of the living. For the life of me, I do not know why none of them noticed me. I was terrified. Why had I chosen to stay? Henry. "Henry! Where are you?" I shouted myself hoarse.

Oh, please let him be alive. If something horrible happened... Blood soaked down Henry's chest and arm. My hands ran over his blood-soddened coat, looking for the source. I edged his coat off his arm, careful to not yank it and minimize the movement. A hole in his shirt showed me they had shot him below his right clavicle. I didn't want to say it was lucky they shot him there, as it would have been best if they didn't shoot him at all. I wanted to tell him at least it was not near his heart. No foamy blood, which meant it hadn't punctured his lung.

Henry was shot, and I didn't know what to do. I checked his back. There was no blood, no hole. It didn't go through. He had a bullet somewhere in him, possibly causing internal damage. He winced when I pulled his shirt away from his chest.

"I'm going to have to dig it out." I gulped down the

tears. There was no time to cry. I needed to stay strong for him. "Sterilize it. Dig out any material that went in with it."

"You are injured, Amelia," Henry wheezed out as he looked towards my arm. Blood soaked my left sleeve. My arm burned, but I didn't have time to worry about myself. A bullet or a shard of wood from flying chunks of wagon had skimmed past my arm and left a superficial injury. I would live. Henry might not.

"I'm fine. It's only a scratch." Blood continued to seep out of my arm with every movement. I took the small camp knife I kept in my pocket and cut a piece from the bottom of my shift, held one end between my teeth and wrapped the other end around my arm a few times. I attempted to knot it using my hand and teeth. A makeshift pressure dressing would get me through until I could dress it properly.

"Do you have any of the brandy left?" He choked out a laugh. "I do not believe I could do this sober."

"Hell, I'm not sure I can do this sober." I stroked back a lock of hair out of his face. "I'm really worried about internal bleeding and damage. And then there is infection to cause worry. We cannot stay here."

"Find the bullet and sew it up." Henry was losing a lot of blood. If I didn't do something soon, he would bleed to death before he could die of sepsis. "We must save my men."

"You cannot save yourself right now, let alone your men," I said. "I've got to stop this bleeding and get you on a wagon." If I could find a wagon with horses.

Henry tossed his head back. He tried to hide the pain, but it was no use.

"Looks like Louis is going to have to get us out of here." I looked around to search for someone to help me take him away from there. Men had taken the horses off the wagons to ride away. Louis was all I found to take Henry to safety. "I need to stop the bleeding right now, so you don't bleed to death. We can worry about mending you when we are safe."

I pulled another strip from the bottom of my shift. Round and round my shift, I continued to tear the fabric. The piece looked as though I could get it around Henry two or three times. My shift was going to end up as a mini dress by the time I was done. It certainly was not clean, but it would at least stop the bleeding. "This will hurt... I'm so sorry, my love."

I held a piece of wadded up fabric over the wound and applied pressure. Then I wrapped the cloth around Henry's shoulder and chest and tied a knot over the wad of fabric. Louis was eager to get us out of there. He stomped his hoof in agitation, as if to tell me to hurry. Gun fire continued in the distance. Shouts and screams echoed around us. Bullets no longer whirled at us, but we were far from safe.

I stood up and looked down at Henry as he sat propped up against the tree. "I can help, but I can't pick you up." My fists dug into my hips as I tried to assess the moving of Henry. "Do you have enough energy to walk?"

"My legs work fine," Henry said as he wiggled his feet back and forth. "Mayhap, you could help me stand?"

Crouching down on his left side, I said, "Wrap your left arm over my shoulders. Use me as a brace. We'll stand up together. One, two, and three." I grunted and strained to stand with him. I immediately regretted not doing more squats when I worked out. If we lived through this, I would attempt to get in better shape. I couldn't continue fighting in a war at my age if I didn't make a change to my workout routine. A small laugh escaped me as I thought about my concern to get in better shape in order to fight in a war. "Sorry, not laughing at you. Just thinking about how stupid this all is."

We hurried over to where Louis stood in anxious anticipation. "Just so you know, I have no clue how I'm going to get you on Louis," I said to Henry as we approached his agitated horse.

"I cannot use my arm to pull up."

"Cheese and rice. Let me think." Sizing up Henry and Louis, I had to come up with a plan. "Okay, I think I got it. In order to minimize you trying to pull yourself up, you will need to use my leg as a step stool, and I can help push you up."

As we stood looking at the stirrup, I bent my leg to make a step. "Grab the saddle with your left hand and use my leg."

"That will not work. You are overthinking it." He looked up at the saddle. "I can get up well enough without using my right arm, but stay sharp to give a push."

He clumsily got into the saddle, yelling out in pain as he pulled himself up. A riderless horse ran out of the wood line. I thought it would continue to run, but it stopped near us.

"Lady luck is on our side." I whooped. Although skittish, the horse allowed me to approach it. I led it next to Louis and handed the reins to Henry. This must have been a horse Benjamin Franklin sent from Pennsylvania for the officers. I hiked up my petticoat, grabbed hold of the saddle, and stretched my leg up to get my foot in the stirrup. My arm screamed in pain as the binding dug into it. My wound refused to allow me to use my strength to pull myself into the saddle. It looked as though my luck was about to run out. I was too short to get my foot up and in too much pain to climb. Tears pricked at my eyes. My nose stung. I wanted to collapse on the ground and cry. "We don't have time for this. You've got to get out of here. They'll take me hostage before they'll kill me. Just go"

"I'm not leaving without you."

"I'll figure out how to get on this damn horse and I'll catch up."

"Didn't you tell me the time lord sent you here to protect me?"

"That was probably bullshit, and you know it." I continued to size up the horse. "And I think I called it the god of time. He or she isn't *Doctor Who*."

"No, your insistence on staying here while I leave is bullshit. I can try to pull you up here with me."

"Louis has been through too much. He cannot carry the both of us." I took the reins from Henry and walked toward Wills Creek. "I'll walk and find something to stand up on." Shouting was getting louder as the French and their indigenous allies were getting closer to us. They would not stop until we were all dead. In the distance, I could see a wagon with men in the back and others on horseback headed towards Fort Cumberland. In the distance, a man appeared to look like George Washington, but I couldn't be certain from this distance. I wondered if General Braddock was among the men in the back of the wagon. "We cannot stay here."

Not too far down the rugged path, I found a tree on its side from when men had cut the trail. I used it as a step stool and climbed onto my horse. "We need to make some distance," Henry winced out as he pulled the reins and gave Louis a nudge with his heel.

Women and men alike sprawled on the ground. Lifeless. Bloody scalps exposed. Souvenirs. We found supplies thrown from wagons and rifled through strewn about the ground. There were more women missing than laid upon the ground. No one was moving or crying out. We didn't stop. In the distance, I saw women and children corralled and imprisoned by the tribesmen. Flaxen-haired Millie was among the group; her hair stained with her mother's blood. I had to believe she would be safe and cared for by the women. I kicked my horse to push it harder.

We rode as hard as we could and stopped for the night, in hopes safety and luck stayed on our side. A nearby creek allowed for me to clean up some of the blood and for us to drink water. The horses drank their fill and ate grass, while Henry and I ate what little piece of dried meat and a chunk of stale bread we pulled out of the saddlebags. It wasn't much, but it would give us a little sustenance. "Are you not going to the creek and just pull out a fish?" Henry tried to joke. His voice was flat. I knew he was in pain with every wince and grunt he made in response to the slightest movement and breath. He would not let me look at his wound. He was afraid it would bleed, and we would have nothing else to wrap it up. I shot him a look, letting him know I knew it was worse than he was letting on. I gathered wood, lit a fire with a piece of flint Henry had in his saddlebag.

"Ha! That was pure luck." When Henry and I first traveled together, early one morning, I had gone to a nearby creek to clean up. There were at least twenty fish in the section swimming around and coming up for the bugs that skimmed across the surface. The spot was thick with fish, fighting for their meals. I rested my hand in the middle of the battle. They scattered away from me. Cold water swirled around my arm as I left it in there, waiting for the time to strike. The fish came back, looking for their meal. One brushed up against my arm. I wanted to pull my arm and scream, but prolonging our meager rations was a priority. The fish came back, thick and oblivious to my arm. My fingers dangled in the stream, like fat worms waiting to be devoured. Curiosity led to my finger in a fish's mouth. I hooked my finger into the side of its mouth and with the other hand, I grabbed around its slippery scaled body. Triumphantly, I headed back to where we had camped. Henry thought I had run away, back to the French and Ensign Jumonville and Bouchard, who I had recently escaped from. Henry was livid and pointed a gun at me. Thankfully, he didn't shoot. I didn't have that type of fishing luck on our escape from the battlefield. We were stuck with whatever we could scrounge from my pockets and the saddlebags. We would leave early in the morning and continue to Wills Creek. If we pushed hard, my guess was we could arrive late the following day. Henry informed me that was an unlikely timeline. The bacteria lurking in Henry's wound would cause deadly damage, and travel would become more treacherous.

We slept close to each other, using the fire and body heat to keep us warm. I tore more from my shift to make another wrap for my arm and Henry's chest and washed it in the creek. I wanted to clean our wounds and bandages and would have to do it in stages. Clean the new bandages. Dry them next to the fire. Remove dirty bandages. Clean wounds. Put on clean bandages. Clean dirty bandages. Dry them next to the fire and have them ready to switch out tomorrow.

I peeled away the bandage from my arm. The blood made it stick like glue. In return, it burned in protest. The cool stream of water helped calm the fire. I wrapped up my arm and got ready to tackle my husband. "You have got to let me clean this."

Henry sucked in air through his teeth as I removed the pressure bandage from the wound. The bleeding had slowed until I had awoken the wicked beast and the blood oozed out of the wound again. I wiped the blood as best I could. It was a losing battle. A wad of clean cloth, a wraparound to apply pressure, and I hoped it would be enough to get him through the night.

We arrived at Fort Necessity, or what was left of it, the next night. A few soldiers had met us there on the way to Fort Cumberland. What they lacked in provisions, they made up for with the sense of comfort that we were not alone. "Colonel Washington and General Braddock are where?"

"They are not but a mile or two away, Mistress Spencer. General Braddock was shot. Might not make it."

CHAPTER THIRTY

*B*raddock was going to die. As much as I wanted to blame the French or their allies, it was his own fault. The same reason Washington lost Necessity, thinking that they could only fight using the English methods. This was not England. The indigenous didn't fight by English gentlemen's rules. The dismissive attitude that Braddock showed to our allies left a foul taste in my mouth. I could only hope that they would not base their entire attitude of the colonists over the behavior of Braddock. If we had to fight the French with no allies, we would surely lose. I was not to blame for this misstep, like Washington had tried to blame me for the death of Jumonville or the surrender conditions at Necessity. That blame would lie on Braddock's dying shoulders.

Amidst the chaos of the ambush, they had shot Braddock. I was angry with Braddock. There were so many lives lost that day, but Braddock's arrogance, or lack of flexibility for the changes in warfare, was the cause. I told him they would not meet our troops on even ground on the battlefield. The terrain and the fighting style of the French allies differed from what he had experienced. His arrogance and unwillingness to listen to those that he considered beneath him—such as me and the Haudenosaunee—would lead not only to his death, but possibly Henry's. I was livid.

Henry laid on a makeshift bed, his eyes closed. I watched his breathing—shallow and labored. He was in a great deal of pain. I touched his forehead; no fever... yet. He required real medical care. More medical care than my Girl Guide's first aid. "They shot Braddock," I said as I handed a mug of water to Henry. He tried to sit up, but fell back down in his struggle. I knelt beside him, placed my right arm around him as he attempted to sit up again.

"How bad is it?" He coughed as he sipped the water.

I took the mug in my hand and sat it to the side. "He's probably going to die. He is a couple of miles down the path from here." I pointed toward where Washington, Braddock, and Orme had stopped. "Do you think I should see if I can help?"

"Can you?"

"Probably not. Maybe I just want to make sure the bastard dies. He caused this slaughter and I'm so angry I just want to scream and cry and... I don't know." My shoulders sunk. "Whatever I do, it won't bring back Johnson, or McDaniel, or Lovett's arm."

"No, no, it will not. I am... was," he choked on his words. "I was their commanding officer. 'Twas I that lead them into battle. They were my responsibility."

My heart ached for him. He was following orders. Even though we knew they would use terrible tactics to secure trading, we had to take the forks of the Ohio–Fort Duquesne. Well, that wouldn't happen now. Our forces were decimated, and the battered men limped home. "Well, if you live through this, you can apologize to those who survived. And help make recompense to the widows. Mistress Lovett will deal with the one-armed Mister Lovett. She will keep him from sulking. Until then, we must get you patched up."

"We can leave for Fort Cumberland in the morn. Mayhap, we can find a surgeon." He winced as she shifted positions.

"I hope so..." I didn't trust 18th century surgeons. They sterilized nothing. People died more from infection than from their injuries. I would tackle digging the bullet and any cloth and debris out of Henry's chest before it caused more damage or infection. Our dirty clothes and traveling situation didn't help the prevention of the cultivation of bacteria. My arm still ached and oozed blood if I moved it too much. I would mend myself, somehow. "Fort Cumberland in the morning. I'll let Washington deal with Braddock on his own." Braddock was not my priority.

The night was restless. Nightmares of the events of the last few days startled me awake as soon as I fell asleep. Coupled with the memories of our last night at Fort Necessity when a group of men had attempted to assault me, sleep was out of reach. When I closed my eyes, I could see the look on Jumonville's face as he held out my notebook and Tanaghrisson's ax gave a crushing blow through Jumonville's skull. No. Jumonville had to die with the secrets he held, and I needed my notebook. I couldn't tell anyone of my time traveling secret, other than Henry. Tanaghrisson believed he knew the truth or some version of it from a dream. He felt a need to protect me, and he also despised Ensign Jumonville for his own reasons.

The evening of our defeat, as negotiations occurred, a group of men from another unit attacked me. Henry, Sergeant Lovett, Private MacDonald, and a few others came to my rescue. I never learned the identity of my attackers, but they assured me I would never encounter them again. Not wanting to cause more problems, I didn't ask questions, but somewhere deep down, I wanted to know who to hate instead of just faceless attackers. I wanted... no, needed... the closure that they did not afford me. It caused me to look at the soldiers with a cautious eye, never knowing if they were one of the men.

Laying on the ground, staring up at the dark sky, I tossed and turned. Memories and nightmares of the past and our recent battle flooded my every thought. My attempts to get comfortable would be met with a pull on my arm, which caused the wound to reopen and bleed. If Henry tried to move, I jumped up to help. I was cold, bloodied, in pain, exhausted, and wanted to go home. I finally fell asleep from pure exhaustion, with tears rolling down my cheeks. Really, I was homesick for the safety and comfort of the 21st century.

It was a Monday morning when we rode upon

Washington as he directed a group of men to dig a hole in the middle of the road. Braddock had succumbed to his injuries the night before, and it was not worth the effort to bring him back to Fort Cumberland. They buried him smack-dab in the middle of the road, in the middle of the Allegheny Mountains near Fort Necessity. I took a mental note that if I were to make it back to my time, that I would come visit his grave, if I could find it. They would leave no markers to indicate, "On this spot, General Braddock died." Men fled the battlefield trampling over his grave, without realizing their commander laid to rest under their feet. I was still angered with him and thought he deserved what he got, but I am not entirely heartless. A man died. This was not my doing, and an "I-told-you-so', wouldn't bring him back. We paid our respects, but I insisted we continue to Fort Cumberland to get Henry's medical attention. Washington could figure the rest of the burial without us. We paid our quick respects and continued down the road.

"We could have helped."

"Who could have?" I scoffed. "You can barely sit in the saddle, let alone help bury the man." I shook my head. "No. You paid your respects, and that was more than you should have done. If you survive this, you can do more later. For now, we need to pick up the pace. That bit has delayed our arrival."

If pushed hard, we may have been able to make the fifty-mile ride in one day, but neither one of us could handle the physical toll it took on our wounded bodies. We spent another night under the stars. We tasked scraps of salted pork and stale bread to sustain us through the next two days. I only hoped Louis and Toni could make the journey unscathed. Toni, that is what I ended up naming the horse I had been riding. Toni was short for Antoinette, as in Marie Antoinette. It seemed fitting to go with King Louis, Henry's horse.

We arrived at Fort Cumberland the next day. The surgeon had a line of injured patients waiting for his attention. I stood nearby, holding my injured arm, and watched. He would dig his finger around a wound, looking for a bullet as the patient screamed. Sew up the hole and move on to the next. There was nothing sanitary —whatsoever—in his method. Most of these men would die from infection or some blood-borne disease passed on from one bloody wound to another. I couldn't scream about germs. No one would know what I was talking about and if I tried to explain, I would have been branded a heretic or a witch. It was disgusting that always came rushing into my thoughts. I was not sure what I was willing to do. Have Henry die from his wounds? Or die from the doctor's dirty hands? Either way I looked at it, it was quite possible he would die.

"I hate to ask this, but if I find us some food and whatever else I can find, could you hold out another couple of days? I think we need to get to Winchester before this group moves on."

"Should we not wait for the surgeon?" He winced as he tried to move his shoulder to keep it from getting stiff.

"I'm concerned that the surgeon will kill you quicker than the bullet or debris. There should be more supplies to work with in Winchester. I know we have some coins stashed away. We can get a clean place to stay for a couple of days while you recuperate. If I can't find the bullet, I can at least clean it up better."

He sucked in air and grunted, "If that is what you think is best."

"I do."

Only a few supplies had made it to Fort Cumberland. The supply chain had been a constant struggle for Major Carlyle. He fought with the treasury to get reimbursement. He knew what he was working with and knew they would be slow to reimburse or avoid paying him altogether. Even if he could get the supplies, there would be ruffians along the way that would rob the men and take the supplies we needed on the frontline. I took what I could and loaded up our packs. It was enough to get us through the next couple of days of travel.

Louis and Toni were champions in getting us to Winchester. We could get a room at the inn I had stayed at previously. This time, Henry didn't stay with the soldiers at the nearby field, but stayed in the room with me. I had food brought up, and asked for a couple of bottles of whiskey, and the local tailor. I would need a needle and thread. What we needed was an emergency room and a proper doctor, not me playing one on television.

The innkeeper supplied what he could and brought me the extra linens I had requested. "Are you sure you do not require a surgeon?" A man in his fifties, he was short, thick in the middle, and nearly bald. His square squished face made him look as though he was constantly holding in a fart.

"No. No surgeon."

"Did you shoot the man?" He eyed Henry for his response.

Henry's body winced at the contraction of his attempt to laugh. "No, we would have the French devils to thank for this." Henry looked at the bloody wound under his right clavicle. "My wife can handle this bit of needlework."

I shot a look at him. He knew this would hurt and we would be lucky if I could do this without either of us passing out. I had helped the doctor with the wounded at Fort Necessity. He would dig out the bullet or arrow. I would finish up the stitching. This was different. It was one thing to work on someone that you casually know; it is something else to know I would cause pain to the man that I loved.

Removing the bandages was painful for both of us, but it was only the beginning. Blood dried to the cloth, sticking the make-shift bandages to his open wound. I poured some whiskey on the wound, hoping to soften up the grip of the dried blood and provide some sort of disinfection. Henry howled out in pain. The whiskey stung as it touched the red flesh.

"When I start, I'm going to need you to hold still." I looked around the room for something to distract him or tie him down. How would I keep him still and clean out the wound at the same time? "Do I need to get men up here to hold you down?"

Henry growled out in pain and frustration. He didn't

want anyone to see him weak. I didn't give a crap if they saw him weak or not. I just wanted him to live through this. I placed the bandage back over the wound and ran downstairs to the tavern to look for a couple of men that were more sober than drunk. Across the room in the corner, two men had just sat down to eat their meals. The food smelled good. I hadn't had a proper sit-down meal in months.

"Good day, gentlemen." I said, walking up to them, straightening my tattered blue petticoat. "Might I ask..."

"Can you see we're trying to eat?" said the older man on the right. He looked close to my age, maybe mid-forties, thin except for his distended stomach, with a long-pointed nose, and wore a set of brown-colored clothes. The brown was from lack of frequent washes and less from the dyed color of the cloth.

The younger man, who appeared to be related to the man—perhaps a son or nephew—looked up from his plate of boiled pork. "She is too old for me, uncle." A twisted snicker crossed his face. "Mayhap you can have a go after we eat."

"Mayhap," I began, throwing my hands on my hips in a very don't-mess-with-the-bull-or-you-will-get-the-horns kind of way. The men stared in disbelief at my audacity. "As I was saying, I need a couple of strong men to hold down my husband while I attempt to pull a bullet out of his chest and sew him up. I thought you two looked like you were up to the task, but perhaps I can find someone else with the intestinal fortitude and strength to hold down an injured man." With a quick turn on my heel, I looked around the room. I knew by the shocked look on their faces, they thought when I approached I was offering services between my legs. That couldn't have been further from the truth. I heard the men snicker as I left, in search of someone else. Everyone else looked three sheets to the wind. I didn't need a drunkard to get sick at the sight of the hole or unable to hold on to Henry or to pass out in the middle of me cleaning him up. No. No one else would do.

I spun around to face the men again. "Listen, I really don't give a flying donkey's ass of what you think of me or not. I need two sober..." I looked the men over. "Well, sober-ish men to hold my husband down so I can mend him. I will pay for these meals and if you are still hungry afterwards, I will pay for those meals as well. Please, I wouldn't ask if I didn't need your help."

The older man sighed, crossed his arms over his rotund stomach, and leaned back in his chair. "What else are you going to give us?"

Bastard. I took a deep breath to prevent myself from lunging across the table and grabbing the jerk by the throat. "I don't have time for this. My husband is going to die."

"You should find the surgeon. Did you shoot him yourself and fear the noose?"

"What? No. It's nothing like that." I shook my head in disbelief. Why did everyone think I shot him?

"You either shot him or he did something to get himself shot. Either way, you and your husband sound like trouble." He took a sip of his ale and looked towards my bloody and bandaged left arm. "We don't get involved with trouble for free."

"I didn't shoot my husband," I said as my shoulders dropped in defeat. "Captain Spencer, my husband, was shot in an ambush. We barely escaped with our lives. In fact, I'm wasting precious time explaining myself to you when I could try to save his."

The nephew poked his nose up out of his plate, where he had been steadily shoveling food down his gullet. I wasn't sure he could hear our conversation over the sound of him devouring and slurping his food. "You pay for our meals and give us some coin, the genuine stuff, and I will hold your husband down."

"Fine. Let's go." I spun around and looked over my shoulder. He was still sitting at the table. "Now. Move it," I yelled. The room got quiet, and all eyes turned towards me. I gave a bullshit curtsey to the onlookers. There was no time for that madness. I was not sure how much money this was going to cost or how much we had, but if it meant saving Henry's life, I would pay all the money in the world.

CHAPTER THIRTY-ONE

"Wash your hands," I said to the young man as I pointed towards a bucket of water the innkeeper's daughter had brought up. "With soap, if you don't mind. And touch nothing else. Don't scratch your nose or ass. Nothing." I snapped at him. The opened curtain let the sunlight fill the room. I washed my hands and began preparing the bandages, needle, and thread. I didn't have any tools other than my hands, and was completely unprepared for what I was about to attempt. Henry let out a groan.

"Thank you for helping," I said as I scrubbed my hands with the soap. "I'm Amelia. This is Henry." I nodded towards Henry laying on the bed with his eyes closed, trying to take himself away from the pain he experienced and the excruciating pain he knew he was about to endure. "What's your name? It's easier if I know what to call you." When I poured the whiskey over my hands, any of the small nicks and cuts I had sustained felt on fire.

"Joseph," he said, looking at me in disgust. "You're wasting good whiskey."

"I'm not so sure how good this whiskey actually is." I sniffed the bottle. My nose burned as much as my hands did when I poured the fire water on it. "I'm making sure I reduce the number of germs introduced into the wound. Without antibiotics, I'm trying to hold off infection." Joseph looked at me like I had three heads. It was too late to think of the 18th century version of what I just said. I couldn't take it back now and decided to roll with it. If I am a witch, then I'll be a witch if that meant saving Henry's life. "Hold him on his left. Don't let him buck and pull away."

I pulled the bandage away from the wound. Blood oozed out of the freshly disturbed wound. A large pour of whiskey over the wound caused Henry to buck and arch his back. "Hold him, dammit," I yelled at Joseph.

He gripped down on Henry's left shoulder, pinning him to the bed. I pried my finger into the hole. It was hot, wet, and squishy. I was not sure how deep the bullet went, but with no tools, I could only poke around and hope to find any cloth or the bullet. Resistance when I got to the muscle. I moved my finger around, looking for a hole or the hard round bullet. I couldn't find either. Henry screamed out. Joseph continued to pin him down. He threw more of his body on top of Henry, trying to keep his hips from bucking off the bed.

"Stop it," Henry screamed out. "You will kil..." He howled in pain.

"I can't find it," I cried. "And I can't keep doing this to you." I looked down at the hole. My finger exploring his insides did more harm than good. "I need to disinfect it the best I can and sew it up." That, truly, was all I could do. No wonder why so many men died during war from wounds.

I poured whiskey on the wound again, wiped up the area with a clean linen, wiped my hands of the blood, and picked up the threaded needle. I worked my way through his skin. He called out with every puncture. My heart broke for each stitch, as I felt the needle break through the skin and felt the resistance of the thread as I pulled it through his flesh. It would not be pretty, but it might start the healing process. I wrapped clean linen around the wound to absorb any blood. The sling I tied around him would keep his arm immobile.

It was done. I sat down, exhausted. My left arm throbbed. I looked down, blood oozed out of the open wound, soaking into my sleeve.

"Mistress Amelia," Joseph interrupted my focus. "Allow me to take care of that for you." He nodded towards my arm. I pulled off my jacket, easing it down my left arm. Whatever had hit me had ripped the left arm of my shift open since the day they shot me. It required little moving away of fabric to expose the wound to him. I avoided looking at it over the past few days. Ignore the pain and infection and it might go away, was my theory.

I couldn't ignore it any longer. The wound was about

two inches long and a half inch deep. It was warm to the touch and tender. It should have been stitched up days ago. "Good thing I have some extra padding in these arms. I don't think it got too deep." I tried to laugh it off, but only sucked air through my teeth.

Joseph paid attention to my routine to clean up Henry and followed suit to tend to my arm. He washed his hands, poured whiskey over them, grabbed the needle and thread, laced the thread through the eye, and came at me with the whiskey and needle. "Wait!" I yelled out. "Pour whiskey over the needle. It's not the same as boiling it, but it will have to do."

He looked at me as though I had lost my mind... again. Pouring whiskey over the needle, he moved in to stitch my arm. I could feel the hesitation in my skin as the needle pierced it. Each puncture burned through my body. I gritted my teeth and white knuckled the chair. Heavy breaths shot out of my nose. I tried taking deep cleansing breaths with each lace through my skin. Tears rolled down my cheeks. I looked towards Henry. He had propped himself on his left elbow in order to see me being tortured. There was nothing he could do. He could barely look up. The pain had weakened his body. I clenched my eyes tight and looked away from him. I couldn't look at him laying helpless, while I tried to hold it together while being stitched up. My big toe flicked up and down as I tried to distract myself from the pain. "Almost done, Mistress." Joseph said in a low voice, trying to calm me. It didn't work. I wanted to jump out of the chair and be done with it.

"Cheese and rice," I yelled out. "Aren't you done yet?"

"Two more and I can knot it." He said, his voice a little unsteady. "There. Finished."

I looked down at the white thread, tinged pink from my blood. It would have to do. My arm burned and throbbed. I sucked in a deep breath and let it out slowly. "Thank you, Joseph." I mumbled as tears flowed down my cheeks. "Let me find you some coin." I scraped around my pocket and found a quarter of a Spanish pistole. I had used the rest of it to get our room and food. Even though the colonies used the English pound, it was difficult to find the coin. Most of the time, people used trade, a bartering system. The Spanish coin was happily accepted, and he left us in our pained misery.

Henry traveled with a pouch full of Spanish pistole, which were often used instead of the pound. In modern times, when we think of pirates and pieces of eight, it is referring to the pistole. They could cut the coin into eight pieces to pay for goods and services. Eight pieces of pistole. Pieces of eight. I had seen other people use it, so I never questioned why Henry would have a pistole in his pouch. When I first got here, I would not have been able to identify an English pound. The only pounds I was familiar with was the one- and two-pound coins, five and above paper notes in various sizes and colors, sporting the portrait of Queen Elizabeth II. Whatever the reason, Joseph seemed satisfied to receive it as payment.

Henry laid back down on the bed while I wrapped linen around my arm. "We need antibiotics."

Henry, weakened and barely coherent, asked, "Where would we find that?"

"We don't," I said as I slumped in my chair. "Fancy going to the twenty-first century? We can find some there."

"If only we could." Henry stared at the ceiling. The light that flooded in the room was warm and began to fade. I would need to light candles. "No. We need to get home to Williamsburg."

"We'll leave in a couple of days after you've had a chance to rest." I searched for a flint to light the candle that sat in the lamp on the table.

Henry's voice quivered. "No, we need to leave in the morn. Will you arrange for supplies?"

"Do you think I should try to find a wagon?" I shot out of my chair and made my way next to Henry's side. Death hung heavy in the room.

"We will travel faster on the horses." He recoiled from my hand as I tried to touch his wound. "We might make it in four days, if Louis and Toni and hold up for the ride."

I tried not to panic. He was already counting off the days he had left alive. "Okay, four days to Williamsburg, then you'll be willing to rest?"

"Please make sure we have enough supplies." He closed his eyes and fell into a fitful sleep.

My arm throbbed as I raced up and down the stairs, making travel arrangements and gathering what supplies I could. The ostler would have the horses fed, saddled, and ready by the break of dawn. I purchased salted pork, bread, and hard-boiled eggs. No vegetables. We wouldn't get scurvy in the brief four days it would take us to get to Williamsburg. I needed to make sure we had enough protein to fill our bellies. Yes. We would have enough food for four days of travel.

I gathered and washed extra linens for clean bandages. A couple of bottles of whiskey to get us through as a disinfectant and pain reliever. Extra thread and needle wrapped up and put in the saddlebag. I hoped we wouldn't need it. Four days. Four hard riding days. Closing my eyes, I put a prayer out to the universe. I had to keep Henry alive.

"YOUR HUSBAND IS SICKLY, MISTRESS," the ostler said to me as he helped me climb into the saddle. "Are you certain he should travel?"

"No," I said. I took a deep breath to help ease the pain in my arm. I strained the stitches climbing into the saddle. My arm burned and throbbed. There was no time for me to worry about it. We had to get Henry to Williamsburg. "But travel we must. Thank you for your assistance."

Louis' soft trot kept Henry from jostling about too much. I was concerned he would bounce off the back of the horse and I could not get him back in the saddle. After every stop, I would have to figure out how to get him back in the saddle. He was not doing well. The ostler was correct; he was looking sickly. His skin was pale and clammy, but I brushed it off to the pain and surgery. I used whiskey to disinfect. It should have worked... right?

By the end of the day, we traveled for nearly 14 hours and found a home to stop at for the night. A large family, with eight children under the age of twelve, occupied the small cabin. We happily took a spot in the barn. Louis and Toni were thankful for the rest. Three more days like today were going to be hard on them. It was going to be tough on me. As my arm burned and throbbed, I refused to look at it. I still was under the belief that if I ignored it, it would go away. Nothing could be done for it, anyway. A poultice? Perhaps. But there was no time to figure that out. No. I would worry about it when we got to Williamsburg.

Mister Williams helped me get the horses ready and Henry in the saddle. We left before the morning sun crested over the eastern horizon. The soft glow would have made for a lovely ride, if not for the ride for Henry's life.

As the day progressed, we continued to head southeast. The sun beat down on us. Birds chirped and circled overhead. Flies and gnats hovered over our wounds like miniature vultures. We stopped to let the horses drink and rest. Overheated, I needed to wash my face in the cool stream, and I refused to let Henry out of my sight. He ran a fever and refused my attempts to check the wound. We both knew it would not be a positive outcome for him. With the way my arm ached and burned, my outcome fared just as poor.

We crossed past a few homes and through a few small towns, finally stopping as the sun began to lower behind us. The shadows stretched, long and thin. I looked over towards Henry. He could barely hold on to his saddle.

Louis was agitated. Toni took it all in stride. She followed wherever Louis would go or do whatever he did. She and I made a magnificent pair.

"How much further to Richmond?" I asked Widow Jackson when we stopped for the night. The tiny widow was close to seventy years old and lived alone. I had her by at least three inches and fifty pounds. There were a few homes in the area, but the first house we stopped at suggested we ask to rent a room from the Widow Jackson. A spare room meant we didn't have to sleep in a stinky barn. Her spare room proved to be in line with a barn. The mattress was a sack stuffed with straw that poked and scratched and may have contained lice or a bug or two. I helped Henry to bed and gathered a meal for him. One neighbor came for the horses to house them for the night. A generous tip made sure they would be saddled and ready to go for us by the break of dawn. It would make for another miserably long day, but we seemed to average the forty-five miles-or-so, needed to get us to Williamsburg within the next couple of days.

"Well, now, it is not another day's ride. If your horses do not die where they stand, you can get there tomorrow." She handed me a bowl of hot stew. I was exhausted and beginning to feel weak. I was sure my arm raged with infection. It was hot and tender to touch. "We should look at your man's injury. He is looking sickly."

"I've heard that one before," I said, taking in a deep sigh. "We need to get to Williamsburg."

"I am not sure who is looking worse for the wear, your horses, your husband, or you." She pointed at me with a wrinkled, arthritic finger and looked at me over her squashed nose with her faded blue eyes, that showed age and a lifetime of wisdom.

"Oh, I'm fine," I tried to convince her and me of that statement. "I just have a bit of a nick on my arm. He has a musket ball lodged somewhere in him."

She just lifted an eyebrow at me and made some sort of snort of disbelief. "Well, let us get a clean bandage on the both of you before you settled. No sense in bleeding on my linens."

All I could do was laugh. Grandmothers have not changed over the years. They worry about you and their linens. The laugh caused my aching and fevered body tighten up more than I could handle. I needed to feed Henry, get us cleaned up, and collapse into bed.

"Stop acting like a child and let me check out your wound," I berated Henry. Sweat poured from every pore of my body and his.

"I am not a child, and I won't be spoken to like one." He growled back at me.

"Then let me clean your wound." I pulled back the bandage to find a flaming red, swollen lump. "Oh, sweet cheeses. Why didn't you tell me it was this bad?" Stench from the infected wound pierced through the air like a bullet. I quickly covered it again.

"It matters not how bad it is," Henry said, taking my hand in his. He looked deep into my eyes, pleading for energy for his next statement. "I have to live long enough for you to get me home."

"I will get you a few herbs to help with the pain," Widow Jackson said as she left the room.

"We can stay here and let you rest," I couldn't hold back the tears. I was physically and emotionally spent. "We can go to Williamsburg when you feel better. I just don't understand why we must rush."

"My love." Henry reached up with his left hand and caressed my cheek. "There are things you must be told. Secrets that I need to show you before I die."

"What are you talking about?" I shook my head in confusion. We knew each other's secrets. At least, I thought we told each other everything. What could he possibly have been holding back from me? What could be worse or more embarrassing than the way his late wife and his brother had treated him? He told me about that, but he refused to tell me this secret until he was on his deathbed?

Widow Jackson entered the room with a cup of tea for us and hot water to clean the wound. "We need to drain the wound. It's rancid." We peeled the wrapping off, and the smell hit our noses. The wound was wet from sweat. Widow Jackson held up a knife. Oh no, I knew where this was headed, and I wasn't sure I could hold Henry down. I was weak, but looking into his eyes, I knew he was weaker.

The old woman pulled back her sleeves and pinned an apron over her dark brown petticoat and jacket. "Do you have any whiskey?" I asked.

"If you need anything for the pain, drink the tea. It will help." She said as she wiped the knife off on her apron.

"I was thinking of helping disinfect the wound. Maybe

boil the knife in water to get the ger..." I had to stop myself from saying germs. The understanding of germs and disinfecting everything for medical reasons would not be in practice for over a hundred years. Besides, I doubt germs would make the situation worse. It was bleak, and a disinfected knife made no difference either way. "Never mind," I said as I shook my head. "Please, Mistress Jackson, continue." I turned to look at Henry. "I need you to look at me and hold my hand. This is going to hurt... more than you can imagine."

Widow Jackson took her knife and popped a few stitches out of the center, leaving the rest of them intact. She applied pressure to the top and bottom of the wound. Rancid pus oozed out, stained pink with blood. "Wipe as we go, Mistress Spencer." I grabbed the linens piled on the bed and wiped as she continued to apply pressure. Henry sucked in air through his teeth and let out a guttural howl. "The worse is almost over," she said, trying to reassure all of us. No one believed her.

She took a thin ribbon of the linen and tucked it between the folds of skin where she had removed the stitches. "Leave that in there. It needs to drain." I hadn't thought about the wound needing to drain. I had sewed it up to keep everything in, not to let anything out. She applied a poultice and fresh bandages over the oozing wound to catch any liquid. "Now, mistress, let's look at your arm."

Cheese and rice. She peeled away the bandages I had wrapped around my arm two days ago. I hadn't been as vigilant to keep my arm cleaned and tended to as I tried to care for Henry's wound. Blood and pus crusted on my wrapping, sticking it to my skin like I glued it on. She handed me a wet cloth to hold to it in order to loosen up the blood-dried cloth. We finally could peel it away without ripping off half my skin along with it. It was swelling. It was hot and red, but the stench of infection hadn't cursed it yet. Widow Jackson took her knife and popped a couple of stitches out. Pus didn't ooze out of my wound the with same volume as it had Henry's, but it was a relief to have some of the pressure of the stitches removed. She helped clean the wound, add a poultice, and re-bandaged it for me. It was lovely to have someone else to help take care of me in this situation. I knew Henry was out of commission. His breathing labored, he ran a fever, and he was weak. The grim reaper was hanging out in the other room, scratching his scythe on the door. No, Henry could not take care of himself, let alone me. Being strong for the both of us was taking its toll on me. I couldn't last much longer.

CHAPTER THIRTY-TWO

The smell of food wafted into the room. My stomach made an audible proclamation that it was time to get up. Henry stirred in the bed next to me. He was a fireball lying next to me. "Hey sleepyhead," I said as I propped myself up on my right elbow. We slept closer than I would have preferred, but he was unwilling to let me sleep anywhere else but next to him. His attempt at sitting up was met with failure, and he ended up collapsing back down on the bed. "Do you think you will be able to eat breakfast at the table? Or should I bring it in to you?"

"I must piss." Direct and grumpy at the same time. A pleasant day ahead for us, I see.

"If you hadn't already been shot, I would have shot you for that good morning."

"I'm sorry." He looked downtrodden. "I shouldn't have provoked. I just... just..."

"Feel like a herd of wild horses has run you over?" I asked. "Yeah, my arm is a bit stiff this morning, but I'm sure nothing like you're feeling." Every muscle in my body ached. I dared not move during the night, for the fear of waking or injuring Henry. My arm was a bit more than stiff, but I wouldn't admit to it. It seared with pain, flaming hot. I was sure I was running a fever. My muscles ached as if I was on the cusp of getting the flu, but it hadn't got to where I couldn't function. Typical of a woman, it's not bad until I'm on my deathbed. Then I would still have more people or things to take care of and wouldn't be allowed to die.

"Yes, something like that," he said with a forced half-smile. "I will need help to use the chamber pot, get dressed and," he continued, "to sit at the table like a gentleman, instead of feeling like an invalid."

"Well, you are an invalid," I raised an eyebrow at him, "but I get what you're saying."

Morning faculties taken care of, washed, dressed, and we sat down for breakfast. The windows and doors open, letting in the early morning cool air. It was mid-July in Virginia and by mid-morning, the sun would scorch down throughout the colony, heating it up to miserable proportions. We had to take advantage of the cooler air while we could. The pre-dawn glow made the outdoors a soft purplish blue. Widow Jackson had prepared oatmeal, grits... heck, I'm not sure what it was, but it was warm and filled our bellies. The coffee was bitter but appreciated. The neighbor brought the horses and tied them up to the porch. I needed to finish packing our bags and get us headed towards Richmond before the sun made its full appearance.

I stroked Louis' neck. "Hey there, buddy, I'm going to need you to keep good care of Henry for me," I said to the gentle horse. He was sturdy and well suited for Henry. He had taken great care of the both of us, and I couldn't imagine being able to make this journey without him. Toni was smaller than Louis, but her temperament and size suited me well. I wasn't sure who she had belonged to. I hadn't paid enough attention to the horses of the other officers. One thing is for sure, whomever had ridden her was now lying dead just south of Fort Duquesne.

Mounted on our horses, I waved farewell to Widow Jackson, and turned to watch a slumped Henry, barely able to stay in the saddle. Today would have to be slower, or else Henry couldn't stay on his horse. "Do you think we should get a wagon or rent a carriage to take us from Richmond to Williamsburg?" I asked later that morning, breaking the unnerving silence we had experienced most of the trip. With his injury, Henry had been quiet, avoiding expending more energy than he needed. It took all that he had in order to stay in the saddle. Luckily for us, Louis was a very good boy, and didn't need to take much command from Henry. All that I needed was for Henry to stay in his saddle and to stay alive.

Henry's head lobbed from one side to the other. He looked over towards me. "Hm?" I recognized that look. Last year, that was me, before I ended up in a fevered daze for three days.

"Wagon? Carriage?" I huffed out. I was slightly annoyed at him, but knew it was not his fault that they shot him. No, I still blamed Braddock for that. His stubbornness to get to the house in Williamsburg instead of trying to recuperate anywhere else was incredibly annoying to me. "Should we get a wagon or carriage to take us from Richmond to Williamsburg? The roads are getting much better and I think a wagon or carriage could probably handle the ride. You could lie down instead of expending all your energy trying to stay in your saddle. What do you think?"

"I think... I refuse to think. Just get me home," he snapped at me.

Deep breath, Amelia, deep breath. We would find an inn in Richmond and ask around for quick passage. I would have to check our finances and see if there were any coins hiding anywhere else in the bags or on Henry. I knew I had a coin in my pocket, but Henry may have a pistole or two stashed away. We had used quite a bit of what he had while we were in Alexandria and along the way to Fort Duquesne. The English soldiers destroyed everything in their path and left families with destroyed property and without food. Henry tried to provide some sort of recompense and went through his coins quickly. The colonists would have preferred to eat, instead of a piece or two of Spanish pistole. It still baffled me how he came into so much Spanish coin and lacked the pound. I remembered money moved from Spain to the Caribbean, and then up to the colonies, but his business traded with the pistole more than I realized. When he was feeling better, less grumpy, or on his deathbed, perhaps he would finally tell me the story.

"We've got to stop for a few minutes," I said, rubbing

Toni's wet neck. The humidity felt like a million percent, and the midday sun only added to the miserable journey. "The horses and I need to cool down." My head swirled, and I felt the world spinning around me. I was not sure if it was from the heat or from the ever-looming fever. I pulled Toni to the side, but Louis continued to walk. Henry's head lobbed and his chin touched his chest. Toni and I stood there for a moment, watching Louis and Henry continue down the road. "Come on, girl, let's stop those boys."

A little tap on her hindquarters finally got Toni moving fast enough to catch up with Henry and Louis. I would have been reluctant to move fast, as well, since the day was miserably hot and sticky. We caught up to Louis, and I grabbed hold of the reins with my right hand. My left arm remained plastered next to me. The pain radiated up to my shoulder. Any movement caused me to scream. I gently tugged on the reins, pulling Louis to a stop. I leaned over, rubbed Henry's leg, it twitched. Thank the stars above, he was still alive.

One of the good things about Virginia was the fact that water snaked throughout the terrain. Twisting and turning. Small and wide. Water could be found everywhere. The four of us needed to hydrate. My clothes were heavy with sweat. We drained our canteens about an hour ago and could use a refill.

"Henry," I said as I rubbed his leg. I didn't want to startle him and cause him to fall off Louis. He needed to dismount and rest for a moment. We needed the horses to rest if we were to continue through this heat. The forty

ALEX R CRAWFORD

miles we were to travel would take us the entire day. I couldn't push the horses any harder than I had pushed them. The heat would kill them. The heat was certainly going to kill Henry. If we were to stop, we would need to stop by a fallen tree, a large rock, something to assist me to get him back in the saddle. We had seen the occasional traveler pass by us, but by then, the roads were empty. It was probably too hot for anyone to want to go outside. I closed my eyes and daydreamed of central air conditioning.

Henry budged no more than a head nod. I hated pushing him and the horses, but, against my better judgement, I listened to him and promised to get him to Williamsburg. He knew he was going to die, and he wanted to do it in his own bed. Fine. Whatever. I hoped he would live long enough to make it home. I decided we needed to continue down the road until I was sure I could get him back in the saddle. No sense in stopping for a break if we would be stuck in the middle of nowhere.

Thinking about central air conditioning allowed my mind to wander. If Henry was to die, would I be stuck in the past? I didn't know how I would get back to my time. That part of time travel eluded me. There must be some way to control it. It just seemed to happen to me when I had least expected it. I knew doors, coins, and something else must be the trigger. I tried thinking about what else triggered the slip through time. My head spun, unable to focus. It was too hot. I was too hot. I closed my eyes. I just needed to rest for a moment.

My body jerked awake. I fell asleep thinking about how I was to get home to my time. I swear, I was just going to close my eyes for just a moment. Unaware of how long I dozed off, I took in a breath and reassessed my surroundings. Louis and Toni had continued down the path at a slow walk. The heat and lack of water were taking a serious toll on all of us. I forced my eyes open. The sun blared into them. Sunspots danced around my vision, making it difficult to focus on the road and terrain ahead of us. I wasn't sure if I was seeing things, or if we were approaching a town. Oh, thank goodness, it was a small settlement. I checked my pocket, two and a half a pistole. It would get us a small meal and the horses watered. I put the coins back in my pocket and patted it, just to make sure they were still there. Pulling Toni next to Henry, I grabbed Louis' reins to slow him down. There were about a dozen buildings lining each side of the road—homes, a small merchant, an even smaller church, a blacksmith, and a tavern. It was not much, but it would serve us well.

The heat of the day made for quiet streets. I cannot say that I blamed the people of the town. I would have preferred to lounge around in the shade, instead I was taking my dying husband down a hot and dirty road. The merchant sauntered out of his shop. Dressed in white shirtsleeves, no waistcoat or jacket—it was too hot for that—an apron covered his chest, a pair of light blue breeches, a light pair of stockings, and black shoes. He held the bottom of his white apron in his hand, wiping the sweat off his brow. His dark brown hair pulled back in a leather thong. A stray strand plastered across his forehead. He nodded a greeting towards me. We looked haggard, and he seemed to size us up as non-customers. He was correct. We were close to destitute at this point. What was left of my dress was ripped and dirty. My left sleeve of my coat and shift had been ripped off days ago in order to have better access to my wound. I used the bottom half of my shift to make bandages on the battlefield. All I had left to cover my bottom half was my petticoat. Well, what was left of it. In order to prevent chafing from the saddle, I had pulled it between my legs. Sweat poured down my body; the petticoat saturated and stuck to my skin. I had attempted to pull my hair back in its bun but gave up on trying to detangle it days ago. I lost my cap and brimmed hat who knows where, which screamed to the populace that I must be a poor woman that didn't know any better. With the sun beating down on me for the past few days, I had developed a bit of a sunburn. I looked and felt miserable. I wanted them to see that I was a war worn woman, just trying to give her husband peace. They wouldn't care and, at that point, I didn't care what they thought of me.

Henry looked worse than I did. He barely could lift his head. It lobbed back and forth with every step Louis took. His arm hung down in front of his body, holding on to the reins. If you could even call it that. I placed the reins in his limp hand. His skin was sunburned, but under it you could see the life was being drained out of him. His shirt was ripped and bloodstained. I had wiped off his breeches and washed his shirt, but they still looked as though he had rolled around in dirt, mud, and blood.

"Excuse me," I tried to choke out. The words caught on my dry throat. I tried to make spit and swallow it to lubricate my throat. It felt like sandpaper. I tried again,

"Excuse me, sir. We need to water our horses and get something to eat and drink. Could you point me at someone that can help us?"

"What's wrong with him?" He asked with a flick of his head towards Henry.

"Shot. I'm trying to take him home."

"You'll be taking him to the grave soon."

Tears pricked my eyes. Even if I wanted to cry, I didn't have enough water to create tears. "Yes, well, until then... I need to water our horses and try to feed him."

"You'll be wanting a place to stay for the night?"

"No," I sighed. "Just a meal and water." Of course, I wanted a place to stay. But I didn't have the time or money for that luxury.

"Two buildings down, you'll find the tavern. I'll have Samuel help your husband off his mount." The merchant called over his shoulder for Samuel to help us. An enslaved man, no older than late teens, came running out of the shop. His slight frame gave me concern about him being able to take the weight of Henry. It wasn't like I could have done any better. I was at the mercy of any assistance I could receive.

I gently slid off Toni, threw her reins around the post, and limped next to Samuel as we tried to slide Henry off Louis. It ended up being an attempt to catch him as he fell off the horse. With me on Henry's left and Samuel on his right, we stumbled into the tavern and propped Henry up in a corner seat. "Will you take the horses to the ostler and get them wiped down and watered?" Samuel turned to leave. I reached out to catch him and called out, "Tell him I will need them ready when we have finished our meal."

Samuel nodded and ran out the door. I collapsed in the chair next to Henry and realized that I couldn't last much longer. The hard travel, constantly caring for Henry, along with the infection that raged, took a rough toll on me. Henry raised his eyes when the barkeep came over to check on us. The tavern was empty, except for an old man passed out in the opposite corner from us. "You have to buy something to use that table." He looked us up and down, a disgusted look on his face. I'm sure he thought we were there to freeload from him.

"What can we get with this?" I held out half a pistole. I would need the other half for the horses. We would have to figure out something in Richmond, since we wouldn't have enough money to stay the night at an inn. Things always seem to cost more in the bigger cities. It was true in 1755, just as it was in the 21st century.

He lifted an eyebrow and took the coin out of my hand. "I'll bring you something to eat and drink." The meager meal he brought out ten minutes later showed that I overpaid. Leftover stew from who-knows-when, stale bread, and even staler ale. I helped Henry lift his spoon and tankard. It was only this morning when he could feed himself. Now? Now, it was a different story. He couldn't lift his arms. I was afraid he would choke on the ale, let alone chew the toughened meat.

Leaving Henry at the tavern, I limped down to the stable to settle my bill with the ostler. "Do you want me to change out your horses for you?" He asked as I entered.

"No," I began. "I just need to settle the bill and I will need help to get my husband back in the saddle."

"How far are you headed?"

"Today? Richmond."

"They might hold up long enough to make it there." He stroked Louis' neck while Toni continued to drink water. "You should hold up there for a day or two and let them rest."

"I need to get to Williamsburg by tomorrow."

"Have you ever ridden a horse to death?"

I shook my head. I didn't even know that was possible. "No? Is that something that can actually happen?"

"Aye." He turned his attention to Toni. "These are beasts of burden. As long as you keep on pushing, they will keep on going. They will go until they drop dead beneath you. These two have been riding hard and might not make it to Williamsburg at the rate you push them."

"Thank you for your concern." I was at a loss, and didn't have time to stall our trip. I certainly didn't want either horse to die. Mission focused, I had to get Henry to his house and hope he didn't die before we could get there. "I'll try to take it slow with them. I'll need help to get my husband mounted on Louis. He's the reason we need to push on. He's waiting for us at the tavern."

He grabbed a stool from the side of the stable; I grabbed the reins of the horses, and we headed a couple of doors down to the tavern. We had wasted precious time resting, but it felt good to have a moment to breathe. I handed the reins to the ostler and limped into the tavern to retrieve Henry. He remained slumped in the chair, chin touched his chest, just as it had for the entire day. He hadn't the energy to hold up his head anymore. Sweet stars above, I hoped he would live long enough to see his home. I couldn't get more than two words out of him, if I could get that. It pained him to speak. "I need you to walk. My love, cannot carry you." I said as I put my arm under his left arm and around his waist.

He grumbled a response and pulled his arm out from around me. His body flopped forward on the table. Bracing himself with his left forearm, he used the table to help him stand. He teetered back-and-forth. I grabbed his left arm, threw it over my shoulder, and wrapped my right arm around his waist. "Louis is waiting outside for you." He looked at me through glazed eyes. I wasn't sure he understood what I was saying, but he moved—one hard, unstable step after the other. Outside, the ostler looked at us like he saw zombies. He just might have.

"You don't need help to get your husband in the saddle. He needs a wagon, lest you help into a grave."

"A wagon would be too slow over the roads. Besides, I gave you my last coin." I patted my pocket. "He needs to get in the saddle."

With the ostler's help, the step stool, and the stars above, we somehow got Henry in his saddle. I happily took the offer of help to get saddled onto Toni. My legs ached, and I had the use of only my right arm. The infection was spreading and caused swelling around my left shoulder. It was stiff and painful to move.

We took it easy and made it to Richmond late in the day. The long summer days gave us the opportunity to ride longer into the night. Unfortunately, we were out of money and had no place to stay.

"Do you know anyone here?"

"Hm?" Henry lifted his head.

"Richmond," I was agitated by the constant repeating of words. "We're in Richmond. Do you know anyone here?" He continued to stare at me with a glazed look. "We don't have money for an inn. Do you know anyone we can stay with?"

"Richmond."

"For the love... yes, Richmond."

"No. Not Richmond," he said. I looked at him, confused. We were in Richmond. I knew we were. "Williamsburg. Home. Must get home."

I had to take a deep breath to calm myself. He was becoming delirious. "Louis, Toni," I called out to the horses. "Do you think you can walk for longer?"

Louis snorted at my request. Toni looked over at Louis and stomped her foot in reply. Apparently, the horses had better communication skills than I was having with Henry. "I'm not sure what the equivalent of a horse massage and spa day is, but I will make sure the both of you get one after we get home."

Louis flicked his head down the road, and Toni followed suit. We would ride for a bit longer. I wasn't sure how any of us were going to sleep, but we would worry about that in a couple of hours.

CHAPTER THIRTY-THREE

*T*he glow of the sun that had set a couple of moments earlier was fading fast. It was late. Toni and Louis' stride had slowed down. We needed to stop for the night, and I had to figure out how to get Henry out of the saddle. For the love of all that is good in the world, I did not know how I was going to do that ginormous task. I had kept putting it off throughout the ride. Someone or something had always come along. Now, it was up to me to figure this out.

I pulled Toni to the side of the road, close to a stream, and Louis followed us over. I slid off Toni and let her loose to drink. "Louis, I need for you to get down... all the way down." He flipped his ears at me. Or was it the fly that was swirling around his head? He blinked at me. Either he didn't understand me, or he thought I was crazy—probably both. I grabbed hold of his reins and pulled them down. I could see it in his eyes. He understood what I was asking.

He collapsed down to his knees, allowing me to pull Henry off his back. "Thank you, buddy." I stroked his neck. "Go find Toni and get some water. You're a very good boy."

He sauntered down to the stream as I lugged a barely responsive Henry to the ground. "I will get us set up, but first I need to use the little girls' room," I said as I looked around. "Or bush, I guess. I will help you next."

My thoughts were like when you fly on a plane. They always gave the safety instructions. Help yourself before you help someone else. Or maybe I needed to be selfish for a moment. I found a tree nearby and emptied my bladder. I went to the stream, rinsed my hands, and splashed water over my face. The sweat and dust caked on my face. I grabbed sticks on my way back to Henry. I broke down in tears at the sight of him slumped over. Louis and Toni grazed nearby. Toni lifted her head to look at me. I dropped the wood near Henry, wiped the tears from eyes, and knelt next to him. "Can I take you to use a tree, bush, something?"

His head flopped over to look in my direction. "Pissed myself." I wanted to kick myself for being selfish. I could have held it a few minutes longer and made sure he was taken care of. If I didn't feel bad for taking care of myself before, I did now.

"Okay, deep breaths. I'm going to remove the packs from the horses and make camp. I'm going to start a fire and strip you out of your pants. They will dry by morning." I looked over at Henry, his cheeks wet with tears. "We'll get through this and get you home tomorrow.

But I need you to hold on until then. Can you do that for me?"

He squeaked out a reply. I wasn't sure what he had said, but it might have been a yes. With the saddles pulled off the horses and bedrolls unpacked, I dug around for what we had left for food. I gathered up some dried leaves for kindling, and more wood to get us through the night. I flicked and flicked the flint. I always had trouble starting a fire with it, but I finally got it going. Finishing up with bedrolls around the fire, I stood there assessing the situation, right hand on hip, left arm held tight against my side. I had used my left arm too much throughout the day and it was seizing up. That is what I tried telling myself— ignoring the swelling that had moved from my shoulder and was making its way towards my neck.

"I need for you to help me move you. I can't do this on my own." Tears streamed down my face. Henry needed to get on his bedroll so I could strip him out of his pants and attempt to clean him up. That was easier said than done, and I didn't think it would be easy to begin with. He couldn't use his upper body to brace himself and was a limp rag doll. Begging and pleading with his breeches led to cursing and shouting at them. I finally could get them down by pulling on them. I flew backwards as they pulled off him. "Cheese and rice, that flipping hurt!" I called out as I splayed on the ground and looked up at the sky. My breaths came in hard and labored. The flight to the ground landed me on my left shoulder, which caused the pain to soar through my body.

I flipped over to my stomach, planted my right hand

on the ground, got to my knees, and finally worked myself up to a standing position. I limped myself, the pants, and our canteens to the stream, before I set in to prepare our food and get water down our throats. One more day, I had to remind myself. I can make it through one more day.

I hoped.

CHAPTER THIRTY-FOUR

he drive from Richmond to Williamsburg took less than an hour to cover the fifty miles. I traveled that highway enough times that it would fly by, and I would visit Hannah at her school, College of William and Mary, in no time. What would take me less than an hour by car would take me a hard day's ride on horseback. Traveling with a husband tip-tapping on death's door, slowed the ride further. The early morning glow of the sun crept into my eyes. It felt as though I had just laid down. Stuck somewhere between Richmond and Williamsburg, the last day of our ride had just begun. I should have felt relieved, but the daunting task of schlepping Henry into a saddle hung heavy on my mind. My shoulder throbbed and burned with pain. It pained me to prop up on my right forearm to check on Henry and the horses. Too exhausted to care or think straight, I forgot to secure the horses that night. If they wandered off in the night, we were doomed. A small clearing next to a stream, somewhere between Richmond and Williamsburg, was not where Henry nor I had intended to spend our last moments. With that foreboding thought, it took every ounce of willpower for me to get up. Henry laid on his back, his left arm held onto his right wrist. He looked deathly peaceful. If it wasn't for the slight rise and fall of his chest, I would have thought he had passed in his sleep. I relaxed for a moment. That moment was short-lived. Louis and Toni were gone. I stood up to look around. Did they wander too far? My eyes scanned over the tall dry grass and searched the horizon and down the path in both directions for the horses. They had to be here. About a hundred yards from where I stood, I could see what appeared to be the side of a horse lying in the grass. Oh no! I killed the horses! I hobbled in their direction, my back muscles tight and sore. What was I going to do? I approached Louis. He lifted his head and shot up in a surprised jolt.

Wait! What? Did horses lie down to sleep? I thought the hard riding had killed him. "Hey handsome," I said to Louis as I stroked his neck. "It's okay. Where's our girl?"

Louis snorted and stomped his foot in response to my question. "Why don't you go find something to drink and eat while I find Toni?" I searched the area. This time, I knew to look down in the tall grass for her. I called out for her until my throat ached and burned. I was out of luck. She was missing. I wandered back over to Henry. He laid still, mouth slightly opened, breath shallower than before. "We need to get you home."

I decided to let him rest a little longer while I packed up and made a note of how much food we had left. Maybe enough for the day if we skipped lunch. Maybe? Heading towards the stream to refill the canteens, I heard a bit of a disturbance. Louis neighed. A defensive neigh. I dropped my canteens and hobbled like a zombie after fresh brains, as fast as I could towards him. As I approached the stream, I found a man trying to catch Louis. He had already thrown a rope around Toni's neck. She struggled to pull away from him.

"What in the hell do you think you are doing to my horses?"

"Your horses? These are my horses." The man laughed and snarled. "And there's nothing some stupid woman can do about it."

"Have you lost your damned mind?" I turned to Louis. "Louis, go to Henry! Now!" I pointed towards the camp.

Louis took off in a full gallop in the direction I had pointed. Toni continued to pull on the rope. "You scared off my horse. I suggest you leave while you still have your life, woman."

"You know what? I don't have time for this," I said as I fought back the tears. I didn't have time to spare messing with that fool as my husband laid dying. *Think, Amelia.* Sweet-talk him? Ugh! "Listen, I can appreciate the fact that you think this is your horse, however...."

He yanked on Toni's rope. She reared up on him. The rope pulled through his hands, cutting deep into his palms. Blood stained the end of the rope. The fool screamed out. "Toni," I called out to her. "Find Louis! Now!"

Toni ran past me with the rope around her neck and the bloodied end flying behind her. Horses were safe. I just had to get myself to safety. Outrunning him was out of the question. I could barely keep myself standing up. I could feel my blood coursing, throbbing, aching through my left arm. It throbbed faster, harder. Pain surged through my body. Blood and pus oozed out of the bandages and down my arm. I reached into the front of my stays and pulled out the knife. I hadn't thought I would have to use it, but was thankful for Henry's suggestion of having the knife sheath added before we left Alexandria. It was a small knife of about 3 inches. It was intended to help me out when I cooked, or if I needed to cut something. I doubted he meant it for a rumble in the backwoods. I could do some damage if it came to it. The man laughed through gritted teeth when he saw me holding it up. "What do you think you are going to do with that?" He plunged his hands back into the water, sucking in air through his teeth.

"More than you can do with your hands." I pointed towards his hands with the knife, careful not to show the weakness I felt in my left arm. It was difficult. My knees were about to buckle from the pain. "Your skin is peeling off in sheets. I suggest you go your way, and I will go mine."

He pulled his hands out of the water and looked at them. Thin sheets of skin hung off his hands like melted wax. He gasped and shoved his hands back into the water.

"If you ever try to steal my horses again," I panted out. "I will slit your throat."

The man lunged towards me. I took off in a limped run towards the camp. Did I have to antagonize the situation more? I should think before I opened my big, fat, and stupid mouth. Think before stirring up things? Nope. Not Amelia Spencer.

I looked over my shoulder as I continued to hobble away from the stream, half-expected to see a skeletal hand reaching for me straight out of a horror movie. A woman running away from the villain required a trip over a log or her own feet, to allow him to catch up. Stupid horror movies always get it wrong. What kind of fool looks back while running away from a murderer and trips over their own feet? I supposed I wanted to see it happen and not be taken by surprise. Inevitably, my mouth would cause my demise, but it would now cause Henry's demise as well.

I looked over my right shoulder, the muscles in my left shoulder pulled and screamed at the strain. He was out of my view. I kept running towards the camp. Henry was half-propped up on his side as he looked in my direction. Louis and Toni stood guard next to him. My foot hit something—a rock?—and I tried to catch myself from making a face plant into the ground. Too late. The momentum kept me flying forward. Mid-air, I twisted my body to land on my right side and not cause more injury to my left. If I were smarter, I would have taken the excruciatingly painful hit to my left side in order to keep one uninjured side. In fact, looking up and seeing a worried look on Henry's face and the faces of the two horses—looking at me like I had lost my mind... again—and the horse thief nowhere to be seen, I could have walked back to camp. Such was my luck. Thankfully, my arm was only had a bruise, and I didn't stab myself running with a knife.

I raised my arm above the tall grass, sat up, and shouted, "I'm fine." I plopped back down on the ground to catch my breath. If only I would've stayed in bed months ago, and not met up with Cora in Alexandria. I would've stayed safe in the 21st century. Still being stalked by Kyle, no doubt, but not in a race for my and Henry's lives in 1755. Oh, what did the Fates have in store for me next?

I limped back to the camp, slowly and painfully prepared the food. Every muscle and joint in my body protested any movement I demanded from them. I had to find where I dropped the canteens and get them refilled before we started our journey for the day. Those darn canteens! That is what caught my foot when I ran from the horse thief.

The sleep had done Henry some good, and he was a little more mobile that morning. His pants had dried overnight, so he could put on somewhat clean breeches. I used the water in the canteens to help him clean up. They were refilled and packed with the rest of our supplies onto the horses. I stood there, right hand on hip, left arm pinned close to my side, staring at Louis and then back at Henry. Would I be able to get Louis down on his knees so I could get Henry on top of him? It worked last night in the dismount. I could only hope that I could do it again. I stood in front of Louis and held his reins in my right hand. "Listen, my friend, you and I both know I cannot get Henry up in your saddle. I'm going to need you to..." and with that bit of pleading, Louis knelt on his knees. "Thank you, my goodest boy."

I helped Henry stand, and we both hobbled over to Louis. With only a little bit of tugging, pulling, and odd negotiations, we got Henry in the saddle. Rocking back-and-forth, Louis stood without jostling Henry out of the saddle.

It was then my turn to attempt to mount Toni. Although I could reach the stirrup, I lacked the strength to pull myself up into the saddle. I looked around for a log or rock to stand on. "Oh, sugar snaps." I continued to look around. "I can walk alongside all of you until we find somewhere for me to mount her."

Henry began to speak. Just the simple fact that he had the energy he did that morning made me hopeful that he might be okay. Louis interrupted whatever Henry was about to say with a bellowing neigh and a stomp of his foot. Toni whinnied in response to Louis. A snort and stomp later, she knelt on her knees to allow me to mount her. I looked over at Henry, his eyes wide. Louis snorted a let's-get-on-with-it snort at me, and I climbed into the saddle, ensuring my petticoats were placed between my legs to prevent chaffing. Well, some chaffing had already occurred, along with the tight muscles in my back, it was the major cause of my limp and hobble. My skin rubbed raw, but I was not about to attempt a sidesaddle. I continued to tell myself it would all be over when we got to Williamsburg later that day.

We headed east towards Williamsburg. The morning sun slowly made an appearance over the trees in front of us. I squinted and wished for my sunglasses from the future that were left in my bag of stuff that was sent to Williamsburg months ago from the Carlyle house in Alexandria.

As we made our way down the woods-lined road, the sun continued to rise and cook my already sunburned skin. My entire body heated. The swelling in my arm got worse. The skin tightened closer to my neck. If the infection moved to my neck, it could cause my airway to close. No, I had to remove that thought from my mind. I had to believe that both of us would make it to Williamsburg alive. I looked over at Henry. His chin was already pressed against his chest again. The energy he had built up overnight was already gone and we had been on the road for only a few hours. This day was going to be long. I could feel the stress creep into my stomach and clench it into knots.

We stopped at midday to give the horses the opportunity to rest and drink. Thankfully, Louis and I now had a routine to get Henry on and off the saddle. I'm sure it was difficult for him, but he seemed to understand the impact he had made on our journey.

We continued our expedition, without Henry or I able to fill our bellies with anything other than water. We could eat after we got to the house. I looked over at Henry, his head lolled further down his chest. We had no time to waste. The horses need to pick up the speed and get us to Williamsburg. I gave Toni a nudge and a click of my tongue to encourage her to move faster. Louis followed suit. I looked towards Henry. His body flopped, hardly able to stay in the saddle. It was no use. Henry risked falling out of the saddle if we picked up speed. I slowed Toni down; Louis kept pace next to us. I wanted to scream and curse the gods.

We continued our slow push throughout the day. Conversation between us was nonexistent. Henry's head lobbed back-and-forth in rhythm to Louis' stride. The glow of twilight filled the sky as the sun set behind us. In front of us, the night crept in and filled me with a sense of doom. Henry hadn't lifted his head or responded to me in hours. He was still seated in the saddle and breathing, and that was all I cared about.

Louis knew his way through the streets of Williamsburg. He led us to the house without my guidance. Men and women were still out and walked down the streets. They watched as we made our way to the house. They were either in shock, or they didn't recognize Henry and Louis. A stout man, dressed in a dark coat and breeches, leaned over towards the man next to him and mumbled something as they both stared at us. I turned and stuck my tongue out at them. If the pain and swelling that had made its way to my neck were any sign, I would be dead before the morning came. So, I really couldn't give two shakes of a lamb's tail at what those men thought about me.

Louis led us to the front door of Henry's house.

Memories of the last time I was here came flooding back. I remembered seeing my portrait on the wall in the library. I felt the infection spread throughout my body. Cold sweats poured out of my pores. It became difficult to breathe. The infection took hold of my throat. Every breath was a gasp for my life.

There was no time to waste. Henry needed to get inside. Toni knelt like a well-trained horse and let me dismount. Thank goodness I would have collapsed if slipped out of the saddle. Louis followed suit next to the steps. Henry was no help. He could barely breathe, let alone climb the front steps.

I strained and pulled him up the step with my right arm. I was out of breath. All I could do was gasp for the air, which struggled to find its way through my throat and to my lungs. My throat constricted around every breath I took. As we approached the door, I reached up and grabbed the handle—it wouldn't open. "Are you kidding me?" I shouted into the void. I banged on the door. No one opened the door. Where were they?

"Coin," Henry choked out.

I looked down on the step and saw a coin at my feet. I picked it up and looked at the round gold metal disk. It was a pistole. The same kind Henry had taken with him to Alexandria. "Who cares if someone left money here? Don't you understand we are going to die? You and I... dead. I need to get you inside?"

"Someone... treasure... inside," he mumbled out. "I love you."

Well, that stopped me in my tracks. A smile crept

across my face. "I know." I grabbed the coin and tried the door handle again. "Now let's get you inside." Tears poured down my cheeks in a steady stream. That was the first time he told me he loved me. Until that point, we were going to die, and he was worried about his money. Was that his concern this entire time? I leaned against the door and banged on it. I begged for help. Men and women passed in front of the house, ignoring my pleas. Someone needed to let us in. I choked on every breath I tried to take. The handle finally turned. I grabbed Henry by the collar, stumbled in, and pulled him inside with me.

That is when it happened. We fell to the floor. I laid there, smelling the sweet scent of cherry wood smoke. The bright light swirled about us. I wasn't sure if I was dying or if I was being sucked through time. My vision blurred, and I felt dizzy. Henry laid next to me, barely breathing. I didn't know if he was experiencing what I was, but he laid there with his eyes closed. I grabbed hold of him. He grabbed my hand that held the coin. If this was going to be the last time either of us saw of each other, I wanted to remember what he felt like in my arms. It was then it all went black.

Somewhere in the middle of barely holding on to life and slipping towards death is where I was suspended. Pain seemed to slip away, but the chokehold the infection held onto my throat still told me I was alive, if only for a short while longer. I couldn't move. My surroundings were void —a black void. I couldn't tell if I had crossed the time or death threshold and if Henry had joined me. How could he? Kyle tried to cross with me in Alexandria, but the door would not open for him. I pushed the thought of him out of my head. In my dying moments, I refused to think about Kyle. I forced myself to think about Hannah and Henry, and Beth and Hector. My thoughts spun around until I accepted my death. I was too tired to continue to fight. I had lost Henry. Hannah would only be a memory. I choked in a breath, my throat closed in on itself. I lost consciousness.

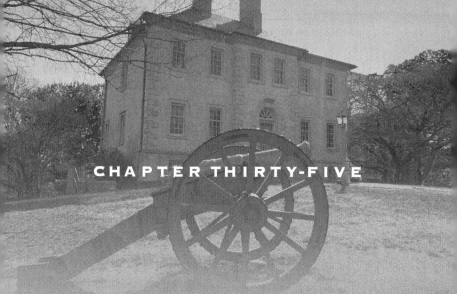

CHAPTER THIRTY-FIVE

Beep. Beep. Beep. Pause. Beep. Beep. Beep. Pause. "The afterlife has rhythmic mechanical beeps? Odd," I thought. My throat and arm ached. I squeezed my eyes tight. I couldn't speak, it felt as though something recently was down my throat. My heart rate skyrocketed in a panic. The beeps increased astronomically. Alarm bells rang through my ears. The blood coursed through my veins and thudded in my ears. My eyes blurred as I tried to focus on what was happening. A bright light above me filled the room. Voices from every direction came at me all at once.

Where was I?

What was happening?

Was I still alive?

Yes. I must be alive. I was in pain. But, how?

I looked around the room and tried to focus on the faces. A woman was speaking to me. Her face leaned in towards mine. I couldn't understand what she was saying.

I tried to speak. My vocal cords were tight. Reaching up to touch my throat, I noticed resistance from something attached to my hand. Someone grabbed my wrist and held it down next to me. Panic continued to course through me. Was that a needle? A warm sensation moved from my hand and up my arm. Whatever had just happened had a calming effect. I could feel my panic and heart slow. My breathing slowed. Thoughts slowed down.

"Amelia," a woman's voice said to me. I looked to my right, towards the voice. A woman with navy blue scrubs stood next to me. Her blond hair pulled back in a bun. "Amelia," she repeated.

I looked at her, unable to speak. I blinked. Scared, a tear rolled down my cheek.

"Amelia," she said again. "I'm Katlynn, your nurse. Doctor Jensen is on her way." She rubbed my right shoulder.

I tried to look around the room. The bright light blinded me. I opened my mouth to speak, but nothing came out. I touched my throat. "You just had an intubation tube removed. Don't speak." Katlynn looked behind her in anticipation of someone walking through the door. I could hear the fast footsteps coming down the hall as well. Someone was running to my room.

The door opened and an older woman rushed in, her mousy brown hair laid around her shoulders. She had a white lab coat worn over her dark blue scrubs. A stethoscope hung around her neck. Identification tags hung off the pocket of her lab coat, but I couldn't make out the words. It was all a blur. She looked over towards my left arm, lifted a bandage off it, and placed it back down.

When her cool hand touched my neck, it startled me. "I'm checking the swelling. It is looking better." The doctor shined a penlight in my right eye, then my left. "Can you follow my finger?" She asked, moving her finger from left to right in front of my face. I followed with my eyes. "Good. Good. It looks like you are coming around." She motioned to Katlynn, who pulled things out of a nearby cabinet. "I'm Doctor Jensen. You're at VCU in Richmond. You were transported here three days ago." She put the earpiece from her stethoscope in her ears and placed the diaphragm against my chest and moved it around. Next, she held my wrist and looked at her watch. Her expression was unmoving. I couldn't tell if what she discovered was good, bad, or what. "You gave us quite a scare, Miss Murray."

My eyes shot back and forth as Katlynn approached. "We extubated the tube from your throat. You will be uncomfortable, but from what we can tell, you've been through much worse."

Just because I went through much worse didn't mean I wanted to go through more pain. My throat was sore. I inhaled deeply, which caused a coughing fit. That didn't help the pain in my throat. "Henry?" I whispered.

"I take it that is the man found lying next to you?" Doctor Jensen asked. I nodded in response. "They admitted him at the same time. You both sustained quite severe injuries."

Admitted. Injuries. Not dead. "Hannah?" It hurt to

speak. Katlynn brought me a cup of ice chips and spooned one into my mouth. The cold, numbing sensation felt good.

"Your daughter has spent night and day here," Katlynn said as she gave me another ice chip. "She went home to change and shower, but I called her to let her know while Doctor Jensen was examining you. She knows you're awake and is on her way back from Williamsburg."

I pushed my head deep into the pillow. Henry was still alive. I was still alive. And Hannah had somehow found out that I had come back. I wanted to know more, but the simple strain of trying to speak hurt my throat. With my energy depleted, I closed my eyes to sleep until Hannah returned. She would let me know what happened.

Dreams came in vivid flashes. Musket balls whizzed past me. The shouts of men yelling orders. Cries of pain. Calls of victory. Lovett's arm dangled from his body. The searing pain from a bullet or arrow or wood from a wagon pierced through my arm. I never found out what had caused the gash in my left arm. Or I chose to forget it. Someone had wanted me dead; they wanted us all dead. Gunshots and arrows had filled the air that day on the battlefield next to the Monongahela. Wood splintered from the wagons when the bullets pierced through them. So many men and women died. I hoped Little Millie didn't die. Some warriors led her away, along with other women and children. The young Private Johnson, only sixteen years old, laid on the battlefield. He saved me more times than I could count. I jerked awake in a cold sweat. I tried to sit up, only to be stopped by the ache in my arm.

"Mom," called out Hannah, and she raced to my side from the chair that sat next to the window. The afternoon light replaced the blinding overhead light from earlier.

"Hannah," I whispered out and reached my right hand towards her. "I love you." The waterworks started. It was such a relief to know she was with me.

"Why did you leave me?"

"Water." I reached towards the cup that was on my bed tray next to the bed. If I was going to hold any sort of conversation with her, I would need a lot of water and ice to soothe my throat. I reached for the remote attached to the bed and used the buttons to sit my bed up. Hannah handed me the pink plastic cup, and I took a sip from the straw, letting the water coat my throat. "Didn't," I took another sip, "mean to." Another sip. "Kyle chased me." Another sip. "No choice." My throat was on fire.

"What happened to you?" She took my hand and sat down on the bed next to my legs. "How did you end up back here and like this?" She waved her hand over me.

There was not enough water in the world to explain what happened. I took a deep breath and coughed out. Panic raced across her face. I held up my hand to wave her off. When the coughing subsided, I took another sip of water. "Battle," I whispered out. "Shot." Sip.

"You couldn't just go back and keep out of trouble?" She asked, placing her fists firmly on her hips.

I let out a stifled laugh. I swear trouble followed me wherever I went. "Henry?"

"They had to sedate him. He woke up this morning in

a panic," she said as she rubbed my leg. "Poor guy, he has no clue what or where or, I guess, when he is."

Tears poured out of my eyes. I grabbed a tissue to blow my nose. It caused me to cough, out of control. I had to wave Hannah off again. I sat up and threw my legs over the side of the bed. If Henry was in the hospital, I needed to find him. I had to be by his side to let him know he was safe.

"You can't get out of bed." She put her hand on my right shoulder and edged me back into the bed. "You can barely sit or breathe. He will be fine for now." She patted my leg. "When you are able, we'll get you a wheelchair to visit him."

A tearful nod let her know I knew she was right, but I would have crawled down the hall, dragging the IV pole behind me. I had to see him with my eyes to know he was okay.

"How is he?" Sip. "Really?" My throat was aflame.

"The both of you were close to dying. If you hadn't been found when you were, the swelling and infection would have completely closed your throat. As it was, they could barely get the intubation tube in. They wanted to do a trach but thought they would try the tube first." She looked at over at my arm. "They've been pumping some pretty heavy-duty antibiotics through you for the infection. Good thing you had left the drainage hole, or they might have had to take your arm. The doctor explained to me that the infection could have been much worse... for both of you." The Widow Jackson really knew what she was doing.

"Henry?" I had to know. I didn't care as much as how I was doing. I needed to know what had happened to him.

"They found a bullet," Hannah said and rubbed her forehead. Disbelief? Confusion? "No, they thought it was a musket ball. They asked me how he could've been shot. They thought it was a reenactment event gone wrong, considering the way you two were dressed." I huffed out a laugh when she said that. It definitely went wrong. I still held a grudge against Braddock. "I told them that must have been it." She let out a small laugh. "His infection was deep. It was moving towards his lungs. They put him on a respirator and kept him sedated. The doctor was pretty upset that the two of you hadn't found medical attention sooner."

"How did you know?" I fiddled with the cup. Something a little stronger than water was in my future.

"Oh! Emily, the living history interpreter at the Henry Spencer House recognized you." Hannah's eyes lit up. "Her and I had met up a couple of times after you disappeared the last time. I had gone to look at your portrait and tried to find if you had left me any sort of message hidden on a wall or in your notebook. Which, I'm pretty upset that you didn't."

"Sorry," I wept out. "Couldn't..." She waved me off before I could struggle to get out another word.

"Three days ago, while at work, she got the museum ready to close for the day and she found you laying on the floor—again. She saw that you and a man were injured. Called nine-one-one and then me. I got there before the ambulance. They wanted to take you to

Riverside, but the trauma center here could take care of you better."

"Cheese and rice." Sip.

"Yeah, you're telling me. Anyway... so you almost died from the infection closing around your throat. Henry's infection went deep and impacted his ability to take a breath. So basically, the two of you were suffocating to death. And then there's the sepsis. So, yeah. There's that," her words were coming out in an excited hundred miles an hour. "You've been gone for months, and you didn't leave me a message."

"Couldn't." I took another sip. I couldn't keep up with all the sipping and talking. My throat burned in protest. "Wasn't there. Didn't know how." I got frustrated with the lack of ability to communicate.

"Yeah, we found your SUV at a parking structure in Alexandria. Cora called Beth looking for you."

"Why Beth? Not you?"

"That's what I wanted to know. But I guess she figured she talked you into doing another historical story and thought you might have contacted Beth again for some research. I thought you had stopped looking at trying to go back. You promised me."

"I stopped," I said, taking a breath and another sip. "Didn't try. Just happened." Sip. Choke on water. "Promise."

"Well, whatever happened, I'm happy you're home and alive," she said. She got up to give me a hug, avoiding my left arm. "I called Beth on my way here. I'll check in on Henry when she gets here."

I nodded in response. All the excitement had worn me out. I patted her hand, laid back on my pillow, closed my eyes, and fell back asleep.

"I swear, Amelia Murray, you are going to be the death of me," Beth's exuberant voice came flying through the room and woke me up.

"Spencer," I whispered out as I woke up.

"Holy moly! You didn't?" she said. I gave her a half-asleep smile. "Well, Missus Spencer, your incredibly handsome—and sedated—husband is in the next room. I peeked on my way in. Hannah is speaking with Katlynn right now."

I sat my bed up. "You can call me Lady Spencer. Thank you very much." I hated being stuck in bed, unable to run next door and sit by Henry's side. I took a sip of water. My throat felt like it was lined with sandpaper. "I need to," I paused to choke down a swallow, "see him."

"Of course you do," Beth said as she patted my leg. All the leg patting made me feel like they felt sorry for me. It was irritating as all get out. "But you just woke up from being unconscious for the past three days. You can't rush it."

"Video?" I had to see that he was okay.

"Sure, let me see what we can do."

Hannah slid through the open door. "So, sleeping beauty in the next room won't be getting his cannula out today. His right lung still isn't functioning the way she wants it. He had a raging infection."

I struggled to get out of the bed, but the blanket and sheet twisted around my legs like an octopus holding on with all eight tentacles. Knowing he was laying there in such terrible shape and I was lying around my bed was too much for me to handle.

"Hold your horses," Beth held my hand down. "You have tubes and wires hooked up to you. I'm sure you haven't noticed, but there is a catheter up in you, along with this IV, that I know you've noticed. Let's not forget you don't have the strength to just run next door. No. You've worked too hard to get the two of you here. Don't screw up your health now."

I laid back on my pillow and slammed my hand into the mattress. Tears welled up. I was too tired to fight them. "Video? Please."

"Let's do a video call," Beth said to Hannah. They pulled out their phones and made a video call. Hannah went next door while I held Beth's phone.

"Are you sure you can handle this?" Hannah asked, camera facing her. I nodded. She flipped to the camera that showed Henry. My hand shot up to cover my mouth. Henry laid in the bed, not moving, except for the rise and fall of his chest. A small plastic tube ran up his nose to help him breathe. An IV was stuck in his hand. I had expected that. A large bandage covered his wound under his right clavicle from the musket ball. Pads with wires attached were stuck to his chest. Although the lights were dimmed, I could see the color had returned to his skin. He was no longer pale and sporting the grayish tinge of death. Besides being sedated in a hospital bed, with tubes and wires hanging on and in him, he looked healthy. Well, healthier than he had when I last saw him. The shock subsided, so I slowly removed my hand from my mouth. I took a deep breath. Knowing he was doing better, I could relax.

Two days later, they were ready to discharge me. Which was the same day they were going to take Henry off his sedation. I needed to be by his side when he woke up. This entire world would be a complete shock to him, and Doctor Jensen agreed it would be best if I stayed by his side during the transition. I was still weak in the knees and they decided that Scott—the nurse that was now on duty and taking care of Henry—should push me in a wheelchair to his room. I was concerned about how Henry would take seeing me in a wheelchair, but I would not argue with the medical staff if that is what it meant for me to stay by Henry's side.

After removing the cannula and the slowing of the drip, Doctor Jensen left, and Scott wheeled me in next to Henry's bed. I held Henry's hand and waited for him to come around to the land of the living. They said it would take only a few minutes, but with Henry's low tolerance level to the medications, I was sure it would take longer than it took me. I was concerned about his reaction, never experienced being in a hospital like this, and the machines or the tubes sticking in his hand. Scott would monitor his vitals from the nurse's station. I would stay with him while he woke up, to prevent any additional trauma.

I waited by his side, emergency call button at the ready, and watched for any signal of waking up. Hannah, Beth, and Hector waited in the hallway. I could hear them chatting with Scott. Henry's hand was cold, the life drained from him because of his injuries and the sedation over the past week. I continued to hold his hand to give him some of my warmth. A slight twitch in a finger got my attention. He slowly woke up, and I gulped down my fear of his response to the 21st century.

His breathing increased to a normal, but excited, rhythm as he stirred in his bed. "Henry," I whispered as I continued to rub his hand. We dimmed the room to prevent the bright blast of light from piercing into his eyes. "Can you hear me? Henry?"

He let out a grumbled moan. "It's Amelia. Before you open your eyes, I need to warn you about what happened." I immediately doubted my choice in words. He jerked his hand away from me and patted his chest and rubbed his hands on his arms. His left hand touched the IV that they placed in his right hand. "Don't mess with that. It's your IV... for medicine." He touched it again, gently running his fingers over the port and tubing. "Don't open your eyes yet. Just listen to me. When I'm finished, you can open your eyes then. It will be difficult for you to speak. So just nod. Don't answer me just yet." He slowly nodded. Beeps from the machines faded into background noise. "You are in a hospital in Richmond. Our injuries were severe, and the infection nearly killed us. But we both kept all of our body parts and we will live." I took his left hand in mine and gave it a kiss. He started to open his eyes. "Please, not yet. Keep them closed."

He groaned and kept them closed. He could tell he was somewhere new. The surrounding sounds, tubes, the bed, the temperature-controlled room. I could tell he sensed what I was going to tell him. Anticipation filled the room.

"When we went through the front door of your house, I traveled. We traveled. Together. We're in my time. When you open your eyes, please don't panic. Are you ready?"

"Yes," he whispered out. His throat sore from the tubing.

"Don't try to speak. I'll get you some water in just a moment." I gave his hand a squeeze. "You'll feel your bed move under you. It will be smooth, but the sensation will feel... well... I don't know. It'll just feel weird." He nodded, and I used the buttons on the side of the bed to raise the top half of his body into a seated position. "Okay, open your eyes slowly."

He opened his eyes, slow and unsure. His eyes grew to the size of saucers. His body tensed; he jerked back in his bed. The beeping on the heart monitor quickened. He pulled his hand out of mine and grasped the bedrails. Knuckles white, as if he had to hold on for dear life. I followed his eyes as they continued to dart around the room. His eyes fell on mine. The look of terror lingered, but appeared to diminish slowly. I could tell his acceptance of being able to travel through time was a lot different from mine. I had science fiction, movies, and books to tease about the possibility. If he had remained in his time, it would be another one hundred and forty years before H. G. Wells would write *The Time Machine*. The beeping on the heart monitor slowed down to a normal rhythm.

"Are you okay?" I looked at him, trying to read his face. He looked around the room again and nodded. "They had to put a tube down your throat to help you breathe. The infection from the musket ball had spread to your lung.

Give it a day or two. You'll be speaking normal in no time."

He took a sip from the cup of water I had handed him. He squeezed the pink cup, testing the flexibility of the plastic. "It's made from plastic. You'll find that we have a lot of things made from different materials than you have experienced."

He handed me back the cup and pressed his body into the pillow. "Do you think you can handle visitors?" He shot a look at me. "No, no one you know. But they know you. Hannah, Beth, and Hector. You can say no. They will understand. One of them has been here with me the entire time I was a patient in the next room. They've kept an eye on you as well." He shook his head. The room was too much to take in. If we inundated him with new people, it might become overwhelming.

"I understand, but you will have to deal with the nurse and the doctor." He slowly nodded his understanding. At least, I thought he understood everything I was telling him. When we were traveling together and I would talk about things from my time, sometimes, he wouldn't understand what I was babbling on about, but just listened and nodded his head. I had a feeling that was what he was doing now. Not really understanding, but didn't want to tell me he didn't understand. "And since you came in with a gunshot, the police will come in and want to question you." He really shot a look of confusion at me. "Police are like the Governor's men. They protect us from criminals." His confused look shifted to concern; he had committed no crime. "When you can speak, they will ask about your injury. Doctor Jensen was required to report it and they will want to know. And we must figure out what we are going to do about identification." Oh, man, this was more complicated than I had thought it ever would be. "We will tell them you visited and lost your passport. We'll give them your name, I guess. You can tell them you didn't see who shot you. They won't be able to trace the bullet, anyway."

I rubbed my forehead. It was one thing to slip in time to the distant past, where it didn't matter if I had identification or not. But slipping into the future where Henry had no paper trail and was shot? My stress level increased as I tried to think it all through. How could we pull this off? Police would want to see identification. Henry had none. I couldn't even think about the hospital bill. I had medical insurance, most of my bill would be covered. But Henry's? He would be lucky if his bill didn't reach over a million dollars. It was America, after all. People go bankrupt over medical bills. I had to tell myself that things have a way of working out. It had to work out. Right?

I stayed by Henry's side over the next couple of days. Hannah, Beth, and Hector stayed out of the mix until later. I kept the television off, an attempt to help ease him into the 21st century, instead of throwing him off the cliff into the wild world of news and entertainment television.

He spoke in a hoarse whisper, his throat still raw from the tubes. By the time the police came in to question him about the bullet, he had an ambushed down an alley, shot, stolen identification story down and believable. I didn't want to think about how we would explain things when they try to run his identification. We had to go on hoping that there would be no further issues regarding the gunshot wounds. I gave my information. Of course, my previous disappearance record showed up. That only brought in more questions on my wound. Lies and misdirection got me through that line of questioning. I would have to stay out of trouble for the next twenty years just to shake off my recent troubles. I was probably at the top of their suspect list. My first husband had died from someone crashing his car off the road and shooting him. Now, I end up in the hospital with another man that had been shot. Men should stay away from me—I was a bad luck charm to getting shot. A sign worn around my neck or tattoo it on my forehead, stating "Stay Away" might keep the male population safe from me. Maybe I should look at getting a cat instead of keeping another husband?

CHAPTER THIRTY-SIX

"No more electronic leashes," I said to Beth as she drove us to her house after breaking us out of the hospital. Hector sat next to Beth, with Henry and me in the backseat of their car. Hannah planned on meeting us at Beth and Hector's house in Williamsburg. I wanted to sneak out before the police investigation, but we stayed until the proper discharge. I didn't need another reason for the police to come looking for Amelia-the-troublemaker. "Do you realize how difficult it is to hide a cellphone in the 18th century?"

"Can we go back?" Henry asked. The look of terror crossed over his face as we raced down the freeway at 75 miles per hour. His knuckles turned white as he squeezed the life out of my hand. We completed a trip that would have taken us an entire day on a horse in less than an hour.

"I don't know." My shoulders sunk. I didn't know how or why I time traveled. This last time, I pulled him with me. If I hadn't, he would certainly have died. No question about that. "I don't know how any of it works. And I didn't know I could drag you along with me. So, there's that." Rubbing Henry's leg with my hand I freed from his death grip, I tried to comfort him. I was not sure if he wanted to get back home or away from this clearly terrifying road trip.

"She tried finding her way back before, you know?" Hector piped in. "After she came back the first time, we took her to Fort Ashby, and she visited the museum in Williamsburg a hundred times, opening and closing doors she wasn't supposed to touch. She almost got herself kicked out of there and barred for life."

Henry looked at me. "Then how were you able to travel again?"

Beth looked back through her rearview mirror. I closed my eyes to think about the events of each time I traveled. "I'm not entirely sure. Something was always happening when I went through. I wasn't thinking too much about traveling, only that I had to get through the door. Twice, it was because I was running from Kyle. I was excited about..." I looked over at Henry. I didn't want to say that I was excited to get back to his bed in front of our friends, "excited about an upcoming event. Then there was this last time, desperate to get you home to die. Nothing consistent."

"Except," Beth interjected, "it appears there was heightened emotion involved. With each time you traveled, you said you were scared, excited, scared, and terrified."

"You might be on to something. Although, anytime Kyle was around, I was terrified. There is something about him that makes my skin crawl in fear. There was always a coin as well. Emotion. Coin. Door. The time travel trifecta." I looked over towards Henry. By the look on his face, he either thought I was crazy or considered that I could be correct. Either way...

Henry leaned back and closed his eyes. There was a pale tinge to his skin and sweat formed across his brow. He reached over and held my hand. It must have been too much for him to take in. He squeezed my hand in reassurance. "Riding in a car is much like sailing for the first time."

"Oh! You're carsick. I thought I was stressing you out with all the time travel discussion." I gave a half-laugh of relief. "You'll eventually get used to it." Beth cracked the back windows for some fresh air. Henry, startled by the electric window, enjoyed the fresh air. We stopped only five times for him to heave on the side of the road.

"Everyone is in a rush." He wiped his brow.

"Well, we were in a rush during your time. Up and down Virginia. We were always moving."

"Yes, but you get there faster and then turn around and race off to the next location. Do you ever slow down?"

"Of course we do." I had to stop for a moment and think about it. Compared to Henry's time, we really rushed from one place to another. Run to the grocery store. Devour our meal. Then rush off to the next location. Kids went to school. Sat in a classroom for fifty minutes. Rush to their next class. Then their next class. Finally, they rushed home to rush through their homework. We didn't stop long enough to take in the smell of the trees as we did as our horse meandered down the trail. The travel took days, giving the opportunity to have long conversations. We would pull up to Beth and Hector's house in a few minutes, and the conversation would end after only a half hour. This was going to take an adjustment for both of us.

"When Amelia started her research into Washington's battles, she had said that it was much simpler and slower in the eighteenth century," Beth turned the car down their street. Now moving 25 miles per hour, instead of the 75 as we flew down the freeway, Henry looked around at the houses and cars we passed. None of these buildings existed during his time. Everything was completely unfamiliar to him. "I'm sure she discovered things were different, but along with our speed and complications, we have advances in technology, medicine, and politics that you may find difficult to leave behind. The antibiotics that saved both of your lives wouldn't have been possible two hundred-fifty years ago. And as you've discovered, the sanitation of indoor plumbing and central heating and air make life more comfortable as we are racing around in trains, planes, and automobiles at breakneck speeds. I'm not sure how long you will stay here, but you may find it difficult to leave behind." Beth, the college professor for Colonial America, was quite levelheaded with her explanation. Before I traveled to 1754 and met Henry, I told her the past was simple and idyllic. She laughed at me. After two trips to the past, I understood the humor she saw in my naïveté.

We pulled up to the house, all of us silent. While we were stuck in the hospital, everything was controlled. The scenery didn't change. Nurses and doctors came and went, but we saw familiar faces. I felt as though we were thrust back into the future and, knowing Henry, he would be quiet as he tried to take it all in. My excitement to show him everything had to be tempered. I was in my element and wanted to share this exciting world with him. Tonight would be a quiet evening at the house, just the five of us: Henry, me, Beth, Hector, and Hannah. Even then, I thought it might be too much for him to take in. I was wrong.

"I would like to go to the house tomorrow," Henry said to me as we were getting ready for bed. He pulled off the shirt Hector had let him borrow. We couldn't leave the hospital with the ripped, bloodied, and dirty clothes we had arrived in. Beth had brought me clothes from my house in Fredericksburg, and Hector brought some of his clothes for Henry to wear. We would have to go shopping for clothes. Eventually. When I could order another debit card... again. I thought back to my earlier conversation with Beth, stating that I refused to get another cell phone, and laughed. I couldn't survive without a cell phone. Now, I wondered how long I could keep my debit card and key fob before I was whisked off to the 18th century again.

I eased out of my jeans, threw them in the laundry hamper, and entered the ensuite bathroom. I looked at my arm, still healing from being grazed by a bullet or whatever it was, during the battle near the Monongahela. There was too much commotion to find the culprit of my wound. It would leave a scar. "Are you sure you're ready for it? It's kind of difficult to see knowing that it isn't yours anymore. It's like walking into a weird dream where the place is familiar, but it isn't." I grabbed my toothbrush.

"Amelia," Henry said as he leaned on the doorway to the bathroom. His grip on the door handle caused his knuckles to turn white. "Stop treating me like a half-wit."

My mouth opened and closed like a fish gulping for air out of water. It left me speechless. He was correct. I was being inconsiderate in his ability to adapt to two hundred and sixty years into the future. "I didn't think you are a half-wit. Perhaps I just wanted to protect you not understanding things because things differ from what you're used to." I was Amelia-splaining everything to him. As if I knew everything and he knew nothing. I could be such an unintentional jerk.

"Have you considered that I understand things are different?" Henry's voice was fast and louder. "Give me time to take it in. If I have questions, I'll ask. Just stop... stop treating me like a child."

There went that foot of mine, swiftly and firmly inserted into my mouth. I had to trust that he would try to learn and adapt to his new surroundings, much like I had to learn to adapt to his. With him in my time, I became more confused than ever.

"You're right. I'm sorry." A deep breath helped me center myself. "I guess I got overexcited to show you my world, as you had showed me yours." I spit out my toothpaste.

"Slow down." He put his hands on my shoulders. "We have time."

As I laid in bed next to Henry, snuggled up against him, I could feel his chest rise and fall with each breath. He was not asleep, and neither was I. We hadn't been truly alone in quite a while and I neither one of us was up to full fighting strength.

I woke in the middle of the night. My mind raced around the world and to the past and back to the future. How could he sleep when I was apprehensive regarding our planned trip to his house—well, what was his house two hundred sixty years ago—the next morning? With him in the future, I wondered if things had changed from the last visit. I stepped on the butterfly and changed what would have been by bringing him to the future with me. However, if I didn't bring him with me—not that I controlled that little adventure—he would have died.

"Apollo, stop trying to shove your tongue down my throat." I pushed the Irish Wolfhound's face away from mine. "Is this how you're going to wake me every morning, big boy?"

Henry stretched next to me. "Should I be jealous?" A sweet smile spread across his face.

"Maybe?" I scratched behind Apollo's ear. Artemis joined in for the morning rubs. "I mean, he is a Greek god and I think he has a thing for kissing me."

"He does this every morning?" Surprised these giant

beasts were permitted to live inside the house instead of a barn, he shook his head in disbelief.

"Yup. I'm not sure how he opens the door. However, every morning I'm here, he thinks he needs to wake me up with a kiss." I looked towards Henry. He sat up in the bed and studied Artemis's brown eyes looking at him, her head laid on his lap. "The house opens at nine for tours. Knowing my furry alarm clock," I gave Apollo another scratch behind his ear, "it is probably seven thirty. That will give us time to get ready and walk to the historic district."

We dressed and joined Beth and Hector downstairs for breakfast. The smell of coffee wafted up the stairs. Pans clanked on the stove. The slosh of a thick liquid whisked in a bowl told me I was in for a gastronomical delight. Beth and Hector were making my favorite breakfast—french toast. After breakfast, we were to meet Hannah at the ticket office. With my ATM card lost somewhere in 1755, I would be at the mercy of my friends and family.

"It is quite remarkable," Henry said to Hector. "When I look at you, I am reminded of a young lieutenant I served with under Colonel Washington. You are but an older version of him."

"Wouldn't he be two hundred eighty years old if he were alive today?" Hector laughed. "I think I'm the junior version of him."

"Well, and his name was Hector Bennet, so there's that," I chimed in. It really was a fascinating coincidence that my friends Hector and Beth Bennedet looked like the 1755 versions of Hector Bennet and Elizabeth Woods.

"However, that Hector and Elizabeth didn't know each other. Hector was off fighting against the French in Pennsylvania, well... I suppose it was still part of Virginia at the time. Anyway," I waved off the thought of the shifting borders of the colonies, it wasn't important at the moment. "Our younger version of Elizabeth was in Fredericksburg, pining away for George Washington, her childhood friend."

"I'm not sure she was pining for Washington," Henry rebutted, taking a bite of his french toast.

"I think she just didn't know any better because she hadn't met Lieutenant Bennet." Beth stood from the table to take her plate to the sink. Henry's chair scratched across the floor as he pounced to his feet. Hector looked at Henry and tilted his head like a confused puppy, wondering what sent a shot of electricity through him.

I smiled. "You can take the gentleman out of 1755, but you can't take 1755 manners out of the gentleman." I looked over towards Henry and grabbed his hand as he sat back down. "We are a bit less formal, most of the time."

"Yes, of course." Henry straightened his shirt and sat down, looking slightly embarrassed.

"I think it is wonderful and one of the many things I love about you, but I'm afraid Hector might be worried that he has to step up his game." I shot a smile over to Hector and Beth. Hector sat with a sheepish grin on his face.

Beth finished loading her plate and fork into the dishwasher and walked behind Hector. She wrapped her arms around him, kissed him on the cheek, "You could learn a thing or two from him."

I sat back in my chair and savored the last bite of eggy bread before we shoved our dishes into the dishwasher. "And what exactly does that," Henry began as he waved his hand towards the dishwasher, "that machine do with the plates?"

"It washes them, so we don't have to do it ourselves." Hector said, taking Henry's plate from him.

"Fascinating." Henry studied it for a moment, scraping his hand across his chin. He would've studied it all day, if I hadn't forced us out of the house.

We headed towards Colonial Williamsburg, leaving Apollo and Artemis at home. Normally, I would have taken them on a walk with me. It had become our routine while I stayed with Beth. They weren't allowed in the museum, and I had every intention of going inside. Calling it a museum instead of Henry's house left a sour taste in my mouth.

Hannah met us at the ticket office. After a tour with us, she would head to work as a server at *The Salty Dog*, an old pub close to the historic district. As we turned down the street towards the house, my stomach clenched. I laced my fingers through Henry's chilly hand and squeezed. He might not want to admit it, but he was as nervous as we all were. I had visited here with Beth and Hannah after the first time I slipped through time. That early morning, though, it was completely different.

Henry stood stone still. He might have stopped breathing. He stared at the house. It was his old mistress colliding with his new world. His chest quivered with his deep breath. He started up the stairs towards the front door. "We have to enter through the side gate, the one next to the old kitchen."

"What? Why? There is a perfectly good door there," he said as he gestured towards the red door atop of the steps. A family comprising a father, mother, a boy of about seven years old, and a three-year-old girl on the mother's hip exited through the front door. "See, they used the door."

"They only let us out the front. We need to enter through the side and in through the back." I gave a slight pull to our left towards the small white building. The building had been the first kitchen Henry had built. The well in front had dried up within the first year and a new kitchen and well were built on the other side of the house. Henry had used it for storage, but he was going to move his office to the small building in order to give me space in the house. Now, the building was locked and probably filled with lawn equipment and cobwebs. The windows were too dirty for me to confirm my suspicions.

"We're going to give you some space to look around," Hector said as he, Beth, and Hannah wandered into the garden. Henry continued to look at the locked door.

"It's locked." I pulled him towards the garden. The rest of our group continued to work their way down towards the stable. "I would be surprised if anything you had left in there still existed." His only reply was a small nod.

The sun filled the garden, or what remained of the once grand garden, and brought Virginia's summer heat.

The air hung heavy with humidity. Sweat tickled down my back. Henry had divided the garden into two sections. The section on the left was the kitchen garden, which was now relegated to a small patch of about twenty feet squared at the very back. Once, it had taken up the entire section of the yard. Stretching from one end to the other. By this time, the long, neat rows would overflow with fruits and vegetables. Josiah, one of Henry's servants, was proud of the bounty they would pull year-after-year. It would feed the household throughout the season. Beatrice, the cook, would pickle and preserve the rest to help last throughout the rest of the year. The cellar held rows of crock-lined shelves, brimming with Beatrice's preserves, hog heads filled with grain, salted pork, and tobacco. Even though Henry didn't smoke, tobacco was always good to have around to sell or trade. Bottles of wine, whiskey, brandy, ale, and other spirits would fill shelves and rooms in the cellar. With Henry away frequently, the servants would spend their days caring for the house, garden, chickens, goats, and horses. They were now long dead. The alcohol and dry goods are gone. In its place stood what was once Henry's home.

We worked our way through the flower garden. We trailed our way past the flowers to an ivy-covered outdoor room. As we entered, we looked up and noticed the beams holding up the ivy roof. "Looks like the skeleton of a ship," Henry said. Curved thick beams arched over our heads. It looked as though a ship's structural beams had been placed upside down in the backyard. A center beam spanned the length of ten-foot by fifteen-foot room. From the center beam overhead, arched beams, placed every five feet or so, touched the ground like spider legs. Clever.

"Should we make our way towards the house?" We looked out across the garden towards the house. Henry avoided looking at the large, red-bricked house. He built the house with every room and outbuilding placed where he wanted them. Now, it was as though he had to ask permission to enter. He couldn't go through the front door of his house. I shuddered at the thought of reminding him, but it was no longer his house. "Come on, let's go," I said, pulling him by the hand back through the garden and up the stairs to the back door. As we entered, I saw Beth, Hector, and Hannah looking in the old stables, now vacant of Louis and Toni, our horses that helped get us home from the battle.

We entered through the back door, greeted by a female staff member, called a living history interpreter, dressed in colonial period attire. I had hoped to have seen Emily. She had been a familiar face during my previous visits. The woman's brown eyes grew to the size of saucers. The color drained from her already fair skin. I could see her sway; certain she would faint. Henry caught her by the elbow and helped her to a nearby chair.

"Are you okay?" I asked.

"I'm sorry," she said. "I thought you were..." She blinked repeatedly. "Well, you look like the couple that built the house. I thought you were ghosts."

I wondered if the portraits would still be there. With her reaction to us, I could only assume that they were still hanging in the library. "We are not ghosts," I laughed. Of course, we looked like the people in the paintings. We were the people in the paintings. Poor woman, if she knew the truth, she would have a heart attack on the spot. I might have been responsible for Jumonville and a few other men's death, but I would not be responsible for her death. "We are just here to look around the place. If you're going to be okay, we'll finish the tour."

CHAPTER THIRTY-SEVEN

*H*enry and I entered the library. I motioned to him to look at the portraits. "We haven't sat for portraits. How did these..." he trailed off, unable to speak. A sharp tip of a knife touched my back. A hand grabbed my upper arm with force. I immediately knew who it was. Kyle.

"You bastard," I blurted out as I tried to spin out of his grasp.

Henry spun around and came face-to-face with Kyle.

"Teach," Henry growled.

"Where's my coin, Spencer?" Kyle bit through his teeth.

"Who's Teach? What coin? How do you know each other?" I was at a loss. How did they know each other?

I looked around for someone to rescue us out of this situation. The interpreter gave a disapproving look for the noise we were making, but apparently hadn't seen the knife.

"Kyle, you're not supposed to be in here. I thought you were persona non grata for slicing the woman's portrait," I said in a severe tone.

"Oh, you know it's you," Kyle started, leading me out the back door. "If you don't want me to make her my pincushion, I suggest you come with me so we can discuss you getting me my money."

"For the love of... what in the hell is going on?" I demanded as we quickened our pace down the garden path to the ivy-covered room at the back. I looked for Beth, Hector, and Hannah. Surely, they had to see what was going on and call the police.

"Your boyfriend stole my treasure," Kyle said, spinning me around.

"What treasure?"

"Do you want to tell her, or shall I? You can guess which version will make you look like the bigger thief." Kyle held up his knife. "And then, when you think you've explained your way out of this mess, you can get me the treasure. I don't want her to die thinking you are honorable."

"Die? You've lost your mind." My head was spinning. "You wouldn't kill me."

"Do you want to test that theory out?" Kyle squeezed my arm harder. The pressure on my left biceps made me want to scream out in pain. "I've killed before over it. I won't lose any sleep over you dying. If your boyfriend wants you to live, he will tell me where the treasure is."

"What? No villain monologue to stall before we get

away from your evil clutches?" I snarked and tugged my arm from Kyle's grasp.

Henry explained how he met Kyle. When Henry arrived at the port in Norfolk from England, he hadn't much more than the clothes on his back and the portrait of his first wife that he had stolen from his brother, Charles the Duke of Marlborough. I knew he took the portrait as the only punishment he could instill upon his brother. It was there he met Casper Teach, the man I knew as Kyle Smith. After a hearty night of drinking, Casper told Henry of the story of Blackbeard's hidden treasure. Casper wanted to find the treasure to take back to his widowed mother to support her and their plantation he inherited from his grandparents.

"How did you know of Blackbeard's treasure?" I asked. "If you were looking for the treasure in 1748, which was seven years ago... sort of... in a roundabout kind of way. Geez, keeping the time travel timeline is confusing." I ran my hand across my forehead. The humidity only muddied my thoughts. "Wait, Kyle, Casper, whatever your name is... when were you born?"

"Seventeen nineteen. January." Casper—or was it Kyle?—said. "What does that matter?"

"What year did Blackbeard die?"

"He died in seventeen eighteen," Casper's voice choked, "November twenty-second. He was my father."

Henry and I stared at each other. This was news to both of us.

"So, I'm guessing the two of you found the treasure?

Or is there some other treasure that you are claiming Henry stole from you?"

"Aye, we found it," Casper said. "We were to split it."

"Then you disappeared," Henry interrupted. "What else was I supposed to do?"

"Do you remember that barn we were going to stay in?" Kyle turned to Henry.

"You went to check out the house to see if anyone was there. You never came back to where I was waiting. I stayed until morning by the creek, with the wagons loaded up." Henry's voice began to quicken and get louder. "I waited for you. Thought they must have killed you. I wasn't going to wait around for them to kill me as well."

"Well, I couldn't come back. I ended up here." Casper scrunched his nose to chase away his emotions. "I had to learn to survive. I ended up asking someone about you. They did an Internet search and found your house here." Casper pointed towards the house. I looked over and saw Beth, Hector, and Hannah exit through the back door and could see us standing in the doorway to the outdoor room. There was no use trying to wave them off without being noticed by Casper—or was it Kyle? He would harm them as well. "I went inside and saw the portraits of the two of you. I knew you took my money."

"I met you well before I traveled through time." I wracked through my memories, trying to remember the circumstances that I had met Casper. It was after my husband Todd was killed.

"Well, you see," Casper stopped speaking midsentence. In fact, I do not think he took a breath. The blood drained from his face. It was as though he saw a ghost. Hector, Beth, and Hannah approached us with confused looks on their faces.

"Everything good here?" Hector asked as he looked at the three of us. He glanced down and saw the knife in Casper's hand pressed up against my side.

"Grandfather?" Casper looked at Hector. He turned to Beth, "Grandmother? But how? The two of you were supposed to have died when I was but a boy."

"Pardon?" Beth and I said simultaneously and looked at each other.

"Oh, no. Kyle, I mean Casper. I think you have them confused," I said, my head spun. The longer this conversation lasted, the more I was going to melt into a sweaty puddle. The humidity and heat must have contributed to this delirium. "They have ancestors that look like them. Henry and I knew a Hector and Elizabeth in seventeen fifty-four, but they were too young to be your grandparents. Both were in their early twenties."

"That was the name of my grandparents. William Hector Ormond and Elizabeth Ormond."

"Sorry," Hector said. "That's not us. We're Hector and Beth Bennedet, not Ormond. And we're not from the seventeen hundreds. However, if you get rid of that knife that you have digging into Amelia's side, I can be whoever you need me to be."

Seeing that he was clearly outnumbered, Casper lowered his knife. "I want my money, Spencer." He pointed the knife in Henry's direction. "Get it for me. I'll be back." With that, he left us, almost in a run, towards the house.

I wanted to throw up. My stomach clenched and twisted. My pulse raced. Henry drew me into his arms and kissed me on the forehead. I could feel his heart trying to pound its way through his ribs. "Amelia, I," Henry began. I didn't let him finish.

Confused about what had just happened and the fact that Henry lied to me about his money, I had to get out of there and away from everyone. I couldn't process all the emotions that tumbled ferociously throughout my body. I pushed out of Henry's arms and stormed towards the house, emotions on fire, leaving everyone behind me.

The heat and humidity in the middle of summer in Virginia rivals that of the deep south. The sun scorched down, blazed hot. Walking outside from the cool air conditioning will turn someone into an instant puddle of sweat. The shade offered no respite. Quite frankly, my attitude matched the Virginia summer day. I was miserable to be around, and I didn't care who I scorched in my path.

Unfortunately, with no money, I had nowhere to go, but back to heartache. I found Henry, Beth, Hector, and Hannah standing in front of the Henry Spencer House.

"Better?" Hannah raised her eyebrows at me as I approached. "Listen, the two of you," she motioned towards me and Henry, "need to figure yourselves out. And I'm not sure what was going on with Kyle, but you need to figure that mess out, too. I'm heading to work. Call me later." She planted a kiss on my sweaty cheek and left.

"She is beyond her years," Henry said as he watched her leave. He turned towards me. Instantly, I could feel the heat thrust through my body, up my neck, and threatened tears. "Amelia, please, let me explain." Henry reached towards me. I would not offer my hand to him. If he touched me, I would burn with rage.

"We're going to head home," Beth looked towards me and Henry. "We'll see you back there."

"Stay." Henry turned and looked at all of us. "I'm going to need your help to break into the house to steal back Blackbeard's treasure."

"I think the heat is getting to me," Hector said. "You aren't talking about the Blackbeard. Are you? The pirate? Blackbeard?"

"Yes, Blackbeard. Edward Teach's treasure that I dug up with Casper. It hides in an underground room. And I intend to take it back before Casper can find it."

I looked at Beth, gulped, and looked towards the large red bricked house that stood in front of us. How were we going to break in and steal a treasure?

Cheese and rice.

Continue the adventure with
The Time Writer and The Hunt

Thank you for joining me on this adventure. Join my newsletter, *The Chrononaut*, to download the prequel, *The Time Writer and The Cloak*

(ebook and audiobook available), and to keep up to date
with my shenanigans and new releases.
https://bit.ly/CloakMB

Reviews and ratings help readers discover books you love.
Please consider leaving a review or rating wherever you
purchased this book.

AUTHOR'S NOTE

Wow! That was quite a fun ride. If I do say so myself... and I do! I hope you enjoyed reading *The Time Writer and The March* as much as I did writing the historical time travel adventure.

First things, first—my usual disclaimer. This shouldn't be considered a history book. This is historical fiction, heavy on the fiction, and heavy on the time travel. It is written from the point-of-view of a modern-day woman traveling back through time, so you will find historical anachronism throughout the book. *Crucible of War*, written by Fred Anderson, is a wonderful book that discusses the time. He is an expert in the field.

I make stuff up! I research the heck of the events and the time, but ultimately, it is fiction and I let the story take us on an adventure.

Let's get down to business and discuss people, events, and locations from the story.

The Carlyles. Major John Carlyle and his wife Sarah

Fairfax Carlyle's home in Alexandria was the center of the conference, hosting a house full of dignitaries, representatives, and soldiers. Major Carlyle, a Scottish merchant, married into the very wealthy Fairfax family. He joined the Ohio Company and helped create the port town of Alexandria, to help service his own interests. Carlyle imported and exported pretty much anything that he could gain a profit—from sugar to coal to people. He ran the commissary for the Virginia militia and decided that the commissary was more trouble than it was worth and found himself over stressed and taken ill throughout his service. He had difficulties obtaining and transporting supplies to the frontline, causing issues for the soldiers during battle, to include obtaining the necessary wagons, horses, and wagoners to move equipment and supplies.

The Carlyle mansion in Alexandria, Virginia is open to the public and is part of the Northern Virginia Regional Parks Authority.

Who is Braddock? General Edward Braddock was the British Officer sent to the colonies during the start of the French and Indian War, also known as the Seven Years' War, or what we could considered the first world war. The British and French fought for territory and trade rights across Europe, Asia, Africa, and North and South America. The Ohio Valley, Virginia border, and New York's border with Canada, was a hotbed for entanglements and pushing trade boundaries.

During his stay at the Carlyle house, his party emptied the Carlyle's store of wine, ale, and alcohol, harassed Carlyle's enslaved women, and caroused with other women from the area. He left the house in shambles. To say that Carlyle was keen on Braddock and his men to move on, would be an understatement.

Braddock's March would also be called Braddock's Defeat. Whereas it is true that he abandoned heavy cannons, they would not have done them any good. The French and their allies ambushed Braddock's troops from the tree line, and the cannons would have been ineffective to prepare and shoot at the close distance. The British troops, listening to Braddock and his archaic battlefield fighting style, allowed for their easy decimation. By archaic, I am pointing out the fact that Braddock expected them to line up and meet each other on the battlefield to take shots at each other, like gentlemen. Instead, the French followed the Native American battle style and used the trees as cover and defense. The French and their allies aimed at first taking out the officers, then the rest of the soldiers. Braddock was mortally wounded and removed from the battlefield by George Washington. A couple days later, somewhere in the vicinity of Fort Necessity, Braddock succumbed to his wounds.

Money, money, money. Let's discuss the cost of war and who paid for it. The boundary and trade lines that Braddock and the militia were to defend benefitted the Ohio Trade Company. One would think that since the Ohio Trade Company's finances would benefit, that they would pay for the war. One would be wrong. Since the men running the country, also had financial interests in the trade company, and with the approval from the British Parliament, the colonists were taxed to pay for the war.

Taxations would compound and lead to help plant the seeds for the revolution twenty years later.

The missing soldiers' pay is part of Virginia lore. Rumor has it, Braddock had the pay buried along with cannons somewhere in the Allegheny mountains. Its whereabouts, and Braddock's grave remain unknown to this day.

Medical and doctors. Braddock brought along with him a young apothecarist and his sister from England. When they reached Fort Cumberland, Braddock insisted that the women receive medical exams. In *The Time Writer and The March*, Amelia takes the role of **Charlotte Bristowe Browne**. Browne traveled with General Braddock from England and served as the first nurse at Fort Cumberland. When the sick and injured arrived at Fort Cumberland, she led their medical care.

Doctor Craik was Washington's doctor and helped care for him during his bout of dysentery that kept him from staying with the troops for a large portion of the march. Craik would remain Washington's personal physician until Washington's death.

Camp followers. Camp followers were typically the families of the soldiers. They would help maintain the camp and take on other duties so the soldiers could soldier. They allotted the women half-rations, leaving the women to find ways to make do. Many women and children were captured as slaves or killed during the ambush.

Wagoners abandonment, including Daniel Boone. Benjamin Franklin was brought into the planning of the war to help facilitate the movement of correspondence, which was vital in organizing an assault. He proved to be much more than the postmaster when he negotiated with farmers from Pennsylvania for the use of their wagons, horses, and wagoners. During the ambush, the wagoners unhitched the horses and fled. This includes the twenty-year-old Daniel Boone from South Carolina who had joined as a blacksmith. Yes, THE Daniel Boone who would later become a famous frontiersman.

Mind your business. Benjamin Franklin used the phrase "Mind your business," in respect to actual business, instead of the common turn of phrase of today. The Fugio Franklin cent, is the first official coin of the United States and had Franklin's motto "Mind your business" imprinted on it.

French prisoners. The French prisoners from the ambush at Jumonville Glen the previous year, had been moved around until they were settled in Williamsburg and Alexandria. The officers in Alexandria were granted parole, which meant they were allowed to walk around, and in the case of Drullion, stand around and complain loudly and to whomever he could get to listen to him, but remained in Alexandria until their departure for England. They were transported on various merchant ships, when there was room to transport them.

Hard biskit versus hardtack. The words mean the same item–a biscuit that is baked a few times in order to remove all the moisture. It allowed prolonged storage and the ability to transport food on the road or a ship. It was too hard to outright eat; however, soaking it in lard, broth, or wine, made it slightly more palatable. The difference comes in the time of usage. Hardtack usage began around the time of the Civil War.

Henry Spencer. Captain Lord Henry Spencer is a figment of my squirrelly imagination. His home is based on the George Wythe house in Colonial Williamsburg, Virginia. Although there was a Duke of Marlborough, Henry's wicked brother, Charles, is another figment of my story-telling imagination.

ACKNOWLEDGMENTS

Ah, yes. Time for my academy acceptance speech.

It takes a village to raise a child, it also takes a village to write a book. I may not mention everyone before they used the hooked cane to yank me off stage but know that I appreciate your indulgence with your expertise in this adventure.

First and foremost, to the **hubby bubby**: Thanks for staying employed so we can pay the bills and encouraging me to quit my job so I may explore the world of becoming a full-time novelist. You are the best partner in this adventure. A heartfelt, thank you. Additionally, thank you for providing battle and wound feedback.

The Real OGs: Thank you for your amazing support and encouragement. I continue to strive to make you proud of me, and I hope to occasionally succeed in that venture.

Beta and Sensitivity Readers: YOU ARE AWESOME! I received amazing feedback. With your time and dedication, the story became a million times better.

Lars Hedbor: Thanks for being the best cheerleader. I think I'll get you some pompoms.

Spilled Red Ink: Thanks for your editing, story development, and covers support. If not for the team, this would be an unreadable word document sitting on my hard drive, collecting dust and cobwebs.

Northern Virginia Regional Parks Authority: Thank you for maintaining the Carlyle Hose Historic Park and related records. Your volunteers and staff are knowledgeable and patient with my millions of questions. The *Docent Dispatch* provided a breadth of information and insight. I read every publication of the *Docent Dispatch* from 2001 to present, the site reports on the restoration, and John Carlyle's correspondence, and probably a few more documents that helped educate me.

Readers of my historic time travel adventures: Without you, I would be writing into the void. Thank you for picking up a copy of my books and joining me on the adventures through time. I have more exciting adventures planned, and hope you come along for the ride.

ABOUT THE AUTHOR

Alex R Crawford is the author of *The Time Writer*, A Historical Time Travel Adventure series. Alex grew up in Southern California and traveled the world with her military husband and daughters. She has lived in California, Texas, Georgia, Missouri, Virginia, and over six years in Germany. Crawford now calls the history-rich Washington D.C. area home.

Alex obtained a Bachelor of Science in Marketing and International Business and was one class short of having a minor in History. She regrets not completing the history minor (she loves history!). She doesn't regret not completing the two master's degrees she started in International Relations and Human Relations.

Once upon a time, she worked for the United States Federal Government as a writer, copyeditor, social media manager, and webmaster. Prior to working in public affairs, Crawford worked for the U.S. Marine Corps and U.S. Army in managing various outreach programs supporting service members and their families. Now, she is a full-time novelist, avid reader, and dog and cat wrangler.

When her nose isn't in a book or fingers typing away,

she enjoys visiting historical points-of-interest and museums.

Stay in touch! Join Alex's monthly newsletter for updates on upcoming books, adventures in research, and more shenanigans. Your information is not shared, nor will you be spammed. If you like SPAM®, then Alex recommends her favorite SPAM® recipe, SPAM® fried rice.

Visit Alex's website to receive the prequel *The Time Writer and The Cloak* ebook for FREE:

https://bit.ly/CloakMB

Did you find a typo? I wouldn't be surprised. My proofreader hands me a perfectly proofread manuscript and I start changing things, because I can't leave well enough alone. Mistakes, typos, and whatnot happen. If you find an example of my disruptive behavior (typo, missing word, whatever...), please reach out to: editor@spilledredink.com and they will make updates to the book as necessary.

I stink at social media, but I'm getting better! Join me on: Facebook and Instagram @AlexRCrawfordAuthor

facebook.com/AlexRCrawfordAuthor

instagram.com/alexrcrawfordauthor

MORE ADVENTURES

Visit my website for early releases, special offers, and to purchase ebooks, audiobooks, signed paperbacks, and exclusive merchandise.

alexrcrawford.com

Made in the USA
Columbia, SC
17 April 2024